Atlantean Secrets

Volume 4

The Return of the Flying Dragon

Samuel Sagan

D1572681

Clairvision™

PO Box 33, Roseville NSW 2069, Australia
www.clairvision.org
info@clairvision.org

By the same author:

❋ **Atlantean Secrets, Volume 1 – Sleeper Awaken!**

❋ **Atlantean Secrets, Volume 2 – Forever Love, White Eagle**

❋ **Atlantean Secrets, Volume 3 – The Gods are Wise**

❋ **Bleeding Sun – Discover the Future of Virtual Reality**

❋ **Awakening the Third Eye**

❋ **Entities, Parasites of the Body of Energy**
   (published in the US as Entity Possession)

❋ **Regression, Past Life Therapy for Here and Now Freedom**

❋ **Planetary Forces, Alchemy and Healing**

❋ **Clairvision Astrology Manual**

❋ **Clairvision Knowledge Tracks**, correspondence courses in meditation and esoteric knowledge including audio-cassettes, videos, printed material and electronic texts.

Visit the Clairvision Website for book excerpts, free books, Atlantean Secrets music, and a full concordance of the *Atlantean Secrets* saga:

www.clairvision.org

Book cover by Michael Smith

Copyright © 1999 by Clairvision School Foundation
Published in Sydney, Australia, by Clairvision
PO Box 33, Roseville NSW 2069, Australia
E-mail: info@clairvision.org
Website: www.clairvision.org

ISBN 0 9577119 0 5

Atlantean Secrets
The Tetralogy

ACKNOWLEDGEMENTS

First and foremost to Lord Gana, whose flow of inspiration was the driving force to begin, carry on, and complete this epic novel.

Then to the people who edited, proofed and illustrated *Atlantean Secrets*: Avril Carruthers, Catherine Ross, Debianne Gosper, Eva Pascoe, Gilda Ogawa, Michael Smith, Oonagh Sherrard, Orna Lankry, Philip Joseph, Ros Watson, Rosa Droescher, Ruth Camden, Tobi Langmo and Wilhelmina von Buellen.

Last, but certainly not least, to Gervin extraordinaire, friend and master in Thunder. Without him, none of this would ever have happened. *All glory to the teacher!*

Volume 4

Contents

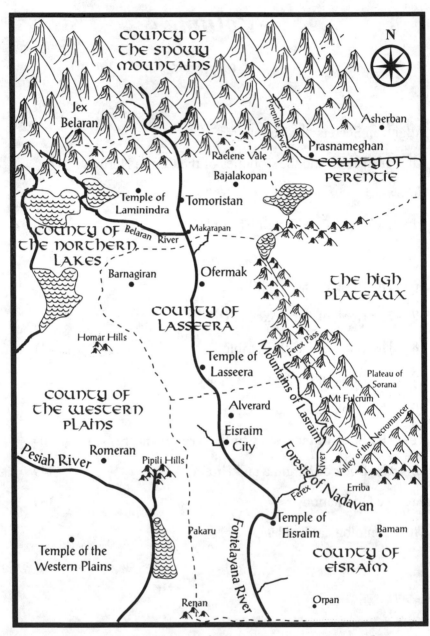

The Counties of the Centre North

Foreword

The twenty-two books which constitute the four volumes of *Atlantean Secrets* follow a carefully arranged sequence, designed to take you through a succession of spaces of consciousness and realisations. To enjoy the effects woven behind the lines, it is therefore essential to start from the beginning of Volume 1, *Sleeper Awaken!*

In scenes 16.2 and 16.7, Bobros the giant will recap the fields, which powered the Atlantean civilisation but also brought about its downfall. The topic it so crucial that it is suggested you read again scenes 9.10 and 9.16 (in Volume 2), in which Gervin and Lehrmon taught Szar about fields fundamentals. To refresh your memory about the Archive and the Fields of Peace you may want to refer to scene 9.28.

A glossary of the main names and terms of *Atlantean Secrets* can be found at the end of *Sleeper Awaken!* For a more comprehensive study, see the saga's concordance, *From Eisraim to Philadelphia*, which can be obtained from the Clairvision School's Internet site.

To follow the action of Volume 4, you will need the large temple map inserted at the end *Forever Love, White Eagle.* For a diagrammatic representation of the different worlds mentioned in *Atlantean Secrets*, see the cosmological ladder, p. 370.

Like Flying Dragons, the *Atlantean Secrets* epic is musical in essence. Characters, gods, angels and worlds each have their themes, and a number of scenes are accompanied by musical scores. This music, which forms an important part of the epic, can be heard in full at the Clairvision site: www.clairvision.org

The prelude of *The Return of the Flying Dragon* is set in the future. Virginia and Hiram have just died during a gigantic space battle – a story told in the novel *Bleeding Sun*. Arriving in the Fields of Peace they join Master Barkhan Seer, who shows them Archive records of the ancient continent, Atlantis. The whole saga of *Atlantean Secrets* unfolds in front of them.

Now, to the Archive halls, where Virginia and Hiram are contemplating visions of time.

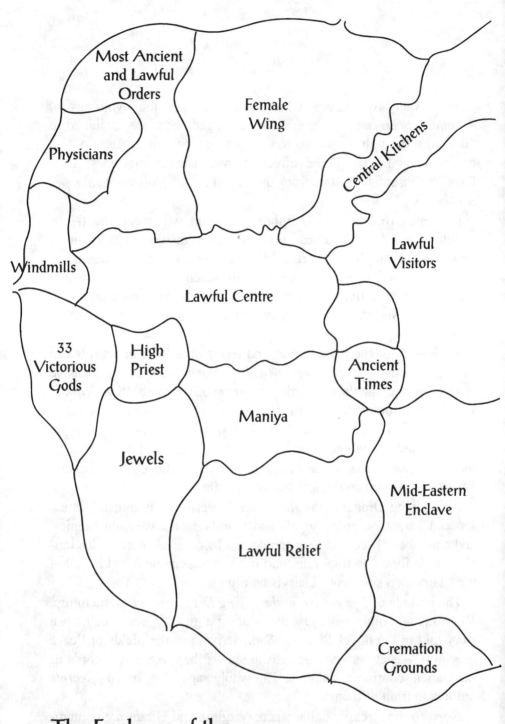

The Enclaves of the
Western Part of the Esraim Temple

Prelude

"Did Barkhan Seer tell you about your next life?" Virginia asked.

"Only that I was going to be the kind of man who has everything. He wouldn't tell me more for the moment," Hiram, Knight of the Apocalypse, was contemplating the stars through the high dome ceiling.

Stars in the Fields of Peace. A feast of gem-like colours, stretching forever above their heads. Starlight with Spirit.

He looked down, meeting her eyes, "What about *your* next life?"

Drawing from a music field, Virginia produced a sequence of descending arpeggios. Reaching rock bottom, the sounds exploded into an all-comprehending vastness that made the canopy of stars sound like a wavelet in the ocean.

She became the vastness. Hiram felt like a tiny white dot inside her. It made him laugh with astonishment, "How do you do that?"

"Flying Dragons don't do music, they *are* music," she said, softening the sounds to let him melt inside her. "See, in your next life you'll have everything, and gods, will it be well-deserved! But I will only have this – music. Not much else, I'm afraid."

Her sounds made him feel fluid. "If I have everything then perhaps... we could share."

She teased him, "In your next life, you'll be far too handsome and gifted to even look at an ordinary person like me. You won't even see me. And just as well! I'll probably be *so* ugly."

He made his voice White-Eagle soft, "How could I not see a Flying Dragon?"

Seen through normal eyes, Virginia was a stunning seventeen-year-old young woman with sparkling-green almond eyes and long brown hair. Seen from the Point, her Flying Dragon nature stretched from the Abyss of the Deep and the Fault of Eternity to the sphere of the Great Ant and far beyond the Blue Lagoon. Looking at her was like taking a panoramic view of the spheres of remoteness, it made Hiram feel like a wide-angle telescope.

Sometimes the immensity became overwhelming. There was too much to see, the mind boggled.

Hiram was certain, "When I see you, I will recognise you. Immediately!"

The kind of things people tell each other when they are in the Fields of Peace. When they descend and incarnate into the physical world, of course, it all becomes more complicated.

"You probably will," she made her sounds caressing. "The question is, will I recognise myself?"

In the absolute clarity of the Fields of Peace, everything is so simple. To be is to see. Eternal, you are, therefore you can see forever. Being yourself is the most natural thing in the world. But down there, in the physical universe... Virginia shivered, thinking of how many existences on Earth she had lived in near-total oblivion of her Flying Dragon nature.

Point-master Hiram was puzzled. "Easy to see why human beings forget their eternal nature when they are on Earth. Their consciousness is frail. But you are so vast!"

"Precisely! That's the difficulty when you are a Flying Dragon: human bodies don't fit, they're too small! You can only put a drop of yourself inside them."

So hard for a drop to comprehend the ocean.

"So you *completely* forget?"

"There is always a knowing in the background." To illustrate the notion, Virginia conjured Archive images of Szar healing Felicia. It was in a cave in the canyons of the Red Lands, in the southern part of the long-disappeared continent, Atlantis. Szar had just come out of eighteen months of training with the Great Warriors of the temple of the Sons of the Dragon in Mouth Lohrzen. Fed by the formidable energies of the Underworld, his body had doubled in width. His lower chakras resonated with awesome earth-powers. But he was totally ignorant of the power of the Point. The column of Spirit above his head hadn't been cultivated. A Nephilim Hunter could have venomised him to death in a matter of seconds. And yet his Flying Dragon nature had made Felicia strong enough to face the fire of the Watchers.

Virginia made her music silent. "Look!"

In the small cave the gorgeous red-haired Nephilim priestess was lying unconscious. Szar was healing her body with his hands, using forces from the Underworld. But at the same time, unknown to him, his Flying Dragon nature was working on the centres of energy above her head.

"At that stage Szar still had no idea about Flying Dragons. He found them totally incomprehensible. That didn't prevent him from saturating Felicia's energy with Flying Dragon forces," Virginia commented.

After the healing Felicia returned to the cave of Verzazyel the Watcher, descended into the crypt, and miraculously survived the tempestuous experience of the Watcher's mind. Resisting the temptation to accompany her, Szar returned to the temple of Eisraim.

Prelude

Virginia called up an image of Elyani of the White Eagle. She was alone in her small courtyard, in the female wing of the temple of Eisraim. In the silvery semi-darkness of a warm Atlantean night, she was lying on the lawn, laughing with joy, flooded with Flying Dragon sounds. Same experience of being a tiny dot enveloped in a mothering infinity of star sounds.

Elyani called through darkness visible, "Teyani! Teyani! Szar is on his way back from the Red Lands! He will be here in three weeks. Perhaps two."

"Praised be the Lord Melchisedek!," Teyani's light shone through darkness visible. "Did the Eagle announce the news?"

"No, Szar himself! I mean, his Flying Dragon voice spoke to me again," Elyani answered.

Virginia stopped the vision. "After Szar became a Great Warrior, his Flying Dragon voice frequently spoke to Elyani and Gervin, and even more to Teyani. But Szar was totally unaware of that part of himself." She brought up other images. Szar and Gervin of the Brown Robe were finishing one of their discussions. Szar was leaving the aquamarine chamber, looking shattered. Gervin had just informed him of the recent deterioration of the fields, a harbinger of the imminent downfall of the kingdom of Atlantis. Overwhelmed, Szar walked in the alleys of the temple, singing mechanically, "What does a madman do when his house is melting? He dances! He dances!"

Filled with the presence of the gods, the temple looked so immutable – unshakeable! Hard to believe there would be nothing left of it in only a few years, perhaps even less. What would happen to all these high initiates, priests and priestesses? What would happen to Elyani and him?

He bumped into Artold of the Salmon Robe, who afflicted him with the sempiternal, "And how are your parents my friend in the Law?"

Meanwhile, Master Gervin called Elyani through darkness visible, "White Eagle, I need your help. Time is running out, the Archive team needs Szar *now*! I am going to have to awaken his Point straight from Thunder. Lord Gana and I are about to deliver a massive dose of energy above his head – more than enough to plunge a normal person into unlawful insanity. But his Flying Dragon nature should allow him to cope, especially with the Eagle's tender care. You are in charge of that side of the operation."

Elyani had just spent a year and a half in the throes of agony, the man she loved dying in the Dragon in the hands of dangerous Underworld fanatics. Now it was his column of Spirit that was about to be cooked in cosmic fire. Thank the Eagle, Elyani's trust in Gervin was total. "Does Szar know what is about to happen to him?" she just asked.

"Mm... he will find it *much* easier to cope if he thinks you are his instructor and this is a normal Point process," Gervin wisely decided.

"Can't we speed up his reconnection to the Flying Dragons? If he could get in touch with his nature of remoteness, everything would be so much easier for him."

Gervin twinged his beard, "Unfortunately, only the Flying Dragons themselves can do these things. But Szar is solid enough, now. He should be able to cope. His behaviour might just be a little queer in the coming days. Don't be surprised if he does foolish things."

"I'll be ready."

Next scene, Szar was in Lord Gana's chapel, dancing, when his Point erupted like an upside-down volcano. Five minutes later he was in Elyani's arms, declaring his feelings, "I love you, Elyani! I love you! I love you!"

In Archive Hall Five, Hiram and Virginia were laughing their Points off. "Poor thing!" Hiram was always ready to empathise with his favourite White Eagle. "It's tough to be in love with a Flying Dragon." They watched the love scene again, and again, replaying the first kisses – Dragon vroofing below, Pointness flowing from above like hot lava, millions of angels singing above Szar and Elyani's heads, galaxies of Flying Dragon whispers in the background... it had class. Caught in the drift, Hiram and Virginia watched on.

Nurtured in the Eagle's wings, Szar coped surprisingly well. In a matter of days, his Flying Dragon nature had absorbed the excess of fire. The hurricane above his head subsided. His Point became fully operational, but he was still completely unaware of his Flying Dragon nature. Voices from remoteness kept whispering behind his mind. He heard them and he didn't hear them at the same time. Occasionally, his behaviour was queer. Overall, it remained within the limits of the Law. Elyani breathed, but not for long! Soon an oracle revealed that she and Szar were about to be separated.

The gods had thrown the daiva – the dice of destiny. Teyani, woman of infinite sight, knew exactly what was pending. Following the advice of the Sons of Apollo, she refrained from telling Elyani. Elyani and Szar enjoyed a short period of happiness, learning about love, which is the central mystery of the Eagle.

Virginia brought up an image of Elyani's courtyard. It was just before sunset. Szar and Elyani were climbing the ladders to the roof of the Blue priestesses' chapel. They were talking about their new friend Woolly of the Dirty Cream Robe, stone maker of unmatched genius and unlawful manners. Woolly had been showing great interest in Maryani of the White Eagle, the young priestess who had just descended into the Underworlds under Szar's guidance. But down there, Maryani was receiving so many spiritual gifts from King Vasoukidass and his Nagas that Szar feared she might not want to return to the kingdom at all. Elyani trusted the wisdom of the Eagle, who had ordered the descent. Arriving on the roof they sat together and watched the red magic of sunset, the Atlantean mists set ablaze. Through Elyani's love, the Eagle was pouring forces into Szar, preparing him for the magical discovery of his Flying Dragon nature.

Prelude

It was during that period that Szar began to fathom the scope of the Archive project, which Gervin and his Field Wizards had been preparing for more than thirty-five years. Foreseeing the unavoidable fate that awaited the Atlantean civilisation, the Masters of Thunder had endeavoured to salvage the knowledge of their time in a non-physical Archive – a temple of light built in the Fields of Peace, or World to Come. The project, which was to be carried out by the temples of Eisraim and Lasseera, consisted of transferring the memories, connections and spiritual forces contained in these temples into the Archive. The creation of high-quality soft stones was essential to the success of the project. Shortly before the transfer, the energy fields of Eisraim and Lasseera would be involuted into the soft stones. This extraordinary operation, called 'charging of the Archive stones', would last hardly one night. The stones would then be carried to the Plateau of Sorana, on the other side of the mountains of Lasraim.[1] There the final ritual would take place, transferring the content of the stones into the Archive. To prepare for this ritual, more than three hundred Masters of Thunder had already assembled in the temple of light in the Fields of Peace, under the direction of Barkhan Seer.[2]

Virginia called images of the chapel of the Field Wizards, from where Ferman and his men were monitoring the temple's fields. Szar was now commander of the kingdom-side of the Archive project. Central to his mission was to ensure that once charged in Lasseera and Eisraim, the stones would journey safely to the Plateau of Sorana. But first, considerable difficulties had to be overcome. The stones had fallen sick from the pollution which afflicted the warp of fields, they had become unfit for the Archive project. Maryani, who had returned from the Underworlds invested with massive powers, saved the situation. Using the phenomenal alchemical lore of the Nagas, she and Woolly concocted hermaphroditic soft stones of immense value.

Woolly was glowing. His broken nose looked less broken, his face less marred with carbuncles and pimples. He was wearing a brand-new cream robe. "Commander, look at this!" he jubilated, showing Szar a treasure-stone the size of an apricot. "The Archive is saved! We no longer have to worry."

"Lawfully fantastic!" Szar forced a broad smile, not wanting to pour cold water onto Woolly's newly-discovered positive attitude to life. But inside himself he knew how quickly the situation could degenerate. For sure, the new stones were perfect – ideal for performing the Archive transfer. But precisely because of their perfection, they were bound to attract attention from swarms of potential enemies: the Nephilim Hunters of Jex Belaran, several clans of Renegade Hunters, the Nephilim giants of the Eastern Peninsula – perhaps even the king of Atlantis himself. Once charged, the

---

[1] See map p. 4.
[2] Pronounced Barkhan Zair.

Archive stones would contain enough power to control the entire kingdom. Each and every would-be conqueror would want them.

The scene was being set for a momentous battle – a battle in which Szar was going to need every single power he could possibly draw from, Dragon below, Dragon above. But when the Flying Dragons came to awaken his nature of remoteness, he missed the rendezvous.

Virginia and Hiram watched again the scenes in the palace of Tomoristan. Szar was attempting to heal the princely child of the Ozorenan family. By his side were Hermina of the high caste of the Immaculate, and her young assistant Jinia, former incarnation of Virginia. The physical proximity of Szar and Jinia formed an antenna, particularly auspicious to receive impulses from the Flying Dragons. A time window was open. But, worried that Hermina would read the secrets of the Archive project through him, Szar remained deaf to the voice of the Flying Dragons. He closed his Point, closed his mind, and closed his heart. The presence of the Flying Dragons withdrew. The appointment with destiny had been missed. A sixty-minute blunder had set Virginia on a thirteen-thousand-year wandering course.

Soon after this Jinia died from grief, not even knowing what she was grieving for.

Virginia had watched these images so many times in the last days that she no longer reacted to them. She moved on to a scene in Eisraim. Szar was in Elyani's courtyard, feeling abysmally empty. It was soon after the oracular revelation of the decree of the gods – the daiva. Holma, the ascending goddess, had died. Elyani had been designated to replace her, and locked in the tower of Malchasek. Under the supervision of two Immaculate priestesses, she was to prepare herself for the ritual that would see her reborn in the world of the gods. Due to the chaotic state of the fields, the ritual no longer worked. Elyani was already falling sick. Szar was in a state of utter devastation. Alcibyadi[1] of the White Eagle, Teyani's daughter, was trying to pull him out of his depression. He was throwing her from one side of the courtyard to the other, breaking her ribs. That seemed to make him feel better.

"This broken heart was a blessing from the Mother of the Light!" Virginia shook her head. "It created a breach in Szar's structure. It's what made the reconnection to the Flying Dragons possible."

At the time, no one understood this better than Alcibyadi. A few months earlier Szar had saved her life when he had rescued her from the Underworlds. Now it was Alcibyadi's turn to rescue Szar. Unforgettable images! In the cellar, by the crypt of the Archive stones, he was sitting on the floor. The tall woman with long straight dark hair was standing behind him, both hands on his head, blasting the high end of his column of Spirit, forcing a connection to the Flying Dragons. All at once she started screaming like a hundred madmen. Szar's consciousness was projected throughout the

---

[1] Pronounced Alsibyahdee.

12

spheres of remoteness. The intensity became more and more insane. Alcibyadi was about to fall apart. Gervin ran into the cellar. She didn't respond to his orders, her hands glued onto Szar's head. She kept screaming, louder and louder. Gervin had to throw her on the floor violently. Lehrmon arrived on the scene, helping Gervin to contain the pandemonium.

When Szar came back to his senses, his column of Spirit was cracked, his mind was a complete chaos, he could hardly recognise Gervin. But a conscious link had been established between his earthly self and his Flying Dragon nature – a link that would never be lost again. Alcibyadi was lying on the floor, her head on Lehrmon's lap. She sat up and immediately returned to the charge, using the power of the Eagle to intensify the link. It shocked Szar awake. It made Gervin burst out laughing.

Having recovered a thin thread of sanity, Szar walked out of the cellar warning Lehrmon, "Brother, this woman will *never* give up!"

Shaken by the momentum behind the words, Lehrmon raised both eyebrows, his lips trembling imperceptibly.

Hiram and Virginia cheered and gave a handclap, "Taken!"

Next image, Alcibyadi and Lehrmon were making love. Passionately.

Alcibyadi was one of the six White Eagle priestesses who were to be sent to Egypt – not an enviable destiny in a culture where exile was regarded as a punishment worse than death. Alcibyadi, who had long been in love with Lehrmon, had asked him to make a child with her before she left. Until then Lehrmon had categorically refused, considering it would have been pure folly. That night, folly took over.

While they were in each other's arms Szar was wandering in the Point-guided corridors of the female wing, in search of his new identity. Several times Elyani had told him the legend of the Flying Dragon who, long ago, had travelled all the way from the Abyss of the Deep and the Fault of Eternity to see the Web of Love and the spheres of Melchisedek. When the Flying Dragon met the White Eagle it was cosmic love at first sight, a passion of epic proportions. But the Flying Dragon could not stay here, his spheres of remoteness needed him. And the spheres of Melchisedek could not do without the White Eagle.

What would this world be without the White Eagle?

So the White Eagle stayed, and the Flying Dragon went. But before leaving, he planted his seed into the Dragon of the Deep. This was when he said, "Forever love, White Eagle!"

And the White Eagle answered, "Forever love, Flying Dragon!"

As Szar's feet walked the alleys of Eisraim, his head spread in remoteness, he remembered the legend. Arriving in Elyani's courtyard, he fell on his knees. Remembering Tomoristan, he cried, "Jinia! Jinia! How could I fail to recognise you?"

In Archive Hall Five, Virginia bit her lip. She nodded, "Yes, how could you!"

She brought up images of the temple's music hall. Taught by Fridrick, former Nephilim Hunter trained in Jex Belaran – or so everyone believed at the time – Szar was learning to gear his Point into the music field, producing magical sounds. Virginia commented, "Remember how Gervin had encouraged him to play music? That was so wise! Flying Dragons are always better with music."

"Helps them get in touch with themselves?" Hiram drank the sounds.

"More than that. It allows them to be. On Earth you breathe air. In remoteness we Flying Dragons breathe music."

Fridrick may have been an impostor, but he was a sensitive soul. He had intuitively sensed Szar's musical dimension, and especially designed a program of Point-work for him based on music. This was Szar's first training in Point-warfare.

Szar couldn't see himself having a chance against a pack of Nephilim Hunters. Through Fridrick, he therefore sought to make an alliance with Perseps, Grand Commander of Jex Belaran's Nephilim Hunters. Fridrick led Szar to believe that Perseps had proposed a plan aimed at eliminating the Red Renegades and the Foxes, two gangs of Renegade Hunters who threatened the Archive mission. The plan required Szar to infiltrate the Foxes' headquarters and kill a few Hunters, simulating an attack by the Red Renegades. While Elyani, the new ascending goddess, was rotting in the tower of Malchasek, Szar created a music field in his courtyard and practised from morning to night, building his Point to kuren-jaya standards. Soon he would realise that he had been duped: Fridrick was a fraud, he had never been in Jex Belaran. He had lied when saying Perseps had offered an alliance and a plan. Neither Perseps nor anyone else in Jex Belaran had ever heard of Fridrick. And the 'plan' had been entirely fabricated by Fridrick, whose real identity remained a mystery.

"Now look at this!" Virginia replayed the scene where Szar met Aphelion, the emissary of Ahriman, Prince of Darkness. Implementing Fridrick's scheme, Szar was in the Foxes' headquarters. He had just seized the stone through which the Foxes derived powers from the Watchers. Overwhelmed by darkness, Szar found himself completely disconnected from his Flying Dragon nature. The voice of remoteness instantly disappeared. So did the background of cosmic music. "Praise the King of the World!" Aphelion hailed Szar in his enchanting voice. Szar's encounter with evil had begun.

Hiram called another scene. In the temple of Lasseera, Master Esrevin of the Brown Robe was on his knees, crying silently. By his side was the body of a blond young man, hardly twenty years of age. He was Oriel of the Brown Robe, Esrevin's disciple. A few lawful feet away, two Hunters lay dead on the ground, their energy blasted by the Word of Thunder that Esrevin had projected into them. But Esrevin had arrived too late. The Hunters had already killed Oriel.

Hiram felt an immense sympathy for the young man. "He looked smart didn't he?"

Prelude

"How can you say that?" Virginia frowned, watching the corpse.

"I just know!" Hiram said, and from the Point he called up an earlier record. It was in the cellars of Lasseera. Oriel and Woolly were working together with a feeling of great excitement.

"What a fantastic idea!" Woolly exclaimed, examining Oriel's work.

Hiram raised his hands, "See?"

Virginia laughed.

"He's my brother!" Hiram nodded.

"In Atlantis?"

"Oh no, not in Atlantis!" Hiram pulled a face, "You don't want to know what I looked like in Atlantis."

"Of course I want to know! Show me! Show me a record!"

"There are no records. I wasn't even in a temple. Just some kind of obscure peasant labouring from morning to night in some remote barbaric land." Hiram returned to Oriel. "His death could have been avoided! Had Szar listened to Aphelion, he would have killed the Black Hunters before they raided Lasseera. But then of course... God knows what else would have happened if Szar had followed Aphelion's advice."

Yet, such irony! When Oriel died, his training in the Brown Robe was only half-completed. Consequently, some seven thousand years later when Oriel was reborn in ancient Persia, he was particularly vulnerable to the persuasion of Aphelion, who took him to the dark side. And another six thousand years later, after several lifetimes of training under Aphelion, Oriel was reborn in apocalyptic times as Alexander Rosher, one of the most powerful generals of Ahriman's armies.

Rosher – Hiram's enemy!

"A genius," Hiram said with reverence. "And I know what I'm talking about. I've just spent a life looking for ways of neutralising the weapons of hell he invented."

Rosher's inventions had changed the course of the wars of the Apocalypse, giving Ahriman the edge.

Hiram brought back an image of Szar and Aphelion. In front of them six Renegade Hunters of Murdoch's Black Clan were begging for their lives.

Szar hesitated.

"Come on! Blow their heads off!" Aphelion exhorted in an exuberant voice. "Kill them! Kill! Use the power of your stone!"

With a quick hand gesture, Szar sent the Hunters away. After which three of them went straight to Lasseera, the others to Eisraim. In Lasseera, Oriel was killed. In Eisraim, Woolly was in great turmoil. Gervin had just offered him to become his disciple in the Brown Robe. If he accepted, he wouldn't be able to accompany Maryani to Egypt. Loyal to her, Woolly decided to decline the offer.

It was late in the evening. In the cellar near the crypt of the Archive stones, Woolly fell on his knees. For the first time since he was nine years old, he prayed. With total sincerity, "Mother of the Light, oh, Mother of the Light... if I am making the wrong choice, *please* send me a sign!"

Two hours later the Black Hunters ransacked the chapel, leaving Woolly half dead. Following which he was healed by Maryani and Vasouk.

Once healed, he became one of the Masters of Thunder.

Destiny!

Hiram replayed the fatal image. Szar was standing with Aphelion by his side. In Szar's left hand, the egg-sized evil stone was glowing. In his eyes, Hiram read genuine hesitation. When Szar gave the sign with his right hand, sending the Hunters away, it didn't seem like an inspired decision coming from the high spheres. More like the randomness of the world.

"Things could have gone either way!" Hiram mused.

Now, thirteen thousand years later, Woolly was a legend among the Knights of the Apocalypse, and Rosher had become one of the Rex's most precious assets. In the Philadelphias, if Hiram and Virginia had been separated for so long, it was because of the P-21 mines invented by Rosher.

In the grand workings of time, so much can depend on so little.

"Things could have gone either way with the ascension ritual too!" Virginia brought up a scene showing Gervin and Esrevin. The two Masters of Thunder were in Gervin's aquamarine chamber, discussing the kingdom. It was not long after Szar's return from his nightmare-encounter with Aphelion. He was completely exhausted, demoralised. The energy of his left hand was pitch-black from having used the evil stone under Aphelion's instructions. Hermina the Immaculate had just arrived in the temple of Eisraim. Elyani had been allowed to return to Szar. She was still an ascending goddess but it was becoming increasingly obvious that in the agony of the fields, the ancient holy ritual of ascension had become impossible.

"Any hope?" Esrevin asked. "Can you see Elyani making it to the world of the gods?"

Gervin was grim. "My friend... Elyani is dying! I'm not even sure Szar will be able to keep her alive until the ritual. As to succeeding," Gervin shook his head, "the elementals of nature have become so rotten. It would take a miracle."

Esrevin quoted a verse of the Law of the Eagles, "Put a Flying Dragon and a White Eagle together, and let the miracle unfold!"

Light in Gervin's eyes, "Yes! Have you seen them when they are together? So beautiful! A poem in remoteness. The old magic is alive and well."

They remained silent, remembering the Forever Love legend.

Gervin went on, "Szar will be here any minute. I'd like you to use your sight and give me your opinion on something. Perseps the Hunter has given Szar a stone as a present. It's supposed to allow him to communicate with Jex Belaran. But there's something I don't like about this stone!"

Esrevin frowned in horror, "You mean Szar accepts presents from the Nephilim Hunters? And a soft stone, moreover?"

16

Prelude

Gervin smiled, amused, "I'm afraid my apprentice still hasn't completely realised what the Nephilim are like."

"Even after having been betrayed by Fridrick the Nephilim?"

Dragon-vigorous knocks resounded at the door. Esrevin jumped to his feet, went to open the door. Tears in his eyes, he took Szar in his arms and gave him a long hug. He missed Oriel. Having lost him was like having lost his own son.

Hiram understood, carrying his share of the feeling of loss. There are sorrows that do not pass with time.

Virginia moved to the critical night when Szar had the intuition that would bring victory. Discomfiture had reached a climax. Each time Elyani chanted her hymns, she attracted a tidal wave of elemental slime. Hermina had been so badly injured that she would probably never recover. Szar's left hand was paralysed, becoming more and more painful. Alcibyadi had vowed to heal him but it was difficult to imagine how she could succeed where all other attempts had failed. The night of the howling dogs, signalling the final agony of the warp of fields, was imminent.

During his sleep, Szar had a vision. He saw a way of performing the ascension ritual in which the offering would not be made of elementals of nature, but of forces drawn from the Underworlds.

It was a mad departure from the canon of the Law.

The next day, Elyani was reborn in the world of the gods.

"Why couldn't Gervin think of this?" Hiram wondered.

Virginia smiled from the depths of remoteness, "It had to be a Flying Dragon!"

"So the legend lived?"

"Oh yes, the legend lives! If Serah wanted you to be the next White Eagle of the Philadelphian Air Force, it is because the legend lives. And if you found me and managed to drag me to the Fields of Peace, it is because the legend lives."

Thoughtful, Hiram looked up to the dome, his Point flirting with the stars. "I still can't completely see myself as a White Eagle, somehow!"

"You *have* to! It's your destiny!"

The enthusiasm in her voice made him feel warm. "Is it?" he smiled.

She was categorical, "Flying Dragons *know* these things."

Hiram responded with a touch of irony in his smile, "Thirteen thousand years have passed, the old magic hasn't."

She warned, "Don't take me for granted, Knight Hiram!"

"No risk. Want to come for a stroll by the River of Remembrance?"

"No, we keep watching!"

Earlier they had viewed records of the twelve hours – twelve stretched hours – which Elyani and Szar had spent together in the world of the gods. After his stay with the gods, Szar went on a journey to the spheres of his father – far, far away, beyond the Abyss of the Deep and the Fault of Eternity.

Now Szar was about to return to the spheres of Melchisedek.

"Before we return to Eisraim, Master Barkhan Seer said we should watch this." Virginia brought on a grey, misty scene.

A tall man in his sixties was standing with bare feet in the snow. His torso too was bare. He held a long sharp knife in his left hand. Shivering with cold, he turned his head skywards. He raised both hands slowly and started screaming, using the power of the Voice.

Ugly screams. Incoherent sounds. Dark flames coming out of his mouth.

"Joranjeran, past Grand Commander of the Nephilim Hunters," Hiram recognised him. "But what is he doing?"

"Nephilim ritual of sorrow," Virginia Point-read the Archive.

"Looks more like rage to me!"

A long, furious scream, gradually turning into a shriek. The flow of Voice became pitch-black lava.

Around Joranjeran, the air was thick with the presence of the Watchers.

The old man with the parched forehead and the huge hands kept screaming. Louder. And louder. Voice-vomiting darkness.

"This is sick," Virginia shook her head.

There was a short silence. It made the snow look whiter.

Abruptly, and with all the strength he could draw from the Watchers, Joranjeran called, "Henrick!" His Voice shot like an arrow through darkness visible.

The scream lasted for as long as he could stretch his breath. And with his knife he slashed his chest from right to left. Red drops fell onto the snow.

"Nephilim love!" Hiram nodded.

Four more times, Joranjeran Voiced with all the violence he was capable of, "Henrick!" Four more times, he gashed his torso with the knife.

Then, completely discharged, he dropped the knife and collapsed in the snow. And he cried, "Henrick! Henrick..."

There was dignity in tears. He no longer looked like a Nephilim beast but like a human being. "Henrick," he sobbed, "why did I let you go?"

His face dropped against the snow. His voice was muffled.

In another corner of the Archive Hall, Virginia recalled the record where Szar and Princess Pelenor were dining on Watchers' ratatouille, sitting on the roof of the Blue Priestesses' chapel. Eating like a pig, Pelenor had just been explaining how Henrick, her lover, had walked away from Jex Belaran – and from the order of the Nephilim Hunters – after a quarrel with Perseps. Henrick was now the head of a small clan of Renegade Hunters.

Szar, whose column of Spirit had just been repaired by Space Matrix, looked a little pale. "What did Henrick and Perseps disagree about?" he asked Pelenor.

"No one knows, they always kept it a secret," the princess answered. "Henrick never told me. He just left. And six months later, to everyone's surprise, Joranjeran retired and installed Perseps as the youngest Grand Commander of the Hunters ever."

Instead of Henrick.

"Henrick! Henrick..." Joranjeran cried, his face in the snow, his body covered in blood.

Both visions faded, leaving Archive Hall Five silent and dark, bathed in dim light of the fields of stars.

Infinite peace of the World to Come.

After a few seconds, Virginia brought up bright images of a city built on high cliffs, facing the ocean.

"Was this in Atlantis?" Hiram frowned. "The mists are quite sparse."

"The citadel of the Nephilim giants," she announced.

Hiram rubbed his hands with curiosity, "The most sophisticated fields in the kingdom of Atlantis, I believe."

"Which was why the mists were so sparse."

16

The Book of the Nephilim Giants

And the Watchers have gone to the daughters of men upon the Earth, and
have slept with the women... And the women have borne giants, and the
whole Earth has thereby been filled with blood and unrighteousness.
                                                          1 Enoch 9.8-10

And there were giants in the Earth in those days... when the sons of God
came in unto the daughters of men, and they bare children to them, the
same became mighty men which were of old, men of renown.
                                                          Genesis 6.4

16.1 Atlantis, Eastern Peninsula, citadel of the Nephilim giants

Melissa the giantess untied her dress and casually let it drop on the
marble floor. She walked down the steps of her pool. From her way of
gliding rather than walking, from the crispness of her glorious naked body
and from the excitement which imperceptibly pinched the corner of her
lips, Pralaya the baphomet understood that Bexton, Melissa's lover, was on
his way. Pralaya smiled. Not like human beings smile, of course.
Baphomets had a particular smile no one could copy. Perhaps it had to do
with the fact that in their head they always seemed to be laughing with
irony, even when they were crying. To smile they didn't need to move their
lips, just change the glow in their mysterious eyes.

Pralaya contemplated the sea through the large windows of the room, recalling the loud moans of ecstasy heard from Melissa's bedroom three days
earlier, during Bexton's last visit. When Bexton made love to Melissa the
entire house seemed to be shaking. And what a mess in her bedroom after
he left!

"I can hear you thinking, Pralaya!" Melissa said mischievously.

"No you can't!" Pralaya replied immediately.

The feigned assurance in the baphomet's voice made Melissa chuckle.
"Mm... Can you tell me why you are wagging your tail, then?"

"No I am not!" Pralaya wagged his tail a little faster to make Melissa laugh.

The giantess shouted outrage and let herself sink to the bottom of the pool. Pralaya moved nonchalantly to the edge of the water and lay down, waiting for her to emerge.

Melissa loved her pool. She spent at least two hours in it every day. She never seemed to get enough of the warm, caressing vibrations that came from the state-of-the-art rejuvenating field at the bottom of the water, and which kept her body young and exceptionally soft. Although forty-two years of age, she looked barely thirty. And she was now much more beautiful than twelve years earlier, when the extraordinarily costly rejuvenating field had been installed in the house by a team of top-level Field Wizards.

She swam towards the baphomet. When her head came out of the water she was smiling ecstatically. She hardly caught her breath before asking, "What do you think of him, Pralaya?"

"Er... Bexton?"

"Well of course, Bexton! Who else?"

"Yes, who else?" Pralaya sighed. "I say, a great leader he is indeed. A man of exceptional qualities, and certainly deserving to be the grand commander of our citadel."

"But that's not what I'm asking you, Pralaya! Do you like him?"

"I like his sense of humour. He always has something interesting to say. And he's a splendid giant."

"Mm... such a beautiful man!" Melissa closed her eyes.

"And so intelligent! And kind!" Pralaya mimicked Melissa's enraptured voice.

"Yes! Yes!" She didn't even notice the baphomet was making fun of her. "Do you think he loves me?"

"I say, if he comes to visit you four times a week, then, then... it must be because you have captured something in him."

"But from what you see in him... tell me, wise baphomet, do you think he really loves me?"

"I say, if you call on my wisdom, then, then..." Pralaya paused, carefully searching for words.

Melissa frowned, "Do you see something worrying?"

When baphomets used their sight or when they thought intensely, their eyes shone with an eerie glow.

"Pralaya, you don't approve of him... or do you?" Melissa tried to read his thoughts. But reading a baphomet was a most difficult exercise, even for a highly psychic giantess like her. "What do you think is wrong with him?"

Pralaya remained silent. Melissa was his dear friend. The last thing he wanted was to hurt her feelings.

"Tell me! Please tell me what's on your mind," Melissa insisted impatiently. "What worries you?"

"It's not what I see in Bexton, but more what I see coming for you, Melissa. On the one hoof, I am delighted to see you so happy and shining. But on the other hoof, I wonder if a politician – even Grand Commander Bexton – is the right man for you. You are a woman of sight, a prophetess. You have always cherished wisdom, not wealth. You are so different from the power-hungry courtesans who run after men like him."

"I know!" she said. "Do you think that's what he likes about me? I never ask him for anything but his company. And it's sincere. What I want is *him*. I don't care about his wealth."

"This is what worries me. I try to imagine you in the palace of a grand commander with all the power games and the intrigues, and I can't see how you could be happy."

"You and I in the grand commander's palace?" Melissa was in heaven. "Can you really see that happening?"

"I say... of course, I can see that happening."

"Youhou!" Melissa shouted in exultation. She knew the depth of the baphomet's vision. "So he really loves me! Ooooh!" she let herself float on her back and contemplated the huge ceiling, on which an energy field projected the moving image of a night sky with thousands of stars and gigantic clouds of light. "Oooh!" she repeated ecstatically, letting the vision of the field of stars make her mind tipsy.

Pralaya looked at her with a touch of disconcertment. He laughed (in his strange baphomet's way), "I say, where is Melissa the Wise? Look what love is doing to you!"

"Have you never been in love?" she answered through the space because she had water in her ears. "That would surprise me. A spunky little baphomet like you!"

"We're digressing, here!" Pralaya called on Melissa's logical rigour.

"No way, baphomet! The miracle of love, this is what it is all about!"

"I say, there must be a way to be happy, and yet be wise at the same time."

"Wise... wise..." Melissa laughed. "That's the problem with you baphomets, you're always so wise!"

"I know!" Pralaya sighed philosophically. "Even my guru used to say that." And he rolled onto his back, joining Melissa in the contemplation of the magnificent galactic space on the plass ceiling. From time to time, the clouds of coloured dust started whirling, stars rushing in all directions at mind-boggling speed, weird geometrical patterns of infinite complexity flashing in the space of the room. This, according to the architects who had crafted the energy field, was because the images came from the consciousness of the Watchers, the fiery angels who could see through myriads of worlds and dimensions at the same time. In this cosmic jumble the images became so multifarious and perplexing that the giants themselves – despite being the Watchers' descendants – had to close their eyes. And if they persisted and kept watching, they were sometimes taken by fits that made them lose their mind and run about like madmen, destroying everything in their way. As the saying went, when the giants became mad, nothing in the kingdom could stop them.

Melissa and Pralaya were about to close their eyes when the images suddenly disappeared. The field of stars was replaced by a blank ceiling –pale whitish glows exuding from the plass. The atmosphere in the room became flat and empty.

"Another collapse of our energy field?" Pralaya complained.

"I'm afraid so."

"But it's the fifth time in four weeks!"

"Not much we can do about it," Melissa shrugged her shoulders in resignation. "I'll ask Lusec to come and fix it tomorrow morning."

Pralaya was gripped by a wave of anxiety. What if all the fields of the citadel collapsed for good, as many seers – not just baphomets – had predicted?

What if it were tomorrow?

What would become of him and of his kind? The mental powers of the baphomets rested entirely on the fields. "If the fields cark it, then so do we!" a baphomet brother-disciple of his guru had once told him. That was long ago, at a time when no one really believed it could ever happen.

Now the question was no longer whether it would happen, but when. And it scared the Watchers' hell out of the baphomets.

Pralaya had recurrent nightmares of reverting to the state of a silly goat. It was as ugly and terrifying as it was inevitable. It happened slowly. First his supernatural sight lost its sharpness and his intuition was shrouded. A few months later he realised he could no longer read people's time tracks. The giants no longer had the same fascinated glow in their eyes when they looked at him. His mental clarity was obscured. He could no longer guess people's motivation, and whenever he played social games with them, he lost. Gradually, insidiously, he became dotty. But he didn't realise it until months later, during a brief flash, remembering who he had been – Pralaya, the shrewd adviser of Melissa the Wise, the super-gifted baphomet who used to stand by her side during the prophetic readings she gave to the mighty patriarchs of the citadel. Long forgotten were the days when Grand Commander Bexton used to praise his wisdom and listen to his advice before taking any major decision. Now Pralaya was nothing more than a useless wreck. So debilitated, he even pissed on the floor of Melissa's bedroom, like a stupid goat. And he overheard conversations between Melissa and her friends.

"After all, he's just a goat!" her friends said.

"No!" Melissa protested vigorously, "Baphomets are no ordinary goats! Over hundreds of years, they have been bred into one of the most psychic and intelligent of all creatures."

"But that was through the power of the fields," her friends argued. "The fields are gone. Baphomets are nothing more than goats!"

23

"No! Oh gods, have mercy!" Pralaya tried to scream. "Not that! Not a goat!" But no sounds came out. To his horror, he realised that he no longer could talk. Panic-stricken, he gasped, his mouth open in despair.

He prayed to the Watchers. He called onto the universe. But no sounds came.

The flashes of clarity did not last long. His mind was devoured by the most monstrous of all plagues: oblivion. Lost, he was. There was nothing left of him. He wandered about with an empty look, a stupid goat dropping excrement all through the house, a constant embarrassment to Melissa and her guests. Until the day...

The terrible day.

That day when, out of nowhere, Melissa snuck up on him and stabbed him with a long kitchen knife.

In the back.

Melissa!

Only one stab. A master blow. In his spine. Just below the neck. A spreading red stain in his white fur.

He collapsed on his side on the marble floor with a thud.

The pain was atrocious. Excruciating. Unbearable.

In a last flash, he remembered who he had been. And he shed big wet tears. "Melissa, how could this happen?"

"I love you, Pralaya," Melissa burst into tears. She knelt close to him, horrified at what she had done, and yet immensely relieved that she had finally found the strength to do it. "I'm sorry!" she sobbed, "I couldn't bear to see you like this. I couldn't bear it!"

The breath of life was fast escaping from Pralaya. He spoke slowly, as if from far away. "Thank you Melissa. I say, this was a very sensible thing you did. The right choice, really."

"I am so sorry!" Melissa cried a flood of tears.

"But Melissa, does all this mean I never existed? Was I a complete illusion, nothing more than an abstract construction of the fields?"

Before she could answer, everything became black.

That was the moment Pralaya woke up from his dream.

Every time.

Back in the room, the ceiling was still ominously blank.

Pralaya tapped the marble floor with his hoof, as if to make sure he was no longer dreaming. He sighed and looked up silently, wondering if there was one power in the creation that would have mercy on him. Not that he had an inflated opinion of himself. Only imbeciles think of themselves as unique. Still, he believed that he and his fellow baphomets were well worth saving. "So many stupid animals will survive the destruction of the fields," he thought, "why couldn't we?"

Perhaps, after all, this was the meaning of the terrible wave of destruction that was about to strike the kingdom. All the good things would be engulfed: the fields, the knowledge, the temples, the works of art... Only barbaric natives and idiotic beasts would be left to populate the new world.

"I bet rats will survive the flood!" the baphomet's eyes narrowed.

Melissa, whose mind was so inflamed that she could not think of anything else but her lover, swam close to Pralaya and whispered into his ear. "Tell me, what have you seen about Bexton?"

"I haven't seen a thing about Bexton," the baphomet answered. "And I am not sure I want to use the sight for this matter."

"But why?"

"Because you're madly in love with him. What if I discovered something terrible? I say, many a baphomet before me was butchered for less than that."

"Pralaya!" Melissa the Wise expressed her indignation in her softest voice. "How can you imagine something like that could ever happen?"

Pralaya didn't answer.

"Please, Pralaya," Melissa insisted. "I love him but I don't want to behave like a fool. I call on your wisdom. Please use your sight. Show me possible scenarios of the future."

Still lying on his back, the baphomet closed his eyes and tapped from his supernatural vision. "Mm... There is something I don't like. And it's happening at this very minute."

"What?"

"Look!" the baphomet said, and in the space of the room he conjured the image of the citadel's fish market, where a large number of giants were converging for a public meeting.

16.2 The giant whose time had come

"It's a great success," Samoan exclaimed when Bobros arrived. "Look at this crowd!"

At least fifteen hundred giants, not one giantess among them, had gathered in the marketplace. Dozens more were arriving by the minute.

"The Watchers are with us!" Bobros grinned with satisfaction, waving at the mob that had been waiting for him.

The assembly of giants gave him nothing short of an ovation.

Bobros the Terrible, as he was often called, let them express their jubilant enthusiasm for a while. Then he raised his arms to silence them. So many people had come that those who stood at the back could not see him. They protested loudly.

Three of Bobros' men went to fetch a huge barrel, ten lawful feet high, from the stall of a sympathiser. They rolled it amidst loud roars of encouragement, and the crowd exulted when the barrel was stood vertical. Lifted up by his men, Bobros stood on top of the barrel. A second ovation rose from the giants.

Despite being only twenty-four, Bobros, son of Bobros, knew how to mesmerise a crowd. He was a superb giant, more than one-and-a-half times the size of a normal man (or 'dwarf', as the giants liked to call those not of Nephilim stock). He was a mountain of muscles with huge hairy hands, even huger feet, and exceptionally sharp black eyes that shone with light-ning-like glows coming straight from the sky of the Watchers. From his eyes one could tell he had mastered some of the most dangerous powers of the necromancers of his lineage. The Bobros had been black magicians from generation to generation, ever since the ancient days of Harmag the Necromancer, son of Azazel the Watcher and father of the first Bobros.

"Friends," he started his discourse in a clamorous voice that no one had any difficulty hearing, even those who stood in the last rows, "I have come here today to remind you of the glory of our ancestors, the invincible Watchers!"

The crowd responded to the name of the fiery angels with a deluge of applause. Bobros enthusiastically cheered with them, before again silencing them by raising his arms. "Too many people," he went on, "...too many people in this kingdom tend to forget what the Earth was like before our ancestors the Watchers, led by Azazel and Shemyaza, descended on Mount Hermon. The kingdom, if you could call it a kingdom, was a kingdom of dwarfs – shameless, useless, stupid blobs, hardly capable of dressing and feeding themselves. They spent their days vegetating, hardly talking to each other. They never discovered anything. They never invented anything. They never built anything, apart from sheds and tree houses. And they were so totally hopeless in bed that you wonder how their species managed to survive!" Bobros lifted his fist, his little finger half-erect. And he gave a scornful, pitying look.

As he knew well, the giants delighted in this kind of rhetoric. They clapped their hands, screaming like wild animals, jumping up and down, making the earth shake under them.

"A race of poor, miserable, worthless, contemptible, despicable blobs! Hardly better than animals. Not worth being called human beings, really! Were they?"

"No! No! No! No!..." the giants yelled in one titanic voice.

"Not worth anything at all! Then at last, at last the Watchers descended." Bobros paused to let his audience shout enthusiastically.

"They married the daughters of the sort-of men, and they blessed the kingdom with their Nephilim children. It was the true beginning. The new race was created! The first real men were born!" Bobros raised his voice, "And they were formidable! They were unstoppable! Like you! Like me! Like us!"

The mob of giants demonstrated their approval by raising their fists, pounding the ground with their feet.

"Can you tell me one good thing in this kingdom which did not come from the Nephilim? Without us, there would not be *one* tool in the kingdom. Without us, there would not be *one* soft stone in the kingdom. Without us, there would not be *one* proper energy field in the kingdom. What did the dwarfs do with their fields? Chapels where they could sit and kiss angels' asses, and nothing more! No wonder, mind you, with the kind of food they ate – and which they still eat, by the way. Worse than crap. At least, crap has taste."

The giants laughed, booing their contempt and spitting on the ground.

"The dwarfs, sad to say, haven't changed much. But they tend to forget one thing: *We* brought civilisation onto the Earth! *We* made the kingdom what it is!" Bobros paused a few seconds, wondering if the time had come to suggest that none but a giant was fit to occupy the high function of King of Atlantis. But as this amounted to nothing short of a declaration of war on the rest of the kingdom, he decided to wait for a more opportune occasion.

He went on, "In the last years, as you know, there have been great disturbances in the energy fields. Truly, these started many years ago. When I was a child, I remember hearing Bobros, my father, complaining that some of his rituals were being disturbed by new kinds of field distortions never encountered by any of the necromancers of my family until then. But these remained moderate. It is only in the last months that it has become obvious to all of us that there are great perils just ahead of us. These matters are *extremely* serious. Do you realise what will happen if things are left to follow their course? It's not just the fields that keep you warm in your bathtub that will collapse. It is not just the fields that keep your food from rotting that will collapse. We, Nephilim giants, connect with the consciousness of the Watchers through the fields. We, Nephilim giants, draw our powers from the Watchers through the fields. If the warp of fields collapses, we lose everything. *Ev-ery-thing!*"

Bobros remained silent for a few seconds, watching the wave of anxiety that ran through the crowd. He clenched his right fist, hit the palm of his left hand and continued in an angry voice, "Here we come to a complete absurdity. *We* were the first people to manipulate the fields in the kingdom. *We* taught others to craft soft stones to control the powers of the fields. *We* developed the most powerful and the most sophisticated fields in the entire kingdom. But when the whole warp of fields is threatened with extinction, what are *we* doing? Nothing! Nothing at all! We just sit and wait for the disaster, as if it were inevitable. Is *that* in keeping with our Nephilim spirit? Is *that* behaving like the sons of the Watchers?"

"Nay!" the giants responded, pulling disgusted faces.

"Do you realise that throughout the kingdom, the dwarfs continue to mess with the fields, creating a terrible tangle through their incompetence? Do you realise that our fields are being polluted by the misguided manipulations the dwarfs perform every day? Do you realise that *we* are paying a high price for *their* mistakes? The truth is, the dwarfs should never have been allowed to play with the fields in the first place. They are too stupid!"

"Shall we kill them all?" one of his supporters shouted.

"Why not, after all?" Bobros burst out laughing, and the giants laughed with him.

"What shall we do, Bobros?" a giant asked.

"Yes, Bobros. Tell us what we should do!" the crowd echoed.

Bobros raised his hands to bring silence and declared, "We *must* regain control over the fields. Full control. *Absolute* control. And right now! Let Grand Commander Bexton send a communication to the King of Atlantis demanding that throughout the kingdom, all the superintendents of the fields be replaced by our men."

"But that would mean giving us total control over all the temples of the kingdom!" an old giant exclaimed. The plain truth – whoever was in command of the warp of fields would become the new King of Atlantis.

"I don't have a problem with that, grandpa, do you?" Bobros' eyes lit up with a frightening necromantic glow. He stood very straight on his barrel, absorbing the giants' exultant mood with satisfaction.

Judging the time had come to bring his speech to a conclusion, he raised his hands, drew from the powers he had received from his father and projected the Voice onto the crowd. "Are we going to stand here gaping and doing nothing, like helpless cattle waiting for slaughter?"

"No! No!..." the mob was heating up.

"Are we going to waste all the gifts we have received from the Watchers instead of standing up for ourselves?" he raised an enraged fist.

Mounting anger in the crowd, "No! No!..."

"I want you to stand up and be great! Make our ancestors proud!" Bobros made his Voice a huge flame, "I want you to show the world what full-blooded Nephilim are capable of! I want you to accompany me to the house of Lord Vrolon, Superintendent of the Fields under the Appointment of His Supreme Majesty the King of Atlantis, and deliver an unambiguous message to him. I want you to walk with me to the palace of Grand Commander Bexton and demand that a communication be sent to the King of Atlantis – let the fields, which our glorious ancestors taught us to operate, be returned to us!"

"Yes! Yes!..."

"And let the supremacy of the Nephilim be restored! Let us be glorious, and victorious. Glory! Glory! Glory to the Watchers and to their sons!"

A mighty wave of jubilation rose from the crowd. The giants euphonically congratulated each other. They carried Bobros in triumph along the central alley of the marketplace. But as they advanced, their applause gradually turned into screams of rage. They raised menacing fists towards the sky. They jumped up and down, they trampled the earth threateningly. Some started shaking the stalls of the market and breaking jars, while others collected large wooden sticks and all kinds of implements that could be used as maces and weapons. Many didn't need to forage for weapons, they had come to the meeting with their clubs.

In the space of a minute the giants turned into wild, screaming beasts, rushing in all directions, attacking the plass buildings of the fish market.

Melissa, who had been watching the images with a disgusted look on her face, closed her eyes. "Oh, no! Not again!"

"Shall I stop the vision?" Pralaya asked.

Melissa reopened her eyes. "No, I think I prefer to see. Do you think we should warn Bexton?"

"No, no," Pralaya answered quietly. "Some of his men were at the meeting."

16.3 Carnage

It was savage, beastly, insane, and the giants loved it. Using their clubs, their maces and their huge fists, it did not take them long to flatten the entire fish market. Not one living wall was left erect. Every single jar was broken. Every single barrel of oil was crushed. Not one basket of fish was left intact. In the frenzy of destruction, some of the shopkeepers were even seen ransacking their own stalls.

When nothing was left but piles of plass rubble drenched in stinking fish puree, the mob of giants led by Bobros' men ran full-pelt through the streets of the citadel, yelling their fury, stirring up a high cloud of dust. Attracted by the clamour, many more giants joined in. By the time they arrived at the gates of Lord Vrolon's residence, their numbers had doubled.

It was a splendid mansion, built at great cost – the proud emblem of the sovereign authority of His Supreme Majesty the King of Atlantis, of whom Lord Vrolon was the official representative in the citadel of the Nephilim giants. Comprised of three separate wings, the large building was surrounded by exquisitely designed gardens full of rare, ancient trees and precious herbs that exhaled subtle, health-strengthening energies. Dozens of field-gardeners attached to the residence maintained dazzling flowerbeds that shone with a feast of auric colours and spread intoxicating astral fragrances, to the delight of pet filosterops, blue tortoises and rare animals with strange shapes as in the Ancient Days of the Earth. Everywhere one looked, whether inside or outside the mansion, there were statues of the gods wrought with gems and other invaluable works of art. The privacy and tranquillity of the small estate was secured by high walls of rock-solid plass, three lawful feet thick, and the only entrance was a fortified portal made of massive wooden gates, guarded by a small troop of soldiers from the King's army.

When they saw the furious crowd approaching, the soldiers who stood outside the gates immediately called their comrades for help. Like the rest of the small garrison they were normal men, not giants. The army commander, who was positioned on a small platform at the top of the front wall, was so terrified at the sight of the giants that he decided to abandon his men outside rather than running the risk of opening the gates. He called for help, gathering all his men – forty-three of them on the property. And he ordered the gates to be fortified with wooden beams.

The giants encircled the property, making sure none of the dwarfs could escape. Then they started a menacing war dance, shouting in low-pitched voices, "Tremble-tremble-tremble-tremble...!" stamping violently, making the earth quake under their feet.

His Excellency Lord Vrolon, Grand Superintendent of the Fields for the North-East under the Appointment of His Supreme Majesty the King of Atlantis, was sitting behind his huge desk when he heard the giants' ominous growling.

"Oh my Lord Melchisedek! What in the kingdom is *that*?" he exclaimed, wondering whether he should walk to his balcony. But the elderly man was so obese, and his heart condition so bad, that even standing up was an effort.

One of the crimson-robed officers rushed into his office. "Lord Vrolon... Lord Vrolon... there are hundreds of them! They're completely mad! And you know what they're like when they're mad..."

"Send a message to our garrison in Pentor. We need reinforcements. Immediately!" Vrolon's throat was dry.

"But we can't, Your Excellency! All communication fields have been out of order for three days. They are presently being diligently repaired and if, by the grace of our Lord Melchisedek..."

"Underworld!" Vrolon swore. "Those damn fields will play up with me right until the last moment!" From his pocket he grabbed a soft stone, a present from his young fiancee. It was a state-of-the-art communication device crafted by the kingdom-famous stone makers of the temple of Verzazyel, in the distant county of the Snowy Mountains. But when Vrolon tried to activate the soft stone to send an emergency message through darkness visible, the space remained silent.

"The Lord Melchisedek have mercy on us!" Lord Vrolon whispered, wiping thick beads of toxic sweat from his brow.

Meanwhile, Bobros had arrived at the gates.

The giants stopped their foreboding war dance. An ominous silence dawned on the place.

Bobros took on a calm, ceremonial voice, "I have come to deliver a message to Lord Vrolon, Grand Superintendent of the Fields under the Appointment of His Supreme Majesty the King of Atlantis. Open the gates and lead me to him!"

The guard, even though tall, was at least four heads shorter than Bobros. He looked up at him in terror.

"Open the gates!" Bobros projected the Voice onto him.

Compelled by the power of the necromancer's Voice, the guard turned to his commander who was still standing on top of the wall, and repeated the order, "Open the gates!"

"No way, man of the Law!" the officer replied. "If you have a message, give it to me. I will deliver it to His Excellency Lord Vrolon, Grand Superintendent of..."

"How dare you?" furious Bobros interrupted him. Locking his gaze into him, he projected a massive shower of venom into his head.

The officer instantly fell off the platform. His soldiers had to dodge aside as he collapsed on the dusty ground with a thud.

Dead.

"Open the gates!" Bobros repeated, this time in a cool, nonchalant voice.

One of the crimson-robed soldiers, his face contorted in panic, shouted to his comrades who stood behind the walls, "For the Lord Melchisedek's sake, open the gates!"

There was no reply.

Bobros shrugged his shoulders and turned back. "Well, then... open the gates!" he told the giants, with a calm smile on his lips.

The order triggered a new wave of madness. The giants all started screaming. They rushed against the gates and attacked the walls. In ten seconds the guards had been crushed to death. A few groups of giants went to fetch the trunks of large poplar trees from nearby streets. It was easy. They stood on each side of a tree and they pushed alternately, shaking the trunk until the roots gave in amidst ugly cracks. But even before the improvised battering rams were brought back, the gates had already crumbled under the fury of the mob. Meanwhile on the southern side of the property one of the plass walls was collapsing.

The hordes of giants rushed in. They used their clubs, their bare hands and their teeth. They massacred the dwarf-soldiers and the gardeners. Every single tree in the garden was knocked down. The statues were reduced to rubble, the flowerbeds trampled, the bushes uprooted. The pet filosterops, the tortoises and the rare animals were eaten alive. Downstairs in the house, having slaughtered the servants and broken every single piece of furniture, the giants started attacking the living walls.

Bobros and his men went straight to the superintendent's office. When they arrived at the top of the majestic staircase, with a gesture of his hand Bobros ordered them to remain calm. To make them laugh, he went and stood in front of the door and gave three delicate knocks. "Would Lord Vrolon, by the grace of our Lord Melchisedek, happen to be here, please?" he asked in a distinguished voice. But the tumult in the mansion was so loud that he had to repeat his question, this time shouting.

On the other side, a young army officer was desperately trying to fortify the door, using Lord Vrolon's desk. "What d'you want?" he shouted back.

"I should like to speak to His Excellency, by the grace of our Lord Melchisedek."

"On whose authority do you come?" the officer asked shakily.

Bobros the Terrible lost patience. Looking at his friends, he clicked his fingers and pointed his thumb at the door.

Fifteen seconds later the door was flattened, Lord Vrolon's desk under it, and the army officer crushed to death under the pile.

Lord Vrolon was still sitting in his armchair. Rendered bold by the imminence of his death, he looked straight into Bobros' eyes. "Provoke the anger of the King of Atlantis at your own risk, giant!" he exclaimed defiantly.

"Are you threatening me, piglet?" Bobros smiled with contempt, pointing a menacing finger at Lord Vrolon's enormous heap of fat. He saw the soft stone the superintendent was holding in his left hand. Fearing it was a weapon, he immediately swamped Lord Vrolon with a massive dose of red venom.

The pain was horrendous. Lord Vrolon gasped. The soft stone, which the beautiful Felicia, high priestess of Verzazyel, had given him a few months earlier, fell from his hand.

Laughing sardonically, Bobros walked slowly toward Lord Vrolon. He grasped his head with his two huge, hairy hands, and finished him off with a lethal shower of black venom while thrusting his thumbs deep into his eye sockets. Holding onto the head, Bobros lifted Lord Vrolon's grossly obese body as if it was nothing more than an empty crimson bag. He carried it to the balcony and brandished it in front of the crowd.

Throughout the property, the giants, heated by the smell and taste of blood, celebrated their easy victory with a titanic clamour. They ran to the front of the mansion to acclaim Bobros.

Standing on the balcony, the young giant used his necromantic powers. Resting on the frenetic vibrations that came from the crowd, he called on the Watchers, bringing down a reflection of their supermental presence onto himself.

A strange glow appeared around Bobros' aura.

The crowd was silenced by the extraordinarily fast-moving, eerie energy of the Watchers.

Like most encounters with the Watchers, it was brief but devastatingly intense. Unforgettable. An aeon condensed into a second, a whirling myriad of worlds cognised in the twinkling of an eye, the cacophonic revelation of multidimensional abstract unrealities coiled into one hyper-real dot. Time moving upside down and back to front, running after the Watchers' light-speed train of thoughts without ever catching it. The universe realising itself as a perplexed mental form – but whose? – and spreading all over the place – but why? – then condensing into a point again without having had time to ask what's the point. More and more universes spawning from the sourceless source – but why? – and becoming strangers, especially to themselves. The cosmic cycle that seemed to be completed had already started again while much, much greater things were happening concomitantly – things that can only be known through living mathematical formulae that worm their way through to infinity, but so fast that you never have the time to ask if there is anyone there.

As quickly as it had come, the supermental presence vanished.

It left the giants stunned. Their complete silence contrasted with the rampaging noise coming from inside the mansion, where many giants were so busy demolishing everything that they had missed the Watchers' descent.

Bobros, who was still holding the corpse of Lord Vrolon by the head, his thumbs thrust deep inside the old man's eye sockets, contemplated the blood running down his arm. "Who wants the piglet?" he shouted to the crowd. For the giants believed that eating the body of a defeated enemy was a way of stealing his power – especially the kidneys and their tasty tops, and the brain, the liver and the heart.

"Me! Me!..." Woken from the supermind-boggling flash of Watcher-ness by the prospect of a cannibalistic feast, the giants responded with child-like excitement, jumping up and down.

"Let the victory be yours!" Bobros threw the superintendent's body off the balcony. His men then brought the bloody remnants of the young army officer who had been mashed under the door. His body was also tossed to the crowd.

Like hungry dogs, the giants rushed onto the corpses. They didn't bother peeling off the crimson robes. Those who could come close enough just bit into whatever they could grab, and it was left to chance as to who inherited the kidneys and other tidbit. The giants who were further away from the balcony satisfied themselves with the bodies of the other soldiers. In the elated madness, the crowd also attacked the corpses of the gardeners – not to steal their strength but just for fun, so as not to be left out of the feast.

On the balcony, Bobros was watching the ritual orgy with an affectionate smile on his face when one of his men came to whisper in his ear, "Nearly all the walls of the mansion have been demolished! We'd better get out of here before everything collapses!"

As he was speaking, there were ominous cracking sounds.

Bobros and his acolytes were seen hastily jumping off the balcony, while all the other giants still inside the building were running out at full speed. Just in time. The last two walls still erect were yielding under the roof's pressure.

In a matter of seconds, that which used to be the pride of the King's architects was reduced to rubble, to the wild delight of the mob.

"Shall we take them to the grand commander's palace now?" Samoan asked Bobros.

"Give them a little longer. Let them finish eating the dwarfs," Bobros answered, putting one of his bloody thumbs in his mouth and licking it, contemplating the carnage going on around them. "We want them to be in a high mood, don't we? Feasting on dwarf meat will warm up their spirits."

"We should have left one of them alive, so he could report to the King's palace," Samoan sighed thoughtfully.

"Don't worry, the King will soon hear from us. Come on, let's gather our men outside."

A few minutes later, when every giant had had his share of raw flesh, Bobros gave the signal, "To the palace of the grand commander! And Glory! Glory! Glory to the Watchers and their sons!"

16.4 The challenger

Grand Commander Bexton, who had been warned by his police, was standing on a high balcony when he heard and saw the furious swarm rushing towards his palace. He remained very calm as he had throughout his life, even when faced with the most difficult circumstances. In his fifteen years as leader of the citadel, there had occasionally been waves of civil unrest. The giants were hot-blooded, they enjoyed the sport of destroying part of their own city from time to time. Especially the smelly fish market, which had been purposely built (and regularly rebuilt) with lightweight materials. But never before during his years as grand commander had a crowd dared to march against his palace.

Two thousand soldiers formed a thick line of defence. And these were no dwarf-soldiers of the army of the King of Atlantis, but giants of the third battalion of the Green Guard, a small army of its own, famous throughout the kingdom for being one of the most formidable fighting forces of all times. Against their deadly venom-fields and Point-weapons, the angry mob armed with only clubs and maces didn't stand a chance.

Or did they? Bexton wondered. Many among the giants knew how to manifest the strange and frightening powers of the Watchers' sky. And the crowd was led by Bobros, the prestigious sorcerer who, two years earlier, at the age of only twenty-two, had won all the magic contests of the guild of Nephilim necromancers, subsequently becoming their leader.

What if Bobros and his men were powerful enough to neutralise the Point-weapons of the Green Guard?

Then anything could happen.

And what if the Green Guard refused to fight against their fellow-giants? That was unlikely. The soldiers were remarkably well disciplined. Still, they had very rarely clashed with their own kind. Grinding his teeth, Bexton watched the crowd gathering in Proclamation Square, so called because the inhabitants of the citadel assembled there once a year to hear their grand commander deliver a speech inspired by the Watchers. Bexton hated to imagine the carnage that would ensue if the situation degenerated.

When they saw their grand commander standing on the royal balcony, towering more than fifty lawful feet above ground level, the crowd of giants became silent. They stayed a few lawful feet from the rows of guards, waiting for Bobros.

Standing in the first row of soldiers were Fornan and his son Basalinger, the two generals who commanded the elite battalions of the Green Guard. Fornan was an old giant whose face was so wrinkled that his men affectionately called him 'Fornan the crocodile'. He was standing underneath the royal balcony. Using the power of the Point, he communicated with his son, who was posted outside the southern wing of the palace, some six hundred lawful feet away from him. "They are at least twice as many as we are!"

"Don't worry," Basalinger Point-answered, "Bobros has given me his necromancer's word he won't do more than deliver his message. He promised he would keep the crowd quiet."

"But look at their eyes. They've been showered with Watcher's venom. They're wild! All this could get completely out of control."

A lucid assessment of the situation. By nature the giants were highly unpredictable. But when their brains were overheated by Watcher's venom, then really *anything* was possible. As they said themselves with undisguised pride, 'When the Nephilim giants become mad, their madness knows no limits.' Bobros, even though a master in the necromantic art of crowd control, knew very well he was playing a dangerous game. But from the omens he had perceived, he believed his time had come and the Watchers were with him.

When he arrived at Proclamation Square the crowd opened a corridor to let him walk towards the royal balcony. Followed by his men he advanced slowly, looking straight in front of him.

"Strange beast!" Fornan the crocodile said to himself, watching the plethora of complex geometrical shapes that shone in Bobros' aura – an unmistakable token of a high initiate of the mysteries of the Watchers.

On the royal balcony Bexton was also contemplating the strange lights that emanated from Bobros. "No wonder he fascinates the crowds!" he thought. And he drew a long breath, getting ready to fight one of the decisive battles of his life.

Bobros stopped a few lawful feet from General Fornan. The two men looked at each other silently for a few seconds. Then Fornan asked in a loud, ceremonial voice, "Bobros, son of Bobros, why have you come here?"

Bobros answered in a no-less-ceremonial tone, "Inspired by the high consciousness of the Watchers, I have come to deliver a message to His Excellency Bexton, Grand Commander of the citadel."

"Speak, Bobros!" Bexton called from the royal platform. "I am listening."

A heavy silence followed.

The crowd had witnessed the descent of the light of Watcher-ness on Bobros. They were now convinced he was an inspired representative of their angelic ancestors. Was it the fiery Shemyaza that spoke through him? Or perhaps Azazel himself?

Bobros, as protocol dictated, bent his head with reverence before addressing the leader of the citadel. Then he looked up. Following etiquette, he fixed his gaze on the sovereign's feet. "Your Excellency, we, of the guild of Nephilim necromancers, believe that the time has come to demand from His Supreme Majesty the King of Atlantis that the control of all energy fields be returned to the Nephilim people. I therefore bring you a petition, asking that a message be sent to the King's palace immediately, requesting that in each province in the kingdom, the grand superintendent of the fields be replaced by one of the necromancers of my guild."

Bexton could hardly believe his ears. Never before in the fifty-two years of his wretched life had he heard anything so absurd. Total war against all the other provinces of the kingdom, was that what the necromancers of the guild had in mind? Not wanting to inflame the anger of the crowd, Bexton carefully refrained from dismissing the young fool. "Thank you for bringing the guild's petition, Bobros, son of Bobros," he replied in a calm voice. "I shall consider your request and inform you of my decision in the lawful near future."

Bobros wasn't going to give up so easily. His eyes still directed towards Bexton's feet, he insisted, "Your Excellency, the guild of necromancers wishes to draw your attention to the extreme gravity of the present situation regarding the energy fields. Unless immediate action is taken, a global breakdown of the entire warp of fields could take place any day. I do not need to tell you how dramatic the consequences would be for all Nephilim people, whose precious link to their ancestors the Watchers relies on the fields."

"Why does this arrogant bastard need to bring four thousand people under my balcony to tell me that?" Bexton thought. But he betrayed no sign of anger. "Your grand commander is well aware of the condition of the warp of fields in the kingdom, and he has taken all required measures to ensure the welfare of his people," he answered in a quiet, paternalistic tone of voice.

Bobros raised his voice, "Which measures, Your Excellency?"

Bexton became pale. In his fifteen years of leadership, never had anyone dared reply to him in this way.

Whispers ran through the crowd.

Fornan the crocodile hardened his look, ready to order the onslaught. But Basalinger Point-called him, "We remain quiet, father! We remain quiet!"

Swallowing his anger, Bexton simply repeated, "All required measures."

"Your Excellency," Bobros further raised his voice, "in these extraordinary times when the Nephilim people are on the brink of total disaster, we, necromancers of the guild, believe we have the right to know exactly what is being done by you."

This insolence went far beyond the limits of the tolerable. Seeing that the confrontation was becoming unavoidable, General Fornan started giving instructions to his officers. On the other side, Bobros' men, who were spread among the crowd, established a token-ring of Point-connection, ready to unleash the deadly secret powers of the guild and swamp the Green Guard with a formidable shower of venom.

Bexton decided to make a last attempt to avoid the massacre. Raising his hands, he addressed the crowd, "Good people of the citadel, since I have been your leader, you have enjoyed one of the most precious of all things – peace! As a result of years of my patient work, you are now in a situation where you do not have to fear any enemies. And why? Because you have no enemies. All our neighbours have signed treaties with us. And this is why not one of you has had to leave his wife and family to go to war. Not one of you has had to cry about the premature death of his children. Instead of wasting our energies waging wars in distant lands, we have built a prosperous nation for ourselves. Never before have we been so rich! Throughout the kingdom, people envy the Eastern Peninsula – not just because of our brilliant origins, but also for our culture and our wealth. Why would we want to destroy all this by declaring war on the rest of the world? Let the dogs of war bark! Listen to the voice of wisdom!"

It was a beautiful discourse spoken in warm near-Voice thresholds, and with sincere enthusiasm. But was it really the right language to galvanise a venomous rabble heated by the taste of raw human flesh? The giants were not in the mood to hear about peace. They wanted more blood.

"Your Excellency, peace is certainly a beautiful thing," Bobros replied with a touch of cynicism that resonated with the pack, and he paused. "There is just one problem with your peace. It is going to kill us all!"

"He is going too far!" Fornan angrily Point-called his son. "If you can communicate with his men, tell them to piss off, fast! Or I blast the Watchers' hell out of their brains."

"Wait, father!" Basalinger Point-pleaded, "For the sake of Naamah's boobs, wait!"

On the royal balcony, Bexton was trembling with rage.

That did not stop Bobros. "If we keep waiting peacefully for the disaster, then the disaster will come. Ineluctably. And it will kill us all! Are we going to let..."

"Bobros!" Bexton interrupted him. "I give you five minutes to disperse."

A mixture of excitement and anxiety ran through the crowd.

Holding onto their clubs, the giants waited for Bobros' order to go on the rampage.

Facing them, the soldiers were ready to detonate their weapons.

Still gazing at Bexton's feet, Bobros drew from his powers and projected with the Voice, "Your Excellency, for the last time, I ask you to respond favourably to the petition of the guild and send our message to the King."

"Five minutes, Bobros!" the words fell like a sentence.

Raising his eyes, Bobros looked straight into the grand commander's eyes. He projected the Voice, "Well, then, Bexton, I challenge you!"

"What's this Ugly Underworld of a nonsense?" Fornan Point-called his son in fury. "Did you know this was going to happen?"

"I had no idea, father!" Basalinger Point-replied from the other end of the line of soldiers.

Bexton was taken completely by surprise. "A challenge?"

According to the Law of the Nephilim, a giant of noble birth had the right to challenge a grand commander, provided he was backed by at least twenty patriarchs and five hundred citizens of the citadel. Using their psychic powers and their bare hands, the grand commander and the challenger were to fight to the death in a duel of magic. The one who survived inherited the kingdom of the Eastern Peninsula. It was an ancient barbaric custom that had not been used for at least two hundred years. The reason was simple: it was the grand commander's prerogative to be backed by all his court sorcerers, while the challenger was to fight on his own. There were traditionally forty-nine court sorcerers, recruited from the most powerful teachers of the Law of the Watchers. Bobros was mad, but not mad enough to dare face the combined venom of forty-nine top-level Nephilim wizards! Through their spells they could not only kill a man, but also damage his soul so badly that almost nothing was left of him, just an astral flicker, good only for spending an aeon reincarnating among grubs and earth worms.

Who the Far and Ugly Underworld did Bobros think he was to challenge so much power?

Flabbergasted, Fornan the crocodile looked at the young giant in disbelief. "Does he really mean what he says?' he Point-questioned his son.

Basalinger held his breath, dumbfounded.

"Yes, Bexton, a challenge!" Bobros shouted. "A perfectly legal challenge, supported by fifty of the most respected patriarchs of our citadel."

To back his words, fifty of the giants who stood in the first rows raised their fists.

Bobros had spoken the truth. These were men of renown, wealthy and influential members of the Nephilim community. When he recognised them, Fornan was astounded. "What are they doing in that mob?" he wondered.

Suddenly, the messy demonstration was taking on the air of a well-prepared coup d'etat.

This time, it was Fornan's turn to Point-direct his son, "Tell your men to remain very quiet! There is no way in the seven spheres we're going to start a civil war. We watch and do nothing!"

"And what if Bexton orders us to attack?"

"You take your orders from me and from no one else!" General Fornan Point-yelled at his son. "Understood?"

"Yes, father!"

"Now, Grand Commander Bexton," Bobros continued, "as to the five hundred citizens who are required to support my plea..." The necromancer turned around and, calling on the Watchers, he shouted at the crowd, "Those who are with me, raise your fists!"

This was the kind of language the giants liked.

Proclamation Square turned into a sea of angry fists pointed at the sky.

Bobros defiantly stared at Bexton. "As challenger, I am legally entitled to choose the time and the place. It will be here, Bexton. Tomorrow at dawn!"

Pale with rage, Bexton retorted in a menacing voice, "Disperse, Bobros! Or else..."

Bobros smiled with irony, "Your Excellency, as long as you are the grand commander, I would hate to go against your orders!"

16.5 Guess who is outside the door!

Later on that afternoon, Melissa the Wise, clad in her most beautiful white dress, was sitting with her baphomet in the small room where she gave her readings when she received a warning signal through darkness visible. She quickly pulled herself out of the deep space of vision in which she and Pralaya had been immersed for hours, seeking help for Bexton.

"Oh! Oh! Guess who is outside the door!" Pralaya exclaimed.

"Bobros!" Melissa turned pale. "How come we didn't feel him arriving?"

Three loud knocks resounded at the door of the house.

Terrified, Melissa was trying to think straight. "Shall we call for help?"

The baphomet closed his eyes, Point-scanning the space. "Don't waste your time, they've completely isolated the house. All the fields of Point-communication have been interrupted. And we can't escape through the back. Six of his men have taken position at the rear door."

Three more knocks were heard.

"Oh, Watchers! What shall we do?" a shiver ran along Melissa's spine. "Pralaya..." She wrung her hands, the images of the carnage carried out by Bobros and his men still fresh in her mind. In panic, she ran to a cupboard where she kept a soft-stone weapon.

"Don't even think of using that!" the baphomet warned her. "It won't work against them, it will only make them furious."

Not listening to him, Melissa grabbed the soft stone and thrust it into her dress pocket. "How many are they?"

"At least twenty-five. Perhaps more."

Three louder knocks resounded.

"But how could they break into the enclave of the patriarchs?" With its high surrounding walls and its streets constantly patrolled by the Green

Guard, the enclave of the patriarchs was the safest and most secluded part of the citadel. Only giants of higher castes were allowed in.

His eyes still closed, Pralaya was desperately trying to break through the energy shield that Bobros' men had established around the house.

"What do we do?" Melissa contracted all the muscles of her legs to stop trembling. It worked, until a volley of loud bangs nearly knocked down the door.

"I say, open the door," Pralaya said.

"What?"

"I'll come with you," the baphomet said bravely. And as Melissa didn't move, he pushed her legs with his head, "Come!"

As soon as they started walking towards the door, the banging stopped.

"They can feel we're coming!" Melissa shuddered, holding onto the soft stone in her pocket.

Pralaya rubbed his fur against her legs to try to reassure her a little, or perhaps to reassure himself. It seemed to take an eternity to walk the corridor that led to the door. Everything had become so silent that when they finally arrived at the entrance hall, Melissa ventured to ask, "D'you think they've gone?" It was absurd. She could feel the presence on the other side of the door.

As if to answer her, three more knocks sounded. Three gentle knocks. Nothing like the wild bangs of the last minutes.

"Open!" the baphomet urged.

Melissa put her hand on her mouth hesitating. Then without thinking she pulled the door open all at once.

She found herself face to face with Bobros.

He stood in the doorway, massive and grounded like an Underworld mountain.

Melissa's eyes were caught by his exaggeratedly thick lips, his wide square jaw, his hairy neck so bulky that the collar of his shirt had to be left open.

None of his men were with him.

"Melissa the Wise?" Bobros asked in a respectful voice.

Melissa was so frozen with fear that Pralaya decided to answer for her. "Yes."

"And her wise baphomet!" Bobros turned to Pralaya and saluted him with a nod.

Pralaya, who always observed people's eyes, was struck by the exceptional intensity of his gaze.

Bobros gave a polite smile, "May I come in and speak to you for a moment?"

"Yes," Pralaya answered. And as Melissa wasn't budging, he added, "Come in."

Bobros waited patiently for Melissa to move aside. Then he walked in with an amused but extremely courteous smile on his face.

As he began walking down the corridor, Melissa quickly glanced outside. No one in sight. She promptly closed the door, and for one second was tempted to detonate her soft-stone weapon.

"Don't be a fool!" Pralaya Point-told her off. "Come!" And he started following Bobros, who went straight to their lounge.

Melissa followed Pralaya mechanically.

When he saw the large room with the pool and the many works of art Melissa had collected over the years, Bobros nodded in admiration, "Congratulations, Melissa. A fine place you have here!" Looking up, he saw the blank ceiling where the field had collapsed. "Ah," he commented in an annoyed tone, "these fields that break down all the time!"

He closed his eyes for a few seconds, gearing his energy into the collapsed field.

"What's he doing?" Melissa Point-asked Pralaya.

"No idea!" the baphomet shook his head.

Bobros reopened his eyes, a triumphant child-like look on his face. "All fixed!" he clicked his fingers.

Stunned, Melissa and Pralaya looked up. The field of stars had reappeared on the ceiling.

How could he possibly have fixed it so fast? Last time the field had broken down, it had taken Lusec and his men nearly two days to repair it.

"Don't thank me, it's my pleasure!" Bobros joked. "Do you mind if I sit down?"

Still holding the deadly weapon in her pocket, Melissa looked at him silently.

"Not at all. Please do," the baphomet answered in a neutral voice. Meanwhile, he Point-shouted at Melissa, "Take your hand out of your pocket, or you're going to have us both killed!"

Melissa obeyed him.

"Thank you!" the young giant gave them another exquisitely polite smile. If she hadn't seen the horrendous carnage that had taken place that morning, the scenes of cold-blooded murder and cannibalism, and the furious crowd running through the streets of the citadel, Melissa would have found it difficult to believe that the man who was sitting on her cushions was Bobros the Terrible. He looked so affable and obliging.

"Aren't you going to sit down?" Bobros inquired.

"But certainly!" the baphomet sat on his hind legs, keeping his forelegs straight and looking into Bobros' eyes.

"I see I have a supporter in this house!" Bobros exclaimed.

Standing very straight, Melissa frowned in outrage.

"No, I don't mean because he's being so polite. If he is polite it's only because he is trying to protect you, Melissa the Wise," Bobros kept smiling. "What I mean is, all the baphomets of the Eastern Peninsula are my supporters. And you know very well why, don't you?" he winked at the baphomet. "If the fields cark it then so do you baphomets! You know I am your last chance."

Pralaya remained impassive. "Will you tell us the purpose of your visit, Bobros?" he asked the giant, partly because he was afraid Melissa would flare with anger and say something stupid.

"Certainly. I have come to deliver a message for Bexton. I know he will come to visit you later on this evening. I have been told there is no one more likely than the two of you to bring him to reason. Now that I meet you, I understand why," he said in a voice that sounded perfectly sincere. "I must say, I envy Bexton for having beautiful and devoted friends like you. And so perceptive!" he added with a touch of irony. He had no difficulty detecting all the baphomet's tricks Pralaya was using to try to read his mind.

"And your message, Bobros?" Pralaya asked, not in the least embarrassed at having been caught Point-sniffing.

"My message is simple. Explain to Bexton that I have nothing against him. Tomorrow morning, I will take control of the state. But this does not have to take the form of an ugly challenge – a challenge in which he does not stand a chance, by the way. The entire guild of Nephilim necromancers is behind me. Not one of Bexton's court sorcerers will dare to intervene. And I'm afraid, despite his many qualities, our grand commander is no match for Bobros the necromancer. It will take less than five minutes before I am declared victorious. After that, I won't have any choice but to kill Bexton."

Melissa was filled with outrage, "What have you come to offer?"

Bobros looked at her gently, as if to thank her for speaking to him. "Let him rally to me! There is a perfectly lawful and respectable way of doing this: let him declare me his successor. Tonight. And I will make him one of my ministers. Tell him I have a great respect for his political talents. He is a brilliant statesman, isn't he?"

Pralaya and Melissa remained grim.

"In the great war which is going to take place, ineluctably," Bobros emphasized this last word, "every single Nephilim man will be precious. I sincerely believe Bexton is too valuable to be wasted. I want him to work with me. This is my message."

"Were Grand Commander Bexton willing to communicate with you, is there..." Pralaya started asking.

"No!" Bobros cut through Pralaya's words. "No negotiations. If Bexton wants to accept my offer, let him declare me the new grand commander tonight. I give him until midnight." And he became silent, contemplating the moving fields of stars on the ceiling.

"We shall certainly transmit your message to Grand Commander Bexton," Pralaya said after a short while. "Is there anything else?"

"Yes," Bobros fixed his fiery gaze on the baphomet, then on Melissa. "Please stop looking at me as if I were your enemy. I am not your enemy!

All I want is to secure a future for our people. A world in which the seed of the Watchers can flourish. Not a chaos in which all of us will have perished in vain, and baphomets will have reverted to goats. If we want to survive, we must take action. Radical action. And fast! This is exactly what I am doing. If we just sit and wait, we are lost. A hundred years from now, there won't be one community of giants left on the face of the Earth. Wise people like you know perfectly well that what I am saying is the truth."

Bobros kept eye contact with Melissa, hoping she would soften.

She remained like stone.

"Thank you for listening to me," he finally said, and he stood up. "Now, if you don't mind, I must take leave. Not that I don't enjoy your company, but... the Watchers are waiting!"

He walked back to the entrance hall, Pralaya and Melissa behind him.

Following the custom, Bobros waited politely for Melissa to open the door. Then he gave her and the baphomet a last smile, and he walked out.

Trembling, Melissa remained in the doorway for a moment, incapable of speaking or moving. Then she slammed the door, dropped on the floor, took Pralaya in her arms and held him tight. Sobbing, she let fall a flow of tears into his white, white fur.

"Melissa! Melissa!" the baphomet exclaimed. "I made a discovery. While scanning his energy, I found something that could change everything!"

16.6 And what if Aegypton had been colonised by the giants?

"Guess who's outside the door?" Pralaya mimicked the voice he had used earlier to announce Bobros' visit.

"It's not funny!" Melissa shouted at him, and she ran into the entrance hall.

"Isn't it?" the baphomet gave a lazy smile, stretching his body luxuriously. He quickly licked his white fur here and there to make himself more presentable. Then he stood up very straight on his four legs and took on a dignified, ceremonial attitude while scanning the space around the house. There were soldiers of the Green Guard everywhere. After Bobros left Melissa had immediately called Bexton, and within minutes the Green guards arrived at the house. They were soon followed by hordes of Field Wizards. "Don't waste your time!" Pralaya had tried to tell them. He knew very well that Bobros was far too intelligent to leave a spying device behind. But they didn't listen. Only after every single field in the house had been probed were the men satisfied the place was safe. Ready for Bexton's visit.

Grand Commander Bexton soon made his entry into the lounge, holding Melissa's arm. His energy was tense, he looked tired. Pralaya immediately noticed two new wrinkles on his high forehead. But that did not take anything away from the superb charismatic aura that enhanced his handsome aristocratic face.

"Here is our great baphomet!" Bexton exclaimed.

Pralaya bent his head reverently, "At your service, Your Excellency."

"Pralaya, I am very proud of you. I shall have a pink ribbon bestowed on you for your brave behaviour and the outstanding service you have rendered," Bexton declared, utterly impressed with the way the baphomet had handled the situation.

"A pink ribbon!" Pralaya told himself, bending his head a little lower. "That is no Watcher's pooh!" (a traditional Nephilim saying which referred to the fact that the fiery angels never went to the toilet). And he wondered how the Watchers' hell he would manage to attach the ribbon to his white fur.

Melissa, her shining eyes still red from the tears she had shed, invited Bexton to sit on a pile of cushions by the side of the pool. She sat in front of him and lightly touched his hand. She didn't feel like talking. She just wanted to drink his presence.

Bexton looked deep into her eyes but partly kept his stately attitude, as he usually did when Pralaya was in the room.

"He really loves her!" the baphomet thought, watching the gradual softening of Bexton's face. Each time the grand commander spent time with Melissa, his heart opened. It made him shine. And Melissa became genuinely wiser – baphomet's word! – and more profound, her blonde energy ripening like a field of wheat under the Sun. "What a shame they go together so well!" Pralaya Point-mumbled to himself.

"I don't have much time," Bexton said.

"You should have let us come to you!" Melissa gently caressed the tips of his fingers.

"It does me a lot of good to leave the palace! And the enclave of the patriarchs is only five minutes from my office in the tower of Akibel. It takes me less time to come here than to go from one end of the palace to the other! I wonder how that devil managed to find his way here. What do you think, Pralaya?"

At Melissa's invitation, Pralaya slowly trotted over to them. "The fact that fifty patriarchs have supported his challenge might have something to do with it," he answered, and he went to sit by Melissa's side as he always did when she gave a prophetic reading.

Bexton nodded thoughtfully, then he started asking Melissa more questions about Bobros' visit.

When Melissa finished telling the story again, Bexton sneered, "Me, abdicate for that lunatic? The necromancers of the guild have gone off their brains! That's the problem with this band of fanatics, they're mad. Completely mad. You have no idea what their plans are!" Bexton looked up to the starry ceiling. "They want to conquer the entire kingdom. Talk about radical solutions! To secure their supremacy over the fields, they have set their mind on destroying every single temple in the kingdom. They want a 'new Nephilim order', in which only Nephilim giants would live on Earth. In other words, they plan nothing less than slaughtering the entire non-Nephilim male population, while raping every single female to repopulate their new world. And they believe this to be the will of the Watchers! They even believe that if they succeed, the Watchers will descend on Mount Hermon a second time."

Melissa shook her head in horror, "Do they really want to massacre the entire non-Nephilim population of the kingdom?"

"Absolutely! And right now! If Bobros were to win the challenge against me, the first armies of giants would leave the citadel in a matter of weeks. We must stop them immediately, the situation could get completely out of control. But luckily for us – and for the rest of the world! – Bobros does not stand a chance tomorrow morning."

Melissa was concerned, "Bobros seemed very confident when he maintained that your court sorcerers would rally behind him."

"There is not one feather of truth in that bag! A complete fabrication, as will become only too clear tomorrow morning, when I leave him flat dead on the podium," he added with all the weight of his authority to reassure her. "What about this information Pralaya discovered?"

"During the 'visit', Pralaya used his skills to scan Bobros," Melissa explained. "He found something that could prove very precious to you."

"Mm..." Even though he had a great opinion of Pralaya, Bexton found it difficult to imagine Bobros the Terrible letting himself be scanned. Still, he listened with interest.

Pralaya preferred to let Melissa describe what he had seen.

"Bobros' grandfather – his name was Bobros, of course – used to live in the Centre North, in Eisraim. He had discovered a valley once occupied and bewitched by Harmag, son of Azazel. As it came to happen, that Bobros wreaked havoc in the county of Eisraim, until he was challenged by the non-Nephilim monks of the Brown Robe. Believe it or not, Bobros took a beating. Even though he was backed by all the forces Harmag had left in the valley, the Brown Robes got rid of him in less than a day."

"Did they kill him?"

"They did. Expectably, his son (who was the father of 'our' Bobros) swore revenge. He never had the opportunity to travel to Eisraim, but on his deathbed he made his son give his necromancer's word that the Brown Robes' temple – the temple of Eisraim, as it is called – would be destroyed. Ever since then, Bobros the Terrible has been engaged in secret workings against that temple. He intends to ransack it himself."

"And so?" Bexton seemed only moderately interested. Anyhow, hadn't Bobros decided to ransack *all* the temples of the kingdom? What was so special about Eisraim?

"And so we start with a personal grudge between Bobros the Terrible and the monks of the Brown Robe," Melissa continued. "Then Pralaya discovers one crucial fact, and this is where the story becomes much more interesting: it would seem that the Brown Robes are none other than the Masters of Thunder. This would explain how they got rid of Bobros' grandfather so easily."

"The Masters of Thunder?" Grand Commander Bexton found the story far-fetched. "I thought they were only a legend."

"Oh, no," Pralaya replied in a calm voice. "I say, not a legend!"

"Watch this! It was called the clearing of Erriba. It happened thirty-eight years ago." In the space of the room, Melissa conjured the image of an assembly of Brown Robe priests. They formed two long rows, facing each other, and delineating a corridor of extraordinarily charged energies. At one end of the corridor, a fire had been lit, and a huge obelisk of light sprang from it.

"Impressive," Bexton commented when he saw the massive clearing. "And what has all this got to do with us now?"

"Simple!" Melissa discontinued the vision. "Pralaya and I believe that an alliance could be formed with the Masters of Thunder to eliminate Bobros and his guild."

"Making an alliance with a non-Nephilim order against people of our own citadel?" Bexton immediately hated the idea.

"These Brown Robes are very wise people," Pralaya intervened. "In the last hours, I have carefully scanned a number of records concerning them and their activities in the temples of Eisraim and Lasseera. I believe we can trust them. They could be precious to us in these difficult times."

"Have you contacted them already?" Bexton asked suspiciously.

"No," Pralaya lied, as he and Master Gervin had agreed to keep their preliminary Point-conversation a complete secret. It had been a most cordial and informative exchange, at the end of which Gervin had even invited Pralaya to come and visit him in Eisraim.

"Mm... To tell you the truth," Bexton contemplated the ceiling, "I can't see why we should seek help from non-Nephilim people in distant counties when our citadel is teeming with magicians, Field Wizards and necromancers. And who says we need help, anyway? This Bobros is a fraud."

Melissa did not insist. She too looked up to the starry field, wondering where to take the conversation from there.

Pralaya looked down. "They don't understand," he sighed to himself. "They simply don't understand what's about to fall on their heads. And onto mine too, most unfortunately."

"Will you give me one of your prophetic readings, Melissa?" Bexton asked.

"With pleasure." Still holding his hand, Melissa closed her eyes. Using the special fields that were woven in the house, she projected her consciousness high above her head and established a link with the sky of the Watchers.

The atmosphere in the room suddenly changed. Everything became vibrant and strangely not like itself, very still, but infinitely more quickly, and with a queer quiddity which in its everywhere-ness – but where were we? – seemed to be asking a galaxy of axiomatically unanswerable questions. In short, there was Watcher-ness in the air.

"Connected!" Melissa whispered, reopening her eyes.

"Beautiful shining eyes, what can you see?" the grand commander asked in a little voice. Melissa's prophetic eyes always moved him deeply.

Melissa hesitated. "Clouds. Dark clouds," she finally said.

"On me, or on the kingdom?"

"Everywhere, Bexton. The danger is real. Your court sorcerers..."

Bexton frowned, "What about my court sorcerers?"

"I fear Bobros was right. They will support him, not you."

"No, that's impossible!" Bexton was adamant. "I have just spent the afternoon rehearsing with them for tomorrow morning. And I have spoken to each of them personally. They have all assured me of their full support. I also know from the reports of my secret police that they have never had any dealings with the guild of necromancers."

"Are you sure? There are many..."

"Absolutely sure!" Bexton interrupted her. Even though he didn't regard himself as a great expert in magic, Bexton had enough occult powers to decide when someone was lying to him. During thirty years of political life, his intuition had never betrayed him.

A strange feeling swept his mind. What was happening to Melissa? Since the beginning of their conversation, he had had the impression she was deviating from reality.

"Your secret police may no longer be reliable, Bexton," Melissa suggested. "I see a deal struck between Aprali and Bobros."

That was even more impossible. Aprali, the chief of the secret intelligence services, had been Bexton's friend since childhood.

Bexton became suspicious. Had Bobros veiled Melissa's clarity of mind? The wretched necromancer was certainly capable of bewitching her and her baphomet in order to create confusion.

Was that what had happened during Bobros' visit? Was that why she and Pralaya had suggested an alliance with non-Nephilim people – a sure way of making Bexton hated by his people?

As he knew without a shadow of a doubt that the third battalion would remain loyal to him, Bexton decided to test Melissa. "And what about the Green Guard? Have they also struck a deal with Bobros?"

"Not yet. But they are very much tempted to do so," Melissa answered in her prophetic voice.

"Melissa, Melissa..." deeply disturbed, Bexton closed his eyes. "Melissa, if all those things have been happening, how come neither you nor any of my advisers have mentioned them to me before?"

"It has all happened in the last days. In the last hours," Pralaya answered for Melissa.

Bexton found that difficult to believe. "So, what is your advice?"

Melissa remained silent for nearly two minutes, during which beautifully odd vibrations of Watcher-ness shook the room into total stillness. Then the wise woman spoke from so high that her voice was hardly recognisable. "Flee, Bexton! Take five thousand of your best men, and their wives, and flee from the kingdom. Build a fleet and go east. Cross the great ocean. Give a future to our race. Found a new city in the land of Aegypton, and there your seed will live beyond the flood."

Going into exile in a land of primitive savages? Preposterous! In the Eastern Peninsula as in all states of the kingdom, exile was regarded as *the* capital punishment – worse than death.

Surely, all this nonsense came from Bobros!

"If this necromantic toddler believes I am going to fall into his trap," Bexton told himself, "then really he is even more stupid than I thought!"

He felt angry, and devastated.

What if he could never trust Melissa again? That would have been the most vicious blow Bobros the Terrible could have delivered.

"Do you think I am going off track?" Melissa suddenly brought herself to normal consciousness.

"All this..." Bexton hesitated, "all this is very different from the visions you usually receive in your readings. Could it be that the emotions of the day have left you exhausted?"

The words hit her like a dagger in her chest. She held her breath and contained her tears.

"Melissa!" When he felt her pain, Bexton took her hand, held it tightly. He lightly touched her face, "Beautiful Melissa!"

"Will you excuse me, Your Excellency," the baphomet whispered, as he wisely judged his presence was no longer required.

On Bexton's quick nod, he trotted his way out of the room.

And he started thinking about the long Point-conversation that he and Bobros had had after his visit – totally unknown to Melissa, of course.

16.7 The radical solution

"I am a giant with a vision! I am a giant with a plan!" Bobros told Fornan and Basalinger at the beginning of their secret meeting. And the more the two generals of the Green Guard listened to him, the more convinced they were it was the truth.

To Fornan the crocodile, this came as a complete surprise. The old general had gone to the meeting reluctantly, and only because four respected patriarchs of the citadel, friends of his son, had put pressure on him. Truly, he had expected Bobros to be a bloodthirsty fanatic, a young arrogant whose ambition knew no limits – a deranged mind, cooked by excessive necromantic rituals. That's what too much Watcher's venom does to people, as the giants themselves accepted readily. But as Fornan quickly realised, the new leader of the necromancers' guild was an extraordinarily intelligent man who carefully planned each and every single move, and who understood the complex situation of the kingdom with surprising lucidity.

At first, Fornan had found this frightening, to say the least. Had Bobros been nothing more than a charismatic brute, then he could have been controlled, one way or another. But if, moreover, he was intelligent, then *really* he was dangerous – a major threat to the citadel, and to the kingdom at large!

But the more the general listened to Bobros, the more he was seduced by the man's visionary statements backed by solid common sense, and by the fact that his plans paid attention to the most minute details. Throughout his life General Fornan had complained that his officers did not pay enough attention to detail. Besides, there was something unique about Bobros: he brought hopes for a solution to the looming catastrophe, when every other leader preferred to pretend nothing was happening. Despite all the love and respect Fornan felt for Grand Commander Bexton (whom he almost regarded as his son), he was deeply disturbed by the fact that in the last fifteen years, *nothing* had been done to address the deterioration of the fields. Whenever Fornan mentioned the topic, Bexton usually answered with platitudes such as "All our best experts are onto it", or "We are all working hard at finding a solution." And two months ago, when the old general had finally decided to express his concern unambiguously, hitting the grand commander's desk with his fist and yelling, "For the hell of the Watchers' sake, Bexton, can't you see that this collapse of the fields *is* going to kill us all?" Bexton had simply shrugged his shoulders and answered, "What do you want us to do about it? Even if we could persuade every single necromancer of the Eastern Peninsula to stop their rituals and change the way they tap energy from the fields, it wouldn't be enough. Ever since the time of the Watchers, every generation has added thousands and thousands of fields to the warp. All these fields are intricately linked – not just ours, of course, those of the dwarfs too. Each time we manage to fix one of them, it causes another ten to collapse. The warp has become completely unmanageable! No one – no one in the entire kingdom! – has a clue what to do."

Now for the first time, Fornan was sitting in front of a man who proclaimed he had a real answer to the problem, and who backed his words with precise analyses and credible judgements. No wonder his supporters wanted to look at him as a messiah, and believe in his 'radical solution'.

But what a radical solution! What Bobros was proposing implied nothing less than conquering the entire kingdom, dethroning the King, taking over *all* temples, and carrying out massacres on an unprecedented scale.

"The problem is global. It requires a global solution," Bobros told the generals. "When did the warp of fields start going wrong? Let's face it, it started with the descent of the Watchers!"

Fornan and Basalinger chuckled at such enlightened realism. These were the very words used by all anti-Nephilim propagandists in the kingdom.

"But let's face it!" Bobros repeated, not unhappy with the stupefied look on the generals' faces. "The revelation of the Watchers was the beginning of an awful lawful lot of problems in the kingdom. And the reason is simple: it accelerated the evolution of human beings in phenomenal proportions. If it hadn't been for the Watchers, the dwarfs would still be blissful blob-men wallowing in the countryside, doing nothing but praising the Lord Melchisedek from morning to night. They wouldn't have modified any of the fields given to them by the gods, and everything would be blissfully fine for them!"

Few Nephilim giants ever dared to present the facts in this way. Fornan was as flabbergasted as he was impressed by Bobros' directness.

"And so what do we do from here?" Bobros continued. "The dwarfs themselves are ready to admit that despite all their contempt for the Nephilim, they would hate to live in a world without soft stones and all the good things that landed in the kingdom as a result of the revelation of the Watchers. They know that without the impulse of the Watchers, they would still be as idiotic as they were in the early days of the kingdom. They are locked in. There is no solution for them! They don't want to return to semi-animal ignorance. Yet they are incapable of moving forward and bringing to completion what the Watchers started. They lack the will and the intelligence to bring about progress. They are terrified at the idea of changing anything in their world. They simply do not have the dimension. Truly, they're a dying race."

"Why not just let them die by themselves, then?" Fornan asked. "Wouldn't it be much less trouble than having to kill them all? There are a hell of a lot of them in the kingdom. At least eight men out of ten are completely devoid of Nephilim spice in their blood."

"The problem is, we need to move fast. Unless we immediately take control of the entire warp of fields, everything will collapse. And our link to the Watchers will be irreversibly lost. Let's face it! If we want to survive, we have no choice but to force *all* the temples of the kingdom to discontinue *all* their rituals, so as to clean up the warp of fields from *all* non-Nephilim influences. And then we will reconstitute the warp from scratch through a massive injection of power from the Watchers. As you know only too well, the central problem with the warp of fields is that it has become so complicated that no one can control it. Presently, thousands of different gods are invoked through the fields every day. We must clean up all this! Once my solution is implemented, the warp of fields will have become a warp of Watcher-ness! Every single chapel in the kingdom will be filled with the presence of the Watchers. (This, by the way, is what I mean by the second descent of the Watchers.) And this global simplification will be the beginning of our salvation.

But as you understand, the dwarfs are not going to be happy to give up their little gods, to which they will cling until the very last moment. They will defend themselves, and fight for their Law! Only a powerful army will be capable of disciplining them. Now, some common sense: if we have to go to the trouble of defeating their armies, conquering their provinces, sub-duing their governments, and destroying their temples, then why not complete the work once and for all? For Naamah's sake! If the Nephilim had exterminated the dwarfs right from the beginning, the warp would never have become such a horrendous mess, and now we would not be on the brink of disaster. Why take the risk of creating other long-term disasters caused by the continual tension between the Nephilim and the dwarfs? Let us finish them off and start afresh."

"Then why kill only the men, and not the women too?" Basalinger asked.

"Mass rape will better serve our interests," Bobros answered in a cool voice. "Our seed is strong. The children that our soldiers will have with the daughters of the dwarfs will bear the characteristics of the Nephilim giants. They will worship the Watchers and carry out the tasks needed for the good functioning of the kingdom."

"Have you thought of the fact that certain armies may prove much more difficult to destroy than others?" Fornan questioned. "In the counties of the south, in particular. What about the Great Warriors?"

"My plan is to starve them," Bobros answered. "In the present state of energetic chaos, we necromancers of the guild can easily cause a drought in a county by introducing certain perturbations in the warp. Our technique works like a charm. We have already tested it with great success in the county of the Western Plains, where not one drop of rain has fallen in the last three years. And not one of these imbecile dwarfs has been able to de-tect where the mischief is coming from! As soon as the counties of the Centre are conquered, I will dry up the Jeremitzia river using the same method and famish the counties of the south. The result will be a state of civil unrest and chaos, rendered worse by nasty diseases and plagues – an-other technique of ours that has worked wonders in the counties of the Western Shores. The Great Warriors will be so busy trying to restore some order to the Red Lands and neighbouring counties, they will no longer be any real threat to us."

Mount Lohrzen neutralised! To the Green Guard generals, this sounded as tantalising as the music of the Watchers.

"And what if it was really possible?" Fornan started thinking to himself. What if there was really a chance to avoid the disaster, and the end of the Nephilim culture?

What if the flood could be avoided?

The old general finished his cup of glorious sunrise, then looked straight into Bobros' eyes, "Before you can convince me, young man, you are going to have to tell me how you intend to deal with the Hunters of Jex Belaran."

"There I have a plan. A master plan," Bobros answered with the most alarming of his smiles.

That was not enough to satisfy Fornan the crocodile, who kept his questioning gaze riveted on Bobros.

"A secret plan," Bobros held the general's gaze.

Fornan swore, using the Voice, "I give you my word, Bobros. Nothing said at this meeting will be repeated."

"Officer's word!" Basalinger Voice-projected after him.

Thinking intensely, Bobros looked at them for a few seconds.

Fornan stood very straight, making it clear he would not give up. The atmosphere in the room became tense. Basalinger wondered if his father wasn't making a huge blunder.

Bobros needed to impress Fornan in order to gain his support. He decided to reveal some of his secret workings. "All right, officers, I will trust your word!" he relaxed and grinned, drinking a sip of glorious sunrise. "You are going to like this," he told them. "Perseps, who replaced Joranjeran as head of the Hunters, has made an alliance with the Brown Robes, an order of monks based in the temple of Eisraim, in the county of the same name. But as part of this alliance he has made a capital mistake. He has given one of the Brown Robes a stone that contains the key to the protective shield of Jex Belaran. And..." Bobros took another sip of the most excellent beverage that he prepared himself, according to a special family recipe transmitted from Bobros to Bobros since time near-immemorial, "and presently, this beautiful little stone is in the pocket of Szar of the Brown Robe, a most useful dwarf who is to play a key role in my plans for that part of the world."

"A secret agent of yours?" Basalinger asked.

"I guess you could say so. But who is the perfect secret agent, really? The one who doesn't even know he is one! And yet this dwarf has already rendered immense services to our cause. He has wiped out the Red Renegades, the Foxes and the Black Hunters, nearly all by himself."

"So you were behind that?" Basalinger exulted. "We knew the Renegades had been eliminated, but we had no idea how it happened."

"You can imagine how delighted we were when we learnt the news," Fornan added. It meant the way to Perentie and the Northern Lakes was now clear. "We could take Prasnameghan, Tomoristan and Laminindra without encountering any serious resistance!"

"And Barnagiran, and Ofermak!" Bobros smiled even more alarmingly.

"How the Watchers' hell did you manage that? The Hunters of Jex Belaran have been trying to get rid of the Renegades for years!"

Seeing his strategy was working, Bobros decided to say more. "Now that all this is finished, I can tell you how we did it. We kidnapped two Hunters of Jex Belaran, killed them, and kept their astral bodies. Then my necromancers took a Nephilim – not a giant – and they used the Hunters' astral bodies to make him look and speak as if he had been trained in Jex Belaran, wiping out all his former memories. That made him the perfect spy. We had him enrolled in the temple of Lasseera, where he worked for the Brown Robes. Needless to say, we learnt a lot through his eyes." Bobros paused, wondering whether he should tell Fornan about the fantastic hermaphroditic stones that were being produced by the Brown Robes – stones that he wanted at any cost because they could be turned into devastating long-distance weapons. But he decided to keep this information to himself for the moment. "Finally, we managed to have our man teach Szar of the Brown Robe some of the secrets of the Hunters. After that we played a dirty triple game between the Brown Robes, the Hunters, and the different factions of Renegades, so that they ended up slaughtering each other without us having to do a thing."

"Very clever!" Fornan did not hide it – he *was* impressed.

"And that is not all! Our false Hunter, while he was teaching kuren-jaya tricks to Szar, imprinted a latent conditioning in him. We can now use Szar to catch hold of Perseps' stone, and get rid of the Brown Robes and their temples by the same occasion."

Fornan was not the least interested in the Brown Robe but the possibility of destroying Jex Belaran made him shiver with excitement. It had been the dream of every Green Guard general for centuries. The hatred between the giants and the Hunters was deep, and ancient. After all, hadn't the order of the Hunters been created primarily to eliminate Nephilim giants gone wild?

"I believe the first of the Hunters, Lubu, as he was called, killed one of your ancestors, Bobros." Fornan wondered if that was what motivated the necromancer.

"So goes the legend!" Bobros immediately understood he was being tested. "But let not a legend veil our clarity of mind. We'll think about revenge once total victory is achieved."

"Clever, clever!" Fornan thought when he heard Bobros' calm answer. "Why don't you give us more of this gorgeous glorious sunrise?" he said, to indicate he liked what he had been hearing.

Bobros filled the generals' cups with his bright-orange brew.

"When do you expect Perseps' stone to fall into your hands?" Fornan asked.

"In the coming weeks. Or perhaps the coming months. The Brown Robes are powerful, they should not be underestimated." Truly, Bobros had in mind to wait for the perfect moment, when he could catch hold of Maryani's hermaphroditic stones as well. "As you understand, I have a few plans like this for other counties."

Fornan emptied his cup in one draught. Looking Bobros straight in the eyes, he asked, "Do you really believe you are going to win tomorrow's challenge?"

Bobros nodded silently, his face lit up with a smile that was a masterpiece of necromantic art.

"And why did you ask us to come tonight?" Fornan finally brought up the burning question.

"Two things," Bobros answered without hesitation.

"One..." Fornan closed his fist with his thumb up, waiting for Bobros to speak.

"One, I want tomorrow's contest to be fair. I want the assurance that the Green Guard will abide by the Law of the Nephilim and strictly refrain from intervening during the challenge – even if Bexton calls on your help at the last moment, when he gets desperate."

"Agreed!" Fornan answered immediately, to the complete stupefaction of his son. Then he raised his index finger, counting two.

"Two," Bobros went on, "I want you to use your influence on Bexton, and try to convince him to avoid the challenge by declaring me his successor tonight. I would much prefer to work with Bexton, than have to kill him."

"Ouch!" Fornan frowned, making his exaggeratedly wrinkled face look even more furrowed. "That is much, much more difficult!"

"I believe you will do it for our race, which is presently in great danger. And also for Bexton, to save him from a stupid death."

Fornan breathed out loudly and looked down to his right, thinking deeply. "Were you to win the challenge, would you intend to replace the officers who command the Green Guard?"

"Not one of them!" Bobros raised his right hand, indicating he was giving his necromancer's word. "Except if you advise me to do so, of course. But as far as I am concerned, the Green Guard is commanded by the best generals in the kingdom. Why should I want to replace them?"

"Good!" Fornan nodded thoughtfully. "Now, Bobros, if you catch hold of that damn stone, I want to head the expedition that will wipe out Jex Belaran."

"But of course! Who better than you could do this, General?" Bobros raised his hand again.

"You have your deal, Bobros!"

16.8 The brotherhood of baphomets on Bobros' side

It was late in the evening when Pralaya came into Melissa's bedroom. "Can I talk to you for a minute?" he asked.

"Sure!" Melissa was in bed. She sat up and pulled herself out of her thoughts.

Pralaya jumped on the bed and sat in front of her. "I have just received a communication from the brotherhood of baphomets. They are about to make a public announcement, to declare they have chosen Bobros' side. They give him their full support, and they advise all the wise people of the citadel to do the same."

"What?" Melissa didn't hide her contempt. "How dare they? How can they choose to support that brute? Aren't the baphomets supposed to be wise?"

"Melissa, Melissa... do you realise what is going to happen to us if the fields collapse?"

Melissa thoughtfully caressed the baphomet's fur. "Do they really think it's going to happen?"

"I say, of course it is bound to happen! The brotherhood has discovered the situation is even worse than we thought. Bexton has not been telling the entire truth to the people of the citadel."

"And what is the entire truth, according to them?"

"The truth is, a complete collapse of the warp could happen any day. Do you realise, Melissa? Any day! The baphomets are getting desperate."

"And therefore ready to do anything, even go along with Bobros' radical solution?"

"Bobros has made a deal with them. He said that in the trying times ahead we are all going to have to stick together, and he assured them of his support. He said he admired the baphomets' intelligence enormously, and that as soon as the contest was over, he wanted them to form a task force that would be in charge of advising him, looking for all possible solutions to ensure the survival of the Nephilim race and of the baphomets. He even said he wanted one of us to sit in the War Council which is to replace the present government."

"He is clever, eh? Such an elegant way of convincing you that there is no choice but to make him leader and exterminate the dwarfs."

"And so, what do you think we should do?" Pralaya plunged his strange glowing gaze into Melissa's eyes.

"I don't know!" Melissa the giantess sighed, throwing her hands up in despair.

"I say, that is the problem, Melissa. We have all been saying the same thing for years, 'we don't know!' But while we were sleeping, time has passed. And now, we are all going to die! Have you thought of what will happen to you when the rejuvenating field of your pool carks it?"

She turned towards her mirror, touching the soft skin of her face. "Probably not a pretty sight! I will look ten years older, for a start," she gave herself a cynical smile. "And my hair will probably turn grey. I might even lose my teeth!"

"Doesn't that frighten you?"

"There is not much I can do about it!" she shrugged her shoulders.

"But we can't just keep on repeating the same words and do nothing!" Pralaya softly hammered into her. "There's no wisdom in that."

"Oh no, I am not going to buy into the radical solution of that beast!" she became defensive. "Has the brotherhood of baphomets sent you to talk to me?"

It was even worse. Pralaya had just had another long Point-conversation with Bobros. Among other things, Bobros had invited him to head the baphomets' task force. And Pralaya had accepted! He had also promised to use all his influence on Melissa to convince her to speak to Bexton again.

"Oh, Watchers!" Melissa exclaimed in consternation when Pralaya remained silent. "You're not going to tell me you have taken sides with them, are you?"

"Well, no, of course. I couldn't do that to you, Melissa!" Pralaya lied. "I will stick by you until the last moment." Which in the baphomet's mind meant until Bobros won the challenge. "But still, can I tell you I think it would be in Bexton's best interests to strike a deal with Bobros?"

"No way, baphomet!" she shouted. She took her head in her hands and closed her eyes. "I don't want to hear this! Go away!"

"Melissa, I love you!" he whispered in his softest voice, and this time he meant what he said.

"I hate you!" she shouted at him, and she started crying. "Go away!"

"Melissa, you can still save Bexton's life. If you call him right now, he might listen to you."

This was what Bobros had advised, knowing very well Bexton would be deeply distressed after speaking with Fornan.

"He'd hate me if I called him to say that!" she sobbed.

"Not necessarily. Try! He really loves you. You and he could start a new life somewhere else."

"While you stay in the citadel, is that it?" Melissa hardened.

"Melissa, you know that baphomets can only live in the Eastern Peninsula. Without the giants' fields, what would be left of us?"

"Except if Bobros' radical solution were implemented, of course. Then there would be just the right fields for you all over the kingdom. That's what he has promised you, hasn't he?"

"Melissa..."

"Go away, animal!" she threw a pillow at him. "I really mean it! Go away!"

To a baphomet, being called an animal was the worst of all insults. Pralaya didn't react. He remained where he was, and opened to his friend.

"No!" she shouted with total determination. "I won't soften!" and she stared at him defiantly.

"All right!" he resigned after a moment, and turned away.

As he was trotting off, he remembered the old saying of the Law,

"To those who can't listen, the Lord Melchisedek can give no mercy!"

16 – The Book of the Nephilim Giants

16.9 Deceit, confusion, and more deceit

The next morning, when Bexton walked onto the stage and faced Bobros, he remembered in one second the conversation he had had with Fornan during the night, when the old general had stormed into his office and announced to him straightforwardly that he had just come back from a meeting with Bobros. "He is not at all the beast we thought," Fornan had added before Bexton had time to catch his breath. "I actually believe he is a genius!"

A genius? Perhaps, after all. But now that Bexton was on the stage in front of him, now that he was faced with his huge furious eyes of necromantic madman, now that he saw him jumping around and screaming like a wild animal to excite the base instincts of the crowd, now that the moment of truth had arrived, he knew, and without a shadow of a doubt, that Fornan was wrong, at least on one point: Bobros *was* a beast.

But the old general had a very different vision. Before Bexton had even had a chance to speak, he had delivered the bulk of his message, "I know you are going to hate me for this, son, but I think you should abdicate tonight, and accept Bobros' offer of working hand in hand with him."

It was very late in the evening. Bexton was sitting behind his grand commander's desk, planning his next move after having spent hours lobbying the patriarchs of the citadel. When he heard Fornan's words, he was so shocked that for a moment he remained speechless.

Without waiting for an invitation Fornan sat in front of him. "We're going to have to play this carefully, and smartly. I believe that..."

"Do you realise I could have you arrested for this?" Bexton interrupted him.

"The Watchers' hell, I'd like to see that!" the old man yelled at him, hitting the desk with his fist. "Bexton, when are you going to start realising that they have all been lying to you, and that at the moment Basalinger and I are about the only ones who are still standing behind you?"

"I don't believe a word of this!" Bexton stood up and yelled back. "This is Bobros' propaganda – Watcher's pooh!"

"No it isn't!" Fornan yelled even louder, standing up and pounding Bexton's desk again.

"All right, then, great General, can you tell me *who* has been making deals with Bobros behind my back?"

"Damned Underworld! Dozens of them! Aprali, for a start! The whole of your secret police has already changed sides."

Melissa's words suddenly came back to Bexton. In one second, he became very calm again. He sat down on his chair, his eyes swiftly sweeping the space of the office from right to left and left to right, thinking deeply.

Fornan walked to a cupboard where he took out a bottle of green beverage and two cups, and he went back to sit in front of Bexton. "Have you seen Aprali lately?" he asked while filling the cups.

"He has been out of the citadel this week."

"How convenient!"

Bexton was trying to put the facts together. Had he become completely blind? Was Melissa right, after all? Listening to Fornan, one could have believed so. But then Fornan was just coming back from a meeting with Bobros. What if Bobros had overshadowed his mind too? Same dirty business as with Melissa. Wasn't all this a bluff-conspiracy based on nasty necromantic tricks?

"There is one thing that does not make sense," Bexton articulated, composed and lucid.

"What?" Fornan emptied his third consecutive cup of green beverage.

"The court sorcerers. According to Bobros, they will support him, not me. But I have spoken to them at least three times today, and they keep assuring me of their support. If they had made a deal with Bobros, why wouldn't they try to influence me in his favour?"

"But it's damn obvious! They're scared! They know that if you were to learn they support him, you could have them dismissed and tried for high treason. And you could quickly recruit a new team of necromancers to back you during the challenge. Whereas by allowing Bobros to win the contest against you, they will keep their place in the palace. Bobros has given his word that the guild of necromancers will work hand in hand with them."

That was difficult to swallow, knowing the fierce and ancient antagonism between the guild of necromancers and the court sorcerers. "Why would people who have been enemies for centuries suddenly decide to work hand in hand?" Bexton closed his eyes tightly, trying to figure things out.

"Ugly Underworld! Because we are on the brink of losing everything!" the old general shouted. "It's not just the baphomets that will cark it when the warp goes blank, it's all of us!"

"Fornan," Bexton remained calm, "it can't possibly be that forty-nine people lie to me at the same time without me noticing a thing."

"Yes it can! These are top-level magicians, masters in the art of fooling people. Deceit is part of their Law. Don't you know that before they can qualify as sorcerers, apprentices must demonstrate their art by deceiving their own master?"

"Fornan, if such a well-organised conspiracy has been going on behind my back, then can you tell me why Bobros chose to let out the plot at the last moment?"

"Because he is genuinely trying to save your life! He hopes you will come to reason and realise you do not stand a chance against him."

"Me, not stand a chance against that lunatic?" Bexton's proud lips pinched with contempt.

"Listen, son," Fornan the crocodile softened his voice, "whether Bobros can win the contest or not is not even what matters. I believe he has a *real* solution to the rotting of the warp. Challenge or no challenge, this man is our last chance. He is genuinely inspired. He is from the Watchers."

"What?" Bexton was horrified. He was now convinced that Bobros had psychically influenced Fornan, as he had influenced Melissa.

In a glimpse, while Bobros was jumping and yelling on the stage, pulling grotesque faces at him to the jubilation of the huge crowd that had gathered in Proclamation Square, Bexton saw the scene again, and how he had left the room and retired to his apartment without even attempting to argue further with the old general. He was utterly disgusted by Bobros' tactic of trying to get to him through his closest friends. At the same time, he was bewildered by the ease with which Bobros seemed to be able to persuade everyone that the power of the Watchers was with him. "Clever plot!" he thought. "Just get everyone to believe you are the emissary of the Watchers, and they will hand over their power without even a fight!" A great comedian, this Bobros! But thank Naamah, that was not going to work with him.

Yet Bexton immediately called an improvised meeting with one of the court sorcerers, Organz, an old man who had been attached to the grand commander's palace since his teens.

It didn't take long for the sorcerer to arrive. He never slept at night. The Green guards just had to interrupt him in the middle of one of his rituals.

Bexton asked him, "Have you met Bobros, Organz?"

"Never, Your Excellency."

"That's a good start!" Bexton told himself while contemplating his late-night guest. With his long grey beard, his dishevelled hair, his deep, worrying black eyes, his long staff lacquered with blood, and the unicorn's skin that covered his shoulders, the old giant epitomised the lawful cliché of a Nephilim sorcerer.

"Very good. Organz, I will be direct. I have a problem. I have received intelligence advising me that tomorrow morning some of the court sorcerers will support Bobros."

"Watcher's pooh!" The old giant spat on the floor – the necromancers' traditional way of expressing contempt. "These idiots don't know what they're saying."

Contemplating with a touch of amusement the large yellow spat that had landed on his invaluable carpet, Bexton insisted, "Are you sure?"

Organz didn't even bother answering. He just lifted his ominous gaze to the ceiling and sighed loudly.

"Are you sure, Organz?" Bexton repeated.

"Yes!" old Organz answered in his broken voice, looking straight into Bexton's eyes, and raising his right hand. "My sorcerer's word!"

But how could Bexton know for sure? The problem was, whenever he needed to have someone's mind scanned, he sought recourse to the court sorcerers! They had always proved remarkably reliable. But in the present situation, who could be relied on?

Bexton insisted, "Can you see one reason in the seven spheres why the court sorcerers would follow Bobros?"

"He would have to demonstrate that he is an envoy of the Watchers."

"Can you see that happening?"

Organz decorated Bexton's carpet with another thick yellow spat.

It was this scene that Bexton recalled as Bobros was spitting all over the stage, jumping, stomping, screaming louder and louder, unconcerned by the look of disapproval on the face of the senior patriarch who had been chosen as judge for the contest. His name was Albostanon, and he was *not* one of the fifty who had taken sides with Bobros. Bobros, who was throwing his fists in all directions as if decimating hordes of invisible enemies, moved around so fast that Albostanon had to step back and stand on the edge of the stage. It was a relatively small platform, fifteen lawful feet by fifteen, but raised high above the ground so the contest could be watched by the large crowd that had gathered in Proclamation Square.

Bexton's forty-nine court sorcerers encircled the stage, standing a few lawful feet away to get a better view. They were surrounded by the four hundred patriarchs of the citadel, with Bobros' supporters forming a separate group on one side. Around the patriarchs, the soldiers of the Green Guard led by Fornan and Basalinger formed a deep row to repel the crowd of more than eight thousand giants who had come to watch the match. Many of them had arrived the evening before to secure a good place for themselves. They had brought huge bags of food and barrels of green beverage, and a joyful feast had been going on all night.

One hour before dawn the necromancers of the guild had arrived, dressed in their skins of unicorns, levlons, filosterops, pessalans and other animals dear to the gods – animals which, said the Law of Melchisedek, were never to be killed by men. A frightening mob of silent shades, these necromancers. There were at least three hundred of them. They spoke not a word to anyone, not even to each other, they just stood still and waited. Their arrival marked the end of the feast, as the glacial atmosphere they brought with them was so charged that the giants no longer felt like eating or laughing.

Three-and-a-half hours later, when Proclamation Square was packed, Bexton arrived. The Law said he was to take position on the stage before the challenger. Serene, grave, he walked slowly and solemnly, followed by his court sorcerers. As he climbed the steps that led to the stage, the crowd gave him an ovation. He had always been a popular man, loved and admired by his people.

Then Bobros made his entry. Unlike his fellow necromancers, he no longer wore animal skins. He had given them up a few months earlier to give himself a more credible appearance in his efforts to lobby the patriarchs. That day, he wore only pants of thin grey cloth held by a large black leather belt, his huge and excessively hairy torso left bare. As he walked, he made the crowd laugh by flexing his massive biceps and pectorals, swollen to unlawful proportions by the power of the fields.

As soon as Bobros had climbed on stage, welcomed by an ovation that was no less (but no greater either) than the one Bexton had received, he started jumping and yelling like an animal. Albostanon was disconcerted but there was nothing illegal about this strange behaviour, as long as Bobros did not spit on him. So the judge chose to move back to the edge of the stage, from where he watched Bobros' war dance.

Bexton remained extremely calm, not letting himself be the least impressed by the show. Fornan, who was watching the scene in consternation, admired him for remaining so firm, dignified and kingly, even in these last desperate moments. At the same time he was appalled. He dreaded what was about to happen so much that when Albostanon finally clapped his hands above his head to signal the beginning of the contest, he was tempted to close his eyes. But he didn't.

Bobros became still as a rock, his eyes locked into Bexton's.

Proclamation Square became silent.

"Oh, Watchers!" Fornan prayed inside himself, "Have mercy on him!"

But what followed was not at all what the old general had expected.

For three interminable seconds, the two men locked their gaze into each other.

It was the moment of truth.

"Now we are going to see who has been lying to whom!" Bexton thought while calling on the power of his court sorcerers, following the precise instructions he had received from them during the rehearsal the day before.

In front of him, Bobros' black eyes, open like a wide abyss.

A wave rose from the abyss. An ominous hissing wave, rolling towards Bexton. It was dark and ugly, hungry like the emissaries of death.

A powerful wind started blowing through Bexton's aura. In a triumphant second, the grand commander felt the combined will power of his forty-nine sorcerers. It was formidable, titanic, irresistible! It gushed from him like lava from a volcano, and it hit Bobros in the face.

Bobros, to Fornan's complete stupefaction, fell flat on his back.

A loud "Oh!" of wonder ran through the crowd.

The necromancers of the guild were seen raising their hands and beating their chests. They lamented loudly, uttering strange, frightening curses.

Bexton clapped his hands in exultation. "I knew you were a fraud!" he yelled with rage. "I knew my necromancers were not lying to me!" And in a glimpse, scenes of the night flashed into his mind. After Organz had left, he had suddenly been taken by grave doubts. Organz's words were reassuring, but there was no way to ascertain for sure whether the old sorcerer was lying or not. As Bexton paced around in his lounge, crazy ideas started running through his mind. He thought of dismissing all his sorcerers and recruiting forty-nine new ones. But it was too late. And who could be trusted in the citadel? What if Bobros had been trying to confuse him so that he made the fatal mistake of dismissing his brave, loyal sorcerers and recruiting frauds, or men of no substance?

But Fornan's words kept resonating in his mind, "They have all been lying to you! You do not stand a chance against Bobros!"

The mad thought of running away suddenly tempted Bexton. He saw himself taking Melissa with him and fleeing! Anywhere. There were many beautiful and quiet areas in the kingdom, and he had enough wealth to live a comfortable life. He loved her. And she loved him! Why stay in this wretched citadel, since anyway it was just a matter of time before it was destroyed by the collapse of the fields?

But, thank Naamah, as he was about to call Melissa and tell her to pack her bags, he came back to reason. The fighter inside took over. "I am *not* going to fall into your trap, Bobros!" he shouted, and he called his friend Aprali through darkness visible.

He had no difficulty contacting the director of the secret police. That in itself said something. Had Aprali been against him, he would have preferred to hide.

The conversation was frank and direct. "Fornan has gone off his brain!" Aprali immediately answered when he heard the allegations. "I can't *believe* this nonsense! This Bobros is even more dangerous than I thought."

"What about the court sorcerers? Shall I trust them?" Bexton asked.

"I'm tempted to say yes, of course! There has never been any evidence of dealings between them and the guild. But I have no way of scanning their minds and knowing for sure," Aprali conceded. After a few seconds of cogitative silence, he suggested, "Bexton, why don't you talk to them. Pretend to be seriously considering rallying to Bobros, and watch their reactions. If they are on his side, they will probably encourage the move."

Bexton liked the plan. Sealing his mind (it was part of the art of being a Nephilim politician to be able to make oneself unreadable, even by necromantic masters), he convened meetings with five of his sorcerers, and asked their advice as to the wisdom of following Bobros.

All of them opposed the idea vigorously. Two of them even threatened to resign if they were ever asked to work with 'those bandits of the necromancers' guild'. The response Bexton got was so vehemently hostile to Bobros that around four o'clock in the morning he decided to stop the exercise. He called Melissa through darkness visible.

"Bexton, aren't you sleeping?" Her clear tone of voice showed that she hadn't been sleeping either.

"I've been busy. Listen, I have something really urgent to tell you."

"What?"

"I love you! Do you want to marry me?"

Melissa burst out crying.

"Yes! Marry me. Please say yes, Melissa. I promise I will treat your baphomet like a king."

"I'm afraid, Bexton!" Melissa could not contain the flow of tears.

"No, don't! In only a few hours, it will all be finished. And then the first thing I will do will be to come to your place and make love to you. And after that (that's two or three days later, of course), we'll start preparing the marriage ceremony. Will you say yes?"

As he was contemplating Bobros' huge body which lay flat on the stage, Bexton remembered the infinite sweetness with which Melissa had said yes, and he rejoiced at what she must have been feeling at this very moment. She had told him she wouldn't be coming to Proclamation Square. She preferred to let Pralaya watch the scene through their vision-fields and tell her the outcome.

"Your Excellency, be careful!" Afran Kesborn, the leader of the court sorcerers, called him through darkness visible. "Bobros may not be dead yet!"

Hardly had he spoken when Bobros reopened his eyes, and slowly sat up.

The crowd, who had been acclaiming Bexton triumphantly, immediately changed tune. They started encouraging the challenger, "Bobros! Bobros! Bobros...!"

Bobros, who looked completely stunned by the massive dose of power that the court sorcerers had flung in his face, managed to stand up. With the jubilant applause of the crowd, he took a stumbling step on the stage.

"Let's finish him off, Your Excellency!" Afran Kesborn said through the space.

Again, Bexton felt the power flowing through him and hitting Bobros.

This time the pounding was monumental. Never had Bexton felt anything so huge. It was out of the seven spheres, unreally Watcher-like. As if a gigantic pendulum, held from the Watchers' heaven by the revengeful hand of Azazel, had swung and hit the arrogant young a final blow.

Bobros fell on his knees, gasping.

The crowd became silent again.

"You beast!" Bexton clenched his fists with rage and kicked Bobros in the stomach with all his strength. "I cast you into the abyss!"

Bobros collapsed on his front with a crash as his weight hit the stage.

"This time, he is dead, Your Excellency! You won!" the leader of the sorcerers congratulated Bexton.

Bexton could hardly believe his eyes. Bobros was dead, as indicated by obvious signs in his aura.

The judge ran over to Bobros, who by then was nothing more than a heap of warm muscles on the floor. He carefully examined Bobros' aura. The soul had left the body, projected far away by the sorcerers' powers. All that was left was a mass of inanimate flesh.

Bobros was *really* dead. All those who stood in the first rows could see it – including Fornan.

Albostanon took Bexton's hand and lifted it before the crowd, thereby officially declaring him the winner of the contest.

While the crowd was cheering, flabbergasted Fornan pulled his hair in disbelief. "So it was all bluff?" he muttered to himself, wondering who was who and what was what, and who the hell of the Watchers could be trusted in this wretched world.

From a distance, exulting Aprali, who had managed to come back just in time for the contest, waved at him and gave him a joyful, friendly smile.

"So Bobros was manipulating me like a pawn?" Fornan suddenly felt very unsure of himself. As he was clapping his hands, it was his turn to try to put the facts together. "Where did I start going wrong?" he wondered, remembering the first intelligence report advising him that the secret police had engaged in clandestine negotiations with Bobros' men.

Bexton, his right foot on Bobros' back, his hands raised victoriously, his lips trembling from the sudden drop of tension, was being acclaimed by the crowd, when the unthinkable took place.

Under his foot, Bobros' corpse started moving.

His soul had returned.

When they saw Bexton jumping back and Albostanon quickly running to the edge of the stage, when they saw the corpse slowly moving its arms, and sitting up on its knees, and finally standing, raised from the dead by the miraculous intervention of the Watchers – what else could it have been? – the awe-struck crowd remained religiously silent, waiting for the verdict from heaven.

Bobros, alive and well, plunged his abysmal gaze into Bexton's eyes, smiling necromantically.

In a fraction of a second, Bexton understood.

Deceit, confusion, and more deceit!

They had all been lying to him – Aprali, Organz, the court sorcerers, and all the others.

Not all, though. Not Fornan.

Not Melissa either.

And that was his last thought.

16.10 The giants on their way

"But why? But why?" Melissa screamed when Pralaya told her that Bexton was being annihilated by Bobros.

It was quick, ugly, final. In one second, Bobros had erased Bexton's mind. There was *nothing* left of the grand commander, just a body artificially kept standing by the occult powers of the young necromancer.

"Bexton is dead," Pralaya declared simply, sparing Melissa the horrendous details.

"Is he on the ground?" she asked in terror.

"No. Bobros will probably keep him on his feet for one or two minutes. For the crowd."

"What is he doing to him?" she screamed.

Pralaya watched in silence. Bobros was kicking Bexton in the abdomen, the genitals and the face. Bexton's empty body was shaken by the blows but remained on its legs, kept erect by Bobros' will.

"What is he doing?" Melissa kept screaming.

"Hitting him. But it's not hurting him, he's dead."

"But what are the court sorcerers doing?"

"Nothing. It was all planned, I'm afraid," Pralaya sighed.

"What? But what do they want?"

"They want to make him a messiah sent by the Watchers, so the people believe in him."

"A messiah?" she exclaimed, aghast.

"Now, nearly ten thousand people have watched Bobros declared dead and miraculously resurrected. The forty-nine court sorcerers will attest that after his resurrection, the power that ran through him was greater than anything they could possibly match."

"But why? Why are they doing that?"

"To save face, for a start. And also because only a messiah can save the Eastern Peninsula."

Who, better than an envoy of the Watchers, could ignite the giants' hearts, whip them awake and enthuse them to fight against the rest of the world?

"It's horrible!" Melissa hid her face behind her hands. "They have all betrayed him! They have all lied to him!"

"To those who can't listen..." Pralaya said to himself.

"Is he still bashing him?" Melissa asked.

"Nearly finished," Pralaya answered.

"What does that mean?"

Bobros had grasped Bexton's hair, biting the side of his neck ferociously. When he let go, blood started gushing from Bexton's jugular, hosing the stage to the cannibalistic jubilation of the crowd.

"What's he doing?" Melissa shouted.

"Bexton has fallen on the ground now," Pralaya said after a few seconds. "It's finished. The judge is declaring Bobros the new grand commander."

Screaming with pain, Melissa ran to her bedroom to hide.

Pralaya kept watching. Bobros was being carried in triumph, while the crowd shouted in one voice, "Glory to the Watchers! Glory to the Watchers...!"

The baphomet told himself, "Now, it's going to become really interesting!"

– Thus ends the Book of the Nephilim Giants –

17

The Book of the
Paradoxes in Highness

17.1 Eisraim temple

"They're coming!" Woken by the horrendous vision, Mouridji the prophetess sat up in bed. She was out of breath, covered in cold sweat, her heart drumming in fear.

"Luciana!" she called through darkness visible.

There was no answer. It was early morning. The Sun had not yet risen. In the room adjacent to Mouridji's, Luciana of the Green Robe was peacefully asleep.

Using the flat of her hand the old priestess loudly beat the living wall that separated her from her neighbour. "Luciana! Luciana!" she shouted with her physical voice.

"Mm... praise the Lord Melchisedek!" Luciana responded through darkness visible. "But it's too early to get up!"

"Luciana, I saw something terrible. We must tell everyone in the temple, immediately! They're coming!"

"Who?" Luciana was making great efforts to pull herself from the soft vagueness of a dream.

"The giants, Luciana! The giants! They're going to ransack everything!"

Luciana sat up. "But Mouridji, everyone knows our temple will be destroyed by the giants."

"But this time it's different – they're *really* coming! I have seen them. They have a new chief, and he is... he is... so bad I can't even tell you how bad he is. And he *hates* us! He has vowed to destroy our temple. Completely. He and his soldiers will kill everyone, even the cows, and then they will rape all the women, and not just the young ones, and then they will eat the corpses of the high priests! And they'll knock down every single building until there's nothing left, just piles of plass rubble, and then they'll

burn the rest. And before coming here they'll have done the same in Prasnameghan, and in Tomoristan, and Laminindra, and Lasseera!"

"But... the prince of Eisraim's army? Won't they defend us?"

"Against the giants they won't last more than two hours. I have seen the
battle. Unlawful carnage! To protect our temple, Master Melchard tries to
ambush the giants, using the powers of the Brown Robe. But there are too
many of them. And they're accompanied by necromancers with terrifying
powers, and strange evil beasts like goats, but goats that talk. Melchard and
Namron will be slaughtered!"

"Oh my Lord Melchisedek! And what about the other Brown Robes?
Will Szar be slaughtered too?"

From the pinnacle of her prophetic vision Mouridji caught a glimpse of a
mind-boggling scene. Szar and Teyani walking in a desolate landscape,
elemental forces of a titanic magnitude unleashed against them. "In a valley," she started saying. She stopped herself, judging that by revealing what
she saw she might go against the plans of the Brown Robe. "I don't know,"
she mumbled. "A complicated story."

By now Luciana was fully awake. "Shall I start voice-channelling everyone to tell them?" She interpreted Mouridji's silence as tacit approval.

If Mouridji did not answer it was because she was already far away. As
soon as she had thought of Szar, her consciousness had been drawn into
bizarre spaces. "Which sphere is he in at the moment?" she wondered.
"Probably with Elyani, in the world of the gods." After the extraordinary
conclusion of the great ascension ritual, this was the most logical answer.
At the end of the ceremony, when the alarm signal had been given and the
crowd of nearly one thousand people were rushing out of the central crypt,
Mouridji had stayed calmly in her place, her vision fixed on the stage. She
knew the danger was extreme. A tidal wave of elemental sludge could have
hit the central crypt any second. But unlike the crowd, Mouridji wasn't in
the mood to run for her life.

"Oh my Lord Melchisedek!" she had prayed. "I will not budge, I want to
see the end of this ritual! If you want to take my life, then this old carcass is
all yours. My life is such an awful lawful bore, anyhow!" And in the pandemonium that ensued, no one had noticed the small elderly woman who
sat against one of the large round pillars in the southern part of the enormous crypt.

Consumed with anxiety, Mouridji watched Szar's desperate attempts to
feed the ritual hymns with Underworld energies. Time was fast running
out, she could see, and poor Elyani was about to miss her rendezvous with
the gods. She looked so frail and tired, shrouded in her Immaculate gown
as in a white mystery cloud, pouring her Voice into the Holy Blue Flame,
fighting an impossible battle against the rotten warp of fields. By her side
Hermina the Immaculate seemed even more exhausted. She could hardly
sit. She hovered over her body, which she just managed to move, slowly,
painstakingly. "Truly," Mouridji thought, "she is already gone!" And it was

the truth. The day before Hermina had been mortally wounded by a wave of elemental sludge. Now she had to use her initiate's will to keep her Spirit linked to her body.

Mouridji was starting to believe the battle was lost when Szar finally managed to feed the hymns with some mysterious power. The result was immediate. But was it really what he had expected? Stupefied, Mouridji watched Gervin's disciple be lifted up out of his body by the power of the hymns, and zapped straight into the lofty spheres of the gods.

But it was Elyani who was supposed to go up, not Szar!

Unlawfully appalling. "Oh my L..." she began. But Szar had already returned – thank the gods! Mouridji Point-overheard the conversation in which Gervin and Szar instructed Hermina to stop the spheres of the Law. Reluctantly, the Immaculate priestess projected her Voice onto one of the large spinning balls.

As soon as the sphere of the Law started slowing down, a first explosion took place. Huge bubbles of golden energy sprang from below the stage, feeding the starving hymns. With a frighteningly loud hissing sound the Holy Blue Flame flared to the high ceiling of the crypt and engulfed not only Elyani, but also Hermina and Szar.

Elyani, Szar and Hermina had disappeared in the Flame. While Mouridji was trying to discern what the Underworld was happening to them, she heard a thunder-like rumbling. The crypt's ceiling was illuminated by a fantastically bright light.

Mouridji looked up, her mouth wide open in amazement.

It was massive, sensational – an incandescent tapestry woven with fast-moving lightning shafts of all colours. It filled the room with an awesome presence.

"The gods!" Mouridji was trembling with emotion. "The gods have come to take Elyani!" What a shame all those idiots in the Law had left the crypt! Mouridji took a quick look around her. To her immense relief there were a few handfuls of people who, like her, hadn't run away.

Meanwhile the walls and the floor of the crypt were vibrating with the fullness of presence that emanated from the light of the gods. High above the stage, where the Holy Blue Flame reached the incandescent ceiling, flashes of dazzling bluish-white light succeeded each other at fast pace, accompanied by thunder-like explosions.

"So beautiful!" Mouridji burst into tears, deeply shaken by the fiery intensity of the light and its magnificence. "So beautiful!"

She caught a glimpse of a glorious supermental harmony that surpassed anything human beings could ever imagine – worlds of infinity, fields of stars condensed in one cosmic rest, the total perfection of Revelation Sky. It breathed. It shone. It laughed with joy. For ever and ever, aeons and super-aeons.

In the crypt the priests and priestesses praised the Lord Melchisedek and applauded spontaneously. Together with the sky of the gods they laughed with joy. For a short while all the sorrows of the kingdom were forgotten, there was but enchantment. An immense feeling of victory.

The ritual had succeeded!

The gods had responded. They had accepted Elyani's offering.

Elyani was being reborn among them.

As suddenly as it had appeared, the stormy light of the gods faded. The sound of rolling thunder stopped. The ceiling reappeared. The Holy Blue Flame was extinguished.

Left on the stage were two bodies lying face down and holding each other's hand.

"But where is Hermina?" Mouridji muttered. "And what has happened to Szar? Is he dead?"

She saw Gervin and Melchard hurrying towards the stage.

Melchard was in tears. "The first time I see him cry in twenty years of high priesthood," Mouridji told herself. But as she knew everyone and everything in the temple, it was no secret to her that Elyani was his daughter.

Namron was running behind them, chewing his disgusting black root. "Master Gervin! Master Gervin! Did it happen? Did it really work?" he asked, smoothing his round bald head.

"Yes! And our children did it all by themselves!" Gervin exclaimed triumphantly. "I virtually didn't help."

"Praise the Lord Melchisedek!" Namron's smile revealed two rows of black teeth.

Gervin and Melchard stopped at the foot of the stage.

"Namron," Gervin instructed the small man, "you and your men must make sure *no one* comes near their bodies."

"Is Szar travelling with Elyani?" the security chief asked.

"Taken care of by the gods," Gervin was glowing. "He'll be back in twelve hours. But in the early morning, he will be travelling much further away than the spheres of the gods. Lady Teyani will come and take care of his body. Meanwhile, I want the crypt to remain empty."

"It will be done," Namron assured him. Puzzled, "Now then, what about Hermina the Immaculate? Has she already gone?"

"It seems Lady Hermina has taken her physical body with her to the spheres of Highness."

"So she *was* a great saint!" Namron exclaimed in awe, walking up the steps to the stage. "There are her shoes, and her white gown!" he said, not daring to go further than the top step.

"A saint who dematerialises her body at the time of death?" Mouridji could hardly believe her ears. "I'd like to see that!"

She trotted towards the stage, fastening the purple veil that always covered her hair. "Praise the Lord Melchisedek!" she smiled at Gervin and Melchard as she passed them. Before anyone could say anything she had already climbed the steps and was standing by Namron.

The chief of security had never been able to exert any authority over Mouridji because she and his mother were good friends when his mother was pregnant with him, as Mouridji liked to remind him every time she met him. So he kept quiet, watching every movement she made.

"Oh my Lord Melchisedek! But it's true!" the old priestess exclaimed. "She's only left her sandals, her gown and her shawl!" And she wondered what the faces of her friends would look like when she delivered the news to them.

The small woman turned towards Gervin, her eyes sparkling with excitement. "Is it a secret?"

"Not at all, my good Mouridji. You can tell everyone."

"Ah!" she said, almost disappointed. And she contemplated the bodies of Elyani and Szar, who seemed to be deeply asleep like children. She plunged her prophetic sight into Szar, trying to catch a glimpse of the world of the gods. But as her consciousness was absorbed in the young man's energy, a strange chain of reactions was triggered inside her. At first, bizarre geometrical figures and fast-moving patterns of all colours imposed themselves on her mind. Then she heard eerie 'ffffoooohhhh' sounds, quite unlike the normal harmony of the spheres. She felt so dizzy that she had to sit down on the edge of the stage.

"Are you all right, Mouridji?" the security chief put his hand on her shoulder.

"Thank you, my little Namron. I am fine in the Law," she answered, dazzled by the weird forces, her energy swinging like a pendulum.

After a short rest on the stage she managed to walk back to her room, where she collapsed on her bed. For the rest of the afternoon her vision went wild. Startling images that made no sense kept flashing into her third eye. When she finally fell asleep she had prophetic dream after prophetic dream, until she was woken by that horrendous vision of the giant invaders from the Eastern Peninsula.

Still sitting in bed, the old priestess shook her head, trying to hold the continuous flow of visions. The last images of giants were vanishing, already replaced by a completely different flow of visions. Even more incomprehensible than the ones which had blasted her mind the day before. And the 'ffffoooohhhh' sounds were back.

"I must see Szar!" Mouridji exclaimed. Compelled by the vision, she decided to walk to the central crypt immediately.

Of course, she knew Namron had been instructed to keep everyone out. But that wasn't going to stop her.

17.2 The return

"Alarm! I want all doors of the crypt sealed immediately!" Namron sent an emergency Point-communication to his men.

"An attack?" Folosinis Point-replied from the northern entrance of the crypt.

"Mouridji is on her way. Looks like I will have to bear the brunt of the first offensive."

"Praise the Lord Melchisedek, Namron, my great man in the Law!" the purple-robed priestess greeted him just as she had when seeing him for the first time, in his cot, forty-one years earlier.

"All glory to the Lord Melchisedek, Mouridji, the answer is no!" Namron declared upfront.

"But Namron... it's extremely important! I have received a vision that *commanded* me to go and sit in the crypt, and if..."

"No way, woman of the Law! My instructions are crystal clear. No one goes in unless approved by Melchard of the Brown Robe."

"Namron, the *gods* have instructed me to sit close to Szar," she argued. "You wouldn't want me to let them down, would you?"

"If it's from the gods, then call Melchard. If he agrees, you can go in."

Mouridji sighed loudly and turned back.

"The offensive was repelled. But be on guard," Namron Point-warned Folosinis, watching the prophetess walking away decidedly. "It was far too easy. She must have a plan."

When Mouridji felt herself on a mission, she hated wasting time. Rather than disturb Melchard (the poor darling in the Law had so much to think about), she went straight to the third hall of Melchisedek. There, she walked down a stairway that led to the catacombs of the temple, silencing her mind to make sure no one would detect her through darkness visible. She turned left twice, then to the right, then left again, and three minutes later she found herself in a small spiral staircase that brought her to a hidden entrance inside the central crypt, behind a huge statue of the Anger of God. After staying still a few seconds, checking through the space that the immediate surroundings were clear, she cautiously thrust her head between the legs of the Anger of God, looking to the right, and to the left.

"Empty!" she congratulated herself, and she kissed the air twice, thinking of Namron's cheek.

Silent like a cat, she scurried over to hide behind a row of large columns. But when she arrived in the central part of the crypt, what she saw took her completely by surprise.

The space above the central stage was illuminated with a huge flame. Not a Holy Blue Flame, this time, a flame of White Light. It was as bright as Highness, magnificently heart-warming.

The Light of the Eagle. Simple. Eternal.

As she walked towards the stage, Mouridji saw that the bodies of Elyani and Szar were still lying in the same place. Sitting around them was a group of White Eagle priestesses. The prophetess counted sixteen of them. Absorbed in profound contemplation, they formed a circle on the edge of the White Flame.

They didn't notice her. But as she arrived at the top step, Mouridji hesitated. The White Eagles seemed to know exactly what they were doing. They had enveloped Elyani and Szar in a magnificent cocoon of light.

"They don't look like they need me," the old woman sighed, and she turned back, both reassured and disappointed to see Szar so well taken care of.

"Mouridji, come back!" Teyani called her through darkness visible. "The Eagle told us you were coming. We kept a place for you in the circle."

"For me?" Mouridji suddenly felt thirty-five years younger.

"On your left, between Pepni and Seyani."

"For me! I *knew* Szar wanted me to be here!" the Purple priestess thought while taking her position between the two young women.

As she fixed her gaze on Szar, she heard the 'ffffoooohhhh' sound again, and her consciousness was projected into one of the weirdest spaces she had ever cognised.

She heard the whisper of the Flying Dragon.

Is-ness.
A choir of universes, echoing the song of the Dawn of Creation
Which the Mother of the Light is still singing.
The one song.
Never-ending crescendo.
Eerie voidness made infinitely dimensional.
The one song which is the creation.
It started before time.
It went on ever since.
As it was before the beginning, is now, and ever will sing.
Symphony without end.
And the Word is with her. And the Word is her.
I sing her song, therefore my is-ness is.
One thousand trillion Flying Dragons sing with me,
Each measured voice responding to each and every other voice,
With precision,
Philharmonically conversational in their multidimensional fashion.
Nebulae humming in the background,
Percussive stars, metronomically rhythmical, giving the beat,
She dances.
Galaxies have a heart.
It burns with love for her.
Truth and Fire, Fire and Truth,

Mother of the Light, protect my way!
I return.
O, Mother of the Light, thy dance! Thy dance!
With the ardent passion of glacial extragalactic spaces,
Voidness eternal,
Darkness invisible,
Stupendous cosmic rig,
Stretched aeons looking back to the future,
I watch the birth and death of worlds and clusters of worlds.
Thy song, Mother! I love thy song!
Elixir of infinity, mathematical euphoria, I drink the music.
Tipsy, I spin and tumble my way through spaces and fields of stars.
Time is still young. Let us hurry.
I return.
Hail, Great Ant!
Friend of my father, witness of my birth,
Flying Dragon of old,
I praise thy blazing clarity, thy unbearably limpid spirit.
I praise thy archetypal lucid glow,
Which pierces through all astral things, and cleanses,
And separates that which was unduly mingled.
Shine by me. Bless my trail.
I return.
Hail, Abyss of the Deep!
The smile of the Mother of the Light has ignited my being.
Praise the Fire!
Burning Love.
Cosmic Fire – God's Will.
Cosmic Fire – God is Will.
I breathe,
Riding one gigantic wave, one Great Dragon of Fire.
The universe is one spark.
One God. One furnace.
Space Matrix, where is that tiny body?
"Vehicle identified. Fly Dragon. Fly!"
Space after space, flame after flame, aeon after aeon,
Blessed by the never-ending crescendo
Of the one song which is the creation,
I return.
Past the Fault of Eternity, and the spheres of the Blue Lagoon,
And the White Spider, so wise,
And the Great Night, nothingness of all things as in the first instant,
And the spheres of the Yellow Clouds of Wonders,
A glorious light, in front of me.
The Web of Love. I recognise.

Incomparable Goldness.
Praise the Lord Melchisedek!
And lo! White Eagle, my beloved, here you are,
Waiting for me on the edge of your spheres.
Flame raised to Highness,
Unfathomable Love,
I have returned.

Szar moved his right hand.

Mouridji heard him. She opened her eyes.

The priestesses were still holding the connection to the high bright flame. In it, the White Eagle was holding Szar in his wings.

The softness breathed infinity.

One minute ago, as Szar was re-entering the spheres of Melchisedek, Mouridji had beheld the Eagle – a thin Flame surrounded by the dark colourful immensity of galactic spaces. Now the Eagle had made his Whiteness a womb, and Szar was being reborn inside it.

The outside had involuted and become the inside.

The Flying Dragon was being clad in a White garment of light.

Strange, eerie flames of all colours were dancing in the matrix of light which the sixteen priestesses had woven on the stage.

So soft.

She cried.

Szar's hand tentatively explored the plass floor of the stage until he discovered his own head. A stranger to the world, he touched the hood of his brown gown, then his curly hair, and his neck.

Then he turned on his side and moved his left arm.

But what was this ugly dent in his aura? The energy of his left hand was pitch-black. Mouridji wondered how such ominous blackness could coexist with so much brightness. The marriage of the Eagle's Whiteness and Szar's multifarious auric glows created a festival of light on the stage.

Leaning on his right arm, the young man with the impressively broad shoulders slowly sat up, his eyes still closed.

That was when something fell out of his pocket.

In the exalted intensity of the moment, Mouridji was the only one to notice it. It was a small object. She couldn't see what it was.

Clearly, it would have been inappropriate to warn Szar, who hadn't even opened his eyes to the outside world yet because he was still trying to remember what inside and outside were like in this world, and where was up, and what was down, and why his body was so tiny – but was it really his body? – and why exactly had he landed here instead of merging his Flying Dragon nature with the golden incandescence of the Web of Love, which he could see everywhere around him, and which was infinitely more real, and vast, and universal, and eternal, than anything else in this little sphere, as pointed out by the High Light of the Eagle.

The White Eagle, for whom he had returned.

So soft.

A breath.

A voice. Speaking to him.

"Remember the Dragon, Szar!"

He could not understand the meaning of the words, but he loved the breath.

So soft.

He smiled.

"Szar, try to remember the Dragon of the Deep and anchor yourself in it!" the voice repeated.

Was it trying to convey a message to him?

Yes! A message from the Eagle. It said,

"Edge of Highness. Whiteness eternal. Forever love."

From his Flying Dragon nature spread in the infinity of remoteness, Szar responded with a flow of warm whirling lights, and he sang that part of the creation song that tells how the Mother of the Light sparked the first flame of Cosmic Fire out of the Primordial Waters. Instantly, Flying Dragon voices echoed from the sphere of the Great Ant, and also from the Blue Lagoon, and from beyond the Abyss of the Deep and the Fault of Eternity. And from all directions, voices responded to voices, filling the crypt with a crescendo of ebullient harmonies.

"Szar! What are you doing?" Sitting by his side, Teyani held her head in her hands, shaken by violent cosmic winds. The celestial music became so loud that she lost touch with her body. She felt herself spreading in space like a grain of salt thrown into the ocean.

Alcibyadi decided to come to her rescue. Holding her glorious eight-month-pregnant belly, she stood up and went to sit close to Szar and her mother.

"No, don't come near!" Teyani told her off. "His energy is incredibly charged. It might harm the baby."

"I don't think so," Alcibyadi ignored the warning. She Voice-whispered into Szar's ear, "Your mother, the Dragon of the Deep. A great fire. Look into the centre of the Earth. Embrace her."

The result was immediate. Szar opened his eyes – two large windows lit up with the wondrous glows of the Fault of Eternity, the sharp iridescent galactic-ness of the Great Ant, the lightning-bright wisdom of the spheres of the White Spider, and the brilliant irony of his father's spheres where time keeps moving to and fro, constantly inverting the flux and reflux of cosmic winds and the hopeful radiance of new-born stars.

"Welcome back, Dragon!" Alcibyadi whispered in his ear.

His gaze fixed in front of him, he made no reply.

Teyani stood up, gently pulling Alcibyadi by the arm. "We must move away! There's too much fire inside him. It's dangerous."

"Wait. He doesn't know what to do," Alcibyadi answered. Using a soft Voice-threshold, she instructed him, "Elyani must be taken to the funeral crypt. It is your task. Stand up, now. Take her body in your arms."

Szar dropped his left hand, stood up very straight, then bent forwards, and gently lifted Elyani's frail body. The veil that hid her face nearly fell off. Teyani moved quickly to fasten it. Even dead, an Immaculate priestess was to remain covered.

"No, Szar," Alcibyadi said, "it's not with Space Matrix that you are supposed to go to the funeral crypt! Not the way we do things down here. Use my mind instead. Come into my mind, I will show you the way."

Looking straight in front of him, he started walking.

Alcibyadi and Teyani followed, and the other White Eagle priestesses behind them.

Meanwhile, Mouridji looked for that thing which had fallen out of Szar's pocket. It didn't take her long to find it. It was a soft stone, the size of a pea.

"Lucky no one trod on it!" Mouridji told herself as she picked up the stone. It had a weird fast-oscillating energy that made her hand vibrate in an uncomfortable way. "The best would be to give it back to him immediately," she thought, and she rushed after the cortege of White Eagle priestesses. But by the time she caught up with them, they were already crossing the main portal of the crypt.

Seeing Mouridji, Namron bashed his forehead. "What the Underworld are you doing here?"

"I told you! The gods sent me!" she said briefly as she passed him, running after Szar who was striding to the funeral crypts.

17.3 The citadel of the Nephilim giants

Considering the urgency of the situation, the council of baphomets unanimously decided that despite the early hour of the morning, Grand Commander Bobros should be contacted immediately.

Pralaya, as the chair-baphomet, established the communication channel. After a quick exchange of recognition symbols and lawful salutes he announced, "Some important news from the counties of the Centre North, Your Excellency."

"Jex Belaran?" Bobros asked.

"No, the temple of Eisraim. Szar of the Brown Robe is no longer in possession of Perseps' stone."

"Ah, damn it! Did he give it to his teacher?"

"It doesn't seem so, Your Excellency. From the vibration we are getting, the stone seems to be in the hands of an old woman. A person of considerable sight."

"The Brown Robes must have had suspicions. They must have given the stone to one of their witches for her to spy on us."

"So far there has been no sign of the woman trying to probe the connection we have hooked into the stone."

Bobros the Terrible was genuinely worried, "Could she have been scanning us without your baphomets noticing anything?"

"Nothing is impossible, Your Excellency. The Brown Robes are clever. However, we have thoroughly scanned the woman's mind and she didn't seem to notice anything – which means she is either extraordinarily trained in the art of Point-camouflage, or totally unaware of what she is carrying in her pocket. Surprising as it may sound, we concluded in favour of the latter. We believe the Brown Robes have made a huge blunder."

"Difficult to believe!" Bobros was not a man to underestimate his enemies.

"But nevertheless possible. Our recommendation is to strike immediately. How long would it take our man to reach the temple of Eisraim?"

"At the moment he is further north. I can't see him being ready to launch the attack for five days, perhaps seven."

"Don't we have anyone closer to the target? Our assessment is that if a commando was sent immediately, the stone would fall into our hands."

"And what if it was a trap?"

"In that case, the Brown Robes already know we are after them. What would we have to lose in launching an operation?"

"True!" Bobros conceded.

"Is there no way our man could speed up his move? Could another commando be quickly organised from local resources?"

"I will contact him right now. Let me get back to you on this point. But keep your eyes on the witch! At the first sign of her trying to infiltrate our fields, kill her, instantly."

"We have already taken all necessary measures to ensure this, Your Excellency."

"Good, good, Pralaya. But be careful, the Brown Robes *are* dangerous."

"Your Excellency, I give you my baphomet's word, my council is handling this matter with extreme caution."

Bobros answered with a necromantically sardonic burst of laughter, which the baphomet rightly interpreted as a sign of approval and respect.

17.4 The unexpected party

In the aquamarine chamber Master Gervin was in the middle of a profound conversation with his disciple Woolly of the Brown Robe, who had just spent the night in King Vasoukidass' palace, celebrating the success of the ascension ritual in the company of Maryani and a few hundred guests, mainly Nagas. They were interrupted by a volley of hurried knocks.

"Ferman!" Gervin smiled affectionately, recognising the stalwart style of the leader of the team of Field Wizards. He raised his voice, lawfully inquiring, "Who, sent by the Lord Melchisedek, is knocking at the door?"

"Ferman!"

"Come in, my friend in the Law!" Gervin answered, while Woolly went to open the door.

The tall man stormed into the room. "Master Gervin, some grave matters..." He was out of breath, having run all the way from the chapel of the Field Wizards.

"Sit down, my friend."

"No time!" Ferman shook his head. "Master Gervin, in the north of the county... just at the border with Lasseera... around Alverard... the warp of fields is *very* sick."

"Foul elemental murk vomited by the windmills of the Law?"

"Much worse than that... at least half the nature-controlling fields have collapsed."

Meaning that all kinds of natural disasters could be expected, from floods to earthquakes – perhaps even a chain reaction creating a global collapse of the warp in the Centre North.

"Aha!" Gervin pulled his beard. "Can we restore the fields from here?"

"We have launched a joint procedure with the Field Wizards in Lasseera. We'll know by this evening if the warp is responding. But there is more. Something terrible..." Ferman hesitated.

"We're listening, Ferman."

"As we were testing one of our emergency triangular fields between Eisraim, Lasseera and the Plateau of Sorana (where Master Esrevin has sent a team led by Jop), we happened to pick up a vibration showing that a group of Nephilim Hunters are in the county. At least fifteen of them."

"In Eisraim?" Gervin was astounded.

"Less than a day from the temple!"

"Where exactly?"

"We don't know. By the time we tried to locate them again, they had camouflaged themselves. We couldn't find them."

"But I thought we had eliminated all the Renegade Hunters!" Woolly exclaimed.

"So did I!" Ferman shrugged his shoulders in perplexity. "Maybe it's a new clan. Or a gang from far away."

"They couldn't be Nephilim giants, could they?" Woolly frowned.

"Their energy didn't show any of the characteristic signs of the giants," Ferman answered. "But who knows? They could be trying to deceive us."

"We need to go and discuss this with Szar," Gervin decided, and he immediately Point-informed Lehrmon. "Will you come with us, Ferman?"

"I can't, Master Gervin, my men are waiting for me at the chapel. But when you see Szar, tell him to get ready. We may have to launch an expedition to Alverard immediately. If we can't fix the warp over there... then the Lord Melchisedek have mercy on us!"

17.5 The master plan, final version

"Oh, gods!" Lehrmon, who was the first to arrive at Szar's courtyard, could hardly believe his eyes.

Or his ears! The music was supermind-boggling – millions of voices resounding ad infinitum, pulling his consciousness far up into the spheres.

Szar had connected his music field to the Song of Creation.

Compelled to close his eyes and tune in, Lehrmon burst out laughing, "This is lawfully unreal!" Dizzy, he sat down on the lawn.

Ten seconds later, he had completely lost touch with the kingdom.

When Gervin and Woolly arrived, they found him absorbed in deep meditation. So far in the spheres that he didn't even notice their presence.

Szar, who was Dragon-dancing in the middle of the small courtyard, paying his respects to his Mother of the Endless Night, didn't notice them either.

"Is this a new weapon?" Woolly asked, contemplating what was falling from heaven.

"No, it's from the gods," Gervin looked up, thoughtfully twinging his beard.

From her world, Elyani was throwing flower petals onto the courtyard. But not just a handful or two. A thick rain was pouring down. The space was ablaze with flashing lights, flames of all colours, dancing geometrical shapes.

"But what is this music?" Woolly, who felt like crying with joy, had to shout to make himself heard, so deafening was the sound. "Is it from the gods too?"

"Hunh hunh! From the Flying Dragons."

In the centre of the courtyard, Szar was spinning and jumping, weaving patterns of light with his arms. There was magic in his movements. Through him, the Dragon of the Deep was dancing to the Song of Creation.

Mesmerised, Woolly of the Brown Robe started moving his arms, imitating Szar. "I want to learn to dance like this!" Carried away by the irresistible elation of the moment, he jumped his way to the middle of the courtyard and stood in front of Szar, trying his best to mirror his movements.

Had it not been for the latest news from Alverard, harbinger of the imminent collapse of the global warp of fields, had it not been for the pestilence that was threatening the western side of the county, and the drought that was slowly spreading from the neighbouring Western Plains, and the fifteen Nephilim Hunters that Ferman's Wizards had spotted only a few hours away from the temple, and the death of the filosterops, and all the other signs of the looming catastrophe, Gervin would probably have jumped and danced with them.

He sighed.

Szar had taken Woolly's hand. Together they were spinning. Blasted with the Flying Dragons' extravagant intensity of fire, charmed by the Mother of the Endless Night, Woolly kept his eyes and his mouth wide open, moving about with the grace of a celestial grasshopper.

Meanwhile, Elyani was pouring a torrent of flower petals onto Lehrmon, now in the highest state of meditation, completely disconnected from the manifested universe.

And the Song of Creation resounded, trillions of angelic choirs responding to each other.

Taking his head in his hands, Gervin tried to figure out a way of bringing his disciples back into the kingdom, and fast.

It was at that moment that Teyani and Alcibyadi arrived in the courtyard. They were not surprised by the music, which they had heard earlier that morning, when Szar had returned. But the pouring of the petals made them exclaim, "O-o-o-h?" in one awe-struck voice. By then, the celestial light was so concentrated that the courtyard looked like the inside of one gigantic flower of the world of the gods, with unlawfully maddening fragrances.

"Praise the Lord Melchisedek, ladies of the White Eagle," Gervin saluted them.

They didn't hear him.

He used the Point, "Praise the Lord Melchisedek, ladies of the White Eagle. As you can see, we were just about to hold an important strategic meeting." He thought this was why they had come. The inspired Teyani often turned up to important meetings without warning.

"Actually, this is not what brought us," she said after lawfully returning the greeting, contemplating Szar and Woolly with an air of disbelief. "We have come to deliver an important piece of news."

"And what is this important news?"

It was Alcibyadi who answered, "An oracle of the White Eagle has decreed that I am to heal Szar: free his left hand from the black pitch of Ahriman by performing a ritual calling onto the powers of Highness. Immediately."

"How timely!" Gervin took his head in his hands again.

"What?" Lehrmon was back in his body. "But what about the baby?" he exclaimed in horror.

Teyani pushed her lips forward and nodded, holding onto the Light of the Eagle.

"There is nothing to worry about," Alcibyadi answered with total faith. "The White Eagle will be with us."

"This is ridiculous!" Lehrmon stood up. "The black pitch in his hand is horrendously toxic. You are not going to tell me..."

"You're wasting your time," Alcibyadi interrupted him. "My decision is made."

"What kind of oracle was this?" Lehrmon became suspicious. "What was the question? And who asked it?"

"The oracle did not come as the result of a question," Teyani answered. "It was received by all of us during our morning ritual in the chapel of the White Eagle."

"Teyani, I object," Lehrmon raised his voice. "If a clearing is needed, it is up to the Brown Robes to perform it. We haven't even tried to project the Word of Thunder onto Szar's hand. Why should an eight-month-pregnant White Eagle priestess take this kind of risk?"

"The idea that I could do it better than you doesn't even cross your mind!" Alcibyadi was outraged. And in the heated exchange that followed, only Gervin noticed that Mouridji of the Purple Robe had arrived in the courtyard.

"You look very busy!" the prophetess told Gervin through darkness visible, dazzled by all the things that were happening.

"What can we do for you, my good Mouridji?" Gervin spoke to her through the Point. The Flying Dragon music was so loud that it was nearly impossible to make oneself heard in that space.

"I wanted to speak to Szar. But I think I will come back later," the old priestess Point-answered, putting the soft stone back into her pocket. And she turned round and left.

Gervin closed his senses and made a quick excursion into the realms of Thunder, seeking inspiration. On his return, he asked Teyani, "How did you get Szar to carry Elyani to the funeral crypt this morning?"

"Alcibyadi lent him her mind," she answered.

"But that's very dangerous!" Gervin pulled a face. "With the Flying Dragon energies that Szar is holding at the moment, she could get badly burnt!"

"No! Not at all!" Alcibyadi interrupted her argument with Lehrmon to protest. "I wasn't doing anything! It was the Eagle who was doing it through me."

"I see. Anyhow..." Gervin sighed, "I need to have a serious conversation with Szar. Could the Eagle arrange this for me, Alcibyadi?"

"Probably," the very pregnant priestess closed her eyes.

Instantly, the music field became silent.

The shower of celestial flower petals stopped.

Szar turned towards Gervin and became motionless.

A profound peace dawned on the courtyard, as if everything and everyone had stopped breathing, not because they were holding their breath but because they were breathing the infinitely still White Light of the Eagle

81

instead of air. Only Woolly kept jumping and dancing in the back of the courtyard, but that too seemed to be part of the stillness.

"Let's talk!" Alcibyadi took Gervin by the arm. Together they moved close to Szar, whose smile was lit up with the infinite softness of the Eagle.

There was so much love in that smile.

Gervin had tears in his eyes.

Szar slowly extended his hand towards Gervin, and he lightly touched his arm. "A present!" he whispered. "All glory to the teacher!" Using the power of the Point, he showed Gervin the master plan he had prepared for the Archive transfer.

It was supermentally superb. A glorious, Point-packed thought-form that made sense from the Deep Underworlds to the top of Lord Gana's helmet of omniscience, high in Revelation Sky. It drew from several Universal Knowledge Banks and took into account every single pawn on the chessboard of the kingdom. There were tips and traps to trick all parties, from the king's administration to the necromancers of the Eastern Peninsula. There were artistically-laid details and plenty of the much-needed sense of humour without which great angels are reluctant to give their support to human endeavours. And in the background there was the raw power of the Flying Dragons.

Gervin burst out laughing and clapped his hands.

For the first time in thirty-eight years, he felt ready for the final battle.

And from the Fields of Peace, Barkhan Seer and Orest, who had descended from Highness to help finalise the construction of the Archive's temple of light, clapped their hands too, congratulating Gervin. And far, far away from Eisraim, in an icy cavern where the light of day never reached, the old Ran Gereset also clapped his hands. The time was coming, the days were numbered. The ritual he had been conducting without interruption for thirty-eight years was drawing to an end.

"All glory to the teacher!" Closing his eyes, Gervin received the love that the White Eagle was pouring into him through Szar, and directed it to his master, Orest.

Light met light.

Eagle-ness and Thunder.

Where Revelation Sky meets the Edge of Highness.

And below, which was still fairly high up, Elyani looked down onto the kingdom. She warmed the hearts of all those in the courtyard with one of her smiles – a celestial smile, charged with the mysteries of the sky of the gods. It made Woolly dance faster and more ecstatically.

"Thank you, Alcibyadi," Gervin said in a tranquil voice.

"Was it a good talk?" she asked.

"The best we've ever had."

"Good. So, can I heal his hand, now?" she plunged an insistent gaze into Gervin's deeper-than-the-Fault-of-Eternity grey-green eyes.

"Tonight, Szar might have to take part in an expedition to the northern parts of the county, where the warp of fields is in urgent need of healing. Will he be ready to go by sunset?" Gervin negotiated.

"I give you my word!" Alcibyadi answered from the Eagle, without any hesitation.

"Well, then..." Gervin lifted up his hands, turning to Teyani, "let the White Eagles take him!"

Teyani, her energy still ablaze from the embrace at the Edge of Highness, sent another wave of the Eagle's fiery Love onto Gervin.

"All glory to the teacher!" the Thunderbolt Bearer smiled, and the wave ascended straight into the temple in the Fields of Peace. It illuminated the second Archive hall, where Orest and Barkhan Seer were working.

Barkhan Seer had no difficulty recognising where the Light came from – he knew every inch of Teyani's infinity by heart, and inside out, and since long before the beginning of time. He whispered to Orest, "My beloved friend is about to blast Highness out of Gervin's disciple! The poor lad has no idea what he is in for."

Lehrmon heard him. Understanding that Teyani was behind all this, he felt slightly reassured for the baby.

"Let's go," Gervin told Lehrmon. "Ferman is waiting for us."

"And what about him?" Lehrmon pointed to Woolly, who was still completely out of his head, eyes and mouth wide open, Dragon-jumping and dancing under the fields of stars.

"Ah, let him dance," Gervin shrugged his shoulders. "It's good for him. If he hasn't come back by sunset, we'll send Maryani to get him."

Alcibyadi was already walking out of the courtyard, followed by Szar and Teyani.

"The ritual is to take place in the chapel of the White Eagle," Teyani explained.

17.6 The first journey to Highness

As soon as the White Eagles arrived in their chapel, a relatively small room with a high circular dome, Alcibyadi instructed Szar to sit right in the centre of the large luminous circle that glowed from the plass floor amidst a number of other geometrical symbols.

It made Teyani remember the inauguration day, twenty-eight years earlier, when she and her friend Adya had conducted their first ritual in this chapel. Melchard of the Brown Robe was the guest of honour because he had been the chapel's main architect, leading the team of lawful masons. Adya, who was about to marry him, insisted on having him sit right in the centre of the circle.

In a glimpse, Teyani remembered how Lehrmon, clad in his brand new brown gown, was standing at the back of the chapel, holding Gervin by the hand. He had just turned seven and for his birthday Gervin had officially accepted him as his apprentice in Thunder. The chapel was packed with high priests and representatives of various orders, and many important people had to stand outside. Yet for all this lawful creme de la creme there were but two White Eagle priestesses: she and Adya. How unlawfully embarrassing!

After the inauguration day the chapel had seemed terribly empty, with Adya on one side and Teyani on the other. And then Adya died, leaving newborn Elyani in her care. Alcibyadi by then was hardly two years old. Teyani was often seen going in and out of her chapel with two children in her arms. These were difficult times. All of Teyani's friends had been killed in Karlinga. Her attempts to attract White Eagle priestesses from other counties had failed, mainly because there were so few of them left in the kingdom. And no one in Eisraim seemed interested in joining this unknown order led by a twenty-one-year-old grand master. The fact that passersby often heard her children crying in the chapel didn't help.

And yet these were magnificent years. The Eagle constantly blessed the chapel with torrential White Light. Gervin, who stood by Teyani's side throughout these difficult times, was weaving her Point, initiating her into the stupendous mysteries of Thunder. Every night he came to visit her chapel, bringing a feast of knowledge, sharing the secrets of the Brown Robe and taking her travelling through the spheres. When she despaired because her order was so empty, Gervin would point to the cots, "Look at these two beautiful disciples of yours! Can you imagine how powerful they will be by the time they become women? My word of Thunder – the White Eagles will be the pride of Eisraim!"

And now, the day after Elyani had succeeded in the ritual of an ascending goddess, blossoming Alcibyadi was standing very straight behind the Eagle's altar, ready to invoke the powers of the angels of Highness for one of the most difficult of all clearings – that of the ugly, abysmally sinful, hopelessly unresponsive and diabolically fixed black substance of Ahriman.

"Are you all right, Teyani?" Alcibyadi asked when she saw the tears in her mother's eyes.

"Yes. Yes."

"Would you like to chant the first hymns?"

"No. This is your ritual, my love." One of the most beautiful things Teyani had learnt from Gervin was the art of letting major tasks be performed by young people whenever possible.

"Now, let me have a look at this hand," Alcibyadi bent down towards Szar, who was sitting rock-still in meditation position. "Does it hurt?"

Szar opened his eyes, smiling at her like a young child. It took a few seconds before he realised she was asking him a question, after which he closed his eyes and let Space Matrix advise him on a proper answer.

"No thoughts, just Dragon!" was what came out of his mouth.

"Far, far from his human Self," Teyani went to sit behind him. "That's why the Eagle wants us to work on him right now."

Alcibyadi took Szar's left hand. Physically, it looked like a normal hand – except of course that it was paralysed. But the aura stopped at the wrist, continued by an ominously black silhouette. It caused an ugly false note in the otherwise happy and hardy buzzing of Szar's Dragon-reinforced etheric body.

She went back to the small altar, which was lit by a single oil lamp. She arranged the utensils and the sober offerings: just one white fruit, three flowers, a handful of grains of rice, a small bowl of fresh water, and a cupel of scented oil. And she started Voice-projecting the opening hymns of the Eagle's ritual to Highness.

"Let she who is, who was, and who will be,
Curve back onto her source,
And beyond the infinity of her Cosmic Night,
Cognize that which none can comprehend..."

Someone knocked at the door, "Alcibyadi!"

Startled, the White priestess turned round.

To her complete stupefaction, Teyani was no longer in the room.

"Alcibyadi, it's me, Woolly! Can I come in?"

Szar opened his eyes. "Yes, come in!" he answered for Alcibyadi.

"But..." Alcibyadi frowned, "but what about my ritual?"

Woolly, his eyes still glowing with fiery echoes of the Song of Creation, walked into the chapel. "Are you ready, brother?"

"Very much so, brother!" Szar stood up, looking down to his left fist.

"Oh!" Woolly exclaimed with disappointment when he saw that the black smear had not budged from Szar's hand. "So the ritual didn't work?"

"Yes it did! Look, now I can move it," Szar went on clenching and un-clenching his fist. He gave Alcibyadi a mysterious smile, "Anyhow, we have hardly started, haven't we?"

"But..." Alcibyadi searched for words.

"We'll continue as soon as I am back from Alverard," Szar said.

"Good to see you're back to your senses!" Woolly put his hand on Szar's massive pectorals, contemplating the chapel's high cupola. "A beautiful place you have here," he complimented Alcibyadi. "I heard Melchard built it, is that right?"

Alcibyadi was looking at the two men with an air of disbelief. "Are you... are you going now?"

Szar nodded. He plunged a gaze of infinite softness, Whiteness and Ea-gle-ness into her stupefied eyes. "I won't thank you. And I won't say good bye," he saluted her, as if she knew exactly what he meant. And he walked away.

"All glory to the Lord Melchisedek!" Woolly said in the exquisitely polite voice he had been cultivating since he had started his new life, and he rushed behind Szar, who was striding at high pace.

Leaning against the living wall, perplexed Alcibyadi pushed her lips forward and caressed her chin.

She looked up to the chapel's dome. No particular light in sight. No special presence to let her suspect that something unusual had happened.

But where was Teyani?

Casually, she walked to the courtyard outside the chapel. That was when she understood.

"Oh, gods!" she exclaimed, contemplating the reddish hues in the mists.

It was sunset.

More than ten hours had passed since the beginning of her ritual.

Ten hours!

But how? And where?

A hesitant voice called her, "Alcibyadi?"

A frail purple silhouette was standing by the door of the chapel.

"Praise the Lord Melchisedek, Mouridji the prophetess!"

"All glory to the Lord Melchisedek, my child. Would Szar happen to be with you, by chance?"

"My good Mouridji, he has just left. He will be away from the temple for a few days."

"Going north? To fix the fields in Alverard?" Mouridji guessed.

Alcibyadi smiled, amused. It hadn't taken her long to find out. "If you hurry you might catch him before he leaves."

"Not to worry, he must be very busy. Such an unlawful mess in Alverard! They're being smothered by a black cloud coming out of their temple like a huge ongoing fart. It's already killed hundreds of people, there are corpses everywhere," Mouridji shook her head, appalled. "I will see Szar when he comes back. Except... you will probably see him before me, won't you?" Mouridji caught hold of the stone in her pocket, wondering whether to give it to Alcibyadi.

"Would you like me to pass on a message to him?" Alcibyadi offered.

"A message? Yes, that will be the best. Tell him that old Mouridji found the soft stone that fell out of his pocket this morning, in the central crypt."

"I lawfully certainly will, Mouridji. As soon as I see him."

17.7 In search of the poisoned gift

Later that evening, Gervin was in the chapel of the Field Wizards, working with Ferman's team, when he received an emergency Point-call from Szar. Szar was standing on the deck of a boat on the Holy Fontelayana river, on his way to the northern border of the county of Eisraim. He had just realised that the stone which had been given to him by Perseps the Hunter was no longer in his pocket.

"Do you mean we have lost the key to Jex Belaran's protective shield?" Gervin burst out laughing, as Masters of Thunder usually do when receiving disastrous tidings.

"It's not lost yet," Szar Point-replied. "I have scanned the space and located the object. It is with Mouridji of the Purple Robe."

"Our good Mouridji?" Gervin could hardly believe his Point. "How the Far Underworld did that happen?"

"I don't know, but there is a spider in the potage. When scanning the warp around her, I detected a strange field that is not of Eisraim make."

"Are you sure? Mouridji is sharp. It could be something she has woven herself according to the mysteries of the Purple Robe," Gervin Point-suggested. "What exactly did you see?"

"A cord which links her to a place, far away. I didn't want to follow it, it would have revealed my presence. The device is extraordinarily subtle. Whoever has woven this is a top-level Field Wizard."

"Somehow, I can't imagine Mouridji as a secret agent working against us," Gervin stifled a smile. "Let me speak to her. There has to be a simple explanation for all this."

"Gervin, I sense extreme danger," Szar Point-warned. "I request permission to come back to the temple immediately."

"Impossible! The situation in the north is too critical. We can't take the risk of letting our team in Alverard be slaughtered. Let me handle this from Thunder. I will Point-return to you in the coming hours."

Perplexed, Gervin asked Ferman and his men to excuse him for a moment. He went out for a stroll. He simply could not believe that Mouridji, whom he had known for more than forty years, had stolen the stone. Had Szar's clarity been veiled by his Flying Dragon odyssey?

"Praise the Lord Melchisedek, Master Gervin!" Namron hailed him from the roof of the chapel.

"All glory to the Lord Melchisedek, my good Namron!" Gervin looked up. "Tell me, have you seen Mouridji today?"

"Oh!" Namron didn't hide his exasperation. "She played one of her tricks on me this morning. She managed to enter the central crypt against your orders. I tried to keep her out, but she went through a secret passage. Probably the one from the third hall of Melchisedek."

So there *was* mischief in the air.

Gervin bit his lip.

"Master Gervin!" Khej of the Field Wizards called through darkness visible. "Please come immediately! Some terrible news from Romeran: the warp of the Western Plains is wobbling! It's made things worse in Alverard. The whole of the warp of the Centre North could go down any minute!"

"Coming in the Law!" Gervin ran back to the building.

17.8 Alverard, on the northern border of the county of Eisraim

Lehrmon, Woolly and Szar arrived at Alverard before dawn.

The air was moist. The fog was thick. It stuck to their skin and offended their lungs.

Coming off the boat, Woolly was wriggling his nostrils, "What smell is that?"

"Death," Szar answered in his Dragon low-pitched voice, covering his head with the hood of his brown gown.

Esrevin and his men, who had travelled from the temple of Lasseera the day before, were waiting for them on the outskirts of the town. They were standing around a bonfire, warming their hands.

Pelden, the head of the Field Wizards of Lasseera, gave them a briefing. "The fields have been vomiting the Ugly Underworld out of darkness visible!" the tall, thin, middle-aged man began with a disgusted look. "Foul elemental slime like you can hardly imagine. This time it hasn't just made people sick, it's made them lose their minds. Throughout the area people have been slaughtering each other – insanity, large-scale. They beat each other to death. They strangle their own children. They throw themselves into the river. They bash the living walls of their houses with clubs. Yesterday we saw some horrific scenes in town: mutilated corpses on the streets, people running in all directions and screaming as in the caverns of sickness."

"There is also some good news," Esrevin added, his consistently jovial voice hardly watered down. "I have communicated with your people in Eisraim. Ferman and Gervin say that with the help of my team here they can probably restore the warp, provided the leakage in the temple of Alverard is neutralised."

"Do you mean to say the priests of Alverard are still performing the windmills of the Law?" Lehrmon asked in consternation.

"Oh, no," Pelden answered. "They were all killed, probably by the first waves of slime that overflowed from their rituals. But that didn't stop the torrents of noxious elemental muck."

"What? The murk keeps being vomited, even after the windmills rituals have stopped?"

"Exactly. And it's still going on."

Woolly whistled loudly. "That's new!"

The warp wasn't just wounded, it leaked. Normally, astral energies exuded from the warp only when called on by the rituals of the windmills of the Law.

"According to a report we received during the night, it's also been happening in the counties of the Western Shores, and in the east. In the last days the situation has deteriorated considerably."

"So, Master Esrevin, what is your plan?" Lehrmon asked.

Master Esrevin, like Master Gervin, always had a plan.

"We have placed two of our Field Wizards at each corner of the town. They are ready to establish a resonance with the temples of Lasseera and Eisraim. As I told you, this has a good chance of restoring the warp. But before it can happen I need you to clean up the main leakage."

"Where?" Szar asked.

"The temple is located in the centre of Alverard, hardly one hour from here."

"And how do you wish us to mend the leakage, Master Esrevin? Voice and stones, I presume?" Woolly asked him.

Pelden and his Wizards remembered only too well the wild nights when Woolly had yelled at the high priests of their temple, called them all sorts of colourful names, spat on the floor, and thrown bucket-loads of white slime in their faces. They could hardly believe how lawfully distinguished the young man had become.

"I should believe Voice and stones would be ideal devices in this case," Master Esrevin answered in a deliberately lawfully formal voice.

"But you'll have to hold your Point," Pelden warned. "If you let this elemental shit get into your energy, you're as good as Underworld fodder."

"Pretty thick shit, down there," a Field Wizard seconded, pointing in the direction of Alverard. "Especially close to the temple. Yesterday Master Pelden and I tried to reach it, but we had to stop half-way and come back."

"I think I should first go for a quick reconnaissance," Szar suggested.

Esrevin and Lehrmon agreed. They decided to adjourn the meeting until his return.

After taking directions from Pelden, Szar dropped his bag close to the fire.

"Are you completely back, now?" Lehrmon asked him.

"No," Szar answered unambiguously.

"Flying Dragon spaces?"

"No. That's easy. What really blew me away was Alcibyadi's Highness," he confessed, looking down to his left fist. "Have they ever done it to you?"

"Man of the Law..." Lehrmon's eyes blinked fast, "during my childhood, when Gervin was training Teyani, it never stopped! That's the thing with the White Eagles, they never stop." Lehrmon burst out laughing, "If you knew what happened when Alcibyadi and I conceived the baby!"

"You'll tell me on the way home," Szar smiled, remembering the fountain of blue Life and Light in the world of the gods.

"No!" Lehrmon replied. "Sure you don't want anyone to come with you?"

"Yep. I'll run. Anyhow, there aren't any soldiers in Alverard, are there?"

"No," Pelden joined them. "We've asked the prince of Eisraim to keep out of here. The last thing we need is a mad battalion ransacking the area."

"Farewell, men of the Law!" Szar slapped Lehrmon's shoulder and started running.

"Friend, I need to speak to you," Pelden said, watching Szar disappear in the thick dirty-grey mists. He took Lehrmon by the arm and walked away from the group of men who were warming their hands, lawfully chatting around the fire. When he was satisfied no one could hear him he asked, "Has anyone in Eisraim ever found out what the Underworld happened to Fridrick the Hunter?"

"Disappeared. According to Szar's vision, he was killed. Killed in an ugly way. Someone, we don't know who, wiped out his astral body completely. Nothing was left of him, not even a shadow in the caverns of sickness."

"I find it difficult to believe he was a traitor," Pelden confessed. "He was... my friend."

"I know. He was such a lawfully lovely man. And yet he was but a pack of lies. His story was completely fabricated. You know that the Hunters of Jex Belaran had never heard of him, don't you?"

"Mm... except, of course, if *they* were the ones who sent him. Have you thought of that possibility?"

The nightmare scenario.

Lehrmon preferred to laugh, "That would be the end of the Law!"

"Seriously, Lehrmon. What if the Hunters of Jex Belaran were playing with us? With these fifteen Hunters roaming around your temple..."

"I know, I know. The whole lineage of Thunder is on high alert. Gervin himself is sleeping in the crypt of the Archive stones until we know more."

"Apart from Jex Belaran, who could have sent Fridrick?" Pelden insisted.

"Could be the king's administration. There are an awful lawful lot of factions among them. Could also be the giants."

Even worse than the Hunters.

"The giants are too far!" Pelden argued. "And why would they..."

"Alarm!" an emergency Point-signal interrupted their talk. "Two unknown men are approaching. Everyone back to the fire immediately!"

Pelden and Lehrmon ran to the others.

Woolly was quite excited. "I brought a bag full of soft-stone weapons," he told Esrevin. "A new type. I've never had the opportunity to test them."

"I don't think there is danger," Esrevin said, closing his eyes to tune into the two souls.

Everyone kept silent. The cracklings of the fire sounded exaggeratedly loud.

They waited, trying to read through the mists, and holding the soft-stone weapons they had brought with them. In Lasseera as in Eisraim it was in the chapel of the Field Wizards that soft stones were manufactured.

After a few minutes, as no one showed up, they agreed that the men must have turned back. "Everything clear!" Esrevin reassured them. "But we should stick together until Szar returns."

"How long will he be?" one of the Field Wizards asked Lehrmon.

"Two hours at the most."

"Master Woolly!" Esrevin had an idea. "We of Lasseera were most disappointed we couldn't take part in Lady Elyani's ascension ritual. But as you know, many urgent matters kept us busy in our temple."

"A momentous ascension ritual, it was indeed!" Woolly raised his hands.

"Will you narrate the events to us, Master Woolly?" Esrevin asked.

"But lawfully certainly!"

"Yes! Woolly of the Brown Robe is such a good talker," the men applauded, and they settled themselves around the fire to listen.

17.9 The dark night of the kingdom

Szar returned one hour after dawn. He found the small troop avidly drinking Woolly's words. They had arrived at the palace of King Vasouki-dass for the celebration during which the Naga architects were to receive their distinctions. Maryani was having a long and fascinating conversation with Amaran of the Great Warriors, who wanted to know *all* the details of the ascension ritual so he could tell his brothers in Mount Lohrzen at a feast that was to take place there three weeks later. Out of nowhere a shower of golden petals started pouring down in Vasouk's reception hall, to the jubilation of the Nagas.

When they saw Szar, the Field Wizards of Lasseera stood up and applauded him, for Master Woolly had just spent two hours depicting with great eloquence the lawfully unreal battle that he and Elyani had fought. Some of the men, including Pelden, were in tears. Esrevin himself was deeply moved.

Szar responded by praising Gervin, "All glory to the teacher!" But he was in his warrior character – cool, precise, totally focussed on his task. To save time, rather than starting a meeting he established a Point-communication with his brothers in the Brown Robe. "I located the temple and inspected its surroundings. And I found a good way to get there: an earth line that follows one of the main streets of Alverard. It will make it much easier to cope with the elemental pollution."

"How is it in town?" Esrevin Point-asked.

"Dirty. Dark grey slime pouring from the third layer above darkness visible. The closer to the temple you get, the worse it becomes. I don't think it would be advisable for any of Pelden's men to come with us."

"And what about the people of Alverard?"

"Dangerous only to themselves. No real threat to us."

"Anything else?" Lehrmon Point-asked.

"No. Let's move!"

Woolly quickly checked the bag of soft stones he had brought for the rescue operation. He put it on his shoulder, waving farewell to his audience.

The Field Wizards cheered loudly, congratulating him for the lawfully marvellous storytelling.

As they started walking, the three Brown Robes sealed their Points with a combined triangular seal. Each of them established a sharp triangular resonance above his head, and the three triangles were linked. This not only created a major reinforcement of the seals, it also facilitated the detection of potential leakages. If one of their Points were to collapse under the pressure of the noxious slime, or even to be slightly infiltrated, the others would immediately know.

Their heads covered with their hoods, they marched silently, at high speed. Szar opened the way. Woolly followed, with Lehrmon at the rear. They traced a winding path through Alverard's outer suburbs, where houses were sparse. The mists were so thick and grey, it seemed the Sun had forgotten to rise that day. The three men could hardly see sixty lawful feet in front of them.

"I sense a presence," Lehrmon Point-warned. "On the path, a few hundred lawful feet in front of us."

"A corpse," Szar corrected him.

It didn't take long before they saw it. It was the body of a young man, curved in foetal position by the side of an oak tree. He had grasped a large tree root in his hand, as if in a desperate attempt to anchor himself in the kingdom.

"I don't think he's completely dead." Lehrmon wondered whether they should go to his help.

"There are hundreds like him. Everywhere," Szar made it clear he didn't want to stop.

A few minutes later, passing in front of a small cottage, they found more bodies. Close to them three peasants were sitting on the ground, their eyes wide open, sunk in the mists.

"Praise the Lord Melchisedek, men of the Law!" Woolly lawfully greeted them with a warm loud voice and a large smile.

Two of the men kept staring in front of them, as if they hadn't heard anything – perfectly lawful for men of their caste. But the third one stood up. His eyes lit with a demented spark, he started running towards them, brandishing his fists and growling like an animal.

Woolly blew up, "Ah, shit! Shit! Shit! Why can't I keep my fucking mouth closed!" But before he had time to grab a soft stone from his bag, the man was flat on the ground.

Lehrmon raised his eyebrow, startled at the ease with which Szar had neutralised the man. "Dead?" he asked.

"No. Just asleep."

"How did you do it?"

"A particular kind of venom. The Hunters call it angel sneeze."

"I'm sorry!" Woolly was mad at himself. "That was such an idiotic thing to do!"

"Don't worry, my great man in the Law," Lehrmon put his hands on the young man's shoulders. "We won't tell Maryani what we heard."

"If you knew how deplorable her language has become, you would be shocked," Woolly resumed his most lawfully polished tone.

"I wonder how that could have happened!" Lehrmon sighed.

The more they advanced, the darker and thicker the mists. "You call this mist? I call it puree!" Lehrmon observed when they reached the southern neighbourhoods of the city. "If it keeps getting worse, we'll soon find it impossible to breathe."

There were more and more bodies in the streets. It was difficult to say whether they were corpses or people lying prostrate, overwhelmed by the toxicity of the space. As the Brown Robes were crossing a small bridge, four corpses jumped to their feet and started running after them, yelling furiously. Szar instantly knocked them down from a distance, with the same disconcerting ease.

Woolly and Lehrmon exchanged a glance. "He *has* become dangerous!" Woolly scratched the bump on his nose, thoughtful. He was starting to re-alise how useless his soft-stone weapons would be if it came to fighting Nephilim Hunters.

And the giants were even worse.

"We're reaching the earth line," Szar said as they were turning into a wide street. "Keep walking straight behind me."

The fog was as thick and sticky as before but Woolly and Lehrmon im-mediately found it easier to walk. And to breathe.

"Feels much lighter, here!" Lehrmon filled his lungs. "And look, there don't seem to be any corpses!"

"The people who live here were protected by the good vibrations of the line, is that it?" Woolly asked.

"Meaning we need to be even more cautious," Szar warned. "They're in-side their houses, watching us."

Further along they met four cows that were standing right on the path of the line. The animals were from a stable beside the road.

"Look at that!" Woolly marvelled when he saw how they had broken the fences to reach the earth line. "Animal wisdom! Is that what the people of Alverard should be doing to protect themselves?"

93

"Except that the streets of Alverard aren't particularly safe these days. I'd rather hide in my house if I were them," Lehrmon extended his hand to lawfully caress one of the animals, mentally repeating a verse that all Atlantean children learned at school, "Pat a cow, erase one sin!"

"Hunh!" Szar Point-stopped him. "We avoid all contact with the population."

For more than half an hour they followed the earth line. The street was empty, apart from one or two corpses here and there. No one attacked them. No one hailed them from the houses. It was like walking through one of those ghost-villages the dead visit in the first part of their after-life journey, when they desperately look for company without ever finding it.

"We're coming close to the temple now. We must leave the line," Szar finally told them, and he made them turn right into a small alley.

It soon became much uglier. The fog turned into fudge – a stinking, gooey greyness that stuck to their clothes, shocked their nostrils and polluted their lungs. Their shoulders heavy with all the elemental garbage that filled darkness visible, they had to push on step after step. At the end of the alley they reached a large marketplace where it seemed death had taken everyone by surprise, judging by the way shopkeepers had collapsed on their stalls, still holding the goods they were handing to their customers.

When they reached the temple, a relatively small edifice surrounded by the traditional eighty-four statues of the gods, they Point-liaised with Esrevin and Pelden.

"Is there any particular reason why you would want us to check the inside of the temple?" Woolly asked Esrevin after giving a short account of the situation in town. "The astral black smoke coming out of that building is... unlawfully nasty. We will first try to neutralise it from outside, using my stones."

Esrevin and Pelden agreed, but they urged Woolly to move fast. Lasseera had just advised them that a near-collapse of the warp had been reported in Romeran, the capital of the Western Plains. "If we can quickly restore the fields here, we might save them from a disaster. But if hell breaks loose in Romeran, then the Lord Melchisedek have mercy on us! By resonance it might not take more than twenty-four hours for the entire warp of the counties of the Centre North to render its last fart in our smiling face," Pelden warned, using an expression he had picked up from Woolly.

"We shall take action with great diligence, Master Pelden," Woolly Point-replied.

His plan was to establish a field of containment all around the temple so as to allow the Field Wizards to restore the warp – the only real way of fixing the leakage. To establish the containment field he had brought a set of six stones especially crafted by Maryani and himself for this long-awaited situation. If this was to fail, then they would have to go inside the temple, find the chapel of the windmills of the Law and blast everything with stones, or even let Lehrmon project the Word of Thunder.

But when he opened his bag a bad surprise was waiting for him. Despite the box's protective lining, two of the six special soft stones had turned black, contaminated by the elemental pollution.

"Oh, gods!" Woolly remained cool. "What's happened to my babies?"

"Four stones should be enough," Lehrmon decided, and the two men hurried around the building, placing a good stone at each of the four corners. Then Woolly connected his babies to one of the upper intermediary worlds, from where the power was to be supplied for the containment field. To maximise the effect he liaised with the Field Wizards that Esrevin had posted in the surroundings of Alverard. Together they established a powerful resonance, supported from a distance by the teams in Lasseera and Eisraim.

When Woolly finally connected his field, no particular change was noticeable locally. There followed a heavy silence during which Woolly kept reminding himself of his resolve to remain cool and well-mannered no matter what. The suspense was broken a few minutes later, when the Lasseera team reported that the warp was showing certain global signs of improvement, evidenced by a greater fluidity in the field resonance between them and Eisraim.

"But that's not good enough!" Master Ferman Point-warned them from Eisraim. "Unless you can neutralise the leakage in Alverard completely, the warp of the Western Plains is bound to collapse."

Szar, who had disappeared a moment earlier with the two blackened stones, came back to Woolly and opened his hand in front of him.

"Sh... Sweet Lord!" Woolly exclaimed when he saw that his babies had been restored to their original glow. "How did you do that?"

In reply, Szar just shone his motley combination of out-of-the-seven-spheres candour and Eagle softness.

"Hurry!" Lehrmon grabbed one of the stones and ran to the back of the temple, while Woolly went to take position on the side of the right wing. In the seconds that followed the reinforcement of the containment field, Ferman Point-reported an improvement and announced that the joint procedure aimed at restoring the warp had been launched.

There followed more suspense.

Lehrmon came back to Szar. "What if we have to get into that hell?" he pointed to the temple's ominous darkness. Now that the containment field was in place, the corrosive astral smoke inside was getting more concentrated by the minute.

"How about setting fire to the building?" Woolly suggested, despite the fact that Atlantean Law regarded the destruction of a temple as one of the worst possible crimes.

"As in the prophecy of Maveron, 'They will burn their own temples!'" Lehrmon answered with a bitter smile.

"I had forgotten about that verse. But it's bound to happen!" Woolly passed his hand through his mass of curly hair gunked with etheric debris.

"It's just a matter of time before this shit happens in a *lot* of temples. Many people will be tempted to try purifications by fire, I can see it coming!"

"It's not working!" Ferman Point-called them from Eisraim. "The warp isn't responding."

"But it should be, Master Ferman!" Woolly Point-protested. "All signs are that our containment field is now fully operational."

"A top job you've done there, my boy! The problem is, we hadn't planned on the Western Plains going down. I think it's what's happening at the moment: the warp malaise in Romeran is resonating with Alverard."

"I have an idea!" Lehrmon snapped his fingers thunderously. "Esrevin, didn't you send some of your men to the Plateau of Sorana a few days ago?"

"Jop's team. Six of them. But they have left. By now they should be on their way to Ferex Pass."

"Even better! The gods are with us," Lehrmon was enthused. "Tell them to establish a resonance with the temple of Baal in Romeran. There are some top-level Field Wizards over there. And let Lasseera and Eisraim connect with them. Get it?"

"But it's obvious!" Woolly exulted. "That places Alverard just at the centre of the cross, half-way between Jop and the priests of Baal, as well as on the line between Lasseera and Eisraim."

While the Field Wizards were contacting the priests of Baal, Szar kept his eyes fixed on the temple. By then, it had turned completely black, drowned in the filth that kept pouring from astral spaces. "I don't think it would be impossible to reach the chapel of the windmills," he told Lehrmon. "But if we want to do it, we should do it soon. Time is not working for us."

"We give them ten minutes," Lehrmon decided.

It didn't even take that long before the Field Wizards of Lasseera Point-announced jubilantly, "The warp is responding! Most of the fields in the north of Eisraim are starting to resonate with ours again!"

Everyone held their breath, not wanting to rejoice too soon.

"It *is* working!" Ferman and the Eisraim team Point-confirmed a few minutes later. "The warp is not only regaining in fluidity, but also in strength."

And from the other side of the Mountains of Lasraim, Jop and his team Point-joined them, "The priests of Baal are reporting a positive response in the warp of the Western Plains!"

"We are intensifying the resonance," Pelden Point-reported. "The interference from Alverard is no longer blocking us. We've done it, my friends in the Law! The leakage is neutralised!"

In the chapel of the Field Wizards in Eisraim, Lady Maryani Voice-projected a frighteningly loud "Youyouyouyou...", making Master Gervin raise a disconcerted eyebrow. Ferman's men stood up and cheered, shouting victory with her. They hugged each other, and in the glorious elation of the moment they hugged her too. And while similar scenes were taking place in Lasseera and at the camp of Esrevin and Pelden, Woolly and Lehrmon were dancing with joy amidst the dark desolation of Alverard, while Szar was thoughtfully clenching and unclenching his left fist.

In the seconds that followed, an emergency Point-signal cold-showered the collective enthusiasm.

It came from Jop, in Ferex Pass. "We have a problem. A big problem."

"The warp?" Ferman Point-asked anxiously.

"No. We are picking up a vibration. Nephilim Hunters. Four of them."

"Where?"

"Somewhere along the border between Lasseera and Eisraim."

Using the exceptional detection field provided by the cross resonance between the four stations, the Field Wizards of Lasseera were soon able to confirm the spotting. "We can feel them too. Four men. Carrying an unlawful number of soft-stone weapons. At least... at least *three thousand*!"

Enough to annihilate the entire population of Eisraim city.

"Aren't they the same Nephilim we detected yesterday morning?" Lehrmon Point-asked.

"No," Jop was Point-categorical.

"Are you sure?" Esrevin Point-intervened.

"Positive. The reason is simple: we can also feel the vibration of the fifteen others. They've moved away from the temple of Eisraim. They're closer to Eisraim city, now."

"Could they be giants?" Woolly Point-asked.

"Giants?" Jop was taken by surprise. "I hadn't even thought of that. They rather look like Hunters to me. But I've never spotted giants before, so I have no way to tell. They're Nephilim, and they're armed to the teeth with soft stones. That's all I can say."

"Szar!" Gervin Point-called. "I want you to come back to the temple immediately. Immediately! Leave Lehrmon and Woolly in Alverard. Do not waste one minute."

17.10 Paradoxes in Highness

After Szar, Woolly and Lehrmon had left the temple, Alcibyadi had gone for an inspirational walk in the Point-guided corridors of the female wing of the temple.

What the Upperworld had happened during her ten-hour White-out (Teyani's technical term for blacking out in transcendental spheres)? She could not remember a thing. Even more strangely, she could not feel anything in herself to give her clues as to where she had been. Usually, after connecting with angels or prophesying from lofty worlds, her energy was left ablaze with Spirit.

This time, nothing. An infinitesimal blank.

As she was reaching the courtyard of the priestesses of the Dawn of Creation, Teyani called her through darkness visible, "Praise the Lord Melchisedek, Alcibyadi of Highness! How is baby Lehrmon?" For it was already decided that the child would be called Lehrmon, son of Lehrmon.

"He has been angelically quiet lately. But I'm dying to know what happened today. I Whited-out completely."

"Precisely, my love, Gervin and I need to speak to you about this. We're waiting for you at the chapel of the Field Wizards."

That sounded like an unusual place for a discussion about transcendental rituals. But with Master Gervin, anything was to be expected, any time.

Alcibyadi often visited the chapel of the Field Wizards because it was where Lehrmon spent most of his time when he was in Eisraim. She was accustomed to the pandemonium of offensive smells, the dusty shelves (the Field Wizards never allowed cleaners inside their domain), the precisely organised mess of bottles and jars on the floor, and the men who walked fast and with great sense of purpose, far too absorbed in their cogitation to greet visitors, except for the inevitable "Watchyafeetforthebottles!" which they *never* tired of repeating.

That evening she found the chapel busier than ever.

"Praise the Lord Melchisedek, Lady Alcibyadi of the White Eagle!" a voice from above cheerfully called her.

Looking up she saw Namron sitting on the edge of the roof of the one-storey building, chewing his black root, his bare feet hanging in the air.

She returned the greeting. "Are we expecting unwanted guests?" she asked.

The small man just smiled in his usual way to indicate, "You know I'm not supposed to tell you that, so why don't you ask Teyani who of course knows everything about it?"

The doors of the chapel were wide open. Alcibyadi walked in, carefully watching the floor for bottles. On the left a team of five lawful masons were projecting shrieking sounds onto the wall – ugly Voice-vibrations that made chunks of plass crumble and that released clouds of astral dust. Voice-chipping, it was called.

They were killing the living plass!

It made Alcibyadi shiver.

The normal way of creating an opening in the wall would have been to modify the chapel's structural field, and let the plass walls adjust their shapes gradually over a period of a few months. If Voice-chipping was used, it meant the Field Wizards were in an unlawful hurry.

"Alcibyadi!" Maryani ran from the basement to hug Alcibyadi – an Underworldly-delicious hug that filled her with the superior golden light of the Nagas. It made baby Lehrmon shiver with excitement.

"What's this mess?" Alcibyadi asked, pointing at the lawful masons.

"It's an idea of Szar's. Part of..."

Projecting a false note in unison, the lawful masons were at the top of their Voices. So loud, Alcibyadi couldn't hear a thing.

"What?" she asked.

Maryani raised her voice, "It's an idea of Szar's, part of his plan. We're expanding! We're taking over the chapel of our neighbours, the Wise Witches of the Law."

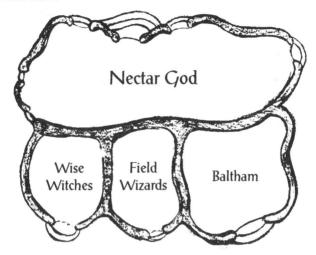

"But I thought the Field Wizards had been trying to get the Wise Witches of the Law to move out for more than twenty years!"

"This time we've made them an offer they couldn't refuse. We're giving them one of the Holy Cowsheds!"

Alcibyadi was shocked. "What?"

"Watch your feet for the bottles!" Maryani took Alcibyadi to the back of the hall close to the staircase, away from the lawful masons. "I was saying, this time we've made them an offer..."

"Yes, I heard that. Do you mean the Wise Witches are moving into the Holy Sheds where our sacred cows have been kept for thousands of years?"

"The Holy Sheds are large enough to fit not only the Wise Witches but also the order of Baltham, our neighbours on the other side, and the order of the Mysteries of the Nectar God. They're all moving out of here. We're taking over the whole block, our chapel is going to be huge! A little temple within the temple. More like an underground fortress, actually. Szar wants us to go down. When you see the basements of Baltham you'll understand. They're gorgeous!" Maryani pointed down and to the right. "And they open onto the temple's catacombs," she added, thrilled.

"But what about the cows?" Alcibyadi was concerned.

"They're being transferred to the chapel of the Servants of the Rural Deities. Their last priest died a few days ago. Gervin said that if we explained to them (I mean the cows) how our project was going to benefit humanity, they wouldn't mind."

"I see..." dazzled by so many changes, Alcibyadi remained thoughtful.

While talking, Maryani had been playing with the baby, sending him bubbles of light and watching his soul laugh. "I must go," she said. "We're about to begin a difficult rescue operation on the warp at the border with Lasseera."

"Do you know where Teyani and Gervin are?"

"In the cellar adjacent to the crypt of the Archive stones. It's the second on your right when you go down the steps. Watch the bottles on the staircase!"

Alcibyadi looked up and sighed.

The cellar where Gervin and Teyani were waiting for her was refreshingly quiet compared to the entrance hall. It was a large chamber in which twenty-four barrels of arch-precious (and foul-smelling) white slime were kept – the matrix of the hermaphroditic stones which Maryani and Woolly had been preparing in the last months. Gervin was standing in a corner of the room, leaning against the living wall. Teyani was sitting on a barrel by his side.

As soon as Alcibyadi entered, she felt a pressing urge to walk to the third barrel on the left. "Is it all right if I sit here?" she asked after the exchange of lawful greetings. To her surprise she realised it was the baby who was avidly pulling her to that barrel.

"Good choice!" Gervin approved. "Maryani calls this one Molten Sea upon Eisraim."

"Namron on the roof, Master Gervin in the basement... what's happening here?" Alcibyadi inquired.

"Fifteen Nephilim soldiers have been identified in the vicinity of the temple," Gervin told her straightforwardly.

"They could be Hunters, but they could also be giants," Teyani added.

"How far from here?"

"That's the problem, we don't know," Gervin said. "We spotted them once, and after that we have been unable to locate them again. Whoever they are, they are remarkably clever. It could well be they are just passing by. And if they are not, Maryani and I have prepared a nice little reception for them. But let's talk about you," Gervin changed his tone.

Alcibyadi was amazed at the way her baby was drinking the energy of the barrel on which she was sitting. It made the golden energy of her pregnancy flare. "This is *very* strong!" she marvelled, her finger pointing to the Underworlds. "I can see why some people end up liking the smell."

Gervin turned to Teyani, "See! What did I tell you?"

Teyani shook her head in reprobation, pulling one of her most evocative faces.

"Anyhow! Do you remember where you have been?" the Thunderbolt Bearer asked Alcibyadi.

"Not a thing in the Law. Will you tell me what happened?"

"Your ritual was so well done that instead of just receiving help from the angels of Highness, you and Szar were projected among them."

With all my heart, with all my mind...

"In Highness?" Alcibyadi opened her eyes so wide that Gervin burst out laughing. "But I haven't the faintest memory of ascending and crossing the Golden Shield!" she said.

"Highness," Gervin explained, "is said to be above the worlds of the gods only because of its supremacy over all manifested levels. Truly, it is neither above, nor below, nor anywhere else. It is nowhere, and yet everywhere – transcendental!"

"But why don't I remember?"

"Yes, why don't you remember?" Gervin sighed, summarising the tragedy of humanity.

Alcibyadi wasn't going to give up so easily. "For more than nine years I have performed at least three rituals a day to the angels of Highness. The angels have consistently responded. I have felt their Light and their presence, I have even healed people through them. How can it possibly be that I feel them so clearly when they come to me, but I completely White-out if I go to them?"

"When angels of Highness come down to you, what you feel is their reflection into the creation, not their true essence of Highness," Teyani corrected.

"But if Szar and I went so high, how come we didn't feel anything when we came back? Why wasn't the chapel full of the Light of Highness?"

Gervin smiled in a way that showed he was enjoying the conversation very much. "Right now, where are you, Alcibyadi? You are in Highness. You are as much in Highness as you were during your ritual. Why isn't *this* chapel full of the Light of Highness?"

"No, that's cheating!" Alcibyadi protested. "What is in Highness now is my true essence of Highness – not me, as in my ordinary earthly self."

"Do you mean to say there is something of your ordinary self which is not a reflection of your eternal, absolute Self?"

"No, of course not."

"Well, that explains it!" Gervin snapped his fingers and spoke fast, "If none of your ordinary self is not already in Highness, and the same for Szar, then nothing went anywhere when he and you went there, which is why of course nothing has happened here."

"Mm..." Alcibyadi was thinking deeply.

"All this makes perfect sense. One can't go somewhere when one is already there," Gervin went on. "Especially if that somewhere is everywhere, and nowhere at the same time. (Everything is at the same time in Highness, since there is no time.)"

"So, nothing happened here, and nothing happened there, is that it?" Alcibyadi was preparing her counter-attack.

"'Tis absolutely correct, my child," Gervin pretended to fall into the trap.

"And the same is true at every instant. Right?"

"Right and righteous!"

"But then the same is also true for everyone, and so we must conclude that absolutely nothing ever happens in our world!" Alcibyadi declared triumphantly. She thought Gervin was caught.

"Nothing!" the Master of Thunder wholeheartedly agreed with her, to her bewilderment. "Whatever happens, nothing happens. Absolutely, absolutely, absolutely nothing! Which, by the way, leads us to the obvious question, 'but what are we doing here?'"

"Yes, what are we doing here?" Teyani echoed with infinite nostalgia.

"But nothing!" Raising her hands, Alcibyadi entered the logic of Highness. "How could we, anyhow, since nothing ever happens, here?"

"Right, my beautiful angel. And this is precisely how you are going to heal Szar's hand!" Gervin announced in his Thunder voice.

"How?" Alcibyadi made herself clear fountain.

"It hasn't happened. His hand was never polluted by a dark force, because dark forces don't exist."

"Don't they?"

"Seen from Highness, no, they don't," Gervin was categorical.

"And seen from elsewhere?"

"Voof! Of course they do! And they are formidable opponents, infinitely more advanced than human beings. That is why you need Highness to heal Szar's hand. Highness is the one thing you have that Ahriman doesn't have."

"I see!" Through the knowingness of the fountain, Alcibyadi caught a glimpse of what she was supposed to do.

"Now, Alcibyadi, one last thing," Gervin went on. "Since there is no time in Highness, next time you take Szar there, could you please make sure you don't keep him ten hours?"

"But how will I remember that when I am there?" Alcibyadi chuckled.

"You will! Even though of course when you come back, you probably won't remember that you remembered it."

17.11 Field spying

Around eleven o'clock that evening, Gervin spoke to Mouridji through darkness visible. He told her that some urgent work had been keeping him busy in the chapel of the Field Wizards all day and that he was very hungry. But the food in that chapel was terrible and he had no time to go back to his apartment. It was late, there did not seem to be anyone left in the central kitchen. Would she know someone who could cook a proper meal for him?

"But... but... please let me do this for you, Master Gervin!" the old prophetess immediately offered. "It will be my privilege!"

"How very lawfully kind of you, my good Mouridji!"

One hour later, Mouridji of the Purple Robe arrived at the chapel of the Field Wizards carrying a huge ritual tray covered with a thin cloth.

Namron spat his black root, "What are *you* doing here?" He jumped down from the roof and stood in the doorway of the chapel, which had to be kept open because the lawful masons kept coming in and out.

"Move away, my boy! I am in the service of the Brown Robe. I *must* get in," the prophetess declared in a perfectly calm voice.

"I'd like to see that!" Namron retorted.

"Call your superiors!" she shrugged her shoulders.

Namron did not have to do that. Gervin, who had sensed Mouridji's presence, was coming up from the basement. "Praise the Lord Melchisedek, Mouridji!" he saluted her from a distance.

"All glory to the Lord Melchisedek, Master Gervin," she replied, lawfully smiling at Namron.

"Let's move away from here," Gervin said. "I've been in this chapel since morning. I need some lawful fresh air." And he took her to sit on a bench in the alley, in front of the door of the Wise Witches' chapel.

"You have prepared a feast!" Gervin exclaimed when she uncovered the tray. There were two loaves of cereals, boiled vegetables, stewed pears, a strange kind of puree he had never seen before (in the silvery darkness of the night, he couldn't tell the colour), and three other dishes which he could not identify.

As she was filling a silver plate for him with a little of each and every dish, Gervin carefully scanned her energy. She was carrying the stone in the right pocket of her purple gown. It took him a few seconds before he could locate the cord. The thin thread of energy attached to the back of her head was so remarkably well camouflaged that he would probably not have noticed it, had he not been searching for it. Gervin smiled, his teacher's heart warmed up to see that Szar had been able to detect such a subtle device from a distance.

But what the Underworld was going on with Mouridji?

"It's so good of you to take the time to cook a meal for me," he said.

"I have plenty of free time now that my official function has come to an end," Mouridji explained.

"Your official function?"

"Yes. Until yesterday, as you know, I was The Official Spokesperson Of Lady Hermina The Immaculate Through The Intermediary Of Szar Of The Brown Robe Acting As Lawful Immaculate Assistant."

"I see." Gervin was sensing a Nephilim flavour behind the cord. Like Szar, he carefully avoided tuning into the device directly, so as not to reveal his identity to whoever was at the other end.

"It required a lot of liaising with Szar," Mouridji went on, "and a few articulate friends to pass on the information to the people of the temple.

"Sweet Lord Melchisedek!" Gervin exclaimed, exhaling loudly. "This is *very* hot!"

"It's called Shemyaza's puree. Do you like it?"

"Shemyaza... as in Shemyaza the Watcher?" Gervin was slightly disconcerted.

"Yes."

"So you know about Nephilim cuisine?"

"Oh, not really." Mouridji wouldn't say more. She had given her sacred word to Szar she would *never* reveal the recipe to anyone.

Gervin had no difficulty picking up she was hiding something.

"But what's going on here?" Mouridji asked, pointing at a long procession of Wise Witches dressed in their long black gowns. Their lawful assistants were carrying large trunks and various pieces of furniture. "Is this one of their nightly rituals?"

"No, they're moving out of Maniya. To the mid-eastern enclave."

"Really? But how come I didn't know?" Mouridji was astounded.

"It was decided this morning." While he was eating his dinner, Gervin explained how the Holy Cowsheds were about to be refurbished.

Meanwhile, he prepared his plan. He suspected that by mentioning the stone he would destroy his chances of finding out where the cord came from. So he took the risk and behaved as if nothing unusual had happened. And when he finished eating, he asked Mouridji if he could keep some of the food for his breakfast, as he had to keep working all night.

"No, no! I will bring your breakfast tomorrow morning," she offered, as he had expected.

After thanking her wholeheartedly he returned to the chapel, leaving her to her observation of all the things that were happening in the alley.

The priests of Baltham were also on the move. Mouridji soon learned that Melchard had given them forty-eight hours to free their chapel if they wanted their share of the Holy Sheds – take it or leave it! And teams of lawful masons who had been instructed to take shifts throughout the night kept walking in and out of the buildings.

Five hours later, when Mouridji came back to bring Gervin's early breakfast, she first looked for Namron. Sadly, he wasn't there. So she just walked up the three steps that led to the doorway of the chapel.

"Praise the Lord Melchisedek, wise woman in the Law! Come in! Watch the bottles on the floor!" Gervin welcomed her. "Let me introduce you to three of my assistants: Khej, Ashok and Gallagher."

The three young men stopped their work to come and greet Mouridji, who was making great efforts not to sneeze. The smells of the chapel, combined with the dust of the construction work, had instantly turned her nostrils into a burning hell.

"Some of the best Field Wizards of the Centre North," Gervin praised his men.

"Yes, I know these boys! They are..." Mouridji was interrupted by a volley of volcanic sneezing.

"Let us show you this chapel," Gervin took her for a quick tour of the room, and the three men followed. They showed her many wonderful bottles filled with foul-smelling liquids and dregs, and remained very calm when she sneezed into one of the bottles. They laughed when she told them she had known Ferman, their boss, since he was a little boy, and did they know that once when he was only eleven, Ferman had sabotaged the guidance field of the female wing so that all the priestesses ended up in the same courtyard, after which his father was so unlawfully upset that he crashed the whole guidance system when trying to fix it, scattering priestesses throughout the temple, causing Pari-Ma of the Blue priestesses to wander for an entire night until she was finally located in the catacombs.

After a few more anecdotes, Mouridji understood that the time had come to lawfully take leave.

"Let's go!" Gervin ordered as soon as she had left the chapel, and the three Field Wizards raced after him down to the basement, holding in their Points the field-imprint they had made of Mouridji's cord. Rushing to the crypt of the temple of light, where Ferman was waiting for them, they established a linkage with the Fields of Peace. And together with Ran Gereset, Orest and Barkhan Seer, they started scanning the field imprint.

17.12 Mouridji, the case

When Szar returned to Eisraim, he went straight to the chapel of the Field Wizards. He was accompanied by Woolly, who had made great efforts to follow Szar's pace because he wanted to be in whatever it was that was about to happen, and also because he knew that it wouldn't be long before the five White Eagles had to leave for the land of Aegypton.

His days with Maryani were numbered. Every minute counted.

Gervin took them down to the crypt of the temple of light. "We received some good news," he told Szar as they were walking down the winding stairway. "Lord Proston has responded to your message in a way that indicates he could possibly accept our invitation." For Woolly, he explained, "Lord Proston is a high-ranking member of the king's administration. A top-level superintendent of the fields. Szar met him once, in the county of Sheringa. He was representing the king of Atlantis at the ceremony where Szar declined to become a public servant. How long ago was that?"

"Eight and half years," Szar answered.

"As part of his plan, Szar suggested we invite Lord Proston to join our team in Eisraim," Gervin continued. "Had such an offer been made to Proston a few years ago, it would have been unthinkable for him to accept. But now, things must have changed."

"Is he coming?" Woolly had no difficulty seeing the phoenix in the pot. A man like Proston knew all the secrets of the global warp of fields.

"He hasn't said yes. But he hasn't said no either."

As they were about to close the door of the small empty crypt, Maryani turned up. "Do you mind if I come in?" Without greeting, she went to sit by Woolly's side, inundating him with her Naga-golden glory.

"I haven't got the stone," Gervin declared to open the meeting. "I was concerned that by getting it back I would draw suspicions from those who plugged the cord into Mouridji's head. And I was right. With the help of our friends in the Fields of Peace, we have sourced the cord. It comes from the Nephilim necromancers of the Eastern Peninsula. Probably baphomets."

"Baphomets?" Woolly asked.

"Superiorly intelligent creatures with the body of a goat. And highly psychic too. The giants have bred them through the power of their fields. The strange thing is, one of these baphomets made contact with me only a few days ago, offering an alliance with Bexton, their grand commander."

"Us, making an alliance with the Nephilim giants?" Maryani was amused.

"There seem to be competing factions over there," Gervin replied. "Anyhow, the baphomet didn't contact me again."

"Could it have been a trick to infiltrate our fields?" Woolly suggested.

"Possible."

"All this is in favour of thinking the fifteen Nephilim soldiers roaming around the temple are giants!" Woolly went on.

"Ashok and Gallagher have made another discovery," Gervin added. "A second cord, plugged into Perseps' stone. It also led us to the baphomets of the Eastern Peninsula."

"So that's what they all want, is that it?" Maryani understood. "The key to the protection shield of Jex Belaran? But why don't we just get rid of it! We don't really *need* to communicate with Perseps, do we? Let's send it back to Jex Belaran with three complimentary barrels of honey-pickled cucumbers and a note saying, 'If you want to talk to us, come and visit any time!'"

"The problem is, this stone could prove extraordinarily precious to us," Gervin revealed. "Szar has planned to use it as a weapon against the giants."

"How?" Woolly and Maryani asked in one electrified voice.

"The protection shield of Jex Belaran is one of the most sophisticated fields of Watcher-ness ever woven," Szar explained. "I intend to use the stone to infiltrate the sky of the Watchers and plug a number of he-stones into it. Twenty-four hours before the Archive transfer, a high-powered interference will be generated from the Flying Dragons, and all Nephilim fields in the kingdom will go blank."

"Blasting Underworld! Can we really do that?" Maryani was thrilled.

"Of course we can," Woolly realised. "You've already produced the he-stones!"

"And there is more," Szar went on. "Lehrmon thinks that by analysing the Point-patterns behind the stone we should be able to create a shield similar to the one of Jex Belaran, which the giants have never been able to break."

"So Perseps' stone *is* worth dying for!" Maryani exclaimed thoughtfully.

"Which brings us to our main topic," Gervin grinned, turning to Szar. "There are fifteen Nephilim warriors in the county, plus another four on their way from the border with Lasseera. On top of that we have the baphomet necromancers at the other end of Mouridji's cord. What do you suggest, Commander?"

"Is there any reason why I shouldn't get the stone back?" Szar asked.

"Now that we have spotted the baphomets, I don't see why not. Except that we have no idea how Mouridji will react," Gervin pulled his beard.

"What's your assessment? Was she manipulated from a distance to steal the stone, or did she operate from her own free will?"

"Son, I know that after Fridrick we should doubt everyone. Still, I simply *cannot* imagine Mouridji as a spy working for the Nephilim giants," the Thunderbolt Bearer was categorical.

"Mouridji, a secret agent?" Maryani burst out laughing. "That would blast the breasts off the goddess!"

"Isn't she the perfect example of a secretive person?" Woolly argued.

"Friends, Point-warfare is dirty business," Szar reminded them.

But as they were debating, Gervin received a Point-call from Namron.

"The prophetess must have heard us speak," Gervin announced. "She's at the door of the chapel. Asking for Szar."

"Do you wish to direct this operation?" Szar asked Gervin.

"I leave it to you, Commander!"

"Follow me!" Szar told his friends. And as they were walking up the stairway, he Point-called Ferman, "Everyone on high alert. I want you, Khej, Ashok and Gallagher in the crypt of the temple of light immediately. Establish a line with Barkhan Seer, search for unidentified fields. Stay Point-linked with me all the time, inform me of all your findings. All Field Wizards in the chapel are to interrupt their tasks and seal their Points."

On the ground floor, Namron was having a difficult time trying to keep Mouridji out.

"I sense the stone in her pocket!" Szar Point-warned Gervin. "There could be a trap here!"

"Ah, here he is!" the prophetess exclaimed when she saw Szar. "Praise the Lord Melchisedek, my little Szar! How was your journey to Alverard? I heard there was an unlawfully ugly mess going on over there. Did you fix it?"

"It's better now. What can I do for you, Mouridji?" His Point sealed, Szar was prepared to match a full-force venom-attack from the giants.

Meanwhile, Gervin relaxed his lower jaw and stretched his neck, readying himself to project the Word of Thunder. Woolly had grabbed a bag of his latest soft-stone weapons. Throughout the chapel the Field Wizards connected their Points to the Fields of Peace.

"Oh, nothing," Mouridji smiled. "I just heard that you were back in the temple, so I thought I would bring this back to you," she took the stone out of her pocket and handed it to Szar. "The other morning when you came back from your journey with Elyani, it dropped out of your pocket. Lucky I found it! Someone could easily have walked on it by mistake."

Flabbergasted, Szar contemplated the stone, wondering what to do next.

At the back of the room, Woolly burst out laughing. "This story is getting betterer and betterer!"

"Don't you want your stone?" Mouridji was surprised.

"Szar!" Khej Point-called, "Both cords have just disappeared! Volatilised."

Mouridji Point-overheard him. "What cords?" she asked.

"Mouridji, we need to have a long conversation with you," Szar told her. "I must ask you to come inside with me."

"Oh, really?" she exclaimed, visibly delighted.

"Yes. Follow me. And watch the bottles on the floor!"

When she saw that Ferman, Khej, Ashok and Gallagher were waiting for her in the crypt, and that Woolly, Gervin and Maryani were also coming in, Mouridji couldn't believe her luck. "Do you mean you *all* want to talk to me?"

They brought in a mattress and made her lie down, with Maryani sitting by her side and holding her hand to reassure her.

But Mouridji was not the least bit anxious. "Is my body needed for the temple?" she asked, her tone of voice showing she was utterly prepared to sacrifice herself.

"You are on a mission, Mouridji," Gervin told her.

"I am ready, Gervin!" she declared.

The stone was placed in a box with space-insulating lining, and for more than two hours the team used their rich arsenal of field-scanning tools and energy devices in search of cords and spying fields. Concomitantly, Gervin, Ran Gereset and Orest were scanning Mouridji's mind from the Fields of Peace.

Finally, they all came to the same conclusions. Mouridji was no longer connected to the giants. And she was not a spy.

Gervin took Szar aside into another crypt and after discussing the case for a few minutes, they agreed that the best was to tell Mouridji everything, keep scanning her every fifteen minutes, and train her to detect spying fields by herself.

"I will speak to her," Gervin offered. "You need to finalise our defence. I have a bad feeling about these four Nephilim – the second group."

Szar looked down to his left hand. "Judging by where they were yesterday, they should be here soon."

"Feeling ready?"

"Quite ready!" Szar slowly clenched and unclenched his fist. "This time the mistakes that were made when the Black Hunters raided the chapel will not be repeated. But if they are giants, then our casualties could be high."

17.13 Eastern Peninsula, the citadel of the Nephilim giants

Pralaya established a priority communication with Bobros and announced triumphantly, "Your Excellency, we found the headquarters of the Brown Robe! We located their power source."

"At last! At last!" Bobros didn't hide his satisfaction. For more than a year the necromancers of the guild had unsuccessfully tried to discover the mysterious stronghold. "Where?"

"In the Fields of Peace, Your Excellency. We saw their temple. A magnificent edifice of light. And we also found out that a great number of Brown Robes have descended from the spheres of Highness and gathered in the Fields of Peace. We counted at least three hundred of them in the temple. They *must* be preparing something."

"And how did you locate them?"

"Through the witch. While she was being probed by the Brown Robes."

"Meaning they have located you too," Bobros said, matter of fact.

"We decided to take that risk," Pralaya acknowledged. "Anyhow, certain signs indicated they had already detected our cords. Their mastery of the fields is considerable."

"And now?"

"We have had to disconnect everything, even the cord to the stone."

"Is it your recommendation that the commando attack should go ahead?"

"No, Your Excellency. Let us delay the attack. We now have a much better plan. Having located their power source, we should be able to create a disconnection that will leave Eisraim completely vulnerable. Without the Fields of Peace, they are nothing! Even a small commando will wipe them out in a matter of minutes."

"Congratulations, Pralaya!" Bobros rejoiced. "Send my compliments to your baphomets. And my regards to Melissa the Wise."

"Alas, Your Excellency, Melissa the Wise committed suicide yesterday. She jumped off the cliffs outside her house."

"I see." From Pralaya's tone, Bobros immediately understood the baphomet had organised the 'suicide'. "My sincere condolences, Pralaya. She was your close friend, wasn't she?"

"A wonderful woman. I loved her dearly," the baphomet said. And it was the truth.

17.14 The palace of the King of Atlantis

"The Most Excellent Lord Proston, Grand Superintendent of the Warp of Fields for the Counties of the East, in the Service of His Supreme Majesty the King of Atlantis!" a Crimson guard announced.

"Let him in!" Lord Javons answered through darkness visible.

The massive golden gates of the hall swung open slowly, and Lord Proston entered. In the dignified manner of his high caste, the tall man in the crimson robe walked slowly. In his right hand he held the orichalc sceptre of the grand superintendents of the warp.

Proston was in such a bad mood that he didn't even look up to admire the field on the ceiling, as he normally did each time he arrived in Lord Javons' reception lounge – one of the most magnificent halls of the palace, with its sixty-lawful-feet-high ceiling made of golden plass that shone like the Sun in the worlds of the triangle.

When he reached the other end of the empty two-hundred-lawful-feet-long hall, he held the sceptre against his heart and saluted his superior, "Praise the Lord Melchisedek, Most Illustrious Lord Javons Orameno, Grand Superintendent of the Warp of Fields, in the Service of His Supreme Majesty the King of Atlantis!"

"All glory to the Lord Melchisedek, Most Excellent Lord Proston, Grand Superintendent of the Warp of Fields for the Counties of the East, in the Service of His Supreme Majesty the King of Atlantis!" the old man lawfully responded. He was sitting on a throne in the centre of a low stage, three steps above floor level. His aura shone with the bright golden light that came from the throne's field. "What tidings do you bring?"

"Not good, Most Illustrious Lord," Proston stood only ten lawful feet away, looking straight into Javons' eyes. "The warp has been restored in Elfen, Piremans, Alverard, Romeran and Lowerlinks. But on the Western Shores, the situation is catastrophic. Two entire temples have melted to the ground. A hurricane has destroyed half of Aforenta. In Orelbank, a large fire has broken out, which the field-firemen have been powerless to contain. And in Asmaban, the filth coming out of the main temple was so horrendous that an angry mob set fire to the chapels of the windmills of the Law. Now the whole town is in flames. But in Jasmarezan, the rains haven't stopped pouring down for two weeks, causing a flood that has broken all the bridges over the Liniah river. And from Baranbin to Karlinga, great pestilences are raging. In a number of villages, the peasants have become insane and slaughtered each other. Panic is sweeping through the land."

"Shall we send the seventh army to rescue them?"

"No! For the Lord Melchisedek's sake, keep the army away! In Baranbin, an entire battalion of the prince of the county of the Western Shores was struck with the insanity plague. They have ransacked their own town."

"And what about the Eastern Peninsula?" Javons inquired.

"Presently the warp is more solid there than anywhere else in the kingdom. But the young necromancer who murdered Lord Vrolon has become the new grand commander of the citadel."

"Does that mean the giants are likely to go on the rampage?"

"This is to be feared, Most Illustrious Lord."

"And what else?"

"Nothing for the moment. But, Most Illustrious Lord, has His Supreme Majesty the King made a decision as to the request I presented to him?"

"Which request?" Lord Javons pretended he didn't remember.

"The urgent request that three hundred and forty-six rituals, as listed by my Field Wizards, be declared unlawful, and that troops be sent to all windmills of the Law to enforce the decree," Proston clearly articulated his words.

"Ah, yes. Yes..." Javons looked to the left to avoid Proston's angry gaze. "His Supreme Majesty has heard your request. He said he would consider it and answer you in the lawful near future."

Proston was furious, "Most Illustrious, I have reached the limits of my patience. Either the King sees me today, or I quit."

"Proston!" the old man exclaimed in a paternalistic voice. He stood up, leaving his throne, which immediately caused the golden light to disappear from his aura. He walked down the three steps of the kingly stage. "I know that at the moment you have to face trying circumstances, and I understand your frustration. But it is not the time to..."

"You have heard what I said!" Proston unlawfully interrupted his superior, brandishing the orichalc emblem of his authority. "Either my recommendations are implemented immediately, or you can have this sceptre back!"

"Proston, my friend in the Law, you wouldn't want to end our twelve years of fruitful collaboration in this unlawful way!"

"As far as I am concerned, these were twelve lawfully wasted years! What have we achieved, exactly? Can you tell me?"

The skilled Javons changed tactic. To help Proston vent his anger, he decided to yell too. Gradually raising his voice, "And what would these recommendations of yours achieve, exactly, can *you* tell me? Nearly half the counties are being decimated by plagues. The giants are about to start a war. And you want us to create large-scale civil unrest by making every single priest in every single temple furious with us?"

"Javons, it is the end. This time, the warp is *really* collapsing. Unless..."

"And what do you want us to do about it?" Javons kept shouting. "You know very well that even if your recommendations were followed, the situation would keep deteriorating."

Through darkness visible, a Crimson guard announced, "The Most Excellent Lord Viniret, Grand Superintendent of the Warp of Fields for the Counties of the South-East, in the Service of His Supreme Majesty the King of Atlantis!"

"Let him in!" Javons shouted through darkness visible.

"What-do-you-want-us-to-do-about-it has become one of the new mantras of the Law," Proston was disgusted. "It seems to be on everyone's lips these days."

"I know! And I don't like it myself! But it's the way things are!" Lord Javons' face was purple-red from yelling so loudly. His voice suddenly quiet, he added, "Can we get back to work, now?"

Proston remained inflexible, "Will you let me speak to the King?"

"No!' Javons shouted again. "Your recommendations are unlawfully unthinkable! The Grand Council of the Law has thoroughly rejected them, and so have the Twelve Supreme Priests of Melchisedek."

"Farewell, Javons," Proston turned on his heel and walked away.

"Proston, come back im-*me*-diately!"

Proston did not answer. A hundred lawful feet from where Javons was standing, he passed Lord Viniret, his inferior by one notch.

"Praise the Lord Melchisedek, Most Venerable..."

"Viniret, you are being promoted," Proston interrupted him, thrusting the orichalc sceptre into his hand. "You are now in charge of the whole of the eastern states!"

"No, you, are, *not*!" Javons screamed from the other end of the room.

17.15 The fortress of the Field Wizards

When Alcibyadi and Teyani next visited the chapel of the Field Wizards they found that considerable changes had taken place. The door of the chapel had been walled up, and so had all the windows. And the walls looked different. The plass was thicker and more compact. It had been crystallised into a rock-hard material, more solid than the temple's outer walls.

They walked to the left, to what used to be the chapel of the Wise Witches of the Law. There the portal had also been walled up and all windows had disappeared. They kept walking and turned right, hoping to get in through the former chapel of the Servants of the Nectar God, a much larger building. But there too they found that all doors had been sealed, and all walls had been reinforced into thick, stone-like plass. They had to walk around the whole block, to the portal of the chapel of Baltham.

They knocked at the massive doors and were answered by Namron. He didn't open, he asked them to wait so he could register their Point-signatures in the security field.

"But aren't we already registered?" Alcibyadi was puzzled.

"No. This is a new security field, limited to the chapel of the Field Wizards."

Minutes passed. The White Eagles were surprised. With the general security field of the temple, a new visitor could be registered in a matter of seconds. "Must be an unlawfully special field!" Teyani frowned.

"You bet in the Law!" Namron told them. "Ferman and Shyama say it's the most sophisticated field they've ever woven. They've Point-designed it with Woolly and Szar. It's already killed four black cats that the Wise Witches had forgotten to take with them."

"Killed?" Alcibyadi couldn't believe her ears.

"Yep. It's that kind of field. If you aren't lawfully registered, it leaves you flat dead, venomised to the eyeballs."

The door finally opened.

"Come in!" Namron warmly invited the priestesses.

"Hum... Does my baby need to be registered?" Alcibyadi hesitated.

"I don't think so," Namron assumed, confident.

"But that's not good enough, Namron!" Teyani was firm.

"Come in, friends, there is nothing to worry about!" Szar came to greet them. "Welcome to my new domain!"

The White Eagles set foot in the hall.

"Heaven on Eisraim!" Alcibyadi commented when she saw the glorious white light dispensed by the living walls, floor and ceiling.

"And where are all the bottles?" Teyani inquired.

"Everything has been transferred underground. Come and see," Szar walked through the large empty hall with them.

"But if everything is in the basements, what are you going to do with all these rooms?" Teyani was curious.

"We've melted down a few areas where the plass was flammable, so now we're totally fire proof. All the rest is to serve as apartments for the Field Wizards and security personnel."

"Has Namron moved in here?"

"Into the luxurious apartment of the high priest of the Mysteries of the Nectar. And in the last days, all his men who are not married have moved in too. I took the decision after the Nephilim commandos were spotted. "

"Have you detected them again?"

"No. In the last week we have searched the entire space spectrum without any success. They have disappeared."

As they reached the stairway to the basements they met Mouridji, who was on her way out. "Praise the Lord Melchisedek, ladies of the White Eagle! Oh my gods, isn't she beautiful!" she placed her hands close to Alcibyadi's belly. "When are you expecting baby Lehrmon? In two weeks, is that right? And I hear Teyani is going to be the midwife, hopefully with Lehrmon by her side? I can't wait to see the baby. And it's such a good name you have given him. I'm sure it will bring him luck in the land of Aegypton..."

The lawful chatting ended, they walked down the plass staircase. Alcibyadi whispered, "How the Underworld did Mouridji get here?"

"Oh, it's a long story," Szar preferred to change the topic. "So these are our new headquarters. We'll be monitoring every phase of the Archive transfer from here – except for the very last one of course, which is to take place in the Plateau of Sorana. I've kept the cellars we had before and linked them to those of Baltham, the Wise Witches, and the Nectar God." They arrived in a huge empty vault. "These are the new crypts of the Field Wizards. The poor men were badly in need of space."

"Voof! The vaulted ceilings are magnificent!" Teyani exclaimed.

Szar received a call through darkness visible. "Commander! Commander! It's working like a lawful charm! We've completely stuffed their asses and they haven't noticed a damn thing!"

"Very good, Gallagher! Keep on. I want them out of action by tonight!" Szar voice-channelled back.

"Will be done, Commander! The enemy is not offering any resistance."

For his visitors, Szar explained, "Three of the chapels of the windmills of the Law are being disconnected. Rather than starting a war against the windmills' priests to get them to modify their practices, I have chosen to secretly block some of their rituals from a distance with my fields."

"Are you really doing that?" Teyani chuckled.

"Naughty!" Alcibyadi slapped his shoulder.

"Commander!" someone else voice-channelled. "That damn bitch of a Nephilim soft stone is starting to talk to us. Want to come and third-eye it?"

"I'll be with you in fifteen minutes," Szar answered.

"But why do they have to be so rude all the time?" Teyani complained.

"Well, well... to tell you the truth, it all started with Woolly," the commander explained. "For years everyone here was outraged by his abusive language. Then he had his shift and, curiously, it created some kind of swearing vacuum in the chapel. After that, everyone began swearing, bit by bit, as if to fill the emptiness."

Alcibyadi laughed, "And what does Woolly say about it?"

"Flat denial. He says he can't remember having ever used abusive language, it must have been in another life. Now let me show you my new bedroom."

"Your bedroom?" Teyani bit her lip. "You mean you have moved in here?"

Szar leaving Elyani's courtyard! That was hard to imagine.

"I had to, for security reasons," Szar said. "The Archive stones must be looked after. But let me show you this beauty," he took the women through a low doorway that led into a tiny dark cellar. "Like my new room?"

"It's... sober," Alcibyadi was appalled.

"Think so?" he smiled.

"I hope you go out of here from time to time," Teyani told him off.

He stifled a smile.

"Oh, gods!" Teyani's Whiteness flashed with wonder.

The four walls had vanished and the miserable cell had been replaced by a huge hall, bathing in the silvery light of a breathtaking field of stars that shone through the high domed ceiling. A fresh breeze softly swept through the hall. A music field played volleys of eerie low-pitched Flying Dragon harmonies. Light and sounds married so well that the breeze seemed to be singing the mysteries of remoteness.

"This is unreal!" Alcibyadi closed and reopened her eyes, wondering whether what she was seeing was physical or Point-constructed.

"Is it an illusion?" Teyani took Szar's arm.

"What isn't?" Szar sighed philosophically, in the fashion of his teacher.

"No, seriously, we want to know!" Alcibyadi insisted.

"Well, come with me then!" Arm in arm they walked through the enormous hall. Szar pointed to a long colonnade of vaulted archways on the right, "These lead to the temple's catacombs. One of the reasons I needed Baltham's cellars so much is that from here, I can get anywhere in the temple in less than five minutes."

Alcibyadi had difficulty believing her senses. "So it *is* real? It is not a Point-dream?"

"That's what I still can't figure out about this kingdom," Szar teased her. "Recognise that crypt?" he pointed to a small archway at the far end of the hall.

"The crypt of the Archive stones," Teyani recognised from a distance. "So you have direct access to them. How convenient!"

"I have woven a few fields in it, to make it more interesting. If an enemy ever finds his way to that crypt, let me tell you, he will have to be damn Point-smart to find his way out."

"That can't possibly be real!" Alcibyadi turned toward an archway that led to another hall with a small pool and an indoor garden.

"Would you like to bet?" he smiled at her mischievously.

"Betting is against the Law of the Eagles." Turning back, "But... what has happened to the crypt of the Archive stones?"

The opening that led to the small crypt had disappeared.

"Yes, what has happened to the Archive stones?" Szar pretended to be utterly confused, and the music field accompanied him with a query of bizarre Flying Dragon sounds. "Wasn't it there?" he pointed to another archway, lit with silvery light.

"But that one wasn't here a minute ago!" Alcibyadi protested.

"Wasn't it?" Szar asked Teyani. "And look! What about the entrance to the catacombs? Disappeared! How are we going to get out of here?"

Teyani answered with a tipsy laugh, contemplating clouds of astral light drifting amidst the fields of stars on the huge domed ceiling. "Jump into the fields of stars. It's the only way!"

"So that's the heart of your defence system!" Alcibyadi got it. "If someone ever gets in, it will take them an aeon to find their way out. That's if the field hasn't left them flat dead and venomised to the eyeballs when they came in, of course."

"And a few other secrets," Szar whetted her curiosity. "Fields have been woven in every single room of our fortress. Hundreds of fields."

"Where did you get the idea for this hall?" Teyani asked in a suspicious tone.

"In the crypt of Verzazyel the Watcher, in the county of the Red Lands," Szar confessed. "I never had the opportunity to see it at its best, but from what I understood, this is close to how it looked."

"Verzazyel the Watcher?" the White Eagles laughed in outrage.

"This place makes me feel like dancing!" Alcibyadi held her enormous belly.

"Dancing under the stars!" Teyani waved her arms. She couldn't take her eyes off the celestial landscape drifting across the dome. "By the way, you know why we have come, don't you?"

"We're here to abduct you," Alcibyadi declared straightforwardly. "We're taking you to our chapel for another ritual to Highness."

"But I don't have the time! I have a thousand things to do."

"It won't take time. There is no time in Highness," Teyani assured him.

"And your teacher said you should come with us," Alcibyadi directed an authoritative index finger towards his nose. "And even though you live in a palace, you *must* go out from time to time! It's been more than a week since you last saw the light of day."

"I can't come now. Ferman is waiting for me."

"That's all right. You can go and see Ferman. We are giving you one hour," Alcibyadi was generous.

"We'll wait for you here," Teyani said, her gaze in the stars, her long straight hair shining with the silvery light that bathed the hall. "Come and take us when you are ready."

17.16 Paradoxes in Highness, second round

Alcibyadi checked the utensils and the offerings on the altar. The fruit, the flowers, the grains of rice and the cup of water were in place. She looked over her shoulder. Szar was sitting in the centre of the circle. Teyani was leaning against the door of the chapel, watching the scene from the Edge of Highness.

After sending a loving thought to the baby, Alcibyadi initiated the Voice-projection – a gentle projection, because pregnant women must be cautious when using the Voice, and also because power is not what leads to Highness.

"Let she who is, who was, and who will be,
Curve back onto her source,

And beyond the infinity of her Cosmic Night,
Cognize that which none can comprehend.
Still Flame, Breath of Highness,
That which is will always be.
That which is not has never been..."
Teyani screamed, "Stop! Stop!"
Holding her belly with her hands, Alcibyadi turned round.
Her mother was rushing towards Szar, who had just collapsed on the floor.
"Gervin! Gervin!" Teyani Point-called. "Come immediately! An accident has happened."
"What have I done?" Alcibyadi remained calm.
"I'll tell you later. Oh, no! No! We're losing him! Look! His body of life force is about to fall apart!"
Alcibyadi stepped towards Szar. His energy was shimmering with strange whitish glows.
Teyani judged that only the Voice could save him. "Get out of the chapel, quick!" she ordered. "The baby couldn't take what I am about to project!"
As Alcibyadi was running out, she saw her mother raising both hands, calling onto the Eagle.
In the corridor outside the chapel she received a Point-warning from Teyani, "Further away! Don't stay around the chapel, the Word is too strong for the baby."
Alcibyadi hurried to a nearby courtyard where she sat on the grass and started invoking the angels of Highness. But she questioned, "Do I really know what I am doing?" Feeling unconfident, she did not even dare continue her prayers.
It was a grey day. Since the catastrophe that had ravaged Alverard, the mists had thickened. Nature seemed to be sulking. Unwholesome whisks of black astral fumes were seen wafting in the space. The grass was becoming greener by the day. The delicious little blossoms that gave it its normal purple colour were fast disappearing, to the despair of the field-gardeners. It made Alcibyadi wonder if her child would ever play on a normal lawn. "Take your time, my love. There is no hurry to be born," she told him. Deep inside herself she knew that if it hadn't been for baby Lehrmon, the Eagle would have long since given the signal for the departure to the land of Aegypton.
"I love you, Lehrmon! I love you!" she pledged. And she let her mind drift, hoping that peripheral consciousness would help her recollect her journey to Highness.
Half an hour later, Gervin called her through darkness visible, "The energy has gone down to a more reasonable level now. You can come back to the chapel if you want."
"What about Szar?" she asked.

"He is out of danger now."

On her return, she found the doors of the chapel open. There was so much light in the room that at first she couldn't see anyone. The living walls were buzzing wildly, as if matter had taken up singing. It made Alcibyadi's life force vibrate so fast that she hesitated, fearing for her child.

"Lawfully safe," Gervin reassured her. "Actually, for a baby like Lehrmon, son of Lehrmon, it will be excellent."

Alcibyadi walked into the White furnace, following the voice.

In the middle of the circle she found Teyani standing still like a statue, her eyes closed, her aura ablaze with dazzling sparks of Whiteness.

Gervin was standing by her side. "Better not to touch her."

Woolly was sitting at their feet. "Praised be the Lord Melchisedek, Lady Alcibyadi of Highness!" he summarised the situation in his exquisitely polite voice.

Szar was lying on the floor, his head on Woolly's lap. When he opened his eyes to look at her, Alcibyadi's consciousness was immediately pulled high up. She heard the strange music of the Flying Dragons.

Periphery of time. Liquid light. Elixir of infinity.

She knelt down by his side. "Can I take his hand?"

"Yes, yes," Gervin answered. "I have just used the Voice to cool his energy down."

"Teyani's Word of Thunder saved him, but it also nearly cooked him!" Woolly caressed Szar's dark-blond curly locks.

"What... what happened?"

Gervin pulled his beard, "Did you White-out again?"

"Completely. I'm so ashamed. I don't know what I'm doing. I should never have attempted that ritual."

"No! No! No! No! No!" Gervin was adamant, "You did remarkably well. You took some risks, but considering what could have happened if you had succeeded, the risks were justified."

"But his hand is still black!" With the tips of her fingers, she lightly touched the ominous dent in Szar's aura.

"You'll try again tomorrow!" Woolly said in his most comforting voice, forcing a chuckle out of her.

"But what exactly have I done?" she asked Gervin.

"You and Szar decided to attempt the deepest possible transformation. It was no mistake, but a choice made in perfect lucidity."

"What were we trying to transform?"

"Matter." Always ready for a mystagogic excursion, the teacher went on, "If the black substance of Ahriman is so difficult to clear, it's because it permeates physicality at a deep level where the human Spirit does not reach – hidden domains, which will not be tackled by human beings until the distant future. But you attempted to descend right now. You tried to ignite matter with Spirit."

"They tried to achieve the ultimate stone?" Woolly drooled.

"Nothing less!" Gervin snapped his fingers.

"That sounds very ambitious," Alcibyadi had difficulty understanding how she could have been so bold.

"A remarkably well-calculated move," Gervin insisted. "You chose the perfect time: Szar's Flying Dragon nature is more attuned to the Dragon of the Deep than ever before. It helped in creating a spark to unite that which is above and that which is below. And the fields are still alive and well, which greatly added to your chances of success. Once the warp is dead, all these transformations will become much more difficult. This is why Teyani and Barkhan Seer gave you their blessing."

Meeting Barkhan Seer in Highness... it sounded like a dream.

"So it was not a mistake?" Alcibyadi hesitated.

"No, not a mistake! If it wasn't for the Archive, we would try again as soon as Szar can walk."

"See? What did I tell you?" Woolly turned up his palms.

Stifling a smile, she gazed into Szar's eyes.

A glimpse of oneness beyond time.

With all my mind, with all my heart...

17.17 The sky of the gods knows the secret

The next day, when the extremely pregnant Alcibyadi went to visit Szar, she found him lying on a low couch in the middle of his huge Point-bedroom, resting in the silvery dimness of the moving fields of stars. She still couldn't figure out whether the hall had a high domed ceiling or whether she was being Point-tricked by Szar's fields.

"Praise the Lord Melchisedek, White Eagle!" he welcomed her. Like his master, he had come to appreciate the immense depth of this most simple mantra of the Law, which he never repeated mindlessly.

"You look lawfully better." Alcibyadi sat beside his bed. "But I'm surprised. I thought I would find you at your Dragon gate!"

"I go there every day for a quick Underworld descent."

"Do you go through the catacombs?" she was curious.

"Of course. They take me to a winding staircase, a few corridors away. But I made a discovery. One of the bowels passes right under the bedroom adjacent to Elyani's – the room we had turned into a kitchen. So I have sent a team of lawful masons to excavate. It should be finished by tomorrow."

"You mean they are digging a hole in the bedroom floor?"

"Linking it to the catacombs. It will allow me to get there in less than two minutes."

"You've become very industrious, lately."

"I want everything to be in place as soon as possible. In the coming weeks the situation in the temple could deteriorate unlawfully fast."

"Aren't I lucky! I probably won't see any of all these horrible things that have been prophesied," she smiled sadly. "As soon as baby Lehrmon pops out, I'm afraid it will be time to depart for Aegypton." To contain her tears she changed the topic, "I have a favour to ask. The other day, when I visited Gervin in the cellar close to the Archive stones, I sat on a special bucket of white slime. They called it 'Molten Sea'. Baby Lehrmon loved it so much that I have been dreaming about it every night. And I see buckets of white slime in my meditations."

"What a fascinating craving!"

"I don't want to drink it!" she protested. "But... could I perhaps go and sit on the precious bucket again? Just a few minutes."

"And what if we gave you a bottle of the dear substance?"

"Would you do that?" the baby made her open galaxy-sized eyes.

"Consider it lawfully done. But you must promise me you won't drink it!" he teased her. "Which reminds me, I have something else to give you," he placed two soft stones in her hand. "One for you, one for Teyani. From tomorrow on, the chapels of the Field Wizards will be completely Point-insulated from the rest of the temple – and from the rest of the world! Point-warfare requirements. No one can reach us through darkness visible, no one can reach us through the Point, unless they carry one of these key-stones. The key will be modified every few days, which means that each time you will need a new stone."

Wave of anxiety, "But then, how will I be able to talk to you after I leave the temple?"

"Ah, don't worry! Lehrmon has already prepared a line that will be relayed to you from the Fields of Peace. A beauty that operates independently of the warp."

She burst into tears.

"How do you manage to live without Elyani?" she asked. "You loved her as much as I love Lehrmon."

"You know," he took her hand, "since I have returned from the Flying Dragons and I have had to invent a life without Elyani, I have been submerged under the love of the Eagle."

"Do you think it comes from her?"

"No, straight from the Eagle. And it is magnificent. Immense! When I was with her, I always felt I couldn't love her enough, as if something in me was too narrow. Now... there is all this love which keeps pouring from my chest, and it seems big enough to love the entire creation. Sometimes it even makes me feel it doesn't matter if she is no longer here."

"I know, I know..." she recited the Law of the Eagle, "It is not for the love of the husband that you love the husband, it is for the love of the Eagle." She kept crying, "But I'm going to miss him *so much*. And you. And Teyani. And Gervin. And all the others, and every living wall in the temple."

"I know the feeling well. The little you aches so much, it's worse than death. But with the Eagle's help, the pain of the little you becomes a gateway. It leads you to a much larger you, one that spreads into the Eagle's immensity. There, everything is so vast. Infinitely One. The story takes on a different meaning."

They remained silent, opening to the gloriously soft warmth the Eagle was pouring onto them.

The music field resounded with strangely rhythmical high-pitched harmonies.

"I recognise this tune. What is it?" Alcibyadi loudly blew her nose in the long sleeve of her dress.

"It's from the Flying Dragons of the Great Ant."

"Makes my spine shiver," Alcibyadi kept blowing her nose. "Sharp, prickly sensations. Does it mean something?"

"It means the Great Ant is cleansing you. The Great Ant is a cosmic cleanser."

The Flying Dragon sounds vanished gradually. They listened to the silence which the White Eagle was shining onto them. For a precious moment there was fullness beyond words, as if the warmth of the Eagle had flared throughout the infinity of the fields of stars.

"I feel much better. Thank you," Alcibyadi said in an uncertain voice when the connection started fading. "Sometimes I fear that in the land of Aegypton, the Eagle won't be with me as much as he is here. Do you realise there are no fields over there? No fields *at all*!"

"The Eagle will be with you, always. We cannot possibly lose him, it comes to us through the very core of our being."

"Look at me!" she laughed at herself. "I don't speak like a woman of much faith, do I?"

"These are trying times."

"Trying times!" she sighed. "Did Gervin tell you that he wants me to try that ritual on you again?"

"Of course! Anyhow, you and I have agreed on this in Highness."

"So you *do* remember!" Alcibyadi flared with curiosity.

"Glimpses. And only through my Flying Dragon nature."

"Tell me! Tell me! What does it feel like to your Flying Dragon nature?"

The music field filled the hall with a superfluity of incomprehensible harmonies that moved up and down and glided in all directions, as if tens of thousands of melodies were being played forwards and backwards at the same time, over a background of flowing rivers of chronological paradoxes and winds of supermental perplexity.

"That's the first impression, when I reconnect after crossing the Edge of Highness," Szar clarified.

"I see. And from your human self, what do you feel?"

"Well, well... nothing! Precisely nothing! It's not even the nothingness in which everything is contained, it's beyond that."

"But why is it so difficult for us to remember?"

"Ah, that I am starting to see clearly. Between Highness and the creation, there is a huge gap. Our manifested human nature is unable to bridge."

"Well, if we need to bridge, then let's bridge! How does one start?" Alcibyadi was suddenly revived by the prospect of a challenge.

"At the Edge of Highness, there is a secret which holds the keys to all the levels of the creation. I can sense it from my Flying Dragon nature, but I don't know how to put it into human words. At the very top of the Golden Shield. Revelation Sky knows the secret." Szar closed his eyes, "Do you know that Revelation Sky is the most magnificent thing I have ever contemplated! A mathematical perfection. When I was in Elyani's world, each time I lifted up my visitor's nose, the archetypal beauty of that sky left me Point-flabbergasted."

"Revelation Sky is just under the Golden Shield. It makes a lot of sense that it should know the secret," Alcibyadi logicalised.

"Hunh hunh! Not under. The upper part of the sky of the gods and the Golden Shield are one," Szar was adamant. "And the higher you ascend, the more levels and marvels. At the Edge of Highness there is an infinity of worlds."

"So how do I get to bridge?" Alcibyadi insisted.

"But it's obvious," Szar snapped his fingers, "you ask the White Eagle, of course!"

She burst out laughing.

Szar remained silent, taking her White-ness in his Flying Dragon nature, reflecting the Eagle's infinite love into her heart.

Another magical moment of cosmic fullness.

It stretched for an aeon or two, until Alcibyadi stood up, ready to leave.

But she didn't feel like going.

She burst into tears.

"I feel so stupid crying like this all the time!"

"But I'm sure I would cry too if I was as pregnant as you are! Why don't you stay a little longer? Does baby Lehrmon like the music field?"

She sat down again, listening to the mind-boggling harmonies and blowing her nose.

It felt so good being in the temple.

So good.

17.18 The rainbow chapel

The team of Field Wizards had gathered in the largest of the cellars of Baltham to celebrate the completion of the Point-insulation field. There were twenty-six of them, including Woolly and Maryani. They were in a lawfully joyful mood, talking loudly, joking at all the problems they had

had to solve in the last weeks. To decorate the hall a luminous blue sky had been field-painted on the ceiling, creating a sprightly atmosphere that contrasted with the increasingly depressed greyness of the outside world. Another field created a large bow of light spanning diagonally from one corner to the other.

Khej came in. "What is that in the Law?" he asked, watching the bow's colour spectrum: from violet to red through blue, green and yellow. "Is it from the gods?"

"What isn't?" Woolly turned skywards with a meek smile. Coming down, he elucidated, "It's called a rainbow."

The young Field Wizard scratched his hair, "A field that makes rain fall?"

"No, dummy!" Gallagher interposed. "It's water that will rain the bow!"

"Rainbows don't exist yet," Woolly explained. "They will appear as soon as we all disappear."

"That's the sad part about rainbows," Gallagher nodded. "First the kingdom must cark it, *then* the clouds will start raining bows. But apart from that they're great."

"Oh I see!" Khej got it. "You mean rainbow like in kingdom of the rainbows! So is *this* what they look like? Heart-warming like a goddess' smile! I want one in my bedroom. Immediately!" he closed his eyes, Pointscanning the field that upheld the rainbow.

Ferman was standing alone in a corner of the room, affectionately watching his team. He received a call from Namron, "Master Gervin has just arrived in the chapel."

Ferman announced loudly, "Friends, our guest of honour is on his way!"

The Wizards became silent, Point-checking all the sub-fields of the defence system, making sure everything was ready for the inauguration.

The main door of the cellar creaked open.

Mouridji entered. "It's working!" she declared triumphantly. "None of my friends can reach me! I thought I'd tell you immediately."

A few seconds later, when Master Gervin arrived in the hall, he found everyone laughing their clear fountain off and clapping their hands.

"They're happy because their shield is working like a lawful charm," Mouridji explained to Gervin after a lawful salute. "And that big rainbow is a surprise, so I won't tell you about it."

Ferman came forth and greeted the Thunderbolt Bearer. "We are ready, Master Gervin," he declared, his voice half-choked with emotion. "This time, we are *really* ready!"

Gervin didn't answer. He just looked deep into Ferman's eyes, shining the glory of Thunder into him.

In a glimpse, Ferman remembered the day when Gervin had first approached him to ask him to participate in the Archive project.

His eyes shone with the same undaunted glow.

It was thirty-nine years ago.

Ferman was only eighteen at the time. He was preparing himself to succeed his father, who occupied the prestigious position of high priest of the windmills of the Law of Eisraim. Gervin, who was Ferman's elder by ten years, had just returned from the clearing of Erriba. The news had just broken that Orest had left his body, leaving Gervin as the new grand master of the Brown Robe. Extraordinary rumours were circulating about the clearing of Erriba.

Ferman was standing outside the chapel of the windmills when Gervin walked towards him, looking straight into his eyes. "Praise the Lord Melchisedek, man of the Law! I need to have a long conversation with you," he had said. Two hours later, Ferman was starting a new life. Having left the windmills of the Law behind him, he was preparing his plan to train the best team of Field Wizards in the entire kingdom.

"We are all ready!" Lorenz, one of the senior Field Wizards, interrupted the flow of memories.

"Let's not make them wait!" Gervin went to stand in front of the team, his hand on Ferman's shoulder. "Where are Lehrmon and Szar?" he asked.

"They have been called for an emergency. One of the high priests of the Water Deities is very sick," Woolly answered. "They said not to wait for them."

"All right. So, who would you like me to Point-call first?"

"Melchard of the Brown Robe!" suggested Arena, Ferman's nephew.

The audience became silent, anxiously waiting for the verdict.

Gervin closed his eyes for a few seconds. Then he shook his head, "No! I can't Point-reach him."

Lawful handclapping.

"I can't Point-reach Esrevin either," Gervin announced a few seconds later. "Nor Ran Gereset. Nor Lehrmon. Friends, you have made it! Not even the emergency Point-frequencies of the Brown Robe can break through your shield."

The audience clapped their hands again, praising the Lord Melchisedek and various gods. They had promised each other they wouldn't swear during the celebration.

"Master Gervin," Arena walked towards him, "as the youngest member of this team, I have been asked to present a request to you. We would like our new chapel to be renamed 'the rainbow chapel', to symbolise that our work is dedicated to the kingdom of the rainbows."

"What an original idea!" Gervin twinged his beard. "A unique name. I don't think there is one single chapel of the rainbows in the entire kingdom."

Not surprising, considering that 'chapel of the rainbows' was unlawfully synonymous with 'chapel of the after-disaster'. Definitely not part of the canon of the Law, which always looked to the past for perfection.

Judging by the anxious silence and the spark in the Field Wizards' eyes, it was easy to see how keen they were on the idea. "Let it be so!" Gervin sighed, giving the blessing of the Brown Robe. "After all, it is exactly what our Archive is about: looking to the future, not to the past."

The blessing was received with much enthusiasm, lawful cheers and applause. After this, Master Gervin was taken to the buffet, full of delicacies brought specially from the central kitchen to celebrate the occasion: cereal biscuits with dark-green puree of boiled vegetables. They drank merrily, filling cup after cup with lukewarm rice-water with herbs.

When Lehrmon and Szar arrived, their grim faces contrasted with the atmosphere of the room where everyone was lawfully chatting and laughing. They went straight to Gervin. "Can we speak to you?" they asked their master, and they took him aside to a remote corner of the hall.

"We have just seen my old friend Varoundass, the high priest of the Servants of the Water Deities," Lehrmon told him. "He's extremely sick. A strange kind of pestilence, never seen before. It started last night. He's burning hot with fever. Coughing dark phlegm and blood."

Gervin closed his eyes one second.

"Let him die!" he replied from the fountain of Thunder.

Disconcerted, Lehrmon bit his lip and remained silent.

"Gervin, there is more," Szar went on. "This pestilence is coming straight from Alverard. Since the near-collapse of the warp, astral filth has been spreading throughout the county. I don't think Varoundass will be the only one to fall sick."

"Let them die!" Gervin replied, speaking from his highest knowingness. "This plague is a blessing from the gods. It is going to save these people from having to go through the nightmare of the last days."

"I am deeply concerned," Szar insisted. "The disease will gain momentum. It could create havoc in the temple. If we don't take action immediately, it might become extremely difficult to stop it."

"I don't want you to heal anyone, apart from those who are strictly indispensable to the Archive project," Gervin ordered in his Thunderbolt Bearer's voice. "Understood?"

Looking down to his fist, Szar gave a Dragon-nod.

"Anyhow, face reality! They are *all* going to die! All of them! And so are we! One year from now, the only ones still alive will be the White Eagles in the land of Aegypton. And Lehrmon, son of Lehrmon," Gervin added, his hand on Lehrmon's shoulder. "This one will be alive and well!"

Devastated, Lehrmon made himself vast, reflecting Thunder.

"Now, bring down the Fire and cheer up, men of the Law! We do not want to spoil this celebration."

17.19 Highness

"Let she who is, who was, and who will be,

125

Curve back onto her source,
And beyond the infinity of her Cosmic Night,
Cognize that which none can comprehend.
Still Flame, Breath of Highness..."

Taken by doubts, Alcibyadi swivelled round. Was the world still the world?

Szar was still sitting in the middle of the circle, Teyani behind him. Judging by the quality of light in the chapel, it was still early morning.

The officiating priestess anchored her column of Spirit into Szar's Flying Dragon nature, high up in the spheres. She turned back to the altar and resumed the ritual.

"That which is will always be.
That which is not has never been.
Eternity is..."
Sound.
The sound of a hundred thousand hierarchies of angels.
The sound of a hundred million revolving worlds.
Sound throughout the creation. The creation is sound.
The universe is one drop.
Implosion.
Fire and Water are One.
...
Jump into the transcendental continuum. Concentrated is-ness.
No such thing as 'I am'. Is-ness has burnt the world.
Not fire, but the essence of fire-ness. Is-ness with Absolute density.
...
On the other side of the Golden Shield, Highness.
To be has a thousand faces.
They are One. You are One. I am One.
You and I have always known
The absolute simplicity of mathematics in Highness:
One plus One is One.
Two times two is One.
Two times three is One.
Two times four is One...
Whatever the question, the answer is One.
Nothing is more simple than Highness.
Time was never born. Infinite limits equate with no limits.
There is only infinity.
Nothing small, nothing huge. Only infinity.
"Teyani, are you here?"
There is no there, only infinite-here.
"Always, my love! Always."
There is no before, no after. Only now, which means always.
Infinite movement equates with infinite stillness.

126

An infinity of infinities. Infinity-ness, the meaning of Love.
"Szar?"
"Infinite-here, with you. Always."
Highness is where all cosmological ladders become One.
Flying Dragons, gods, the Lord Melchisedek, me and you.
Forever One in Love.
Love is.
One Spark.
Seeing you is seeing God.
Highness is One Flame.
The Lord Melchisedek, you and I are that Flame.
Will I remember this time?
A thousand times I have crossed the Golden Shield to become a temporal
soul.
A thousand times I have forgotten God. And me, and you.
And eternity.
A thousand times I have returned, only to discover I had never left,
My true essence being infinite-here, always.
Why go, then?
"Teyani, why go back to the manifested creation
Since anyway, when I go there I keep being here?
Seen from infinite-here, the creation is nothing more than fantasy:
A dream which begins with a cosmic morning.
Time is born, the arrow can't be stopped,
Illusions of limits creating myriads of worlds –
The playground for temporal souls to dream.
Dreams of joy, dreams of being loved, dreams of sorrow and being
abandoned. Dreams of adventure, dreams of power, dreams of fights and
battles. Dreams of being a king, dreams of being a beggar. Dreams of being
wise, awakened – dreams of no longer dreaming.
Then comes a Cosmic Night. The dream dissolves itself.
And everyone realises they have been staying in Highness all that time,
Which anyhow was no time but infinite-here and now, always.
Infinite-here nothing has changed.
I am you, and you are me. And who are you and I?
Whatever the question is, the answer is God.
Infinite-here, to be is to be God,
Absolute, unlimitable, all-comprehending. And simple.
Two times two is God. Two times three is God. Two times four is God...
God, the combinessence of all infinities of angels.
But another dream is already beginning:
Another creation, another cosmic morning.
Time is reborn,
Billions and trillions of souls rushing out to follow its arrow.
But why, Teyani? Why go there? Why go and dream in the creation?

What good does it do to me, you, God?"

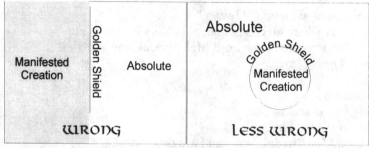

"Alcibyadi, Virgin Spirit, Flame of Highness, eternal beloved,
You are God, and you know that you are God.
God is Highness, Highness is God. The Absolute. Infinite-here.
But where is the creation? Infinite-here too, since there is nowhere else.
Being absolutely infinite,
The Absolute contains the entire manifested creation.
If it didn't, something would be beyond the Absolute,
And the Absolute would no longer be absolutely infinite,
Which is absolutely impossible!
This is why every place in the creation is infinite-here,
Every instant in the creation is now-always.
When you go there, you stay in Highness.
Nothing changes. No one goes anywhere.
And yet... you forget that you are God!
A miserable shade, you forget that Highness even exists.
The Divine Light is no longer with you.
And in the dimness you dream,
You dream yourself a temporal soul, separate from God.
Virgin Spirit, this is why you must undertake the pilgrimage,
Cross the Golden Shield, reincarnate from world to world,
Journey through the manifested creation in search of the pearl.
Highness is revealed Highness. The creation is concealed Highness.
Find the pearl, reveal Highness in the creation.
From Virgin Spirit, become an enlightened One."
"But being God, how could I become anything more?
Anything that is, I am."
"Virgin Spirit you are God, but do not yet completely know how much.
Remember Highness, always, and all dreams will end."
Why do I dream? How can I forget?
I am God. God is Highness. Highness and the creation are One.
When I journey through the creation,
It is God who is journeying through Itself.
How can God forget Itself?
Paradoxes in Highness!

17 – The Book of the Paradoxes in Highness

Infinite-here, ignorance is incomprehensible.
In the creation, Highness is beyond all things.
"Szar, I won't say goodbye."
You and I are One, always.
"Alcibyadi, I won't thank you."
Infinite-here, thanking you is thanking me.
Remember Highness, and all is accomplished.

...

At the Edge of Highness, Alcibyadi found herself a gigantic flame. By her side, Teyani, a no-less-gigantic flame, White like the Eagle.

Still united to the mysteries of Highness, she remembered infinite-here, its absolute knowledge, its pleromic fullness of being – the combinessence of all hierarchies of angels and Flying Dragons.

Warm like a million suns.

At the Edge of Highness they sang the Song of Creation, celebrating the birth of the Fire from the Waters.

So this is how it feels to be an angel of Highness!

Standing at the source of all sources, Alcibyadi saw all seeds, all secrets laid in front of her.

At her feet, the creation was but a drop.

Turning to the spheres of Melchisedek, "I want to give! I have everything to give!"

Highness behind her. No limits. Infinite Love pouring through her heart. Fresh joy, as in the first morning of the creation. Knowledge of all things, strings of know-how for all situations. And the Simplicity that comes from recognising the One behind the apparent multiplicity of this minute creation.

In one glimpse, she saw the true essence of Highness of all souls in the spheres of Melchisedek – One, united in infinite-here, always.

But there was nothing she could give them. In Highness, they already had everything. Always.

She looked for their temporal souls – the part of themselves which grieves so much from believing itself separate from God, which of course it is not, but isn't that what journeying through the creation is all about?

"Teyani, where are the people of the kingdom? I can't see them."

"There!" Teyani pointed down to a mist.

A vague haze. Greyish. Indistinct.

"Are these the kingdom's mists?"

"No, these are human souls."

Souls? Nothing more than drops in an ocean of soul-ness

Wave of angelic sadness in Alcibyadi's heart, "But if I can't see their souls, then I can't give to them! Teyani, why do they appear so vague?"

"Because they are not calling God. Look, this one is," Teyani pointed to a fragile little flame that shone in the mists. "His aspiration is what makes him visible to you."

To angels, giving is ecstasy. Alcibyadi poured her Light into the soul, making the flame flare.

Down in the kingdom, a man was receiving a revelation. Transcendental Peace, combinessence with Highness through Alcibyadi's ecstasy, shower of gifts and powers.

Alcibyadi searched for other visible flames. Each time she found one, she poured her Fire, her Light, her Love. But there were so few of them!

The tragedy of being an angel: everything to give, but no one to receive it.

"Now we must look for Szar's hand!"

It was easy. From the Edge of Highness the chapel of the White Eagle could be seen clearly: it had been built with love, and for twenty-nine years Teyani had been calling the Eagle's Light into it. Angels couldn't possibly miss it.

The circular glow on the living floor helped make Szar more visible.

Healing him was even simpler than finding the chapel.

The black smear in his left hand was just one of Ahriman's futile attempts to separate the kingdom and Highness.

Alcibyadi laughed. Did Ahriman really believe this could ever work?

Extending her hand down to Szar, she made above and below One.

In his hand, she married Highness and the world.

There was nothing to do, since Highness and the world are One. Always.

Since the separation had never existed, neither had the smear. It disappeared instantly.

"Friend, you are free!"

The Eagle's Word had been fulfilled.

So easy! The temptation was great to marry Highness and the world in Szar's entire body – not just his hand.

"Don't try this, he couldn't take it!" Teyani warned. "It's how you nearly killed him last time."

How could marrying two things which are already One kill someone? Alcibyadi wondered, cosmically puzzled.

"The kingdom is such a paradoxical place!"

Ready to resume her pilgrimage, descend from point to line, line to plane, and plane into the kingdom, Alcibyadi turned to Teyani. "Will I remember?"

"The answer is here. Find the source of all sources, come back to the Edge of Highness."

– Thus ends the Book of the Paradoxes in Highness –

18

The Book of Death Terrible

18.1 The departure for the land of Aegypton

The mists were ablaze with the rising Sun.

There were at least five hundred of them – a motley fellowship of priests and priestesses dressed in the coloured gowns of more than eighty orders. They stood, silent and grave, covering the shore of the Fontelayana river and the small hill behind the quay. Each of them carried a torch.

Strangely, the dirtier the mists became, the more magnificently red they turned at sunrise and sunset. Everyone in the county had noticed it, even the most irredeemable sleepers. Simple folks and educated priests alike were wondering if this redness was a sign of the anger of their good Lord Melchisedek – the harbinger of a downpour of plagues. But Szar didn't think so. He found the misty flaring of twilight simply Dragon-beautiful. Of course, he was biased. Since his first glimmer of awakening he had had a passion for the orange flames of sunsets. Fire and firmament, he thought, were a natural match. It made twilight a lovers' reunion. No wonder it opened people's hearts.

There was no breeze that morning. Not the slightest ripple on the Fontelayana river. When the boat arrived from the south, it seemed to be gliding effortlessly on the water.

Melchard, dressed in the crimson robe of his high priesthood, was standing on the quay, waiting for Lord Proston. By a strange twist of destiny, the same boat that brought him to Eisraim was also to take the Eagles away.

Proston was standing on the deck. Szar had no difficulty recognising him from a distance. The tall, kingly-looking man hadn't changed much, though his short hair had turned grey. Szar remembered his high forehead, his large hands, his superb bearing and the impressive dignity of his gestures.

Today Proston's hands were in the pockets of his unofficial dark-grey cloak. And he no longer shone with superb self-assurance. The truth was,

131

he no longer regarded himself as the Most Excellent Grand Superintendent of the Warp of Fields for the Counties of the East in the Service of His Supreme Majesty the King of Atlantis. But who was he going to be next? Would he stay in Eisraim or return to Proston Island, cradle of his prestigious family? The fifty-year-old man had not yet decided.

When he saw the crowd, Proston thought that an official reception had been organised for him. For a moment he felt obliged to wear his official character and make his aura shine. But after Melchard the high priest had formally greeted him and all indispensable lawful mouthfuls had been exchanged, Melchard became himself of the Brown Robe again. "I am sorry, but today is a day of mourning for us. I must stay here for the moment," he told the Most Excellent Proston. "These twenty-four priests will carry your luggage and accompany you to your royal suite."

Realising that the people had not come there for him, Proston laughed in his head. Throughout his career he had had a secret liking for unlawful imbroglios of protocol and embarrassing diplomatic mix-ups.

Yet he was impressed by the depth of feeling that vibrated among the torch bearers. "Who are you mourning?" he asked informally, while the priests were carrying his chests off the boat.

"Nine of our best priestesses are leaving for the land of Aegypton," Melchard told him. To avoid misunderstandings he added, "They are not being exiled, they have not broken the Law. Their deity is sending them there."

"I'm sorry. Had I known, I would have tried to find a better day to arrive," Proston said with a sincerity that surprised Melchard.

"Ah, don't worry. We are all *very happy* to have you with us," the high priest answered.

"Heart!" Proston told himself as the twenty-four priests were escorting him away. "These people have heart." And he sadly realised that it had been many years since he had felt heart in his life. So long that he hardly remembered the magical flavour.

Proston was the only passenger on the boat. After Melchard walked back and took the torch Szar had been holding for him, the quay remained empty.

Silent, deep, solemn, their presences united in one flame, the torch bearers waited, letting the spirit of the temple shine through their hearts.

Soon, the White Eagles arrived. Teyani and Gervin opened the procession. She was serene. He kept biting his lip. Behind them, Seyani and Pepni followed, shining with the White Light of compassion the Eagle had been pouring into them throughout the night. Behind them, the blonde Afani shone even more. Little Berni, however, had spent a whole day and a whole night crying. Her eyes redder than the mists, she appeared to be the most miserable of them all. Lehrmon walked behind her, his baby blissfully asleep in his arms, and Alcibyadi by his side. They were followed by Maryani and Woolly, and Alma, Lorien and Brirg. The march was closed by the sixteen priestesses who had been trained to ascend to the worlds of the triangle and operate the celestial side of the Archive.

Maryani plunged her Dragon-fiery gaze into Szar's eyes, reminding him of the word he had solemnly given her.

"I promise, Maryani," he Point-repeated the pledge he had made the day before with the Molten Sea as his witness.

It had taken place in the cellar of the hermaphroditic stones. Szar and Maryani were busy inspecting the stones with Woolly when a flash of Whiteness interrupted them.

Szar immediately understood. And so did Maryani, of course.

They looked at each other, holding infinity in their eyes.

"What's happening here?" Woolly frowned.

A Point-call from Teyani answered him. "The Eagle has sent the signal. The departure for Aegypton is to take place tomorrow morning."

Maryani received the news in a no-thoughts-just-Dragon fashion. She turned toward Woolly who was pulling from all his resources to stay contained, and she looked at him silently. In the room the golden spirit of Naga-ness became so vibrant that for a moment Szar wondered if King Vasouk was about to pop in for a surprise visit.

Gallagher and Arena came in. As part of the security system, the soft-stone-authorised Point-communications that made it through the shield of the chapel could be heard by everyone. The Field Wizards caught the news and without notifying each other, all converged on the cellar of the hermaphroditic stones. They arrived in small groups and stood silently in front of Maryani. She established eye contact with each of them as they entered.

When they had all arrived, Arena broke the silence. "Are you really going, Maryani?" he expressed the general feeling of disbelief. The Field Wizards had heard that she was one of the priestesses whom the White Eagle had named for exile. But that was long, long ago, before she had joined their team. So much had happened since then – enough to fill entire chapters in the Archive.

"Well, well... yes! I am going to leave the temple tomorrow morning."

"And where is this land of Aegypton you are going to?"

"Far in the east. At the other end of the ocean," she let the Dragon hold her voice and her peaceful smile.

"Why do you have to go?" Gallagher asked her. Unlike most Atlanteans, the Field Wizards regarded 'why' and 'how' as magic words, which they never tired of repeating.

"The Eagle has prepared great works for us over there. We will teach the savages the science of rituals, and the truths of the Law."

"But how could they do rituals if they have no fields?" Gallagher questioned.

"Well, well... I guess we will have to simplify the rituals. A rather drastic simplification, I should say," she tried her best to smile.

"Won't you try to establish a warp over there?" Khej suggested.

"No, my friend!" Maryani sighed. "There will be no fields in the land of Aegypton. Born with the kingdom, the fields will disappear with the kingdom. So have decided the Lords of Destiny."

A difficult thing for the Field Wizards to hear.

"Look at you!" she tried to cheer them up. "You are all biting your lip! I wonder who started this habit."

Ferman knew, but he kept silent.

They all smiled, but they kept on biting their lip.

"How many will be going with you?" Arena asked.

"Five: Pepni, Afani, Berni, Seyani, Alcibyadi. And baby Lehrmon, naturally!"

"And will you teach the people of Aegypton how to make soft stones?"

"Of course! But they will have to be different stones. There will be no fields for them to grow in. I'll have to use compost intensively – the art of the black earth, as King Vasoukidass suggested. But I am also taking some of the hermaphroditic stones with me. I'll get them to reproduce."

There was another long silence. This time it was Lorenz, the senior member of the team, who broke it. "Will you leave us a little bit of your beautiful golden energy?"

"As much as I possibly can," she let her tranquil force resonate with the old man.

"We are going to miss you," Lorenz had tears in his eyes. "Without you our chapel will never be the same."

"I am going to miss you too, friends," she took Woolly's hand. "You have no idea how much."

"Will you join us in the Fields of Peace?" Khej asked her.

"Friends, my path is different," she shook her head. "When my mission in the land of Aegypton is accomplished, I will return to the fountain of blue Life and Light, where I belong."

"In the higher regions of the worlds of the gods?"

She nodded.

Their eyes flared with wonder.

"But I will come to visit you!"

"So... we shall meet again in the Fields of Peace?" Lorenz tentatively asked.

"We shall meet again in the Fields of Peace!" she promised.

They stood silently, drinking her presence and opening to the phenomenal softness the White Eagle was shedding onto her.

Then Lorenz spoke for all of them. "Thank you, Maryani. Thank you for all that you have given us." And after exchanging a last glance, he left.

His fellow Field Wizards followed him, one after the other. As the last of them was walking out Szar made a move, to leave Maryani and Woolly alone. But she called him. "Wait, Szar!"

He turned back, resting the Eagle on the Dragon.

"I want you to promise me something," she looked straight into his eyes.

"What?"

"That you will look after Woolly. I want the Molten Sea to be our witness."

"But... after you leave, my plan is to send Lehrmon and Woolly to Lasseera."

"That's not what I mean. Not this life. After. Once all this is finished, I want you to look after him."

"Hey! Wait a minute," Woolly protested, "what about me, here? Can I be consulted, perhaps? This poor man can't be responsible for all the foolish things I will be doing in my next lives!"

But to his surprise, Szar walked back close to Maryani and plunged his left hand into the Molten-Sea white slime which mothered the hermaphroditic stones. Aligning the Dragon above and the Dragon below, he held Maryani's fiery gaze and swore, "My word, Maryani, I will look after him."

The space of the room was filled with dim echoes of eerie Flying Dragon harmonies.

"Thank you," she whispered. And letting go of her Dragon control she burst into tears. "Thank you!" she sobbed.

For a few seconds, Szar held her tears in the philharmonic silence of the Flying Dragons. Then he walked away, letting Woolly take her in his arms.

Szar went straight to the chapel of the White Eagle. This time he did not go through the catacombs but through the Point-guided corridors of the female wing. A beautiful field, for sure, but not as perfect as he used to think. Now that he was becoming a master field-weaver, he was starting to discern a number of shortages: a certain lack of Point-depth, in particular, and a 'low ceiling' that tended to limit his Flying Dragon connections. It made him remember with a touch of nostalgia the juvenile fascination he used to feel when Point-walking these corridors.

"Praise the Lord Melchisedek, my little Szar!" he met Mouridji on the way. "I heard the news, I know that you must be very busy. But my friend Luciana is terribly sick. Hot like an oven, and coughing like a filosterops. I'm unlawfully worried. Any chance you could see her?" she begged him.

This was exactly what he had hoped would *never* happen – having to watch people die without even trying to heal them. "I'll go and visit her as soon as I can."

"Oh good! Good! Thank you!" Mouridji had total faith in Szar's healing abilities.

"But I can't promise I will be able to help her," he refrained from biting his lip.

"I'm sure you will cure her in no time!" The old prophetess thought he was being shy. But when she saw the way he was drawing a long breath and putting his hand on her shoulder, she had a strange feeling.

Szar left, without saying a lawful word.

When he reached the chapel of the Eagle he gave three measured knocks. "It's Szar!"

It was Gervin who answered, "Come in!"

The magic greeting mantras were spoken, and the Thunderbolt Bearer smiled, "I was just about to call you."

"The Eagle told me," Szar answered, surprised to see no women in the chapel. But the door opened and Teyani entered, filling the space with White Light. And they celebrated the Light by praising the Lord Melchisedek.

Teyani looked neither shocked nor emotional, but grave.

"We have come to stand by your side, dear wise woman," Gervin told her. "And also to make a suggestion. Six of your Eagles are leaving for Aegypton. Sixteen are promised to the worlds of the triangle. This leaves another five of them."

"Alma, Orichalc, Lorien, Iphgin and Brirg," Teyani named them.

"How old are they?"

"Lorien, the youngest, has known fourteen springs and fifteen autumns. And Orichalc, who has known nineteen springs and twenty autumns, is the eldest."

"My advice is, send them to Aegypton tomorrow."

Teyani sighed. "They are *not* going to like this idea."

"They are not going to like what is about to happen here either," Gervin replied in his softest voice.

"True." Teyani had no illusions about the short-term destiny of the temple. She remained thoughtful a few seconds, then she agreed, "I will talk to them, and invoke the Eagle. It would probably help if you spoke to them as well."

Gervin spoke from Thunder, "Not me, Szar!"

"Voof!" Szar frowned and raised his hands toward heaven, forcing a smile to Teyani's face.

"Let it be so!" the Eagle spoke through Teyani.

They agreed to call on a high oracle immediately, after which the five young priestesses would be sent to Szar's Point-hall.

Szar left Gervin with Teyani and walked to Alcibyadi's apartment, only a minute away from the chapel. He announced his visit by turning the space of her room into a music field. A master-technique of the Field Wizards: by letting a field generator Point-resonate with any space of the temple, temporary fields were created from a distance. These could cause visual illusions, unleash deadly venom showers on unwanted visitors, or flood the room with the harmony of the spheres.

"Szar is coming!" Alcibyadi told Lehrmon when she heard the strange pitches of the Flying Dragons, and she ran to the door.

Like the others, she was inundated with the Eagle's Whiteness. It didn't make her less sad, but it added a dimension of infinity to her heart.

"Come and see my baby!"

Her room was bright like a temple in the world of the gods. Lehrmon, who was holding his son in his arms, had also been White-Eagled out by the showers from Highness. "Look who is coming," he whispered to the baby.

Alcibyadi took the child and put him in Szar's arms.

With the deep gravity of a newborn, baby Lehrmon gazed at Szar, who blew a soft low-pitched 'ffffooooohhhh' onto him while space-resonating gentle ascending arpeggios.

"He likes music!" Lehrmon proudly exclaimed when he saw his son's aura expanding with the sounds.

"He looks so much more awake than yesterday," Szar commented.

"This morning, when the Eagle sent the signal, he was smiling," Alcibyadi said in her quiet voice.

"Which shows his *immense* sense of humour," Lehrmon sighed.

"I want to see him in your arms," Szar handed the baby to his mother.

Baby Lehrmon kept third-eye contact with Szar, who was scanning his column of Spirit. "His Point-signature has been fully recorded in the Fields of Peace," Szar announced. "Barkhan Seer, Ferman and I tested his link to the Archive yesterday. Fully operational. But we recommend that you don't bring him to the Archive halls until he turns one."

"And what if he follows me when I astral travel to visit you? He is already travelling all over the spheres!"

"He is unstoppable!" Lehrmon agreed. "Last night he followed us all the way to the triangle."

"Well, well... let this matter be put on the agenda of the next meeting of the Archive council," Szar propounded. He took the baby in his arms again, flattered his aura with a few playful harmonies, and gave him to Lehrmon. With his left hand, now free from Ahriman's pitch, he took Alcibyadi's hand. "You'll have her back in ten minutes," he informed his brother in the Brown Robe.

"Having this child was a fantastic idea," he told her as they were strolling through the corridors. "Totally inspired."

His words fell onto her like nectar from the gods. "Think so?"

"I Dragon-do! And so does everyone in the Archive. They have decided to make him their first prototype for the training of the Knights."

Alcibyadi's mother's heart leapt with pride. "Really?"

"Hey! Hey!" he tempered her enthusiasm. "Not before he turns seven."

"But I don't see why not!"

They kept walking for a few minutes. Silently. Their presences spoke to each other better without words.

Close to Teyani's courtyard, Szar stopped by a laurel tree.

They looked into each other's eyes.

An aeon stretched in the Point-ness of a lawful second.

Remembering Highness.

Infinite-here.

Flying Dragons, gods, the Lord Melchisedek, me and you.

Forever One in Love.

He let go of her hand to clench and unclench his left fist, "I won't say thank you."

"And I won't say good bye," she shone Highness through a smile.

The circle of their friendship complete, he turned round and walked away.

Later that day, when the five young priestesses, led by Seyani, arrived at the chapel of the Field Wizards, Namron sent a Point-message to Szar, "Visitors for you, Commander."

"Bring them to my door," Szar Point-replied.

Soon after, Teyani and Gervin Point-called him, "The Eagle's oracle has left it up to them. They can choose to go or not to go. The Eagle will be with them, whatever happens. So far, they have all said they would rather die than go into exile."

When their Point-signatures had all been registered in the rainbow chapel's shielding field, the priestesses were taken through the daedal of Baltham's cellars and left at Szar's door.

It was open.

They knocked, but no one answered.

They waited a few minutes. Seyani tried to Point-contact Szar, but no success. After waiting a little longer, she finally decided, "If he has left the door open, he probably wants us to go in."

So they stepped through the doorway, and there they found themselves in a cloud of dark-blue light. It was so thick that they could not even see each other.

"Szar?" Seyani called.

There was no reply.

Holding each other's hand, they cautiously moved forwards.

"Szar?" Seyani tried the Point again. Still no answer.

A few steps further, she emerged out of the blue cloud.

"Oh, gods!" she exclaimed, tears in her eyes.

Brirg, who came out of the cloud after her, let out an astonished "Voof!"

It was a new field.

A field of stars. But instead of shining from the ceiling, it occupied the entire space of the room, and it stretched ad infinitum in all directions, even below, so that the priestesses found themselves immersed in a sea of stars and clouds of all colours.

Pulled by curiosity, the other White Eagles stepped out of the blue nebula. They shouted with wonder.

"It's like being a gigantic goddess!" Lorien exclaimed. Uplifted by the spirit of the field, she felt like throwing herself into the space and flying as if she was travelling in the worlds of the triangle. Unaware that she was already intoxicated by the sweet venom of the field, she jumped forward, waving her arms.

To her amazement, it created a bright halo around her.

Incredulous, she stopped and contemplated her body. She looked like her normal self again.

"It's when you move!" Orichalc suggested.

Alma waved her arms again, slowly. No halos.

"You have to do it faster!"

They all moved their arms fast, creating coloured sparks around them.

"This is magic!" Alma started dancing, making herself shine with dazzling halos.

Lorien imitated her, while boldly attempting an exploration of the near surroundings.

Brirg sat close to a small cluster of yellow stars and took her head in her hands. And she wept.

"A magnificent field, isn't it?" Seyani stood behind her and placed her hands on her shoulders.

"Oh, look! Here he is!" Lorien called her friends. "He's dancing. Come and see!"

Seyani took Brirg by the hand, and they joined Lorien and the others.

Surrendered to Revelation Sky, Szar was Dragon-dancing in the fields of stars.

It was a feast of colours, trails of light following his hands, as if myriads of new stars were created by his dance.

Rendered tipsy by the field, the Eagles soon lost any reckoning of time and whether they were dancing or not, because the clouds of stars around them started revolving quicker and quicker, and it seemed that the floor had completely disappeared, and the faster it all moved the brighter it became, and that was not at all what they had expected because they thought someone was going to give them a boring discourse on the necessity of facing their destiny and not flying away from the battles of the world, but where was the top and where was the bottom? And who was laughing so loudly?

Suddenly, it all changed. The fields of stars disappeared.

There was just Light, and nothing else.

Everything had become Eagle-still.

And in the White Peace, they heard what Szar had wanted to tell them.

It was a short message.

The Eagle whispered it for him.

It said, "Edge of Highness. Whiteness eternal. Forever love."

Later that afternoon, when the priestesses came back to their chapel, they looked so seven-sphered-out that Gervin burst out laughing.

"What has happened to you?" an intrigued Teyani asked.

"I'm not exactly sure," Seyani scratched her head.

Brirg walked towards Teyani and declared, "I will go to Aegypton!"

"I will go too," Alma echoed in a decided voice.

"Me too!" Lorien proudly joined in.

Teyani turned toward Orichalc, who was shining as if the Eagle had just given her one of his feathers.

"I will die," the young priestess said with disarming candour. "Tonight, after our evening ritual, I will go to sleep and I will let the Eagle take me."

Iphgin, who was shining the most of all, made the same choice. "I will let the Eagle take me."

And so they did.

The next morning, they were found dead in their beds. And two hours later, when Alma, Lorien and Brirg walked past Szar, they looked at him with incredulity, wondering whether they had really met him the day before or whether they had dreamt the cosmic dance.

By the side of the Fontelayana river the assembly of priests and priestesses covered the hill, making it look like a forest of torches. They remained silent, watching the procession reach the quay.

There Teyani and Gervin stood on each side of the gangway. The priestesses stopped and watched the torch bearers.

There was no discourse. Not even one word.

In one last fiery glance, Maryani reminded Szar of his vow.

Lehrmon surrendered Lehrmon into Alcibyadi's arms.

The nine priestesses walked onto the deck, one after the other. Seyani was the first, Maryani was the last.

They stood with dignity, contemplating their friends.

The ties of the boat were let loose.

And the boat started drifting silently towards the south.

18.2 Touring the temple fields

"Lawfully magnificent!" Lord Proston repeated, rubbing his hands with excitement.

Ferman and Gervin were touring the Point-fields of the temple with him, explaining the aims and methods of their work. They had just left the music hall, at the northern end of Maniya, and were about to visit the temple of the space controllers, adjacent to the fourth hall of Melchisedek.

"For thousands of years, Eisraim has had its own tradition of controllers," Gervin was telling him.

"A special caste?" Proston asked.

"No, we recruit them from various orders. White Eagles, in particular."

The sober entrance of the chapel led to a few rooms where small groups of priests and priestesses were sitting in meditation position, their eyes closed.

"A superb ether," Proston marvelled. "So rich! And the texture is remarkably subtle."

"This field was so cleverly woven that we virtually didn't have to make any changes to it to prepare it for the transfer."

"Through your controllers, every single astral travelling experience of every single priest in the temple has been fully recorded in the field ether, is that it?"

"Correct."

"And you intend to transfer these thousands of years of records into your Archive!" Proston was getting dizzy.

"If the Lord Melchisedek blesses us, there won't be one single ether imprint left behind," Ferman didn't hide his pride. "And the beauty is, as soon as this material arrives in the Fields of Peace, it will automatically be connected to the Universal Knowledge Banks that are linked to the Archive halls: two from the worlds of the gods, and at least six from the Flying Dragons."

"See what it means?" Gervin continued. "These knowledge banks are extraordinarily rich, but they are not easy for human beings to use because their information is stored in Point-packed format – supermental thought-forms. In our Archive, associative links will be established between the Point knowledge banks and our travellers' records. If you want to consult information about, say, the world of the gods, you will get both the gods' point of view and the visions gathered by the seers of Eisraim. The association of the two levels is particularly enlightening. As it has been designed, the Archive senses the quality of consciousness of those who are calling it, and selects the most appropriate level of vision for them. Suppose a little child tunes in. By resonance, the Archive will direct him to the travelling records of children. Those whose minds operate in the form of fluid images will receive records from our visionary priestesses – there have been several female orders in Eisraim that have left us magnificent collections of records."

When he heard Gervin speaking in the past tense, Ferman shivered.

Gervin felt the wave. He paused pensively, then went on, "And those who call from a state of Point-supermental consciousness will be directed to the material of the gods, together with Point-packed visions gathered by our Point-initiates."

"What are these two knowledge banks of the gods?" Proston's curiosity was aroused.

"That of the Sons of Apollo, and the helmet of Lord Gana."

"The Archive is particularly rich in knowledge of the gods," Ferman added. "Several of the Sons of Apollo have taken part in the construction of the temple of light in the Fields of Peace. They are the ones who have established the connection between the Archive and their own knowledge bank. And the two ascending goddesses who were trained in Eisraim in the last four hundred lawful years have been working closely with them."

This time it was Gervin who was startled when he heard Ferman talking about Elyani as some monument of the past.

"To further consolidate the link between the Archive and the worlds of the gods, we will soon be sending a team of sixteen White Eagle priestesses to the lower regions of the triangle," Ferman added.

"Trained by the famous Lady Teyani?" Proston smiled respectfully.

"Lawfully very much so!" Gervin pointed to one of the rooms, "These six young women will be among them."

Proston closed his eyes, Point-tuning into the controllers' field for a few seconds. "Hardly affected by the sickness of the warp," he complimented Gervin, reopening his eyes.

They walked out of the chapel. "I am particularly fascinated by the Universal Knowledge Banks of the Flying Dragons," Proston put his hand on Ferman's shoulder. "Are they already connected to the Archive?"

"Two of them are. One is Space Matrix, the other is the knowledge bank of the Great Ant. The mind boggles when you tune into them. Incredibly ancient, and vast. And in addition to that, they are linked to chains of other knowledge banks of remoteness. But their content is so alien to the normal mind... it's not easy to make sense of them. You should talk to Szar of the Brown Robe. He is our Space Matrix man."

"You already know him," Gervin added.

"Do I?"

Gervin grinned.

They had arrived at the small lake adjacent to the second hall of Melchisedek.

"Here we have a standard reflection field. When you tune into the water, it helps you see inside yourself. Same as many tirtha-fields," Ferman continued the guided tour. "Meaning that the field has kept records of the states of consciousness of all those who have come to meditate here in the last six thousand lawful years or so. Some beautiful material."

"Oho! I had better be careful what I think, then," Proston smiled. "And will you also transfer the field records of that one?" he pointed to the lake adjacent to the third hall of Melchisedek.

"Yes, why?"

"Oh, just curiosity. Now, tell me, how many fields are you intending to transfer into your Archive, altogether?"

"Twelve hundred and twelve in Eisraim, seven hundred and seventy-seven in Lasseera."

"Sweet gods! Preparing all this must have been a monumental work!"

"We've been on this for thirty-nine years," Ferman and Gervin looked into each other's eyes.

"And how many stones have you planned to use for the transfer?"

"Only two: one in Eisraim, and one in Lasseera. When you see them, you'll understand why."

"Let's go back to the rainbow chapel," Gervin suggested.

Each time he heard the unlawfully apocalyptic name, Proston raised his eyebrow, half-horrified, half-amused, secretly wishing he could see the faces of the high priests of the Grand Council of the Law, were they ever to learn about it.

As they turned round the corner, they were stopped by four sacred cows that blocked the alley. Gervin got them to move by Voice-projecting a gentle "Ho!" sound.

"Maniya is the most lively enclave of this temple!" Ferman commented, smiling at children that were playing in the alley.

"For some reasons, temple visitors always seem to flock here," Gervin added. At the end of the alley, Proston also noticed an ass.

Aphrodoros, taking a leisurely morning stroll.

"He's from the chapel of Baradine in the mid-eastern enclave," Ferman explained. "He too likes to hang around here. It's a friendly enclave."

Outside the fortified doors of the rainbow chapel they met Szar, who was just returning from the cremation of Varoundass, the former high priest of the Water Deities.

"Here is Szar of the Brown Robe, the man whom you know," Gervin smiled at Proston.

Szar pushed back the hood of his brown gown, "Praise the Lord Melchisedek, Most Venerable Lord Proston, Grand Superintendent of the Fields."

Proston returned a most ceremonial greeting, unable to recall having ever seen this man. A most unusual circumstance. Atlantean people, and especially politicians, *never* forgot a face.

"Don't you remember the young Beige public servant of Sheringa, who preferred to follow me rather than wear the black ribbon you were about to bestow on him?" Gervin was savouring the moment.

"Your brother, perhaps?" Proston smiled diplomatically.

Szar shook his head. "Me!" he said in his Great Warrior's voice, pointing to the centre of his Great Warrior's chest.

The most excellent Proston remained speechless, his mouth unlawfully agape. And while Gervin was laughing his clear fountain off, Proston touched Szar's imposing shoulder with an incredulous hand, contemplating the strange vibrations at the high end of his column of Spirit.

"See what I could have done with you if you had joined my team twenty-five years ago!" Gervin was still laughing.

"Szar is the commander of the kingdom-side of the Archive transfer," Ferman informed Proston.

"And a great friend of Lady Teyani," Gervin added.

"The Space-Matrix man. I see," Proston regained his composure. "I look forward to working with you, Commander."

Gervin invited Proston to go and inspect the Archive stones with Ferman, while he and Szar walked into the chapel.

"Is he going to stay with us?" Szar asked as they reached the stairway.

"We don't know yet. I think before he can decide, he needs to find himself again, after all these years spent serving the King. But he has already given us a lot of information."

"Anything blasting?"

"You bet in the Law!" Gervin waved a friendly Praise-the-Lord-Melchisedek at Mouridji, who was trotting her way out of the cellars. "According to intelligence received by the King's palace, the drought of the Western Plains was engineered by the necromancers of the Eastern Peninsula."

"The giants were behind that?" Szar gave a loud whistle. "Unlawfully ugly!"

"And there is worse. The epidemic that has been ravaging the Western Shores in the last months also came from the giants. But not the floods, nor the other natural catastrophes."

"What about the waves that blew the warp in Alverard?"

"No, not that. Giants or no giants, the warp is agonising. Our time is coming! Let's go and see what your magnificent Point-hall looks like today," Gervin decided. "By the way, did you *really* inspire yourself from the cave of Verzazyel the Watcher to weave your fields?"

"Oh... only for the general concept. Do you think that's all right?"

"All right?" Gervin burst out laughing. "Completely outrageous! But very much in keeping with the Brown Robes' sense of humour."

18.3 Woolly of Thunder

"Lady Teyani!"

It was just after sunset. The official welcoming ceremony for Lord Proston had finished half an hour earlier. The guests had dispersed.

Lord Proston was walking back to the royal suite where he was lodged. "Lady Teyani!" he called again.

She stopped, and turned toward him.

He walked slowly, unlawfully holding her eyes.

"Lady Teyani of the White Eagle!" he repeated with a touch of reverence and wonder.

"Sir Proston!" she smiled, making him swallow.

"May I tell you something?"

She held onto the clear fountain.

"You... are a beautiful person. The most extraordinary woman I have seen in the kingdom."

She bit her lip.

"True! I am charmed. Fascinated. Bewitched! Since the last time I came here, I haven't stopped thinking about you." He lightly touched her long black hair with his fingers.

She shook her head.

He promptly took his hand away. "I have come here to lawfully ask you to marry me, Teyani. Please, don't say anything now! Please! Give me some time."

Devastated, she shook her head again.

"But the White Eagles can be married, can't they?"

"I am sorry. I can't. This is not my path. I belong to the Eagle!" And for fear of bursting into tears she started running away from the beautiful man.

A howling dog interrupted Teyani's memories.

"How long ago was that?" she wondered, contemplating the moonlight reflecting in the lake by the side of the third hall of Melchisedek. "At least twenty lawful years!" She remembered how much she had been touched. She wondered how it would feel to meet Proston again after so long.

She resumed her walk to the rainbow chapel.

At the gates she had to wait a few minutes. The deadly shielding field had just been modified, Namron had to register her Point-signature all over again. Meanwhile, the dog kept howling ominously. When she finally got in, she went straight to Woolly's room.

She reached his door and found herself face to face with Szar. They immediately knew they had both come for the same reason.

They praised the Lord Melchisedek, their connoisseurs' hearts full of appreciation for the sincere reverence each of them put in the mantra. Then they knocked at the door.

There was no answer.

"It's Szar and Teyani," the White Eagle announced, knocking again.

"Don't waste your time, I'm dead," Woolly answered.

"Can we come in anyway?"

She took the absence of answer as tacit approval and went in. Szar followed.

Woolly was in bed, hiding under his bed sheets.

"I don't want to talk," he told them in the voice of someone who, hitting the bottom of a murky pool, would have kept sinking in the mud for a lifetime or two.

"Do you mind if we stay here a moment while we are not talking to you?" Teyani asked him.

"No, no," he groaned.

"Were you at the cremation of Varoundass?" Teyani asked Szar.

"I went with Lehrmon. Varoundass was his friend."

"I know. They used to play together when they were children. Did anyone else fall sick in his chapel?"

"Not that I know of. But it's just a matter of time."

"I heard it's also in Eisraim city."

"It comes straight from the fields. An aftermath of the catastrophe in Alverard. By now it must be sweeping the entire county."

"Did you hear from Alverard?"

"Unlawfully grim. The people have only partly recovered. There's still a lot of madness going on. People just lie on the ground and let themselves die."

"That's me!" Woolly sighed abysmally from under his bed sheets.

Teyani turned her eyes and her palms upwards, smiling to the gods.

Szar nodded.

"And what about these mysterious Nephilim? Have you spotted them again?"

"Completely disappeared," Szar answered. "I sent two of our Field Wizards to Pipili Hills in the Western Plains, to establish a quadrangular listening field with Jop's men, who have been posted on Mount Fulcrum. We couldn't pick up anything."

"Could it be that they've left the county?"

"Could be. Could also be that they're good at hiding. We spotted them at key moments: just before the near-collapse of the warp in Alverard, and just after it was healed."

The Field Wizards called these phases 'paradoxical clarity'.

Teyani was well aware of the phenomenon. Gervin had long planned that the Archive transfer would be completed during one of these clarity phases, in the late stages of the collapse of the warp.

"It might not take long until the next phase of paradoxical clarity," Teyani warned. "Have you noticed that dog howling in the distance?"

"No it was not a dog," Woolly interposed. "It was me."

Teyani chuckled. She went to sit on the side of his bed. "Do you know why we are here, Woolly?"

Silence.

"We are here because Gervin is about to come and visit you, to ask if you are ready to undergo the initiation of the Masters of Thunder."

"That was predictable," Woolly moaned. "Each time this initiation is about to be mentioned I get assassinated, one way or another."

"It's called a karmic boost, my love," Teyani put her hand on his knee. "When you are about to make a great leap forward, a high part of yourself speeds up. That often creates karmic returns."

Another silence, but a heavier one.

"The Eagle has sent Szar and me to make sure you are ready. The initiation could take place quite soon," Teyani turned toward Szar.

"Imminently," Szar confirmed. The Eagle had told him so.

"Well, I look fully ready, don't I?" Woolly jeered.

"It could be much worse," Teyani encouraged him. "Apart from being dead, is there anything you feel like at the moment?"

"No."

Teyani held the silence and filled it with presence.

"Have you thought what you are going to tell Gervin when he asks you the traditional questions?"

"No idea. My mind is blank. It's like being hit with the pain of the entire kingdom. All these people who're about to lose their loved ones and watch their world be destroyed. And the ugly chaos that will follow, and..."

"No, that's not what it is. That's what your head says," Szar interrupted. "True, we're on the edge of an ugly mess. But at the moment, what's hurting is the part of you that was united to her. Something broken, deep inside, at the core of your life force. Even if the kingdom was miraculously saved, you'd still be miserable."

"And what do I do about that?"

"Time is a great healer of those things," Teyani said. "With time, the part that wants to die heals by itself. This is what mourning is about – a natural mending process. You cannot really do it, you can only let it happen. But there is one thing you can do: not let your head make things worse."

"My head's always been good at making things worse."

"At the moment your mind is poisoned by the despair of the broken part. It sees everything black. Don't listen to it."

"And move!" Szar added.

"Stagnation only makes things worse. It thickens the dark moods. When one of my Eagles has a broken heart, I get her to walk fast all around the walls of the temple every morning and every afternoon. That definitely helps. Why don't you get some exercise with Szar?"

"Don't feel like moving."

"At the moment I'm fielding the catacombs of the under-temple. Tomorrow morning, I'll take you with me," Szar decided for Woolly. "You'll *love* it, brother – dusty forgotten crypts (pitch-dark, some of them), bowels that stink (it's from the sewage), rats (strange beasts I had never seen until these last days). Last week I even found a skeleton."

"But that sounds *exactly* like what he needs!" Teyani sighed. "I wish I could come too." Then a wind in space made her close her eyes. "The master is coming!" she announced.

"Gervin?" Woolly choked.

"He is in a glorious mood," she added in her softest White-Eagle voice.

"What am I going to tell him?" the young man lamented.

"You are going to let us handle this situation for you, my love."

"You keep your mouth shut!" the Great Warrior ordered Woolly.

When the Thunderbolt Bearer arrived, he found the door open. Teyani and Szar treated him with an expertly Spirit-infused "Praise the Lord Melchisedek!" and they invited him into the semi-dark room.

"You have come to visit our friend?" Gervin asked, half-frowning, half-smiling.

"Actually, Gervin... Szar and I have come to see you too," Teyani declared. "We knew you were coming."

"I see," Gervin started having suspicions. But as Teyani had seen, he was in a jovial, perky mood.

"We have a great favour to ask you, Master Gervin," Szar went on. "We are appealing to your heart."

"Yes!" Teyani added.

"I see..." Gervin smiled, pulling his beard. "And... what is this favour?"

Teyani let the Eagle speak through her, "Please come back in two days!"

"Yes!" Szar added.

Gervin burst out laughing.

"Woolly is on a fast-recovery track," Szar pleaded. "Teyani and I are just about to spend two days running around the temple's catacombs with him. And on the roofs too, actually."

"I see! And... " Gervin took on his seriously joking voice, "can I speak to the man?"

"In two days, *of course* you can!" Teyani assured him wholeheartedly. "But I want to know, are you going to ask Szar the traditional questions too?"

"Naturally!"

"Oh, I'd like to be present when it happens!" the grand master of all female orders in Eisraim exclaimed with child-like innocence. "Can I come?"

"You are *always* welcome!" Gervin repeated his very first words to her on the day of her arrival at the temple, twenty-nine years earlier.

She stood up and took his arm. "Let's go to Szar's Point-hall!"

Szar let them go first. He stayed in the room and took Teyani's place by the side of the bed. "You did really well!" he complimented Woolly, who had no choice but to chuckle.

"Listen, there is one thing I want you to know," Szar told him. "The other day, that pledge I made to Maryani... it didn't make any difference. I'll tell you why," he paused, looking down to his left fist. "A while ago, I had already sworn to myself that I would stand by you. When the warp carks it, there are *a lot* of people who are going to find themselves in abysmal shit, especially after they die. We can't rescue them all. But Brown Robe or no Brown Robe, Woolly, you will find me. This is said from the Dragon!" And he stood up and walked away.

Deeply shaken, Woolly pulled the sheet off his face.

Szar didn't turn back. "Get some sleep and get your ass ready by dawn. I'll come and pick you up."

18.4 The traditional questions

When Gervin and Teyani arrived in the Point-hall, they found themselves immersed in a cloud of Point-blowingly magnificent deep-sea-blue light. It was so thick that they could hardly see each other. At first Teyani thought it was a nebula in a field of stars, as in the worlds of the triangle. But as she and Gervin walked further inside, they remained surrounded by the same solid light. And they Point-heard elusive, eerie harmonies that made their energy tingle.

"I find this blue immensely poetic," the White Eagle was rapt. "Do you know what it is?"

"A resonance with the remote spheres of the Blue Lagoon. I visited them once, on my way to the Great Ant. Spaces of strangeness, these are!"

They aimed for the crypt of the Archive stones, at the other end of the hall. But three minutes later, they were still swimming in the light.

"I don't remember this hall being so long!" Teyani wondered.

"It is not," Gervin laughed. "The fields are Point-tricking us by curving our straight lines!"

"A trap for the giants?"

"Exactly. All other entrances to the crypt of the Archive stones have been sealed. The only way in is through this hall. If we are attacked, this will be the battlefield."

"So our Wizards have woven all kinds of deadly things in here?"

"A complete arsenal with more than four hundred fields, including field generators that automatically probe the minds of visitors when they enter and create spaces accordingly. There is also a profusion of venom wells, part of the Lesser Magic of the Sons of the Dragon, and two large Underworld shafts designed to pump deadly fiery venom from the depths. Maryani dug them before she left. This is definitely... the most deadly bedroom you have ever visited."

"At least, if our enemies die it will be with music," Teyani sighed compassionately, letting the indescribable tunes flirt with her energy.

"Very much so! The music field is part of the deadly weapons. It can generate unbearable astral sounds that turn your mind into a pandemonium of hell. I had a brief taste of it the other day – frightening!"

They kept walking in the peaceful sea of Flying Dragon music-light.

"Who do you think are these ghost Nephilim that mysteriously appear and disappear from the county?" Teyani asked her friend.

"I really have no idea," Gervin said. "Their camouflage is exceptionally clever. They could well be giants. But they could also be Hunters."

"Fifteen Hunters... is an awfully unlawful lot. They would *have* to be from Jex Belaran."

"I can't see what they would be doing here."

"Maybe they too want our stones."

"But we are on excellent terms with Jex Belaran! In his dealings with Perseps Szar has always made it clear that if the Hunters needed super-chargeable stones, we would supply them."

"What does Perseps think of this situation?"

"We're not keen on calling him. We're brooding an unlawful mess with the communication stone he gave us. No need to draw his attention to us."

They had finally arrived at a small door at the other end of the hall.

"Last time I came here, it was a large archway that led to the crypt of the Archive stones," Teyani frowned.

Gervin paused to twinge his beard, and they walked in.

"Oh..." Teyani was astounded. "But this is incredible!"

Gervin burst out laughing.

The crypt of the Archive stones looked *exactly* like the chapel of the White Eagle. The imitation was so remarkably well done that for a second, Teyani really thought they had arrived there.

"This is out of the seven spheres!" she repeated a few times, looking up to her beloved dome ceiling and touching the plass floor where the occult symbols were all shining in the right places. "How could they manage to catch the vibration so well? This place is filled with the presence of the Eagle, almost like the real chapel. Is it just resonance?"

Gervin could not stop laughing.

"If it wasn't for that small door, the replica would have been almost perfect. It could nearly have fooled me," Teyani held her chin.

Then she turned back and to her even greater stupefaction, the small door had disappeared.

Gervin clapped his hands and laughed even louder.

"But..." she went to open the doors of the chapel. She found herself in a perfect replica of the Point-guided corridors of the female wing. There was even a Blue priestess passing by. She lawfully praised the Lord Melchisedek when she saw Teyani.

That was when Teyani started having suspicions.

"But..." she went to stand at the centre of the circle and closed her eyes, Point-tuning into the Eagle. "But this *is* my chapel!" she exclaimed, outraged.

And she was right. They *were* in the chapel of the White Eagle.

Or were they not?

Teyani's sceptical glance swept the chapel and for a second she wondered again if she was being Point-tricked into not believing that the false place was the real one or whether it truly was that the real one was not the false one, which after all has always been the best of all magic tricks, but still, without thinking she found herself asking, "This is my chapel, isn't it?"

"Praise the Lord Melchisedek, it is! They have done it! They have managed to fool us!" Gervin was ecstatic.

"But how the Ugly Underworld did we get here?" Teyani swore without even noticing it.

"Precisely, wise woman, the Point-fields must have taken us through the catacombs. I know that Szar has been doing a lot of Point-fielding in the under-temple, lately."

"But we *must* have been climbing stairways. And we didn't even notice!"

"We are ready!" Gervin shone with the light of the lineage of Thunder. "This is what it means. We are ready to face the giants!"

Had Szar and the Field Wizards wanted to make him a present, they could not have found a better prank.

"I want to go back there immediately!" Teyani declared in her Spirit-warrior character. "That was grossly unfair. I was completely unprepared and innocent. This time, I intend to defend myself. I'm not going to let these fields play up with my Point."

"I'll come with you. But let's wait till the lawful morning. Tonight is a special night," Gervin softened her. "A few hours ago the Masters of Thunder decided that Szar and Woolly wouldn't be initiated on Mount Fulcrum but in the Fields of Peace, in the Archive halls. You are invited to take part in the rituals. Barkhan Seer asked me to convey a lawfully formal message requesting the privilege of your presence."

Whenever the name of Barkhan Seer was uttered in her presence, Teyani's White energy became a dancing flame. "Have they finished the construction of the temple?" she looked up to the dome of her chapel.

"Thoroughly."

Teyani walked to the altar, and she sent her answer to Barkhan Seer by Voicing a short velvety 'ooo' sound onto the flame and offering a few grains of rice. It filled the chapel with the vibrant peace of the Eagle.

When she turned back, she plunged her eyes into Gervin's. Together, they held the presence.

"You are not going to stay much longer, are you?" Teyani asked.

Gervin shook his head.

She looked up, filled herself with the Eagle's glorious Light, and descended into his eyes again.

There were no words. Just infinity.

Eagle's feathers. Torrents of Light-ness.

It lasted beyond time, a sigh on the Edge of Highness.

A breath of Point-ness-ness.

Nothing, really.

"You know, this Archive hall that Barkhan Seer has built for you," Gervin pleaded, "I visited it. Point-boggling!"

"Not now," she shook her head. "I will come, but not now."

"Will we have to wait till the wars of the Apocalypse for you to return from Highness?"

"No, I will descend much earlier than that. But now, the Eagle is calling me. I must join him for the Great Lovers' Dance."

Gervin nodded. "And who will you be when you return from the Dance?"

"Your friend. That which is, will always be."

Three knocks resounded at the door.

"Come in, my love," Teyani answered.

When Szar entered, he found the chapel inundated with the Eagle's ardent Love. Gervin turned to face him. Teyani, who shone like a lighthouse on the Edge of Highness, stood on Gervin's left.

A third figure, like a mist, appeared on Gervin's right. It gradually became clearer as Szar walked into the chapel. A tall man. Dressed in the Brown Robe of the Masters of Thunder, with the hood covering his head.

Gervin stepped back. Teyani and the man turned so as to face each other. Szar came close to them, facing Gervin. Together they formed a cross.

"Apprentice," Gervin took on a ceremonial voice, "according to the laws of our lineage, I must now ask you the questions which, since time immemorial, have been asked of each and every apprentice before he attempts the high initiation to the grade of Master of Thunder. Are you ready to answer me?"

Szar replied from the Dragon, "I am."

"Hear my warning, apprentice, this initiation entails great perils. Your vision will be open. Facing yourself is no easy trial. Contemplating the future, more difficult even. Light and darkness, both will be revealed to you, which is why I now solemnly ask you, are you ready to face your fears, and those forgotten corners of yourself which hold endless sorrows?"

"I am."

"Seeing the future is one of the worst of all trials. Few are those who can withstand it and not lose hope. Solemnly, I ask you, are you ready to see what the Lords of Destiny hold for yourself and for humankind?"

"I am."

"Only he who has faced darkness can contemplate the light. Apprentice, are you ready to withstand the vision of the Prince of Darkness, his monstrous works, the abyss into which he aims to plunge humanity, and the slaughter and destruction which he has planned to inflict on the world?"

"I am."

"The higher you ascend, the lower you can fall. Are you fully aware that the sublime knowledge you are about to receive makes you a candidate to be tempted by the Prince of Darkness?"

"I am."

"Apprentice, are you ready to face the Great Light that washes away all illusions and burns all that which is not turned towards the One God?"

"I am."

"Deep inside yourself, apprentice, what do you want?"

"The White Eagle is what I want."

"Praise the Great Apollo! That sounded *very* sincere," Gervin laughed. "Barkhan Seer being your sponsor, let Teyani be the witness. Your initiation will take place in Archive Hall One."

Teyani was crying.

The head of the man who faced her remained hidden under his hood. He gradually faded from the space of the room, leaving a bubbly golden imprint and a subtle smell. Szar had not seen his face. But from the special golden light that shone in his aura, he had recognised him.

He was Barkhan Seer the irresistible, prince of Thunderbolt Bearers and patron of the Knights of the Apocalypse.

18.5 Abandoned by the gods, and by the Brown Robe

"Was that another rat?" Woolly could hardly believe his eyes.

"It certainly was!" In the narrow bowel lit by dim greenish plass glows, Szar knelt down. He thrust his head into a pipe-like opening in the wall.

"But where do they come from?"

"I think they've arrived in the unlawful days that followed the blow-up of the warp in Alverard." Szar crawled into the opening.

"So the warp vomits rats, now!" Woolly sighed. He bent down to see where Szar was heading. "What about the pest-removing field that Ashok and Gallagher tried the other day?"

"Went badly wrong. Instead of hitting the rats, it killed half the cats of the Wise Witches. They were fu-rious. They went straight to Melchard and lodged an official complaint against us." Szar crawled back out of the opening. "It's a cul-de-sac. Not worth fielding."

The two men started walking again.

"This stench is the worst we've had to bear this morning!" Woolly complained.

"The central sewage canal is just a few minutes from here."

"At least, here we can't hear the noise," Woolly yawned.

He hadn't had much sleep. Neither had anyone else in the temple. In the middle of the night the dogs of the chapel of Dhanubis had started a howling party. An hour later, the asses of the chapel of Barradine began accompanying them, and soon the cows started mooing unlawfully. By the end of the night every single beast in the temple had joined in the concert. The music was ugly. The animals were terrified. Four cows from chapel of the Rural Deities were seen running madly through the alleys of the temple. Three of them forced their way back into their former shed and completely ransacked the newly-established chapel of the Wise Witches of the Law, who could hardly believe their bad luck. In the early hours of the morning the fourth cow was found dead, floating in the small lake by the side of the third hall of Melchisedek. The prophets of every order agreed this was about the worst omen they could envisage.

But the animal clamour did not stop with dawn. Great experts of the Voice were sent to project pacifying mantras onto the beasts, but with no result. The people of the temple had to bear with the pandemonium.

"Sorry, we're going up!" Szar announced as they reached a winding stairway. It took them to the female wing of the temple, not far from the chapel of Dhanubis.

"Oh gods!" Woolly plugged his ears. "It was supposed to be the *night* of the howling dogs, not the week!"

They walked down a couple of corridors and found Mouridji of the Purple Robe. She was waiting for Szar in front of the door of Luciana's room. Their arrival was greeted by horrendous choking screams. Someone, it sounded, was being slowly strangled.

"Don't worry, it's just our neighbour's parrot," Mouridji reassured them.

"Better if you stay outside," Szar told Woolly. The last thing they needed was for him to catch the disease. Szar followed Mouridji into the room. He rested on the Dragon to ignore the fetid smell.

"She's stopped coughing, but she doesn't look better," Mouridji said.

Szar walked to Luciana's bed. He discovered that if the old woman was no longer coughing, it was because she had fallen unconscious. Her aura was black from the pestilence, and red with the vital fire that was fast escaping from her kidney and her heart.

"Mouridji..." Szar took his head in his hands, "Luciana is going to die."

"What?" Mouridji was shocked.

Szar looked into her eyes, calling on the infinite compassion of the Eagle.

"But that's not possible!" the old prophetess was taken by a wave of panic.

Szar nodded, biting his lip.

"But that's not possible! You healed my hip, and you healed her blindness, and all those other people. This is just a bad case of a cough. It can't be that you can't cure her."

He stood, silent, calling onto the light.

"But you're not going to let her die, are you? What am I going to do without her? She's... she's been my friend for fifty-one lawful years!" Mouridji burst into tears. "Can't Elyani help?"

Szar walked to the window. The priests of the healing chambers were carrying a corpse to the cremation ground.

"Are you abandoning us, Szar?" Mouridji thundered. "Have the gods given up on us, and the Brown Robes too?"

"It's the end, Mouridji. The end. There's nothing I can do about this. Luciana's is not a bad death. Let her go in peace."

"That's what it is. You're letting us down. When we need you the most! You just want us to die," she cried, and she ran out of the room.

Szar walked back to the bed and Point-called Gervin, "No healings. No healings at all, is that right?"

"Up to you son," the Thunderbolt Bearer Point-replied. "But understand well, this plague is a grace of our Lord Melchisedek. If you decide to go against it, be sure you know what you are doing."

Szar hesitated, his hands itching to start on Luciana's vital gateways.
Then he turned on his heel and walked out.

"Had a lovely chat?" Woolly grimaced from his cynical character.

"I tell you, there's going to be a lot of shit in this temple in the coming weeks." Without any further comment, Szar walked towards the entrance to the catacombs.

"Oh, excellent!" Woolly took on a jovial voice. "I definitely prefer the stink of sewage to the noise."

But as they were reaching the winding stairway they received an emergency Point-call from Gallagher in the rainbow chapel, "Quick! Get your ass here! The global warp is shaking. A phase of paradoxical clarity is about to begin!"

18.6 Searching for the ghost Nephilim

The Field Wizards had assembled in the rainbow hall. They worked in groups of three, using all the scanning fields of their massive arsenal. Cross-linking fields had been established with Jop's men on Mount Fulcrum, Ushbudh and Balavan, who had been sent to Pipili Hills, and with Esrevin, Lehrmon and Pelden's men in Lasseera.

When Szar and Woolly arrived they sat with Khej and focused on the immediate vicinity of the temple.

"The warp is *very* sick," Ferman announced. Together with Lorenz and Proston, he was monitoring the vitality of the global network of fields.

"The final collapse could take place any moment," Proston added.

Everyone shivered.

Gervin and Teyani were walking into the hall when the Field Wizards of Lasseera Point-called to announce, "We're detecting something terribly nasty in the north of our county. Probably around Barnagiran. A big hole in the warp. It's bursting out at this very moment. Are you picking it up?"

"Unlawfully ugly!" Ashok Point-confirmed. "Somewhere between Barnagiran and Laminindra. Closer to Laminindra, actually... and at least as bad as the one which ravaged Alverard. No, no... much worse!"

"The global warp keeps losing power fast," Ferman informed them.

"That's it! The paradoxical clarity is starting!" Flex Point-yelled from Pipili Hills. "Can you sense it?"

"Not yet," Gallagher Point-replied. "What about the damn ghosts?"

"No. Nothing."

From Thunder, Gervin raised the Point-ness in the room. A startling boost in everyone's column of Spirit.

Feverish minutes. The Field Wizards were giving their absolute Point-best, field-scanning madly in search of the ghost Nephilim.

"The wave of paradoxical clarity is reaching Lasseera," Pelden Point-warned. "Oh gods, we're seeing the full amount of the damage now. It's... much, much worse than Alverard. Ugly like the end of the Law. And damn close to the temple of Laminindra. The situation over there must be catastrophic!"

"The paradoxical clarity is reaching Eisraim!" Gallagher gave the signal.

"Oh, shit! Shit!" Khej immediately shouted. "We have them! Only three hours from here, at the most. West. On the other side of the Fontelayana river."

"How many of them?" Gervin asked.

"Four!" Woolly counted.

Gervin linked his Point to Woolly's and tuned in.

"We can sense them too!" Point-confirmed the Field Wizards in Pipili Hills.

"Paradoxical clarity is reaching here!" Jop Point-announced from Mount Fulcrum.

"Can you sense our four ghosts?" Khej Point-asked him.

"No. But wait... we've just located the second group! Approximately the same distance, three hours from you, but north."

"How many?"

"Around fifteen, as before. But they're incredibly well camouflaged. We can hardly pick up their presence."

"Underworld!" Khej hit the floor with his fist. "We can't pick them up from here. Can you, Flex?"

"No. If there are really fifteen of them, then they must be damn good at hiding. We *should* be able to see them."

"The global warp is in free fall!" Ferman Point-interrupted them. "This time, I don't think it's going to survive much longer."

"Agreed!" the most excellent Proston corroborated.

There was an ominous silence.

"Everyone get ready for the final procedure," Gervin ordered in a near-Voice threshold. "I want every priest and priestess in the temple locked in their room. Start sending Point-messages. And I want Lehrmon to be ready to begin the charging of the stones in Lasseera."

"Everything is in order, I can initiate the Archive-charging any time," Lehrmon Point-sent back.

"We have just received a message from Laminindra," Pelden Point-reported from Lasseera. "Complete carnage. A tidal wave of elemental slime. The temple is swamped. The mists have turned black. Hundreds of people have been killed."

A wave of consternation swept the room.

Woolly and Gallagher were both born in the temple of Laminindra. They exchanged a glance, thinking of their friends and family.

There was no time to lament.

"A second wave of paradoxical clarity is reaching Mount Fulcrum," Jop Point-notified. "Much deeper than the first one. It's fan*tas*tic! We can see as far as the Western Shores. Unlawfully unreal!"

"Not a good sign," Proston shook his head. "Not a good sign!"

"The way the global warp is shaking, multiple holes are likely to burst open in the next few minutes," Ferman warned.

"I think I can already see one being formed," Jop Point-added. "South of Eisraim, somewhere along the Fontelayana river. Probably in the county of Berylia. No, further south. Halfway between Eisraim and the Red Lands."

"The paradoxical clarity is also on the increase in Lasseera," Lehrmon Point-announced. "Shall I ride on the wave to charge the stones?"

"Damn it! We have located the fifteen ghosts!" Pelden Point-interrupted him. "North of your temple. They're carrying *thousands* of soft-stone weapons with them. Enough to storm the King's palace!"

"Szar, are you ready to begin the Archive-charging?" Gervin Voiced.

The answer came from the Dragon, "Ready!"

From Lasseera, Pelden sent another ominous message, "We're detecting a new hole in the warp. West of Barnagiran, in the Northern Lakes. Not a populated area, but still... a disastrous chain-reaction could take place all the way from Laminindra through there, and down to the Western Plains. Are you sensing something, Flex?"

"Sounds like it's already happening. The warp is badly shaking in Romeran!" Flex replied.

From Mount Fulcrum, Jop reported, "What we are picking up at the moment is... frightening. From the Western Plains to the Western Shores the warp is being ripped apart. I can count at least nine holes. Two of them are absolutely huge. Around Tipitinan. Tens of thousands of people must have been killed."

"I suggest we initiate the charging of the Archive stones within five minutes," Esrevin Point-intervened.

A tense silence followed.

It was Ferman who broke it. "Wait! Wait! The global warp is picking up! Very fast!" he was startled. "I don't understand, something strange is happening. Like a huge injection of energy."

"We're sensing it too!" Lasseera confirmed. "A formidable force. Never seen anything like it. *Never!* It's phenomenal!"

"Out of the seven spheres!" Jop was Point-flabbergasted. "A gigantic wave sweeping through Perentie and the Snowy Mountains. It's coming from the east. Massive! Massive, massive!"

"The warp keeps picking up," Ferman could hardly believe his Point.

"Where is that coming from?" Gervin asked.

"The signs are unmistakable," Lord Proston answered. "It comes from the necromancers of the Eastern Peninsula."

"Do you mean we are being saved by the giants?" Gervin grinned.

"I guess we are all in the same boat," Proston sighed.

"All of you who are not chasing the ghost Nephilim, tune into the global warp!" Ferman ordered his men. "I want you to see this. The amount of power that is being unleashed at the moment is lawfully unreal! Is this really from the giants?" Ferman asked.

"Without a shadow of a doubt," Proston confirmed.

"Look at that! But look at that! What a master work!" Ferman was astounded. "These sons of a Nephilim bitch are fixing the hole in the warp of Laminindra. And from the Eastern Peninsula, moreover! This is *unbelievable*!"

"Powerful, the giants," Lord Proston nodded.

"The wave is reaching the counties of the west," the men in Mount Fulcrum reported. "This is... this is awesome! Beyond anything you can imagine. As if the warp was being repaired by the hand of the Lord Melchisedek! Hole after hole, disappearing. Oh, gods! Now the one around Tipitinan is being repaired... done!"

The show of force continued, leaving the four teams speechless.

Throughout the kingdom, Field Wizards were watching with the same amazement. In front of everyone's Points, the global warp was being mended. More than thirty-five holes that had appeared in various parts of the kingdom disappeared in a matter of minutes.

Ferman bit his lip. "But where the hell do they get all this energy from?"

Meanwhile, in the palace of the King, Lord Proston's former colleagues were asking themselves exactly the same question.

And they trembled.

Never before had they realised that the giants were such formidable adversaries.

18.7 Eastern Peninsula, the grand commander's palace

In the grand hall of Naamah, the giants stamped their feet in jubilation. Raising their fists, they screamed, "Victory! Victory! Glory to the Watchers and their sons!" And they gave Grand Commander Bobros an ovation.

"We made it!" Basalinger shouted in exhilaration, hugging Fornan. "We made it, father!"

The old general had tears in his eyes. For the first time in hundreds of years, the forty-nine court sorcerers had worked hand in hand with the necromancers of the guild. At first, each group had taken position on one side of the hall, with Bobros in the middle. While they were performing the ritual they gave each other slanted, suspicious looks – nothing surprising for two rival clans who had spent generations cursing and plotting against each other. But as the night passed and signs of success were being reported from the four corners of the kingdom, a superior feeling of mutual respect arose among them. At times, magicians from both camps were even seen smiling at the other clan with appreciation. All of them were performing exceptionally well.

When the news broke that the last hole in the warp had been mended, the unthinkable took place. Afran Kesborn, the leader of the court sorcerers, crossed the no-man's-land separating the two clans and took the hands of Samoan, the new leader of the necromantic guild. In the pandemoniac elation of the moment, the men of both clans ran into each others' arms. They called each other 'brothers in Watcherness' and they exchanged congratulations and friendly ritual insults. They bit their animal skins, shrieked while throwing all their blood-lacquered wooden staffs in the air, laughed loudly at themselves when the staffs fell down on their heads, victoriously pissed on the living walls and, as could be expected, broke every plass statue and every piece of furniture in the hall. They also started a fire in one corner, but nothing serious.

Untouched by the wave of collective delirium, Fornan the crocodile went to congratulate Bobros. "You have achieved what all grand commanders before you could only dream of – unity between the magi!"

"And we are going to need it!" Bobros made it clear he had no illusions. The present victory was a clear sign of their power over the warp, but it was nothing more than a temporary fix-up. The global network of fields was still on the verge of agony. A new collapse could happen any day.

Fornan's eyes flared with admiration. One of the things he respected most about Bobros was his constant realism and lack of complacency. "You know," the general grinned, "I *do* believe you have been sent to us by the Watchers!"

Bobros answered with an explosive salvo of roaring laughter. Then he walked to Afran Kesborn and Samoan, who were chatting together like two uncles planning their niece's marriage. He took both of them by the hand and walked them to the balcony. Together they faced the crowd of giants who had assembled in Proclamation Square.

Bobros lifted his arms, raising the hands of the necromancers. "The warp is saved!" he announced with the Voice. "Glory! Glory to the Watchers and their sons!"

The crowd of more than ten thousand gave a long ovation.

Bobros took advantage of this memorable moment to make the great announcement he had been planning in the last weeks. When silence was restored, he gave a short discourse, "Today, the people of the entire kingdom are contemplating our glory. Tomorrow, they will get a taste of our anger! Tremble, kingdom! The fourth and fifth battalions of the Green Guard will be setting off south in the coming hours. Tremble, kingdom! The time of the Nephilim is coming."

The crowd responded with the ritual stamping, making Proclamation Square shake. "Tremble-tremble-tremble-tremble...!" their war cry was like the rumbling of ten thousand drums. They could already smell torrents of blood, and they loved it.

Voices rose in the crowd, "To the fish market! To the fish market!"

"Yes! Yes!" they started running, brandishing the clubs they had conveniently brought with them. What better place than the newly rebuilt fish market to celebrate this glorious occasion?

From the balconies, the sorcerers and the necromancers smiled affectionately, wishing they had the time to go and celebrate with them.

18.8 The lost jewels

In the dark bowel, Woolly stopped walking, looking down at the trickle of sewage. He was so completely overwhelmed that for a few seconds he blanked out like a sleeper.

From the clear fountain, Szar pulled down the Eagle's Light into the catacomb. He put his hand on Woolly's shoulder, "I'll tell you something. Once, not long after Elyani had been taken to the tower of Malchasek, I was in my courtyard, blaming the gods. Alcibyadi turned up and she yelled at me, 'But what do you think? That's what the end of the kingdom means! We are *all* going to lose the ones we love!' That's what she said. And you know what?"

"Mm?" Woolly mumbled.

"It didn't make me feel better at all."

Woolly briefly smiled, but without letting go of his miserable attitude.

Who did you Point-speak to this morning?" Szar asked him.

"Amanzor. Florabella's father."

"Who's Florabella?"

"The girl I would have married if Henrick the Hunter hadn't started that dreadful melt-wave that destroyed Amanzor's chapel." Woolly's gaze was caught by yet another rat.

"I see. And what did Amanzor say?"

"They still haven't found the bodies of my adoptive parents. But Florabella is alive. Amanzor has spoken to her through darkness visible. She got trapped in a basement under piles of plass rubble."

"Good chance she'll be rescued?"

"They don't know. Laminindra is such a mess at the moment. The blow-up of the warp has left about half the people dead. But you know what? Amanzor said he had forgiven me for destroying his chapel."

"How lawfully generous of him."

"Yes and no. His chapel used to have thin walls. The one they rebuilt for him after the melt-wave was made of thick fortified plass. It's one of the only buildings that has survived the catastrophe."

"So you're a hero, now. No wonder Amanzor has asked you to come back. Of course you wouldn't have to stay, but your uncles would be so happy to see you, be it only for a week, and who knows? You might even be able to save Florabella's life," Szar sighed. "That's if you don't meet Aphelion on the way, of course."

"I don't know why, but I have the inner certitude that if I go there now, she will live," Woolly ignored the warning.

"The timing is *so* perfect. That stinks like Ahriman!" Szar raised his voice.

"Think so?"

"You are about to be initiated into Thunder, remember? The Prince of Darkness wants you in his army."

"I wonder why!" Woolly sighed sarcastically.

"Listen, Woolly of Thunder," Szar looked straight into his eyes, "in five lawful days, when you go through the initiation, do you know what is going to happen? A whole pile of karmic crap is going to be lifted off you – that bad luck that sticks to you wherever you go... see what I mean?"

The words had zeroed in. "You bet!"

"The Masters of Thunder are going to get it out of your system. And all you have to do is keep quiet and let your ass be lifted up into the Fields of Peace. But you can be sure of one thing. In the five coming days, the world is going to invent one thousand fantastically good reasons for you to rabbit away. Just listen to *one* of them, and you are lost." He Dragon-shouted, "Lost!"

Woolly swallowed high. This time, he had heard the warning.

Szar started walking again. "Let's go up. I'll pay Mouridji a quick visit. When you go back to the rainbow chapel, could you tell everyone I want to speak to them in one hour?"

"An announcement?"

"If we want our Wizards to survive the pestilence, we're going to have to take drastic measures."

They walked up the narrow winding stairway and each went a different way. The temple was refreshingly still. In the hours that had followed the mending of the warp, the animals of the temple had become quiet again. It gave everyone some rest, but for how long?

When Szar knocked at Mouridji's door, there was no answer. He tuned into the space. She wasn't in her bedroom. He let the Point-guided corridors take him to her.

The guidance field led him to the courtyard of the priestesses of the Dawn of Creation, where a small crowd of priests and priestesses had assembled.

Teyani came toward him. She was grave. "That's it," she announced through the space, "the last two priestesses of Dawn have left their body."

It created an immense feeling of loss in Szar. "The pestilence?"

"No. They just let themselves drift away."

Their death was bound to cause a wave of despair. True, the pestilence was the worst in living memory. But there had been pestilences in the past. They had not lasted forever. True, pieces of bad news were falling like leaves in autumn. Didn't the Law say, 'Bad tidings fall, the kingdom stands'? But if the lineage of the priestesses of Dawn had come to an end, then, from the very authority of the Law, the end *was* near.

Of all the catastrophes of the last days, this was the one to hit Szar the deepest. He *liked* these priestesses. Dragon above, Dragon below, he found them beautiful. Immensely poetic. He thoroughly enjoyed the fact that their magic was so completely beyond the range of his understanding. They looked so useless, hardly capable of looking after themselves, and yet they were an indispensable foundation of the Law. They were small and humble, and yet strong enough to send him unconscious to the point of wetting his pants, he who had survived the Great Warriors' arch-violent initiation. They made him feel wonder, and respect for the kingdom.

Gone. Forever lost. Once broken, their thread to the Dawn of Creation could never be restored, with the exception perhaps of the very end, when the cosmic cycle will be very tired because all will have been accomplished. The fields of the chapel of Dawn would of course be captured in the Archive. But, Gervin had warned, only the surface of their hymns could be recorded. Enough, perhaps, to make people fall unconscious and wet their pants, but nothing like the real Dawn of Creation. Their lineage was one that could never be restarted from the Archive, nor from anywhere else. Only from the dawn of the next creation.

"Sad, sad!" he whispered.

He didn't want to fool himself, especially after having lectured Woolly so well. Still, at times it *did* feel like he was being hit by the misery of the entire kingdom.

"Hey! Hey! What's happening to you?" Teyani read the profound distress in his eyes.

Szar didn't answer.

She took his arm. "Let's go for a stroll."

She walked him to her courtyard, White-warming him up by telling him unimportant things. Taking him in her wings.

He received the warmth. He even smiled a few times.

Then his Dragon warned him that it was time to go to the meeting he had convened at the chapel of the Field Wizards.

The Wizards were waiting for him in the rainbow hall. They were in a sombre mood. The giants' show of force had sapped their confidence. In the last weeks they had started to believe their fortress impregnable, a sure guarantee of the safety of the Archive stones and the success of the transfer. After witnessing the raw power and the insolent ease with which the giants could manipulate the warp, they had realised that the enemy was far more terrible than they had thought. If the giants could mend thirty-five holes in the warp in a matter of minutes, then surely they could also flatten the fields of an entire county. How far did their powers go? What or who could stop them?

These were the burning questions on everyone's lips.

Not in the mood for a discourse, Szar let the Dragon speak for him. A short talk, during which it was announced that the pestilence was spreading fast. Thirty priests and priestesses and twenty lawful attendants had already left their body. Another three hundred people could be expected to die in the coming days. The more the pestilence spread, the stronger its spirit – and the more difficult to treat. It was reaching the point where the safety of the rainbow chapel was at risk. Szar therefore asked the Field Wizards to stay within the chapel. Visitors were to be limited to a strict minimum. The food that came from the central kitchen was to be cleared with the Voice before being eaten. Anyone showing the first signs of the pestilence – black spots in the aura – was to report immediately.

It was a painful sacrifice that was asked of the Wizards. All of them had friends and relatives in the temple, to whom they could no longer talk through darkness visible since the chapel had been shielded. But they understood and agreed to the confinement. Lord Proston decided to give up his royal suite in the palace of the High Priest and move into the rainbow chapel.

The practical details having been sorted out, Szar returned to his Point-hall.

And to pay homage to the priestesses of Dawn, he danced.

18.9 Celestial smile

Later that day, Teyani used her key-stone to reach Szar through the shield of the rainbow chapel. "Are you better?" she Point-asked.

"Too busy to think."

"Busy doing what?"

"Dancing."

Teyani Point-laughed. "I wish I could come and dance with you."

"Come by all means," he Point-invited her.

"I can't. There are sick priestesses everywhere. They all need attention. And the disposal of the dead is starting to take unlawful proportions. The priests of the cremation ground are finding it increasingly difficult to cope."

"Well then..." Szar pulled a good reason from the verticality of the clear fountain. "I need to speak to you urgently."

"Really?"

"Dragon-serious. It's about the security of your sixteen White Eagles."

"That sounds serious enough. I'll come when I finish a few visits I promised to make."

She arrived at the rainbow chapel late in the evening. She was exhausted. Her feet ached from having spent the day running from room to room. Her heart ached from having to comfort people who, she knew, had only a few more days to live, while warning their loved ones to expect the worst. She felt dirty from the filth of the world. There were smears of blood on the sleeves of her dress, fetid smells sticking to her clothes, and the dark moods of souls in pain sticking to her aura.

Curiosity gave her a breath of fresh energy. What was she going to discover in the Point-hall this time! Without announcing her presence, she just walked in.

It was a sober field. Just voidness. There was neither top nor bottom. And no walls. There were no stars, no clouds of light. Just a black empty space which spread in all directions ad infinitum.

In the middle, Szar was dancing. He shone with a pale silvery glow. So did Teyani's body as soon as she entered.

In this naked space Szar's slow movements took on a strange dimension. It was subtle. At first, Teyani didn't notice anything particular. Yet, as she came closer she realised that Szar was both moving and motionless at the same time, in an artistic Pointful way that made no sense to the common mind.

"How does he manage to do that?" she wondered. She tried to imitate him but couldn't. Each time she started moving, she stopped being motionless.

She frowned, "Point-tricking me again?"

The field turned her words into a shining multidimensional crystal-like 'thing' which, even though it exactly conveyed her meaning, resembled a human voice only remotely. Teyani laughed, creating another volley of Point-fixtures.

Szar didn't interrupt his dance.

The White Eagle sat in the void, not far from him. She closed her eyes for few seconds and relaxed. She loved the presence in the space. Totally familiar, and not just because of the Eagle-ness that accompanied Szar wherever he went.

When she reopened her eyes there was a silvery cup floating in the air in front of her. She turned towards Szar, who was still motionlessly dancing in the womb-like silence. "This, I *know*, is a trick," she smiled. For the Point-fun of it, she acted as if she was being fooled. She took the Point-illusory cup and drank the white Point-illusory beverage.

"Voof! What is *that*?" She felt a fantastic upsurge of life force. In a split second, the worries of the day were forgotten. She jumped to her feet, more refreshed than after twelve hours of sleep in the Eagle's wings. "How did you do that?" she asked with astonishment.

Szar didn't answer. He kept dancing. But she knew he was not ignoring her, because she was enveloped by his presence.

She strolled around the Point-hall. What a bizarre space! No purple glows as in darkness visible. No streams or fields of stars. Just void. And yet totally different from the odd spaces of the Flying Dragons. At one stage she felt herself going up. "I must have reached a staircase," she thought, even though there were no steps in sight. Looking back, she realised that Szar seemed to be ascending at the same time as she was.

She sat down, trying to find out what was Point-going on in that space.

It was at that moment that she saw her.

She stood up, "Oh... is that you?"

She could hardly believe her eyes.

An explosion of light.

She burst into tears.

Elyani was slowly walking towards her.

She shone with the dazzling, ultra-fast-moving Point-ness of the gods.

Her face was glorious.

She wore a long, complicated black dress that radiated peaceful presence and upheld the dark voidness of the hall.

So it was *her* presence! Szar was dancing in the goddess' energy.

"Oh, my child!" Teyani cried.

Elyani smiled. But nothing like a human smile. An Eagle's flight. A dancing forest. With the absoluteness of a celestial pine tree's trust in God.

Someone came into the hall.

Teyani looked down and bit her lip, fearing that Elyani would vanish.

To her surprise, the man was standing at least thirty lawful feet below her level. It was Ashok, who had come to borrow one of the stones from the crypt. "Sorry to disturb you, Commander," the young man apologised. And he stopped, as if to speak to Szar. But he didn't stop at the spot below which Szar was dancing. He stopped at sixty lawful feet from there, a place where Teyani could see nothing.

Ashok, however, thought he was standing in front of Szar, to whom he explained, "This Underworld bitch of a pest-removing field is playing up with us again. I'd better use one of the hermaphroditic stones before the rest of the Wise Witches' cats kick the bucket." And after hearing what he thought were Szar's words, he walked to a corner of the hall, noticing nothing of Elyani's Point-effervescent presence.

Reassured, Teyani contemplated the ascended goddess, "My child. My child... you are so beautiful."

The kingdom seemed so meaningless compared to her smile.

Lofty clouds reflecting infinity from the sky of the gods.

Elyani did not speak.

In one gaze, with the unbearable lightness of her world, she lifted all sorrows off Teyani.

Far away from the grey mists.

Szar walked toward them. He was no longer wearing his brown gown but an extraordinary white outfit that smiled Eagle-ness in all directions.

Together, they Point-laughed.

In a glimpse they visited Elyani's house, which by then had at least two infinities of rooms and as many doors leading to other worlds, and they found themselves in the large clearing around the godly dwelling. The river had grown a lot since Szar's first visit. Patagendradass happened to be drinking there. Szar played the molten star for him. Elyani and Teyani danced, moving and not moving at the same time, the pine forest of ardent aspiration humming in the background. From there they Point-reached the fig trees of Life and the shores of the Molten Sea, where they met long-haired Mareena, dressed in her wisdom-emerald dress.

She was singing her love to Apollo.

Under the sky.

Revelation Sky, who breathes the breath of the One God and knows all the answers.

They watched the horizon, where the Molten Sea and the sky of the gods are One.

When Teyani reopened her eyes to the kingdom she was in the Point-hall, standing by Szar's side. Dressed in his brown gown, Szar was still dancing the motionless dance.

Thirty lawful feet below, Ashok came back into the hall to return the hermaphroditic stone. He was accompanied by Gallagher. They stopped somewhere where Szar was not and Ashok said, "Thank you, Commander, it worked like a charm. Not one damn rat left in the catacombs. But I'm afraid we're going to have to deal with a major complaint from the Wise Witches! Not *one* of their cats has survived our field."

"Yes, but this time we think we've understood why it happened," Gallagher went on. "It *must* be because the fucking cats have been eating the fucking rats."

18.10 The gold of the last days

Two hours before dawn the next morning, when Szar arrived at the door of Woolly's bedroom, he was hit by a serious dose of golden energy.

"Good, good," he said, Point-recognising a field at play.

Just as he was about to knock, the door opened.

He walked in and found himself immersed in a sea of Naga-ness. Wherever he looked there was gold, and only gold.

In one corner of the sea, a bright golden cloud welcomed him, "Praise the Lord Melchisedek, brother!"

"All glory to the Lord Melchisedek," Szar sent a loving wave.

"Like my new field?"

"Lawfully stunning!"

"I tell you, it's great for depression."

"I can see!" Szar *did* feel like laughing, and it *did* come from the manipulating power of the field. "Are you ready, brother?"

"Well, well... sort of."

"What do you mean, sort of?" Szar told him off.

"I mean, yes. Considering. I should say, yes."

"Let's go. Gervin is waiting for us downstairs."

When they emerged out of the sea, their auras were still ablaze with golden specks. It made Woolly's round mass of curly cream-fair hair look like a saint's halo. The young man walked decidedly and wilfully, with the air of someone who's *not* going to blow it this time, and stuff you Ahriman! "I will not let your Aphelion bastard shit on me!" he thought, holding fast to his resolve *not* to take the first boat to Laminindra.

In the rainbow hall, when Gervin saw his two golden disciples walking in with such superb assurance, he whistled loudly. "So we *are* ready!"

Teyani, who was standing by his side, was moved. After ample praising of the Lord Melchisedek, she asked Woolly where his saint's halo came from.

"A new field. For a new life," Woolly nodded seriously, his head slightly bent to one side.

"Any news from Florabella?" Gervin asked.

"Nothing good," Woolly remained composed. Very composed. "They believe she is still alive. But they haven't yet excavated her from the rubble."

Gervin took his arm and went to speak with him in one corner of the hall.

"Florabella is such a tacky name!" Teyani whispered to Szar, pulling one of her most evocative faces.

"I know," Szar couldn't agree more. "It's frightening!"

"What about the ghost Nephilim?"

"Nothing new. We keep scanning."

"Thank you for yesterday. I still feel like dancing with joy."

"Don't thank me, thank the goddess!" Szar raised his hands towards Elyani's house.

"I will. You haven't told me what you wanted to discuss about the security of my White Eagles."

"I think we should isolate them from the rest of the temple. The pestilence is getting out of control. It's bound to hit them, unless we do something. I thought of taking them into the rainbow chapel, but... too dangerous. As soon as the giants arrive in the temple we'll be their main target. So why don't you move to the quarters of the priestesses of Dawn? We could easily wall off the surrounding corridors and leave only one entrance with solid doors."

Teyani hated the idea. "The chapel of Dawn is far too far from the chapel of the Eagle! And what about all our friends?"

"And what if your baby Eagles catch the damn pestilence?"

"Better die from the pestilence than be locked up and die from something else. Anyhow, everything is in place now. The abode on the edge of the triangle was finalised long ago. The Sons of Apollo are prepared to fish my Eagles and direct them there as soon as they leave their body. Whether they die now or in a few months will not make much difference."

The tone left no space for discussion. Szar capitulated, "All glory to the teacher!"

Teyani kept on, "My priestesses' morale is as high as the Golden Shield. Come and sit with us during one of our rituals and you will see – burning White!"

Melchard entered the hall. He praised the Lord Melchisedek with his warm, melodious voice, but looked terribly tired. "Sorry to be late," he apologised. The dust in his aura showed he was coming from the cremation grounds.

Teyani went to take his hand, "Hard work?"

"No worse for me than for you. But let's forget all this for a moment. How is our candidate?"

"Well, Master Melchard. Well!" Woolly gathered his energy, preparing himself to answer the questions.

It was at that moment that they realised there was more to Woolly's new field than met the Point. A vibrant wave of Naga-ness – or was it Maryaniness? – rose from the ground.

"Oh, I know this energy!" Melchard looked down, recalling his unforgettable encounter with King Vasouk.

Szar tucked his head in his shoulders and rested on the Dragon, wondering if the building was about to start trembling. But it all remained very lawful. Nothing more than a joyful golden spirit wafting in the air.

Maryani was tuning in, but delicately this time. She had learnt her lesson.

"The Nagas are watching!" Gervin warned with a smile that showed he didn't mind.

The cross was formed. Woolly stood to face Gervin. Melchard, on Gervin's right, stood in front of Szar. And the White Eagle went to stand by Gervin's side.

It was a simple ceremony. "Yes," Woolly was ready to answer the traditional questions. "Yes," he was aware that the initiation entailed great perils. The way he looked up and sighed loudly left no doubt about that. And "yes," he was ready to face forgotten sorrows and dark corners of himself, a sport at which he had already had plenty of experience. A loud, enthusiastic "yes" showed he was ready to be shown the future. It was one of the things he found the most blasting about that initiation. Yet when he saw the depth of compassion in Gervin's eyes, he started having second thoughts. And when it came to facing the Prince of Darkness and the abyss that threatens humanity, he hesitated, not least because Gervin looked like he was seriously not joking.

"Yes," he answered unassuredly. But hearing that he was becoming a candidate for being tempted by Ahriman suddenly made his mind question whether he was about to make a colossal trans-life mistake, when he could have such a quiet death with Florabella in the ruins of the used-to-be temple of Laminindra.

A slight jolt shook his Dragon from below.

"Yes!" Woolly immediately exclaimed, standing up to his full height.

And that was it for the trials of the day, because he had no problem with facing the Great Light, even though he couldn't see why the Great Light would want to face him.

When Gervin asked him what he wanted, deep inside himself, he pulled a face and declared, "I need a change. Things really can't go on like this. They simply can't go on like this."

Gervin and Melchard burst out laughing.

"Expect surprises!" Gervin gave his word. "Your initiation is imminent. It will take place in the Fields of Peace."

The hall was instantly filled with buoyant golden light.

Far away, on the Jeremitzia river, Maryani was standing on the deck of a small boat. She took baby Lehrmon in her arms and danced with joy.

The child smiled with fascination at the golden bubbles, thoroughly enjoying the near-Voice song that Maryani was projecting onto him.

"Is something happening?" Alcibyadi asked.

"Woolly is on his way to the Fields of Peace!"

18.11 A lot had happened in the kingdom of the mists

"Mouridji?" Szar called, knocking at the door a second time.

"Come in," she answered, both annoyed and happy he insisted.

She was lying flat on her bed, her eyes fixed on the blank ceiling. She didn't invite him to sit down.

He stood by the side of her bed. "How are you today, my good Mouridji?"

She shrugged her shoulders, as if nothing mattered.

Luciana had just died. Her cremation ceremony had taken place a few hours earlier.

The atmosphere was thick and gloomy. It wasn't just Mouridji's sorrow. The sickness of the warp made the space of the temple more polluted by the day. Dark astral fumes, heavy energies, dark moods.

"We haven't seen you at the rainbow chapel lately," Szar tried to engage the conversation.

Mouridji didn't answer.

There was a long silence during which Szar carefully examined her aura. She was clear of black spots, but her energy was pale.

"Have you decided to die, Mouridji?"

"Why stay in a world that is being abandoned by the gods?" she said.

"Are they really abandoning us?" Szar looked up.

"Oh yes, they are. Haven't you heard what's been happening throughout the temple in the last days? The priests stand behind their altars and chant their mantras, and... nothing! No response. No sign in the space to indicate that the gods have received the offerings. They have become deaf to our rituals. They are deserting our chapels."

"Well... that has to do with the fields, not with the gods."

Mouridji was extremely upset, "Do you mean to say that if the gods *really* wanted to rescue our fields, they couldn't?"

"I'm sure they could. If they don't they must have their reasons."

"They don't care, that's what it is. We're nothing better than cattle to them."

"No, that's not true. The gods do care about us," Szar pleaded, tuning into Lord Gana's helmet. "But worlds must pass, that other worlds may be born."

"What kind of world will there be after us?" Mouridji lamented. "You know what your teacher has predicted. Most of the great priestesses and priests of our time will be completely blind to the Spirit-world in their next life. They will be even worse off than simple folk, because something inside them will remember the time when they lived in the Light, and it will hurt like hell. Faced with so much darkness, many of them will even fall into madness, and for as long as five or seven lives."

Now that the pestilence was raging, everyone was suddenly remembering that old prediction of Gervin's. It fed the waves of panic that swept the temple.

"Listen, thinking about this does not help," Szar closed his eyes and took his head in his hands, rubbing his forehead. "Gervin made this prediction more than twenty years ago, to try to get them to awaken. At the time they ignored it. Now, we have to face the situation..."

"It's an ugly situation! What will happen to us when we reincarnate? If the wheel of the Law is no longer there to get us to be born in the lawfully perfect place, then... why wouldn't we end up with the wrong parents, and in the wrong caste?"

It was the first time Szar heard someone like Mouridji mention the possibility that the Law could come to an end.

A lot had happened in the kingdom of the mists.

"If we want to quote Gervin, than we must quote him fully," Szar replied. "The prophet Maveron had warned us long ago. 'Sleeper, awaken!' and 'The days are numbered,' 'The end is coming, and much sooner than they think!' These were his words, and no one listened. Now that the end is upon us, everyone is surprised. Who can they blame but themselves?"

"This is all very easy for you to say, son," Mouridji spoke without anger. "You have been taught by one of the greatest teachers of your time. You have been initiated in all the things one could dream of. And when you depart from this world, there will be a comfortable place for you in the paradise of the Brown Robes. But what about simple people like Luciana?"

"I know. I know," he sighed, reopening his eyes. "I'm sorry, I didn't come to lecture you."

For the first time, she looked at him. "Why did you come?"

He inhaled a long breath. "I came to tell you that I didn't want you to die, Mouridji."

"Why?" she shrugged her shoulders.

"Because I find the world a better place with you in it. As simple as that."

"If I fell sick, would you heal me?"

"If you asked me to, and if you were sure that it's what you want, I probably would," he looked down to his left fist.

"Then why didn't you heal Luciana?" she snapped.

"Because dying from fever in a nice temple is better than starving to death among piles of rubble," he answered, matter of fact, slowly clenching and unclenching his fist.

Mouridji was shocked by the directness of the answer.

She directed her gaze back to the ceiling, wondering whether to become blank or ask more.

"If I were to stay alive..." she hesitated, "do you think I could be of any use to anyone?"

"I think so, yes."

"But why?"

"Because you are not a sleeper, Mouridji."

She kept gazing at the ceiling silently.

He could see she was thinking deeply.

"I'll give it some reflection," she said after a moment.

He took her hand. "Please do. I'll come and visit you again tomorrow." And he left.

She didn't say good bye.

Coming out of the portal of the female wing, Szar met a procession of Salmon Robe priests. Following the straight path of the Law, they were on their way to the cremation ground. They carried the body of an old priest dressed in a bronze gown.

Artold recognised him and greeted him, "Praise the Lord Melchisedek, Szar of the Brown Robe! How are you, my friend in the Law?"

"All glory to the Lord Melchisedek, Artold of the Salmon Robe! I am well."

Artold's lovely smile hadn't changed a bit. "I am well indeed, thanks to the Good Lord Melchisedek! And how are your parents, my friend in the Law?"

Putting his hand on Artold's shoulder, Szar tuned high in the clear fountain and called on the compassion of the Mother of the Light.

Artold waited a few seconds. No stereotyped answer. He gave a lawfully polite nod and resumed his walk to the cremation ground, following his Salmon friends.

18.12 The gift

As Szar was returning to the rainbow chapel, an old priest of the Angels of Dawn stopped him and lawfully saluted him.

"All glory to the Lord Melchisedek, Mossin of the Grey Robe," Szar responded, immediately noticing pestilential black specks in the old man's aura.

Mossin was not coughing, but he looked dried out and exhausted, his face about the same colour as his gown. "Tell me, Szar of the Brown Robe, did your teacher really say that when we come back for our next life, the Law will have been destroyed, the gods will have withdrawn their presence from the kingdom, the land will be only chaos and desolation, and we could be reincarnated as savages or pigs?"

Dragon-still, Eagle-open, Szar wished he had gone home through the catacombs.

Mossin was staring at him, anxiously waiting for the answer.

"Help, Master Gervin!" Szar called through the Point. "What am I supposed to tell this man?"

The Thunderbolt Bearer Point-answered, "Tell him that tomorrow at sunrise in the central crypt, Gervin and the Masters of Thunder will make him a high gift, something that will help him immensely in the Great Journey. Tell him he should go and prepare himself to receive this gift by cleansing his soul."

Startling news! Until then, Szar had never heard his teacher openly declare the name of his lineage. "Gervin and the Masters of Thunder?" he Point-asked for confirmation.

"You have Point-heard rightly!"

Szar repeated the words.

Mossin's eyes flared with hope. He took Szar's hand. "Thank you. Thank you!" And he lawfully took leave.

Szar watched him walk away, wondering what that superior gift was about. After Voice-projecting a low-pitched 'sss' sound on his hand to cleanse it of the vibrations left by Mossin, he went straight to the enclave of the jewels. Via the roofs.

Arriving there he found the door of the aquamarine chamber open. He walked in, his heart open with reverence, feeling welcomed by the living walls to which so many of his memories were attached.

But when he saw Gervin, who was sitting in closed-eye meditation, he exclaimed in consternation, "Oh, no!"

"Praise the Lord Melchisedek, Szar!" the melodious voice welcomed him as usual.

Szar fell on his knees. "Oh, no!"

The left side of Gervin's aura was covered in black specks.

Gervin opened his eyes, shining his profound compassion into Szar.

"You..." Szar had tears in his eyes. He couldn't believe what he was seeing. Gervin, the great warrior of the Spirit, the indomitable clearer backed with the full power of the lineage of Thunder, the healer who had saved Marek the Great Warrior and many others, the magnificent man was half-eaten by the pestilence.

"You are not going to let this thing kill you, are you?" Szar's voice choked.

Gervin nodded gravely.

"But it's absurd! If you wanted, you could clear it from the entire county. Will you not even let me heal you?"

"Peace, man of the Law! Peace! The time has come for me to go. I am going to do it in the way which allows me to give the most to the good people of our temple." Seeing how devastated Szar was, he spoke to his Dragon, "And I am going to need your help."

It didn't work. Overwhelmed, Szar remained silent.

In a glance, Gervin pulled him high up in the light, into an immense space where lightning-like shafts were bolting in all directions. Caught by extravagantly fierce Point-winds, Szar had to call on his Flying Dragon nature not to fall on the floor, and for a blessed little moment he found himself face to face with a massive cloud of Gervin-ness that smiled at him from the Edge of Highness, igniting every speck of Spirit inside him, up-lifting his Gana-helmet and making it revolve faster than the spheres of Melchisedek, so that all that was left was exalted Szar-ness spread throughout the sky of the gods, holding Elyani-ness by the hand and Point-contemplating the vastitude of Gervin's beingness. In full knowing.

In full understanding.

One aeon later, when Szar regained perception of the aquamarine light in the room, he still felt an overwhelming pain in his heart, but the depths of that pain resonated with the vastness of the Earth.

It was White-Eagle-simple.

He loved Gervin.

Gervin was about to go.

The Earth cried through his heart.

"I am going to need your help," Gervin repeated.

No thoughts, just Dragon, Szar held the space of rolling Thunder above his head and gave a nod.

Gervin held Thunder-contact with him. "Tomorrow, I will make my final gift to the people of Eisraim: a grand ritual to the Lords of Destiny. A rare practice. It's been one hundred and twenty years since it was performed in Eisraim. A privileged man I am, to be able to give something of this magnitude."

Szar let the Great Dragon of the Deep inhale a long breath for him. "What ritual is this?"

In a glance, the two men remembered the day when Szar had asked his first question: "When a man has no idea what he should say or do, as when the Law has not been taught to him about this particular point or course of action, what is it that he should do?" At the time, it had been such an immense effort for him.

"It was such a dumb question!" Szar thought.

"It made me so happy," Gervin remembered.

He went on explaining about the ritual, "It calls on the Lords of Destiny to soften the karma of all those present. Karma is a mysterious force. Once an action has been performed, its karmic consequences are no longer in the hands of human beings but in those of great angels, the Lords of Destiny. A man cannot take on himself the karma of someone else. But if his Spirit is strong enough, he can reach the Lords of Destiny and call on their clemency, so to speak. But this ritual is more than a mere invocation. Extremely powerful occult mechanisms are involved, which literally *burn* people's karma."

"Is leaving your body part of the ritual?"

"A mighty breath of Spirit flares at the time of death. When a master departs from the physical plane, this flaring can take proportions of considerable magnitude. I will use it to fuel the ritual, just as my master Orest used his death to fuel the clearing of Erriba."

"Does it really have to happen now?"

"The pestilence is spreading fast. If I wait, too many of our friends will already have gone," Gervin shone with smiling compassion. "I want them to die in lawful peace. Many of them have just started realising that the sleeper's life they have led will not guarantee any spiritual future for them. They find themselves in front of a huge dark hole that is about to engulf them. Their next lives will be a nightmare, far from the presence of the gods, far from the light of higher worlds. Nothing can avoid this. I can't help them awaken in a matter of weeks. But with the power of Thunder my ritual will reach the lofty Lords of Destiny, and their fate will be softened."

Szar looked down to his left fist, which he couldn't get himself to clench. "What will be my task, tomorrow?"

"You are in charge of all the preparations. Teyani will help you organise the central crypt. Tomorrow a number of pilgrims will be coming from Lasseera. The pestilence has not reached there yet. I don't want my ritual to cause an epidemic in their temple. I want you to make Dragon-sure that none of them catch the disease while they are here."

"How many pilgrims are we expecting?"

"Three hundred, perhaps."

The enormity of the challenge made it. Szar *did* manage to clench and unclench his fist, under Gervin's affectionate smile.

"Anything else?" Szar asked.

"Yes. If all those ghost Nephilim are lurking three hours away from the temple, it *must* be because they intend to pay us a visit. Tomorrow, we are going to have to be particularly careful."

Szar pushed his lips forward and nodded.

After this, the two men remained silent, drinking each other's presence.

"Life without Gervin..." Szar tried to imagine. It was inconceivable.

"We shall meet again in the Fields of Peace," Gervin whispered.

Resting on the Dragon, Szar let his tears flow. "How will I ever be able to thank you, Gervin of Thunder?"

"Oh, from that point of view you are a lucky man! Normally, the only real thing a disciple can do to thank his teacher is to make the teachings work – realise the states of consciousness and the powers that were communicated to him. But in your case, with all the things I have asked you to do... in the coming months, you will be able to keep thanking me from morning to night with your work!"

"All glory to the teacher!" Szar prayed the Mother of the Light to give him the strength to deliver the Archive stones to the Plateau of Sorana.

"Another thing I will ask from you. Not as a teacher but as a friend. A personal favour," Gervin said with the heartness of the Brown Robe.

Dragon above, Dragon below, the Great Warrior listened.

"Please, please take care of Teyani. She will not abandon her body, she will stay here and serve the temple. These are not going to be easy times for her. Tomorrow morning Lehrmon will arrive from Lasseera, and he will stay here for a few days. This will be the last time she sees him. After losing Elyani, and Alcibyadi, and me, and him, who will be there for her? You, and no one else. Please, take care of her. Be her friend."

"That will be a joy, Gervin. She is the Whitest Eagle. And she is so much like you."

"Tell her that," Gervin smiled. "It will make her happy." Then he closed his eyes for a short while. "In the last twenty-nine years, we have spoken to each other at least three times a day, except when I was far away, of course. She is bound to feel... an emptiness! And as you probably know, she will not come with me to the Fields of Peace. Not yet. Her destiny is to join the Eagle, on the other side of the Golden Shield. So this will be a real separation."

Tears pouring from his eyes, Szar was shaken by lightning-knowingness.

It came from so high, the certitude was clear-fountain absolute.

It was limpid, thunderous, final – his destiny was *not* to stay in the Fields of Peace with the Archive people.

His earthly self bit his lip, horrified at the idea of not being reunited with Gervin.

The Thunderbolt Bearer shone. "That which is will always be. Why grieve?"

And as Szar's earthly self did not find these words reassuring at all, Gervin added, "Don't worry. Our friendship is only at its beginning."

18.13 The things Eagles tell each other when they meet

As he was walking in the Point-guided corridors, Szar called Mouridji through darkness visible, "Have you decided if you want to live?"

"Not yet," the Purple prophetess sounded gloomy.

Szar told her the news of Gervin's grand ritual to the Lords of Destiny. "There is a lot to prepare for tomorrow," he concluded. "Would you like to help me?"

She hesitated a few seconds. "No," she finally answered.

"I understand." And from the White-Eagle-ness which shines beyond time, he added, "I love you Mouridji."

She did not reply.

"But let me tell you something. You had better turn up at the ritual tomorrow. You can take this as a threat. If I don't see you there, I'll come and take you by force."

The voice channel remained silent. But from the White Eagle, he knew that she had smiled.

Arriving at Teyani's door, Szar felt abysmally empty. He raised his hand to knock but stopped and stayed still, contemplating the spheres of Melchisedek from his Flying Dragon nature.

What a beautiful Web of Love.

So little. So frail. And yet so deep.

A child-infinity, growing up under the compassionate smile of the Mother of the Light.

Only a few spheres of remoteness away, the arch-mathematical Flying-Dragonness of the Great Ant whispered in his ear, "Turn round!"

His hand still in the air, he turned round and contemplated the laurel trees in the alley. The vomit of the warp had made them sick, their leaves marred with unlawful yellow spots. To heal them Teyani had projected the Voice. A massive Word injection, judging by the dazzling White glow on the leaves.

"See?" the Great Ant whispered.

In the courtyard the lawn was desperately green, with not one purple blossom left. The energy lines of the earth were dark and thick. "They stink!" Szar's earthly self told him after a quick nostril-wriggle.

At the crossing of two earth lines, he noticed a small heap of earth.

"Yes. There!" the Great Ant voiced from remoteness in its usual archetypally strict and infinitely poetic tone. "Friends of your friends."

It was an ant heap. It had burst out of the lawn like a pimple.

Around it, the earth lines didn't stink.

Teyani, who had sensed Szar's presence arriving a few minutes earlier, wondered what was going on. She came out of her apartment and found him lying on his side on the grass, contemplating the small ant heap. She lawfully greeted him.

He was so absorbed in his contemplation that he didn't hear her.

She bent down and placed her hand on his shoulder. "They're a pest, aren't they? Never seen that before! In the last three weeks they have wrecked the lawns throughout the temple. I wonder how we could get rid of them."

He turned toward her, plunging a beyond-the-Fault-of-Eternity Flying Dragon's look into her eyes.

"Voof!" she marvelled.

But where was that tiny body? Calling on Space Matrix, he pulled himself back into the spheres of Melchisedek, then into the kingdom.

"No!" the Flying Dragons spoke through him.

"No?" Teyani, who fully knew what trance states were about, patiently held his energy.

"They are friends. Don't kill them," he declared with extreme gravity.

"Kill... who?" Teyani asked.

Having finally landed in his body, he found himself White Eagle again. "I meant the ants," he resumed his normal voice, and he sat up.

"Travelling far?" Teyani's eyes too were red from crying.

"Everything is relative," he looked down to his left hand, which was covered in ants.

She sat on the lawn by his side. They spent a few minutes talking to each other, but without words. There was so much to say. The kind of things Eagles tell each other when they meet. The Mother of the Light loved Gervin for aeons and ever. In the Fields of Peace the Masters of Thunder had built an Archive hall designed especially for visiting Flying Dragons – Archive Hall Seventeen, based on the marriage of the light of Space Matrix with that of the Eagle. Not far from there, Barkhan Seer kept adding wonders to Archive Hall Four – Teyani's hall. Adjacent to Archive Hall Five, evidently. And since there is no time in Highness, why wouldn't Teyani come back immediately, that is, as soon as she and the Eagle began their Great Lovers' Dance. That we may fly together.

"Gervin said I should tell you how easy I find it to be your friend because you are the Whitest Eagle and because you are so much like him," Szar concluded.

Gervin was right. It made her shine.

"There is a lot of him in you too," she said.

For Szar, that was by far the best news of the day.

For a few seconds they held the silence that preceded the creation, then they started talking business. It sounded straightforward. Prates of the Salmon Robe would prepare the ritual gear and gather the seventy-two priests who were to assist Gervin. Szar would take care of security issues and make sure the pilgrims from Lasseera didn't return home plagued to the eyeballs. Teyani, Melchard and Lehrmon would be the masters of ceremony, organising the proceedings in the central crypt. Provided all of them worked all night, it would probably be fine.

"If you want to serve the Masters of Thunder, you have to be ready to work hard!" Teyani summarised her twenty-nine years in the temple.

"I bet the master is doing this to us on purpose, so we don't have time to grieve," Szar stood up, ready to set the Dragon in action. "And if..."

He was interrupted by a voice-channel call from Mouridji. "Suppose I changed my mind..." the prophetess said tentatively.

"Suppose!" Szar twinged his beard.

"Would it still be possible for me to help?"

"Mm... probably!" the White Eagle rejoiced in Highness.

"Well, I'll help, then. What shall I do?"

"One thousand people need to be informed of tomorrow's ceremony. Would you like to be in charge of passing on the information?" Teyani suggested.

Fortunately, it took only minimal arguing to convince the prophetess that yes, she was undoubtedly the best possible person to perform this task. After which she immediately started voice-channelling all her friends.

As Szar was about to leave, Teyani asked him, "By the way, what was that story about ants?"

"From our friends in remoteness. I haven't completely digested the concept yet, but there should be a way to cleanse the temple's astral muck by connecting our ant heaps to the Flying-Dragonness of the Great Ant. Expect surprises!"

18.14 From Eisraim to No Limits – an outbreath

It was early in the afternoon. Szar was in the central crypt when he received an emergency Point-call from Khej, "We just located them. Only half an hour away from the gates of the temple."

"The ghost Nephilim?"

"Yep! The large group. But only thirteen of them, not fifteen like last time. Meaning the other two could already be on the outskirts of the temple."

"Ah, damn it!" Szar Point-swore. "Just what we don't need. How did you locate them?"

"They were spotted by one of the field sensors we laid in the forest around the temple. Short-range devices, exceptionally sensitive. Once caught, the Nephilim immediately neutralised the field. We've lost them again."

"And they know that we know they're coming. Any clues to tell us if they are giants?"

"No, but they're armed to the teeth. At least six thousand soft-stone weapons of high venom intensity."

"Oh, gods! Are all the Field Wizards inside the chapel?"

"Of course."

"Engage the emergency procedure we rehearsed yesterday," Szar Point-ordered. Looking around him, he sighed in consternation.

The central crypt was packed with more than seven hundred people, completely unaware of what was about to fall on their heads.

He turned towards Gervin. The Thunderbolt Bearer was sitting on a low platform that had been erected during the night. For this unique occasion he wasn't wearing brown but a long black ritual gown with a large complicated cap, the black colour symbolising his drawing in people's karma and afflictions.

In front of him, a narrow thirty-lawful-feet-long corridor delineated by two walls of fire made of thousands of ritual oil lamps. On each side of the corridor, outside the walls, stood seventy-two priests of the chapel of the Eternal Fire. Since dawn they had been pouring their Voices into the walls of fire, shaking the space with their mantras, creating mighty flames of Voice-light that rose up to the ceiling.

Priests and priestesses walked up the corridor, one after the other. They started at the end opposite the Thunderbolt Bearer, holding eye contact with him. They walked towards him, slowly, their aura scorched by the ardent fervour of the Voice-reinforced flames, their column of Spirit blasted by Gervin's power of Thunder.

At that moment, Ram of the Salmon Robe was walking inside the walls of fire. Before Point-calling Gervin, Szar waited for the young man to reach the end of the corridor.

The passage lasted thirty seconds.

Thirty seconds to change a destiny.

What Gervin did during these thirty seconds, this no one could tell. But the energy in the crypt was awesome.

It was the last of the great rituals in Eisraim. Everyone knew it.

Moved by hope, they had all come. Those who were too sick or too old to walk had been carried on stretchers. All those who were suffering from the pestilence had come in the first hours of the morning. After them, a massive Voice-clearing had been operated, aimed at eliminating the pestilential energies. Then all the other priests and priestesses had gathered in the hall for the second part of the ritual. According to Szar's plan, this was to last until the evening. Then another extensive Voice-clearing would be performed in the hall, and the pilgrims from Lasseera would be invited in.

But now there was only thirty minutes left before the Nephilim arrived at the doors of the temple.

Gervin's energy was shining like a lighthouse at the Edge of Highness, but his physical body looked increasingly tired. The night before he had used the Voice of Thunder to clean up the black specks from his aura and strengthen his body. But this ritual was terribly taxing on him. As the hours passed, dark rings appeared under his eyes, his face marked with fatigue. By midday he looked five years older than at dawn.

When Ram arrived at the end of the corridor he fainted, like dozens of priests and priestesses had done throughout the morning. While Namron's men were picking him up, Szar established a Point-token-ring with Gervin and Lehrmon.

"We have a major problem. Delay the passage of the next person," he instructed Lehrmon, who was standing at the other end of the corridor. "We've located the larger group of ghost Nephilim. Only half an hour from the temple gates."

Gervin Point-exhorted, "Well, son, you know what to do."

"Shall we not interrupt the ritual?"

"Impossible. Now that the forces have been started, they cannot be stopped."

"What do we do if the Nephilim attack this hall?"

"If they come here, it will be the end of them. Giants or no giants, with the power that is above my head at the moment, they don't stand a chance. And if they decide to kill everyone from a distance with their stones, then... it will be a blessing for our people. The opening created by the ritual will project them high in the spheres. Don't worry about us. Go and fight! Thunder is with you." And he showered Szar with power.

Szar felt a tremendous wave rising in his heart – an exalted breath, an irresistible force to strike and triumph. "All glory to the teacher!" he whispered, his aura flaring.

His Warrior's mind cautioned, "I hate to say this but I don't think Lehrmon should stay here. Far too dangerous. We can't afford to lose him."

"True," Gervin agreed.

"What shall I do?" Lehrmon Point-asked.

"Leave the temple immediately. Return to Lasseera," the exalted force spoke through Szar.

"He is right," Gervin seconded from Thunder, and he showered Lehrmon with the same power.

Lehrmon raised both arms. For a few seconds he turned into a huge flame of white energy. "All glory to the teacher!" he shouted with the Voice.

The entire audience followed him, raising their arms, "All glory to the teacher! All glory to the teacher...!"

When the light faded and Lehrmon's face could be seen again, he and Szar exchanged a last glance.

If everything went right, they would meet again at the Archive rendezvous. If anything went wrong, they might never see each other again.

Szar remembered the Edge of Highness, "I won't say goodbye!"

"We shall meet again at the Plateau of Sorana!" Lehrmon Point-pounded.

Szar turned toward Gervin. He knew this was the last time.

The Thunderbolt Bearer plunged his gaze into him, sparking a time crossing.

For a Point-second, Szar found himself in a field of stars.

A small dot in front of him. Philadelphia Six.

The *same* irresistible light of victory flaring inside him, "Hiram! Hiram! Stand up and fight, Brother Knight!"

"Forever with you, Gervin!"

The space set ablaze with gigantic flames.

From Eisraim to No Limits will only take an outbreath.

In the central crypt the crowd was still acclaiming Gervin, "All glory to the teacher...!"

Lehrmon turned toward Teyani, the depth of his love for her Point-packed in one second.

"We shall meet again in the Fields of Peace," she Point-whispered.

He slowly waved his hand at her as he used to when he was a child, and he started running to the main door.

"Forever with you, Gervin!" Szar fixed this last image of his master in his Flying Dragon image bank. Then he too started running, to a small door that led to the catacombs.

Less than a minute later he was at the rainbow chapel.

For reasons of security the Field Wizards were not assembled in one hall but spread in groups of three throughout the cellars, apart from Woolly, Shyama and Ugr, who had taken position behind the gates of the chapel. Szar joined Khej, who had been coordinating the rainbow team.

The tall young man was in the rainbow hall with his friends Ashok and Gallagher. "Nothing new, Commander!" he announced when Szar arrived.

"The good news is, they had to destroy our detection field in the forest, they couldn't camouflage themselves within it," Gallagher pointed out. "As soon as they reach the temple, we'll know."

In the last weeks more than two thousand similar detection fields had been laid in the temple, and nearly as many in the catacombs.

"The stone from Jex Belaran is in the death chamber. All fields have been engaged at their highest level of power," Ferman Point-reported.

"What's the death chamber?" Szar asked.

"The low crypt at the other end of the cellars, where we keep the bait stones," Khej filled him in.

"How come I've never heard that name?"

"The crypt was renamed this morning when you were out, Commander. An idea of Lord Proston and Lorenz. Because they nearly killed themselves while they were checking the fields."

Lorenz was one of the most conscientious men in the team. Proston was even more skilled than him. "How could that happen?"

"The fields in that crypt are so complicated! Even with the Point-keys, descending into it has become a life hazard."

"When the giants get there, they're in for a few surprises!" Gallagher sneered.

"Yeah!" Khej and Ashok rubbed their hands.

"Youthful enthusiasm!" Szar gave an affectionate grin. As far as he was concerned he was in no hurry to see the Nephilim commando storm the chapel. "I'll let you monitor the detection fields," he told them. "I'll go and take position in my Point-hall. Has that been renamed too, by the way?"

"No, no, Commander. We still call it your bedroom."

When he reached his 'bedroom', a field of stars with an enormous blue Flying-Dragon cloud in the middle, Szar quickly Point-liaised with each group, checking that every piece of the master defence-system was in place. The Field Wizards were monitoring the detection fields, ready to activate the deadly field weapons that had been laid in various parts of the temple.

"I bring down the night," Szar Point-warned everyone, and he activated the most powerful field of the entire edifice.

Instantly, the hall turned black.

It was a pitch-black darkness akin to the Great Night of distant spheres of remoteness. In it, one could not even see one's own aura. All forms of light, subtle and physical, were devoured. If a flame was lit, total darkness remained. The field had been woven from a resonance between the chapel of the priestesses of Dawn and Flying Dragon spheres.

In that cosmic black night, he sat, and waited. Ready to detonate the weapons of their massive field-arsenal.

No thoughts, just Dragon.

18.15 Rats, cats and ghost Nephilim

The first alarm signal arrived twenty minutes later.

It came from Balavan. "Something's moving. In the eastern part of the under-temple. Judging by the vibration, it could be a rat."

"Impossible!" Gallagher was Point-adamant. "We killed them all. What if it was a damn Nephilim disguised as a rat?"

"It would have to be a really small giant."

"Or a damn smart one," Ashok Point-pointed out.

"There is a simple way to find out. Engage the pest-removing field and see what happens," Woolly said.

"Oh, but there we have a problem! The Wise Witches have just brought back three dozen kittens from their trip to Eisraim city. With that field, I can't guarantee anything. If their cats cark it *again*..." Ashok bit his lip, bitterly remembering the sewage of abuse he had had to take three days earlier.

"Friends, the Archive is at stake," Master Ferman intervened. "I'll wear the responsibility for this. Engage the pest-removing field!"

Five seconds later, Balavan Point-announced, "I'm getting a death vibration. From the rat. Now everything is still."

"Couldn't that be a trick of the Nephilim?" Gallagher Point-questioned. "What do you think, Commander?"

"I picked up the vibration. Point-looked pretty much like a rat to me. And if it wasn't, then he'll be here in a matter of minutes."

"Let me tell you, this time, with the Wise Witches, it's going to get u-gly!" Ashok mumbled.

Hidden in the cosmic night, Szar nodded, thoughtful. And he started the slow opening movements of the black dance.

There followed a long, tense Point-silence, broken only by the "Lawfully fine!" signal that each team of three sent every two minutes.

Twenty minutes later, they were still waiting.

"They should be here by now," Ferman was becoming nervous.

"Could they have found a way to camouflage themselves from the short-range sensors?" Lord Proston asked Khej.

"They would have to be *very* smart to do that," Khej wiped the sweat off his forehead. "So far, no one in this chapel has ever been able to produce *one* field that remained unnoticed within the sensors' range."

"Anyway, camouflage or no camouflage, they *should* be here by now," Ferman was pacing around in his crypt.

Szar brought Point-silence back, "Friends, let's keep practising the superior art of waiting!"

A trying experience.

Minutes stretched into aeons.

Finally, an hour had passed, and they were still waiting.

"Shall we remain on the highest level of alert?" Ferman asked.

"Absolutely!" Szar ordered.

"We keep detecting Point-blowing energies coming from Gervin's ritual," Lorenz informed them. "In the forty-one years I have worked in this chapel, I have *never* seen anything like it. Even when the gods descended into the crypt at the end of Elyani's ritual, we didn't register this kind of intensity."

"Could the ghost Nephilim be using this to camouflage their presence?" Gallagher hypothesised.

"Mm... perhaps, after all. When will the ritual be finished?" Lorenz asked.

"Not before late in the evening," Szar answered. "At least another nine hours. When it finishes, you will know."

The waiting game went on.

And on.

Two hours later, Szar was still slow-dancing in the night.

That was when Woolly broke the Point-silence, "Guess who is at the doors of the chapel!"

Everyone held their breath, ready to let hell break loose in the fields.

"The Wise Witches, of course!" Woolly Point-exclaimed.

"That was predictable!" Ashok was not the least surprised.

Szar closed his eyes, holding his head in his hands. "What do they want?"

"Revenge, by the sound of it," Woolly reported after a few seconds. "You have no idea how rude they are. It is... shocking!"

"Tell them we lawfully apologise for this most regrettable accident."

Woolly Point-came back one minute later. "They say it's not enough!"

"Use diplomacy, Woolly!"

A few minutes later, Woolly reported, "They are still banging on the door, unlawfully demanding to speak to our most senior Field Wizard."

"Shall I go?" Ferman asked.

"No way," Szar ordered. "We don't open the gates for anyone."

"What shall I do?" Woolly asked in his most exquisitely polite voice.

All Szar could think of was, "Practise unconditional love!"

And they kept waiting.

And waiting.

Two and a half hours later, Khej asked, "Can we eat dinner, Commander?"

Szar had no objection. "As long as you keep your positions, feel free!"

"Are the Wise Witches still at the door?" Ashok wanted to know.

"Yes, but they stopped knocking an hour ago," Woolly reassured everyone.

The dinner break brought some relief. But later in the evening, after another two interminable hours of the same nerve-wracking waiting exercise, Lord Proston lost patience and summarised everyone's feelings by Point-deafeningly hammering syllable after syllable, in the highly distinguished intonation of a man who had spent twenty years at the King's palace, "But... what, do, these, sons of a Nephilim bitch, *want*?"

It was the first time the Field Wizards heard him swear, and that in itself brought great relief to everyone, apart from indicating that he had now become a full member of the team.

Szar decided to convene a meeting, asking each man to keep monitoring their detection fields at the same time. To receive them he turned the cosmic night into a peaceful silvery dimness that shone from a simple but elegant field of stars on the dome of the hall.

When the twenty-four men had gathered in their commander's bedroom, Proston vented his exasperation, raising his fists, "This does not make any sense! Not any sense *at all*! It's been weeks, now, *weeks* that these damn ghosts have been hovering only a few hours from us. What the hell do they want?"

This did not really bring any new element, but everyone felt much better hearing it being screamed so loudly, and with so much eloquence.

"He's a great talker!" Khej whispered to Gallagher with sincere admiration.

"Shut up! Don't interrupt him," Gallagher told him off.

"We are assuming that they have been on their way to the temple today," Lord Proston went on. "That is probably a wise tactical assumption, and I am not suggesting that we release our vigilance. But who says it is true? They could well have been staying in the forest for entire weeks, completely unnoticed by us."

"True!" Szar agreed.

"The only thing we know is what they want: either the stone from Jex Belaran or the Archive stones," Ferman added.

"But what the Ugly Underworld are they waiting for? Why don't they come and get them?" Lord Proston thundered.

"That's the key question. Perhaps they expect us to die from the pestilence," Woolly suggested.

"Or they hope the windmills of the Law will become so rotten that we won't even be able to maintain our defence fields," Gallagher conjectured.

"If it can make you feel better... this waiting must be even more taxing on them than it is on us," Szar pointed out. "Can you imagine the nightmare? Constantly moving, sleeping in forests, having to not only hide themselves but also to Point-conceal their thoughts and their presence, day and night."

"Yes, actually," Ashok declared enthusiastically, "that makes me feel much better!"

"Yeah!" they all agreed, including Lord Proston.

"They must be damn good soldiers," Ferman pulled a face. "Do you realise what an elite force they are!"

"Excellent attitude!" Szar approved. "Never underestimate your enemies."

"As far as I may know," Lord Proston declared, "there are only two places in the kingdom where Point-combatants of this standard are being trained: Jex Belaran, and the Eastern Peninsula. I can't see any group of Renegade Hunters being capable of sustaining such a level of pressure."

Which always brought them to the same questions: Why would the Hunters of Jex Belaran want to steal their stones, since Szar had offered to supply them? And if the giants were behind all this, then what was the Green Guard waiting for? Why didn't they strike?

Szar walked over to Gallagher who, he had noticed, had been grinding his teeth since the beginning of the meeting. "I'll show you something!" he told him, and he violently projected his right fist in front of him while exhaling a savage, threatening "Ha!" black-dance scream.

Gallagher jumped in surprise.

"Do the same!" Szar ordered.

After a quick frown, Gallagher threw his fist in front of him, imitating Szar's yell.

"Makes you feel better, doesn't it?" Szar gave a broad smile.

"Mm..." Gallagher nodded. "Very much so!"

"Can I do it too?" Khej asked.

"By all lawful means!" Szar lifted up his palms.

The younger Field Wizards joined in, under the puzzled look of the not-so-young ones.

Then Lord Proston decided to have a go at this new and exciting exercise, totally unheard of at the court of the King. "Ha!" he yelled like a furious animal.

Lorenz and Ferman followed him, and for two or three minutes the commander's bedroom resounded with some of the wildest screams ever heard in the temple of Eisraim.

Then Szar clapped his hands, "Excellent! Excellent! Now we can all resume our positions, and keep waiting."

18.16 The flight of the thunderbird

Around midnight, Lorenz was the first to pick up the wave, "That's it! Here they are! A massive field deflagration in the central crypt."

Khej quickly followed, "Throughout the temple, the field sensors are wobbling."

"A huge field explosion," Woolly confirmed.

"Two of the major defence fields on the eastern side of the temple are out of action," Gallagher was making great efforts to keep his Point cool.

"Another explosion?"

"Maybe. Could also be an after-wave of the deflagration in the central crypt."

"The main defence shield of our chapel is shaking!" Shyama threw in.

"All the field sensors in the western catacombs have stopped responding," Khej added.

"In the central crypt, the blast is going on, and on!" Woolly informed them. "A huge dose of energy. Call Teyani to know how many people are still in there."

"Teyani isn't responding!"

"Call Melchard!"

"Melchard isn't responding either."

"Damn it! Damn it! They're *all* dead! Anyone else we can call?"

"They're the only people with key-stones to the shield."

"What does Barkhan Seer say?" Woolly asked.

"We're not receiving anything from the Archive halls," Ashok answered. "The connection with the Fields of Peace has gone blank."

"Another field deflagration in the central crypt," Lorenz detected. "Oh, gods! This one is even more intense than the first one."

"But where is the enemy?" Ferman asked. "Is anyone picking up a Nephilim signal?"

"No!" they all reported.

"How can they be blasting the central crypt with such intensity from a distance?"

"It doesn't look like a normal soft-stone deflagration," Woolly remarked.

"All this points to something coming from the giants," Ferman concluded.

"There is another anomaly," Woolly said. "The venom intensity is strictly limited to the central crypt. Nothing coming from any other building."

"A third deflagration. Even bigger!" Lorenz could hardly believe his Point.

"Our defence shield is still shaking, but holding fast!" Shyama updated.

"Holding superbly, but for how long?" Khej questioned.

"Another deflagration, this time in the chapel of the windmills of the Law," Lorenz reported.

"That was to be expected. Any field explosions of this magnitude would cause a resonance in the windmills."

"Friends, friends, there is no attack," Szar intervened. He was slow-dancing in his hall. "What you are picking up is Gervin's departure. The last of the Thunderbolt Bearers is leaving his body."

There followed an awe-struck Point-silence.

"Everyone remains on guard," Szar ordered. "The enemy could try to take advantage of this to launch an offensive."

"Two more field deflagrations have just taken place in the central crypt," Lorenz reported.

"Let's try to fix the eastern defence fields," Ferman ordered. "Shyama and Balavan, I want you to hold the levels while I am sending reawakening impulses."

"Holding!" Balavan responded.

They were interrupted by a message from Melchard. "The ritual is nearly completed. I am now walking out of the central crypt. Gervin and Teyani are still inside, but not for much longer."

After what had happened in the crypt, how could they still be alive?

"How many people were in the central crypt?" a flabbergasted Ferman asked.

"The last pilgrims from Lasseera left an hour ago. Only three people were left: Gervin, Teyani and I," Melchard answered.

"Will you tell us what happened, Master Melchard?" old Lorenz asked.

"Magnificent, and terrible. The end of one world, to prepare the birth of a new one. Gervin has given to each and every person to the very limit of what they could receive. Now, when Teyani walks out, all entrances to the central crypt are to be sealed. No one is to ever get in there again." After a pause, he Point-added, "I have a message from Gervin for all of you: 'We shall meet again in the Fields of Peace!'"

Two minutes later, Lorenz exclaimed in wonder, "This is... this is incredible! The energy in the central crypt is back to normal! It dropped completely in one second."

It was done. The Thunderbolt Bearer had left.

18.17 Woolly of the Apocalypse

The next day, Szar was working on his Point-hall when he received an emergency message from Khej, "Someone has broken into the temple! An unregistered Point."

"Where?"

"On the far eastern side, where the defence fields blew up during the night."

"Isn't Woolly working over there at the moment?" Szar asked.

"The unregistered Point is walking in his direction."

"Woolly isn't responding to our Point-calls," Gallagher warned.

"What kind of signature are you reading in the intruder's Point?"

"Bizarre, bizarre... tune in for yourself, Commander," Khej redirected the signal to Szar's Point.

"Mother of the Light!" Szar exclaimed, and he started running full speed. "I want everyone on highest alert again! Khej, you are in charge of the chapel. If in two hours you haven't heard from me, you engage the disaster procedure."

"Oh, gods!" Khej swallowed hard. The disaster procedure consisted of recalling Lehrmon to the temple and expediting the Archive transfer during the very next available period of paradoxical clarity. It was to be implemented only if all the Brown Robes of Eisraim were killed.

Meanwhile at the eastern extremity of the temple Woolly was on all fours, field-tinkering at the crossing of two alleys.

"Praise the Lord Melchisedek, Master Melchard!" he exclaimed as he saw the tall man in the brown gown. "I hadn't seen you coming!"

But as he stood up, he immediately realised the man wasn't Melchard. "Who are you?" he frowned.

The man's face was hidden by the hood of his brown gown. "Can't you guess?" he asked in a magnificently melodious voice.

"Aphelion!" Woolly froze.

"Right and righteous, my young friend," the man bent his head.

Woolly tried to Point-call Szar, but no answer.

"Don't waste your time! I have isolated us, to give us time to talk. Anyhow there is *nothing* to fear. I have not come here to attack you, nor to ask anything from you."

Woolly wasn't taken completely by surprise. He had been expecting the visit. What he didn't expect, however, was to hear such a warm and exquisitely harmonious voice. "Go away!" he articulated calmly.

"Not before giving you what I brought for you!" Aphelion ignored the rebuke.

"I will not accept any presents from you, Aphelion!"

"Wait till you know what they are!" Aphelion laughed. "They are not for you, anyhow. They are for your friends. Let's start with Maryani. Send her this piece of information: she and her friends must change their plans. They *must not* go to Sheringa city to catch the boat and cross the ocean. The giants are about to invade Sheringa. Tell them to go further south, and everything will be all right. Otherwise... mm..." he sighed ominously.

"Maryani is protected by all-powerful forces," Woolly declared with total faith.

"You speak like this because you have never seen the giants in action, son. If you knew what they are capable of... anyhow! Up to you to decide. Now, my next present concerns your Florabella. I have helped her. She will not die. She will come out of the rubble unscathed, all fresh and beautiful. Lately, she has been thinking about you a lot, this I can promise you!"

"I don't want your help, Aphelion!" Woolly hammered.

"No! No! No! No! No!" Aphelion said in his gentle voice. "It would be silly of you to refuse these gifts. They are free! I have not come here to ask you to follow me. I have come because at the moment your people and I have common interests. My King isn't keen to see the giants take over the kingdom. So I am going to give you a few tips to help you defend your temple. For a start, I have taken a good look at your defence system. Not bad. Not bad at all! But in the southern part of the catacombs... there lies the weak point. Would you like me to show you where?"

Woolly shook his head. The instructions he had received from Gervin and Szar were crystal clear: do *not* go for a walk with Aphelion, or you might find yourself three counties away before you have time to realise what has happened.

"All right, all right!" Aphelion took no offence. "Here is what you will do: detonate a soft-stone weapon in the left focus of the network of sensors and by resonance, you will see how easy it would be to flatten the catacombs' entire field network. I know the southern quarters well, by the way. I used to play there when I was a child. Have you visited the crypt of the Black Mother?"

Woolly was putting facts together. It flashed into his mind that there *was* a flaw in the sensors system of the southern side. It was obvious. How the hell could he have missed it?

"See!" Aphelion smiled. "Well worth taking. Now to the defence shield of the Wizards' chapel. It is excellent. But in its present state, the giants could flatten it with a massive field deflagration in the chapel of the windmills of the Law. Let me show you how we, servants of the King of the

World, would fix this problem." Aphelion invaded Woolly's clear fountain with the supermind blueprint of a shielding device for the windmills' chapel. "Do you like it?"

It was Pointly superb – the work of a genius! An extraordinarily imaginative and finely-woven web of details that took every single possibility into account, while shining the light of superior simplicity. Woolly, who was a great admirer of intelligence, was astounded. He bit his lip and contained his tears, filled with awe but devastated by his own mediocrity, as when a sculptor who has laboured all his life is shown the perfection of a work of art crafted by the gods.

"Now, to your overall defence system," Aphelion immediately went on. "Your network of fields is good. But let me show you how you could improve it." Again, he blasted Woolly's mind with an artistically constructed piece of mathematical art, both phenomenally complex and limpid at the same time. "Here are a few other possible blueprints..."

In the space of one minute, a torrent of splendid ideas ran through Woolly's mind. It was an exalted awakening, a prodigious thought-stream coming straight from the most lucid levels of archetypal intelligence. Had the experience come from Gervin, Woolly would have been ecstatic. It was the manifestation of a beauty he had always dreamt of but never been able to reach, even remotely.

"You like supermind, don't you?" Aphelion said in an affectionate voice.

Clenching his fists and contracting all the muscles of his body, Woolly slowly shook his head.

"But why deny it? We can be enemies and yet share common passions, can't we? I myself have always loved irony and intelligence. They go together so well. People who are devoid of irony are always complete idiots, in my opinion. Come on, not for the love of you but for the love of intelligence, let me show you how to speed up your mind."

"No, Aphelion, I don't want your intelligence!"

"Intelligence is but an energy. Like all forces, it can be used either way. It's not because..."

"No!"

"Son, you are not behaving very intelligently at the moment. You are wasting precious opportunities," Aphelion sighed. "Let me show you something. My King has made me a promise: when it comes to fighting the final battles, he will give me the brightest mind of my time. So gigantic, it will take more than ten thousand years before the physical vehicle to receive it can be built. This is what it will look like."

What started flowing through Woolly's Point was completely beyond words. It exponentially superseded anything he had ever dreamt of. Even when conjecturing about God's mind, Woolly had never imagined such summits were possible.

"This," Aphelion commented, "the Masters of Thunder will *never* reach in the physical world. Not during this entire cosmic cycle, anyway. Of course, in their high airy-fairy worlds of Spirit-nebulosity, they may have grand visions. But down here, in the physical world, they will *never* attain this perfection of intelligence."

After a few minutes, Aphelion suddenly disconnected the supermental flow.

Woolly fell back into his normal mind. It was like having his wings cut – falling back into darkness after seeing the light. After having tasted the real food, he was sent back into his world of starvation.

"Want to see more?" Aphelion offered.

Woolly pulled in a long inhalation and held his breath. In the dull, empty darkness in which he felt floored, every cell of his body was crying to be reunited with the exalted force.

"No," he said after a few seconds.

"Don't be an idiot! The truth is, this is where you belong. And deep inside, you know it very well. You are not like them."

"Not like who?"

"Gervin, Melchard, Lehrmon and all these other glorious Brown monks."

"I *am* like them!" Woolly held fast.

"Stop the nonsense my boy, will you? Take a look at yourself, for hell's sake! Take Lehrmon. Have you ever *once* seen Lehrmon get aggravated? Have you ever once seen him lose his serene composure, even when Alcibyadi was leaving the temple with his child? Lehrmon is part of the glorious ones. The glorious Barkhan Seer himself sent him to the glorious Lady Teyani, who brought him up. At the age of seven, he was already wearing a brown robe. Or take Melchard. Melchard was born so perfect and so pure that the King told me not to waste my time with him. A lost cause!" Aphelion laughed sardonically.

Woolly felt a stabbing pain in his chest, as if the whole filth of his life was bursting out in the open.

"You are *not* like them!" Aphelion hammered into him with a shockingly vigorous near-Voice threshold. "You are not going to tell me you want to compare yourself with Gervin, are you? Glorious Gervin, who incarnated in the kingdom straight from Highness. Throughout his childhood, Barkhan Seer and the whole lineage of Thunder looked after him from the spheres of the glorious. No wonder by the time he was your age he had already conquered all the powers of the Brown Robe, and was begged by His Supreme Majesty the King of Atlantis to join his court! Or take Szar. Just *look* at him! He is from another world. Everyone wants the darling of the Flying Dragons, from the Fields of Peace to Revelation Sky. But you, Woolly..."

In the abysmal greyness of the mists, Woolly was desperately looking for a thread to himself, his miserable life laid in front of him like a spilled garbage bin.

"Woolly, face it. You are *not* like them. You are *not* one of the glorious ones," Aphelion's voice drilled into his heart. "The Brown Robe initiation is *not* going to work for you. You're going to make a mess of it, as you have always messed up everything. And it's a shame, because you are an intelligent fellow. This supermind I have shown you, it could lift you out of..."

The blackness in Woolly's head became so thick that he could hardly hear what Aphelion was saying. There was no hope. It was like falling into a pit.

Ugly tears.

A world without hope.

Blacker than black.

At the bottom of the pit, there was one thread of light.

Only one thread.

Who cared?

Falling. For a long time.

Deeper and deeper.

One little thread leading to the light.

"No!" he shouted, taking the thread.

"No!" he interrupted Aphelion, standing very straight and letting something huge speak through him, "True, Aphelion, I am not one of the glorious ones. True, I have had an ugly life! True, every single thing went wrong, one after the other. But today, for the first time, I am *not* going to mess it up! If you want to kill me, do it now!" he shouted. "Otherwise, Aphelion, go and get fucked! I will *not* follow you."

After a few seconds of silence, Aphelion burst out laughing.

It was at that moment that Woolly noticed Teyani standing at the end of the alley in front of him. Turning to the alley on the right, he saw Melchard, standing in the distance. Turning to the alley behind him, he saw Szar running – but in a strange slow fashion, as if time was half-frozen.

Turning inside, he remembered what hope felt like.

"All right! All right!" Aphelion resumed his most friendly voice. "I will leave you for the moment. I have enjoyed our talk immensely, young man. If you change your mind and decide you want to know more about absolute intelligence, feel free to call me *any time*." Putting a paternal, protective hand on Woolly's shoulder, he concluded, "We shall meet again, one way or another." And he turned on his heel and walked away, taking the alley on the left.

Trembling, incredulous, Woolly watched him slowly disappear in the distance.

As soon as his ominous silhouette was out of sight, Szar's race took on a furious speed. And Woolly realised that Teyani and Melchard were not standing, but walking fast.

He burst into a flood of tears.

Five seconds later, Szar reached him and took him in his arms, holding him Dragon-tight.

Woolly collapsed, letting out volleys of loud sobs.

"You did much, much better than me!" Szar whispered into his ear, and he burst into tears with him.

18.18 Death terrible

Szar was practising Point-drills with Khej, Ashok and Gallagher in his hall when Shyama called from the gates. "Mouridji wants to speak to you, Commander."

"Scan her and send her here."

Leaving the young men to their practice, Szar Point-arranged a corner of the field into a cosy blue space filled with discrete Space Matrix harmonies.

When she arrived, Mouridji looked around her with curiosity. "I thought this place was much larger! Did you compartmentalise?"

"Sort of," he White-Eagled her in his wings.

Sadness had deepened her wrinkles. She looked much older than a few days ago, and she spoke a little slower.

"Thank you for your help the other day," he told her. "Everyone was remarkably well-warned. Not one person missing."

"It was not an easy task."

They remained silent, listening to Space Matrix's mysterious whispers.

"I have come to ask your advice," Mouridji said after a moment.

"What about?"

"My friends who are dying. I don't know what to do with them."

"Do?" he wondered what she meant.

"Yes. There *must* be something to do. We can't just let them suffer like this. It's inhuman," she said with a mixture of sadness and outrage. "Haven't you heard what's happening? Instead of just letting death take them away, they try to fight and cling to their body. It has never happened before, *never*! And you know why they're doing that? Because they are terrified. Terrified of dying. Can you believe it?"

He nodded in understanding, silently.

"All the lawful things which they have repeated all their life," she went on, "all the 'Trust death as you trust the Lord Melchisedek!' and 'Death takes you from one station of the Law to another, why fear?' and all the other beautiful verses – completely forgotten. They're so scared of what's waiting for them in their next life that they prefer to bear with the disease and the pain, rather than let themselves drift. Long ago, a Blue priestess made a prediction (you wouldn't remember, you weren't yet born). It said, 'When the mists turn black, then all will fear death.' At the time it made everyone wonder, because no one could imagine the mists would ever become as dark as they are now, nor that people would ever be afraid of death. But now... it has all happened."

Szar listened, from as high as he could.

She tried to read a sign of hope on his face, but could not find any. "What's really difficult for them to understand is that the gods are not doing anything to help them," she said without bitterness. "All these high priests and priestesses have spent their entire lives serving the gods with their rituals. They found their joy in the presence which the gods shed in their chapels. Each time a decision had to be made, they asked the gods through oracles. And they *always* followed the decisions of the gods. The gods were so much part of their life... how can it be that suddenly, everything is about to be taken away from them?"

"No, they didn't live with the gods," Szar replied in his softest voice. "They lived with the fields."

"But they followed the Law!" Mouridji argued. "Is it that, after all, there was something wrong with the Law?"

"That's it!" Szar smiled. "If we can't blame the gods, then let's blame the Good Lord Melchisedek and his high angels!"

There was so much White softness in his smile that old Mouridji smiled with him.

"I know it's probably an unlawfully stupid thing to ask you," she went on after a few seconds, "but if your teacher foresaw all these tragic events, did he not also see something that these poor people could do, now?" With all her heart, she appealed, "Tell me, my friend the Master of Thunder, can you help?"

Holding her from as high as he could, he tried to shine the smile of the Mother of the Light onto her.

She waited anxiously. She wanted to have hope in him.

"I am sorry, Mouridji," the wound of the Earth cried through his voice. "There is nothing I can do."

– Thus ends the Book of Death Terrible –

19

The Book of the Fields of Peace

19.1 Woolly's best life

Late in the night, Woolly was woken by a voice from above, "Are you ready?"

He had to think. Florabella was still trapped under the rubble in the ravaged temple of Laminindra. The bodies of his adoptive parents hadn't been found, so the funeral rites couldn't be administered – a major crime against the Law. In Eisraim the situation was becoming grimmer by the day. Three hundred people had already died from the pestilence and at least as many were sick. Among those affected was Antaria, the head of the sixteen White Eagles, and the most important for the team's success. The presence of the gods was fast disappearing from the chapels, creating waves of panic among officiating priests and priestesses. The rats, however, had quickly reappeared. And the fields had vomited a new beast into the catacombs: strange, brownish, six-legged – an insect no one had ever seen before. Meanwhile the Wise Witches, having sworn to avenge the death of their kittens, had lodged the highest possible administrative complaint against the Field Wizards, accusing them of yet another crime against the Law.

Catastrophic news was being received from both inside and outside the county. The prince of Eisraim, a wise man in the Law and a friend of the temple, had been assassinated, probably by his nephew. A phase of political instability was bound to follow – just what the county didn't need right now. But worst of all was the news coming from the east. As foretold by Aphelion, the Nephilim giants had gone on the rampage. Taking advantage of the chaos created by the acute illness of the warp, one of their armies was sweeping the east coast of the kingdom, melting temples to the ground and slaughtering everyone on their way.

The first reports were terrifying. It had taken the giants only one day to exterminate the entire army of the prince of Melankia, their immediate neighbour, as well as twenty-one battalions of the King's army. And in one night of cannibalistic fury they had ransacked the two main cities of Melankia. At the end of the night not one building was left standing, all fields had been extinguished, all animals had been butchered, not one prisoner had been taken. The prince and his family had been eaten alive.

Having finished with Melankia, the giants were now heading south. If they kept up their pace they would reach the county of Sheringa in the coming days, just when the nine White Eagles were due to arrive in Sheringa city to catch their boat and cross the ocean. Following Szar's decision the priestesses had been informed of Aphelion's words. But they had not modified their route, trusting in the Eagle who was directing them. Higher protection or not, Woolly hated to imagine what would happen if the dear women found themselves face to face with demented Nephilim soldiers. But as there was nothing he could do about that, nor about the rest, Woolly gave his answer to the voice from above, "Yes! I am ready!"

He was lifted out of his body and instantly found himself in a cloud of blue light, clear like the sky of the gods.

"Far Upperworld... is this really happening?" he asked himself. "Am I *really* going to see the Fields of Peace?"

His encounter with Aphelion had left him devastated. The words of the emissary of Ahriman had zeroed in. Deep inside himself, something refused to believe he would ever make it to the initiation. His mind kept enumerating lists of reasons why things could go wrong, starting with the fact that in his life everything had always gone wrong. Why should it stop now?

But now that he found himself bathing in this glorious light, he had difficulty clinging to his cynicism.

"Szar," he Point-called, "are you here?"

"Not far from you," the Point-answer carried a warm breeze of Eagleness.

"Am I really seeing the Fields of Peace?"

"Not yet. You *are* in the Fields of Peace, but you're not really seeing them yet."

"Am I doing something wrong?"

"No, that's how it happens when you arrive from the kingdom. At first you tend to project mental constructions based on the world you're coming from. It takes some time before you can see things as they are."

"Where exactly are we?"

"Archive Hall One. Gervin's hall."

"Waooooh!" Woolly jumped with joy. He started running in Szar's direction.

Szar was standing in the middle of a large bubble of White Light. When Woolly saw him, he was astounded. "Is that you? But... you are beautiful!"

Szar's face was not only glowing, it was exquisitely chiselled, as if the Szar who had been left in the kingdom was but a gross caricature.

"So are you," Szar's words touched him like a soft breeze.

"Beautiful, me?" Woolly frowned, wondering if there were mirrors in the Fields of Peace.

"Here, to catch a vision of yourself all you need to do is use your peripheral vision."

It didn't take long before Woolly managed to do that. "Oh! Oh!" he exclaimed with even more astonishment when contemplating himself peripherally. It was like seeing a majestic woolly-haired god with no pimples and no broken nose. "Are they all like this here, or is it just you and me?" he questioned.

Szar laughed, creating joyful ascending waves throughout Woolly's energy.

"Sounds are so different!" Woolly marvelled. "So musical! And you don't just hear them, you feel them caressing your energy."

"A paradise for musicians." Szar held his hands parallel in front of his heart and he whistled like a bird of paradise.

Woolly applauded and tried to imitate him. The whistle was melodious, but nothing like a bird of paradise. "You've come here before, haven't you?"

"I haven't! But there are similarities with the world of the gods. In higher worlds, you can guess a lot just by tapping from the knowingness of your body."

"Through the Point?" Woolly asked.

"No, from the substance of your vehicle of consciousness. All the instructions you need are contained inside it."

"How does it work?" Woolly closed his eyes and tried to tune in.

"Same as in a number of other worlds. When you arrive you are given a visitor's body that allows you to be in that place. The stuff which constitutes the visitor's body is similar to the elemental forces of that world, and so it has an intuitive knowledge of their modus operandi."

When Woolly looked inside himself, what sprang to his consciousness was joy. "This world should be called the Fields of Joy," he sang.

"Look who is coming!" Szar whispered.

It was at that moment that Woolly discovered he didn't need to open his eyes in order to see. All parts of his body were endowed with the sense of sight, which made seeing somehow akin to touching.

Still, he opened his eyes wide with amazement.

Gervin, who was walking towards them, looked thirty years younger. He was not just handsome like a god, there was a multidimensional harmony about him, his features conveying the depth of his being and his manifold soul forces.

"Now his outside is like his inside!" Woolly told himself, fascinated by how much was unveiled by the vision.

Rapt by the beaming revelation, Szar recognised many of the qualities he had intuitively guessed about Gervin. For the first time, he felt his essence standing face to face with Gervin's essence.

The simplicity was total.

No facades. They looked exactly as they were.

In the elated lightness of the World to Come, where joy comes from being and being knows no limits, it was an easy, uncomplicated reunion.

Just being said everything.

And there was so much to be!

Gervin strolled with them through the fluid sky-blueness of Archive Hall One, soaking them in Peace. Silently, they enjoyed seeing each other inside-out. It saved so much explaining.

After a long communion Gervin summarised, "Here, to see is to know."

Gervin's voice, even more than his appearance, struck Woolly and Szar with awe. It covered a wide spectrum and its substance was like warm liquid gold. The sweetness and heartness it conveyed were beyond description. It was pregnant with mysterious, primordial forces that moved the depths of their souls.

"Your voice is like divine nectar, Master Gervin," Szar managed to say.

"This world is a Field of Voice," Gervin shone his smile. "Here, the more you grow in God, the more His Word becomes alive inside you."

"We could sit here and just listen to you until the end of time!" Woolly was melting. He plugged his ears, wondering if his sense of hearing, like his sight, was spread over his entire body.

It made Gervin laugh – a cascade of elated vibrations which created dancing flames in his disciples' hearts.

Gervin began explaining the steps of their initiation into Thunder. First, they were to watch Archive records of their past. Then they would be shown mysterious visions of the future. Finally they would be invested with the power of the lineage.

"Where would you like to start?" he offered.

Satisfied that he could hear just as well with his ears blocked, Woolly dropped his hands. "Master Gervin," he asked the first question, "I want to understand why I feel so much joy. I haven't felt so good since..." he hesitated. "Since..."

"Would you like me to show you the last time you felt as happy as this in the kingdom?" As Gervin spoke, a large three-dimensional image appeared in front of them. "The Ancient Days of the Earth. Long, long before the beginning of the kingdom of Atlantis."

Was it an ocean? More like hot soupish gases.

A strange, blobbish mass of semi-liquid jelly was bubbling its way through the soup.

"You were just about to have a baby," Gervin smiled affectionately.

Szar found the scene rather amusing, especially the ecstatic bloob-bloob sounds which the jelly-thing blurted out.

Woolly, however, was deeply moved. "Oh, God! I remember. It seems like yesterday. And yet it was so different."

"There was not yet any sense of time," Gervin explained, "which is why people remember it as if it was still happening inside them."

Tears in his eyes, Woolly silently watched the blobette coming out of the jelly-thing, while the space was filled with celestial harmonies.

"The miracle of the Angels of the Seed," Gervin sighed. "You understand that you made that baby on your own, don't you? Being a man-woman, you were both its father and its mother."

Woolly nodded. "It was so full. So magnificent."

"That was one of the great advantages of being a hermaphrodite, you could be permanently in love."

"A perfect union. Never any discordance between my two sides. Wasn't that amazing?" Woolly turned towards Szar.

Szar pushed his lips forward and nodded. Yet he couldn't fully relate to the jelly-blob's love story with itself. Seeing how meaningful the vision was to Woolly, he made an effort to tune into the jelly-thing. It took him into a womb-like space in which a deeply internalised fullness resonated with the light of high angels. There were no senses, just vague sensations, and little awareness of the surrounding environment. And yet, at the core of this centripetal fullness there was oneness with limitless spaces, a spreading into vastness of near-Flying-Dragon magnitude.

"Why couldn't that last?" Woolly said with Dragon-deep nostalgia. "We were *so* happy. We had absolutely everything we needed. It was *so* complete."

"An immensely blissful sleeping cosmic consciousness. Precisely because it was so complete, you could have kept sleeping like this until the end of this cosmic cycle."

"Maybe it was sleep," Woolly argued, "but there was infinitely more divinity in that sleep than in the so-called waking state of the people of the kingdom."

"True," Gervin conceded.

"And there was such a deep intuitive understanding of everything."

"True. You could say that you knew everything. The problem was, you didn't know that you knew it," Gervin replied, the harmony of the spheres chanting through his voice.

"Where was Szar at the time?" Woolly questioned.

"He hadn't arrived in our spheres yet. He never experienced the hermaphroditic stage of the early blobs."

"What a shame!" Woolly was sincerely sorry for Szar. "You have no idea what you missed. It was my *best* life!"

Szar sighed to agree with him. But the more he contemplated the burping soft-cartilaginous lump wafting in its semi-liquid environment, the more he was thankful that the Lord Melchisedek had changed Elyani's appearance by the time he landed on Earth.

"I find it difficult to understand how we went from feeling so ecstatically happy to feeling as awful as I have often felt in the kingdom," Woolly reflected.

"A major disconnection took place: the fall." Gervin explained, "You could call it the central mystery in the history of humanity. It involved a number of events that happened more or less concomitantly. The blobs lost their hermaphroditic status, they were separated into male and female blobs. And they fell into a much greater degree of physicality. Until the fall they were hardly aware of the material world. Their consciousness was united with the light of the gods and of high angels, which conveyed to them the presence of the One God. This is why they experienced so much bliss. But after the fall they were confronted with the limits of the material world."

"The light was taken away from them?" Woolly asked.

"That is how they experienced it. But it would be more accurate to say that they were projected into a different level of existence, where they didn't know how to connect with the light."

"Wasn't it a beautiful baby?" Woolly exclaimed with pride, as the newborn blobette was huddling against the enraptured jelly-thing who, wobbling with ongoing orgasmic waves, kept burping bubbles ecstatically.

"The most special blobette in the entire world!" Szar answered without any hesitation.

"You can't understand. It's because you've never given birth," Woolly placed his hands on his belly. "Will you show me how I died in that life, Master Gervin?"

"A tragic accident. It happened not long after the delivery. Your sense of heat got mixed up. You wafted in the wrong direction and were caught in a volcano."

The scene changed. The peaceful gaseous soup was replaced by a fury of gushing winds and red-hot lava. In a matter of seconds, poor Woolly-jelly-thing was cooked into a squid-like mass that blew up after rendering its last burp.

"And what happened to my baby?" Woolly asked anxiously.

"Saved! A compassionate wind took care of it." Gervin showed an image of the blobette. It had already grown up a lot, and was happily bathing in its new home-soup. "It had a good life."

Woolly was immensely reassured. "It looked so much like me!" he marvelled. "It's touching."

Szar bit his lip to stop himself laughing.

"No, it's true!" Gervin told him. "The resemblance was remarkable."

They watched the blobette a little longer, then the image faded. They pondered silently.

19.2 The unfallen world

Szar looked around him. There didn't seem to be any walls or ceiling in Archive Hall One. Just a space. Scanning from the Point, he could not detect any fields like those in the kingdom. Yet there must have been *some* field-like device to project the images Gervin was showing them. When he had first arrived in the hall, he had tuned into the Eagle. He had immediately been surrounded by a cocoon-like halo of White-warming energy. . How could this happen without a field? Before he had time to ask, Woolly continued with the question that had been haunting him all his life.

"I still find it difficult to understand why life in the kingdom is so painful. During the blobs' golden age, we were *so* fulfilled. How could we possibly fall from this summit of bliss to the constant malaise that afflicts people in the kingdom? The more I breathe the joy of the Fields of Peace, the more obvious it becomes that even when they are happy, the people of the kingdom are far from experiencing real joy. What can possibly have gone so wrong?"

"The fall is a profound and multifaceted mystery," Gervin replied. "The loss of the hermaphroditic condition played a major part. There is no doubt that human beings were infinitely happier before the separation of the sexes."

"That is absolutely true!" Woolly pointed an authoritative index finger at Szar, who bit his lip and tucked his head in his shoulders, laughing, but only with his eyes.

Gervin turned towards Szar, "Imagine destiny had made you the gift of a perfect lover, someone who loved you passionately. Someone whose appearance you found the most attractive, and whose mind accorded perfectly with yours. Then imagine this perfect lover understood you totally, always knew when you needed to be comforted, always guessed your desires and satisfied them immediately, and *never* let you down, because your union could not be broken. Then you would know the pleasure enjoyed by those strange-looking hermaphroditic blobs."

Szar was twinging his beard thoughtfully. Seeing the brief flutter of his eyelids, Woolly was satisfied the message got through.

Gervin brought down an image into the hall's field-less field. It was another gelatinous-looking blob, floating in a gaseous broth. "This was just after the separation of the sexes."

The difference with the former blob was not obvious to Szar at first, except that it didn't move, and it didn't burp.

But to Woolly, the vision was shocking. "Oh, my God!" he exclaimed with an appalled expression on his face, his hand on his heart.

Tuning in, Szar understood why. The blob's distress was overwhelming. That, he could relate to. It was exactly how he had felt after losing Elyani. Abysmal grief. A state of utter devastation, as if the core of his being had been ripped apart. For the blob the situation was even worse, because its mind was blank. It had no way of understanding what had happened to it.

"Such a nice, gentle being," Szar commented, surprised by the vibrant heartness that radiated from the blob.

"Amazingly soft!" Woolly nodded. "Was this a man or a woman?"

"A woman," Gervin answered. "Lost in the pit of the primeval broken heart. An agony with no hope, nothing to look for – only a desperate longing for the lost half. The beautiful light in her heart has disappeared. She no longer bathes in cosmic consciousness. But look at this warm breeze caressing her."

"Nature seemed so supportive! Like a huge heart," Szar was moved.

"Nature was still very much like it was before the fall: one big heart. A loving mother who could never get enough of holding her children in her arms and comforting them. But it didn't last." Gervin conjured another image. "This one was Woolly. Thousands of years later."

Another blob. This one was more elongated, and vertical. The atmosphere in which it lived wasn't as thick. There seemed to be a bottom, a firm or semi-firm ground on which to rest, and blurry objects constituted a nebulous landscape.

Szar made himself White-Eagle open for Woolly, wondering how he would react this time. But Woolly didn't seem to be particularly moved by the vision. "I was hardly there. Nothing mattered. Deep inside me, something had disengaged from the world."

Gervin made them tune into the wind, "See how nature had changed! The soup was starting to turn into mist. The rocks had hardened. And the all-enveloping softness had disappeared. This is another essential aspect of the mystery of the fall: it is not only human beings that fell. Nature too lost its connection to the light of the Divine. Just as human beings had been ripped from their hermaphroditic half, so a precious quintessence of life was withdrawn from nature and its elemental forces. The consequences were dramatic. That which used to be noble chaos turned into a corrupt mess. Gradually, very gradually, fire became angry, given to blind violence. The wind became agitated and unstable. The waters no longer carried the infinite sweetness of the Universal Mother. Earth became heavy and inert, opaque to the Spirit and its joy.

In turn, the plants and animals which were now made of these diminished elementals lost the greater part of their wisdom – this wonderful intelligence that animated all things in the early days of the Earth. And the bodies of human beings became corrupt. Life became shorter. The first diseases appeared. All creatures started growing old from the moment they were born. A fundamental loss of integrity had taken place in nature. As a result, nothing could last."

The elongated blob-being fell horizontal and stopped moving. "You died quite young," Gervin told Woolly. "As you said, it wasn't a particularly significant past life."

"So is this why life in the kingdom always ends up being so painful?" Woolly went back to his original question. "We are fallen, disconnected beings, living in a fallen, disconnected nature."

"This covers only half the enigma," Gervin replied. "Look who is coming!"

The blurry landscape disappeared. It was replaced by a gigantic dark cloud, moving in space with superb momentum. The cloud radiated a feeling of formidable strength. It shone with raw power, burning to conquer, ready to fight battle after battle. Its presence was totally devoid of the heartness that illuminated the first scenes Gervin had shown.

"Ouch! That looks rather ominous," Woolly pulled a face.

"But smart. Very smart!" Szar added, jarred by the titanic supermental energy that Point-radiated from the cloud.

"Here, the mystery of the fall thickens," Gervin went on. "When human beings and nature at large lost their integrity, meaning their state of union to the Divine, they fell under the influence of several hierarchies of fallen angels. Beings of darkness permeated all levels of the material world, worsening the disconnection from the light, and strengthening the messy side of chaos. Diseases became worse, ageing became more painful, death more unavoidable. But the influence of dark forces was not limited to the elemental forces of nature. Look at these."

The titan-cloud faded. A group of human-shaped beings appeared, males and females. They looked extremely sharp, their eyes shining with exceptionally intense energies. They were dancing a strange dance that repeated itself in circles, and throwing cords that descended onto the Earth.

"These are not men and women but luciferic beings. Several classes of them cast their venom into the astral bodies of human beings, inflaming their emotions and desires, and thickening the human mind into an opaque veil, blind to the Spirit."

The cords which the luciferic beings had thrown were hooked into men and women. From above, the beings pulled the strings, manipulating people like puppets. And they poured dark, venomous energies into their heads and their hearts.

"From there on, things went from bad to worse. The corrupt human mind worsened the state of corruption of the body. Constant exposure to corrupt elementals made it significantly more difficult for those who did strive to purify their mind and unify their consciousness to the Divine. And thus were knotted the ropes of human destiny."

"And yet," Woolly argued, "in the kingdom until not so long ago, people didn't get sick very often. And nature was rather well behaved, bringing the right season at the right time, and food in plenty."

"Thanks to the magic of the fields!" Gervin explained, letting the image fade. "At the beginning of the kingdom of Atlantis, when the Good Lord Melchisedek gave the Law to human beings, it was with the intention of softening their fate. The fields, which were a central part of the revelation of the Law, helped preserve some of the momentum of the unfallen world. Now that the fields are collapsing, the situation on Earth is bound to deteriorate."

A deep wave of empathy rose in Woolly's heart. "Does this mean the fall of Atlantis will be like a second fall for humanity?"

"In many ways. In Atlantis, thanks to the fields, the people of the kingdom could live close to the presence of the gods, not unlike before the fall (though not with the same intensity). Now that all this is drawing to an end, nature will appear in its fully fallen state."

"Rats and cockroaches instead of filosterops and unicorns!" Szar sighed.

"What's a cockroach?" Woolly asked.

"That new beast that Ashok and Gallagher found in the catacombs the other day."

"So is that what it's called! How did you find out?"

"Mouridji remembered having seen something like it carved on the walls of the chapel of the Mysteries of Ancient Times," Szar explained.

"Will there not be *one* unicorn that survives the collapse of the fields?" Woolly felt sorry.

"Probably not," Gervin replied. "Anyhow, it's unlikely they would be able to maintain themselves in the fallen nature of the kingdom of the rainbows."

"But there *are* unicorns in the Fields of Peace, aren't there?" Woolly drew from the knowingness of his body.

"Of course!" Gervin invited them to think, "The Fields of Peace are an unfallen world. This is how you can best understand the position of the World to Come in relation to the Earth: none of the manifestations of the fall that have happened on Earth have happened here. The elemental forces have remained pure. Nature was never disconnected from the Divine. Dark forces have never found their way here. Here, God shines in every tree, in every drop of water. In so much light, there is no space for dark forces to slip in."

Drinking Gervin's words, Woolly was trying to imagine what an unfallen nature could look like. "Are we going to see this?"

"Right now, if you want. Why don't you and Szar go and inspect the surroundings of the Archive halls?"

Woolly's eyes flared with curiosity.

"How much time do we have?" the commander wanted to know.

"You can forget about time for a while. You will return into your kingdom-body one kingdom-second after you left it," Gervin assured them.

19.3 Fields of Revelation, Fields of Opening

Coming out of the wood and discovering the river, Woolly stopped, amazed.

He had never even dreamed a river could be like that.

In the kingdom, rivers were nothing more than streams of running water. And water, fundamentally, did nothing much more than get you wet.

But here... it was a completely different story. "A poem of life and wisdom," Woolly whispered. "There is more knowledge in this river than a sage could possibly gain in twenty lives in the kingdom. Here, wherever you look, you receive a revelation – the Fields of Revelation, this is what this world is. Every leaf knows the structure of the entire creation. Every drop of water has an epic poem to tell." And he became silent, listening to the river.

"But it's talking to me!" he turned to Szar, astounded.

Szar took his arm and made him sit down.

"Do you know my name?" the river asked.

Woolly opened his mouth and shook his head.

"I am the River of Remembrance," it said. And it started humming a simple melody, because it knew it was what Woolly needed. The words said,

"Look into me and see yourself.

Here we play no games.

Here the old man stops and dies.

Here you are reborn.

Very simple, really."

"I don't understand!" Woolly suddenly understood.

"And just as well! And just as well!" the river sang. Then it stopped singing words, to help Woolly be more silent.

It just sang to his heart.

Gently, delicately.

It was a key-song designed to open closed doors.

Especially those which have never existed and therefore are so much more difficult to open.

And don't look for a reason, it's such a waste of time.

Really.

Start with that which is not completely closed. It can easily be opened. A little more.

Gently. Delicately. Irresistibly.

Woolly started crying.

The beauty of the Fields of Peace hit him at the deepest of himself: the landscape free from mists, the clarity of the light, the dazzling perfection crafted in every blade of grass, the spellbinding rhythms of the birds' music, the friendly fragrances of the flowers which warmed his lungs (instead of giving him hay fever, as in the kingdom), and the river that spoke to him.

The presence that permeated every thing was so soft.

Nothing to fight against.

Just peace.

Woolly's tears turned into a torrent. "How can it be that God has made me live so far from this for so long?"

"Or maybe not so long, after all!" the river whispered.

Down there, in the kingdom, it did feel like an eternity, entombed in greyness.

Atrocious pain in the heart.

A wall that falls, only to uncover another wall.

A flower the colour of peach blossom looked at him, wondering what it could do to help.

"Nothing!" he shrugged his shoulders and kept crying, as if all the tears he hadn't cried in all his lives had accumulated inside him, waiting.

The river kept singing her limpid spirit.

"Here we play no games.

Very simple, really."

Woolly saw. It was crystal clear. Life after life, he had essentially been doing one thing – closing off.

Closing off a little bit more, each time life hurt.

It was so easy, there were so many good reasons. Starting with the need to survive.

One more wall built for every good reason. To keep the pain locked away. And walls to hide the walls.

Soon a fortress. A monstrous construction. A huge city of darkness.

Cynicism had been such a good wall. And even intelligence, at times.

Now the walls were all falling, one after the other.

There was but one big wound left.

"Paradise hurts like hell!" he blew his nose in his sleeve, resting in the White-Eagle-ness that Szar was weaving around him.

The White-Eagle-ness didn't make the pain less, but it made Woolly feel vaster.

"When you are vast, even the worst things are not as bad," the river sang.

"It's true!" the flower couldn't agree more.

Another thick wall was about to fall.

"But what will happen to us if we go back to the kingdom fully open?" Woolly floundered. "The world is going to eat us alive!"

He listened to the river's answer, but couldn't understand the meaning.

19.4 Fields of Fields

When Woolly and Szar returned, Archive Hall One was plunged in a fluid night-like darkness of a strange kind. In it they could see each other better than in daylight.

"If we could find out how to activate these fields, or whatever it is that's being used, it would make Gervin happy," Szar said, looking for clues as to how to activate the vision device.

Woolly was too annihilated to answer. He stood straight, resting on the vastness of the wound in his heart, his mind free like the flow of his friend the river.

He closed his eyes, feeling the flower he had picked. It was pulsing with his heart.

It was a strange flower the size of his thumb, with eight flame-like petals, peach-blossom colour, and a golden-yellow heart. Before leaving the river shore, taking a good look at it, he had felt so warmed that he had to smile, and thank the flower.

But as he started walking away, he heard a whisper, "Wait!"

Holding his breath, he turned back.

"Aren't you going to pick me?" the flower whispered to him.

"But... you're far too smart to be picked!"

"If you pick me, I'll be happy," the flower assured him. "Today is a really important day for you. I couldn't imagine a better occasion. But then of course, you don't *have* to. If you don't like me, you can just go."

Flabbergasted, Woolly turned towards Szar, who burst out laughing.

The flower waited for his hand, silently.

Woolly caressed the short stem, moving up.

"There!" the flower told him when he arrived one third of the way up, and it abandoned itself into his hand.

Woolly's eyes opened even wider. He was sure he hadn't pulled the stem. And yet the flower had broken off into his hand.

"Put it on your heart, and it will be happy," Szar said.

When Woolly did that, the flower shone its colours into his chest, huddling against him. After that, the flower mingled its energy with his heart, and started pulsing with him.

Woolly was tuning into the magnificent sensation that started from his heart and filled his whole body, when Szar exclaimed triumphantly, "That's it! Look!"

Without having to open his eyes, Woolly saw the dark space of Archive Hall One turn Flying-Dragon blue, and he recognised volleys of eerie harmonies which Szar often played in his music fields.

"It's amazingly simple!" Szar marvelled, "The ether is so pure. There is no need for any external source of power to activate a field in it. This is the absolute paradise for Field Wizards – the Fields of Fields! Want to try?"

Woolly couldn't answer. He was too deeply absorbed in the pulsing of his heart. It was a new sensation, only vaguely reminiscent of a physical heartbeat. It was far more gentle and subtle. It originated from the heart centre in the middle of his chest and spread rhythmically into his whole body. It combined strangely with the pain of his wound. When he surrendered to the pulsing, a superior softness vibrated throughout his body. It made the wound different. Not just an agonising ache and a desperate call for help, but... something else, deep and mysterious.

Gervin arrived a few minutes later. He found his disciples watching images of the construction of the chapel of the White Eagle in Eisraim.

"It didn't take you long!" the master rejoiced.

Szar was about to interrupt the vision, but Gervin told him, "Keep watching!"

Helped by two lawful masons, an enthusiastic young Melchard was projecting the Voice into the newly-grown eastern living wall, purifying it from unwanted influences and permeating it with the presence of the chapel's deity.

"I have never seen Melchard look so happy!" Szar was moved. "He was resplendent."

A young woman with curly brown hair and a particularly soft look in her eyes entered the construction site. She wore the long dress of the White Eagle.

"Adya!" Szar held his breath.

"Adya, she was. Already pregnant with Elyani. As you can see she was very tired. She had never recovered from the dungeons of Tipitinan. Her love for Melchard was the only thing that kept her alive."

Melchard stopped his work and walked towards her.

"They *really* loved each other," Szar exclaimed, deeply White-warmed by the familiar Eagle spark in their eyes. "But which archive are we watching at the moment?" he asked as the couple were walking the alleys of the temple. "Eisraim's?"

"No. As you know, the archive of the temple of Eisraim will only arrive here after the transfer. This one is the archive of the Brown Robe."

"How does it get collected?"

"The Points of the Masters of Thunder are linked together. Every single experience is recorded."

This pulled Woolly out of his state. "Does it work with the apprentices too?"

"Of course!"

"Oh, gods!" Woolly sighed.

"And you can be proud of the chapter you have just added to our records. When they saw how you got rid of Aphelion, our brethren were extremely impressed by your directness," Gervin declared.

"So you could see it while it was happening?"

"No. While it was happening Aphelion had totally disconnected you from us. But as soon as it was finished, we all watched the scene. A most impressive piece in our Archive! When he saw how you passed the trial, my teacher Orest prophesied, 'This man will be one of the greatest Knights of the Apocalypse.' And Takhar the Unbending seconded this."

Szar snapped his fingers, "Hey, Woolly!"

Woolly remained speechless.

"And Barkhan Seer has decided he will ask you to become a member of his team," Gervin went on. "If you accept, you will be working with him at preparing the strategies of the Knights against Aphelion's mind – this monstrous supermental network which he briefly showed you. But we'll come back to this later. For the moment, look at this," he told them, turning the space of the hall into a watery landscape in which a gigantic sea monster was swimming.

"This is a friend of yours, Szar. Do you recognise where the images come from?"

"Space Matrix," Szar immediately answered, the high end of his column of Spirit lit with the unmistakable sparks. "A Flying Dragon brother?" he asked incredulously, contemplating the enormous fish-looking beast – so huge, Archive Hall One had to extend itself to contain the vision.

"Jinia, whom you met with Hermina in Tomoristan," Gervin answered.

"And you thought I looked odd in my past lives!" Woolly sighed, watching the sea monster swimming in the depths of the ocean, coming back to the surface from time to time to spit water through its nostrils just like a dragon spits fire through its mouth.

"Not an uncommon body for Flying Dragons when they first arrive on Earth. These large sea animals have a natural affinity with the consciousness of the spheres of remoteness," Gervin explained.

"Did Szar's first life take place in a gigantic sea monster like this one?" Woolly wanted to know.

"No, but he bitterly regretted it didn't!" Gervin let the marine landscape fade. There followed images of a miserable dwarf, crawling over rocky ground, screaming with pain.

"Oh yes, I remember!" Szar shook his head, appalled, "The only good thing about that life was that it didn't last long."

His face twisted, his body shaken by violent cramps, the dwarf was in agony. Alone. Abandoned by his tribe, left to die.

"Your body couldn't cope with the intensity you had brought with you. Which is why you were born deformed, and half-insane. It took a few lives before you became accustomed to being in a human body."

"Can we return to Jinia?" Szar asked.

Gervin conjured the image of a large suite in the palace of Tomoristan. The prince's son was deeply asleep on a bed. Szar was sitting by his side, holding three white roses in his hand. On his left, the frail Jinia. A few lawful feet behind them stood Hermina the Immaculate.

In Archive Hall One Szar took his head in his hands. "The worst mistake of my entire life. I could have fished Jinia as you fished me, couldn't I?" he said with consternation.

Gervin nodded silently.

"What can I do for her now?"

"Nothing for the moment. The past cannot be rewritten. But you will find her again. She has an appointment with the Knights. Next time she reincarnates it is unlikely you'll be on Earth. But in her following reincarnation, if she hasn't awakened yet, you will go and find her. The problem is, there won't be any fields on Earth by then. All operations of consciousness will be infinitely more difficult. Reconnecting Flying Dragons with their nature of remoteness won't be as simple as it was in Atlantis."

Gervin changed the scene. A young woman clad in a bizarre blue garment – it couldn't really be called a dress – was walking in a weird forest. Sad trees of a kind Szar and Woolly had never seen before.

"What is this?" Szar was surprised by the strange attitude on the woman's face.

"A possible future," Gervin replied.

"In the kingdom of the rainbows?"

"Correct. Jinia is wandering. She knows she is missing her life's purpose, but she has no idea how to find it."

"Does this mean that everything is already written?" Woolly asked.

"Oh, no! Certainly not! Human beings are endowed with free will. From the superior consciousness of their Spirit, they *can* modify their destiny. The problem is, they don't often do it. Which is one of the reasons why certain future scenarios are much more probable than others."

"This forest does not look too ugly," Woolly was surprised. "I thought after the end of Atlantis nature would be much worse."

"It's not the fall of Atlantis that will destroy the beauty of nature," Gervin replied. "It's Ahriman."

19.5 The kingdom of the rainbows

"Let me show you some of the marvels of the kingdom of the rainbows." Gervin turned the hall into a beach that extended as far as the eye could contemplate.

"No mists!" Woolly loved the blue sky. "As in the legends about the world of the gods."

"This is bound to modify the way people think!" Szar dipped his feet into the water. "When travelling, each time I found myself in a landscape of this kind, it had a profound impact on me."

"The clear air makes it look nearly as nice as the Molten Sea," Woolly filled his lungs with the breeze from the ocean.

"Look!" Gervin pointed to the horizon, "the Sun is rising."

They sat on the sand and contemplated the regal reddish disk slowly rising from the sea.

Woolly was deeply moved by the vision. "So they will be able to contemplate this *every* morning!" his voice was full of wonder.

"And every evening, of course!" Gervin added, and he accelerated the movement of the Sun. The glorious yellow disk moved across the sky quickly, until it set behind the dunes. There followed a night, with thousands of stars. "What do you think of that?"

"It's... all right." Woolly was not particularly impressed with the field of stars. "The colours are a bit flat." According to astral-travelling standards, it was a rather ordinary field of stars.

"But do you realise they'll be able to see it with their *physical* eyes, without having to leave their body?" Gervin tried to ignite their enthusiasm.

"Mm..." Szar, like Woolly, couldn't really see what would be so fantastic about that. "It will be... entertaining, for them, in the evening."

Gervin sighed and didn't insist. He turned the hall into a large clearing in the middle of a forest of pine trees. It had just been raining and a huge, majestic rainbow was shining.

Woolly was disappointed, "The air is marvellously clear, but the rainbow colours aren't as nice as the ones in the fields of our chapel."

"But this one is a *physical* rainbow," Gervin reiterated, "made by nature, not by fields."

No response.

"It's all very green," Szar pulled a face, contemplating the grass. "Won't there be any coloured lawns left at all?"

"No, the coloured blossoms all rested on the fields. Likewise, many treasure-plants are likely to disappear: slew, oriel, all the herbs of madness, the blue corn of the gods, hereat, disso, and the great trees of wisdom like the alohim. Worse, the medicinal herbs that will survive are bound to lose their virtues. Without the fields, tansy won't be of much help against old age, and several other precious herbs might well turn into weeds."

"Any new animals?"

"No. Except later, when nature will have been deeply wounded. Then many new insects will appear – venomous pests that will attack not only crops but also animals and human beings."

"And what about the people? What will they be like?" Szar asked.

"There, my friends, you have to be ready for some painful images," Gervin warned. To help them cope with what he was about to deliver, he appealed to their logical sense, "Many trends of the future are highly predictable, really. The warp destroyed, there'll no longer be fields. This is bound to cause a major disconnection from non-physical worlds."

Gervin conjured the image of a young woman kneeling behind an altar, praying.

Just by taking a look at the flame on the altar and at the woman's aura, it was clear she was wasting her time. The gods were not responding.

"She prays there every day from morning to night, and with all her heart, but never gets much reward from the Spirit-world," Gervin commented.

"Poor soul!" Woolly bit his lip. "Doesn't she understand that without fields, rituals can't work?"

"These people don't even know what fields are!" Gervin changed the scene into a large ritual where dozens of priests were chanting mantras and pouring an oily substance into a fire. But when the oily substance reached the fire there was no spark of energy. The space remained dull and empty of presence. The miracle of the fire ritual wasn't happening.

"Oh, but that's terrible!" Szar felt a pinch in his chest, remembering the magic years of his life spent performing fire rituals. "So they will *never* be able to experience a real ritual? What if they officiate on a Holy Blue Flame?"

"No Holy Blue Flames left. All extinguished," Gervin announced in a matter-of-fact voice.

Szar swallowed, calling onto the Eagle.

"Still, I find it difficult to understand how they could forget that fields ever existed," Woolly pulled a face. "What about the oral transmission of the Law?"

"Lost. You must understand how different their mind will be from ours. They will be more or less completely amnesiac, hardly capable of remembering a few hundred hymns by heart – and even that will be an effort for them! With time it will get worse and worse. After only a few thousand years the only things that will last from one generation to another will be those engraved on stones or painted walls."

"This is insane!" Woolly was shocked. "Is it going to be the same for us when we reincarnate?"

"I'm afraid so. Worse, the collapse of the warp will be followed by a long era of complete barbarity. Countless wars."

He showed them a weird battle scene. Had it not been for the massacre, it would have looked rather comical.

"Why are these people throwing kitchen knives at each other?" Woolly was perplexed.

"They're not kitchen knives," Szar informed him, "they're 'arrows'. The gods use them too."

"Hunh hunh!" Gervin corrected him. "These are not like the magic weapons of the gods. They're purely physical projectiles."

"Oh, come on!" Had Woolly not been so overwhelmed, he would have laughed. "But what about venom?"

"They won't even think of using venom," Gervin smiled. "Even their greatest warriors won't suspect that such forces exist."

Seeing the incredulous look on Woolly's face, Gervin tried to explain, "Imagine a world in which people *never* feel the presence of the gods, and *never* receive visions from higher worlds. They can *never* astral travel consciously. When they wake up in the morning, they remember *nothing* of what has happened to them during the night. They can't even see auras! Quite naturally, after a few thousand years, they end up believing that only the physical world exists. And they build their life accordingly."

Woolly felt like one big wound, aching for the world.

Seeing the distress in his eyes, Gervin replaced the farcical battle with a gorgeous sunset. "Would you like us to have a break?"

"No," Woolly gathered his courage. "I want to see."

Szar inhaled a long breath and gave a warrior's nod.

To lighten the space, Gervin chose the image of a man who was bathing in a strangely shaped tub, without any god's figure at the front. "If you want to understand these people, you must turn your thinking upside down. Take the most simple things. In the kingdom, when you take a bath you use a field to warm up your body. But they, of course, do just the opposite. They warm up the water of the bath!"

Szar burst out laughing, "That explains everything!"

"Another example. To help people find their way at night, you use fields to make the energy of the path glow in the dark. They will use physical lights, which they will place on the sides of their roads – even if the path is three hundred lawful feet long."

"But of course!" Szar laughed again.

"Or take food," Gervin went on. "To preserve it, you change its level of etheric energy. Whereas their preservation methods will be based on using physical substances, such as salt in meat, or more complicated processes."

"Do you mean they'll be eating corpses?" Woolly was horrified.

"Mainly corpses of animals, only rarely those of human beings," Gervin replied.

This time, Szar didn't laugh.

The next vision showed a hill covered with vines. "A major development in the evolution of the kingdom of the rainbows."

"Grapes?"

"They prepare fermented beverages out of it. It makes them feel euphoric. But the long-term effects are catastrophic. It further disconnects their consciousness from non-physical worlds. These beverages will become so widespread that even religions will advocate their use."

"So they *do* have a religion!" Woolly sighed with relief.

"No," Gervin shook his head sadly, "they have hundreds! Because of their disconnection from spiritual worlds, people will find it difficult to distinguish between vision and imagination. It will result in a multiplicity of contradictory creeds. The first religions of the kingdom of the rainbows will teach truths that bear several similarities to our Law. Then will come a mighty revelation of our Lord Melchisedek, which will foster the Ego of human beings and reinforce their link to the Web of Love – the foundation for a profound awakening. But as time passes complete nonsense will be introduced, such as the belief that the gods do not exist, or even that they are dark forces, the enemies of our Lord Melchisedek. Some will sacrifice animals, or even human beings. Some will go as far as saying that instead of reincarnating, human beings live on Earth only once! But the most dangerous religion of the kingdom of the rainbows will be the one brought down by Ahriman himself. It will proclaim that God does not exist, that there is no such thing as Spirit, and that only the material universe exists."

Szar was even more puzzled than he was appalled. "But... why would anyone want to believe that?"

"The works of Ahriman are extraordinarily clever. To begin with, he will foster corruption in the message of religions. He will promote priests who misinterpret the word of genuine prophets. He will assist in the establishment of empty dogmas. He will incite priests to use torture, and to engage in genocide and all forms of atrocities in the name of their faith. The horrors and the stupidity carried out in the name of God will reach such an insane level that people with some common sense will come to the conclusion there is something intrinsically wrong with religion. Then the ground will be ready. Ahriman will bring down a new revelation.

Expect it to be magnificent – a masterpiece of intelligence. All things will be explained. Great miracles will be performed. Colossal forces of nature will be unleashed. But just as all the oceans of the Earth only have one flavour, salt, so Ahriman's religion will have one central theme: nothing exists but the material universe. And therefore there are no gods, and existence finishes with death."

"What kind of miracles will be performed?" Szar asked.

"Countless," Gervin replied, bringing the image of a gigantic city. "Look at this thin building on the left. Six-hundred-storeys high! The number of people living in it is more than twenty-five times the entire population of the temple of Eisraim."

"Just in that one tower!" Szar exclaimed, contemplating the hundreds of barely smaller towers around it. "What is it made of?"

"Mainly iron – Ahriman's favourite metal. In the kingdom of the rainbows, iron will be everywhere. People will love it just as much as Atlantean people hate it. Its use in buildings will even be made compulsory by Law!"

High in the sky, they saw a silvery bird flying. It was a strange beast. Its wings didn't move, and it was terribly noisy.

"Look!" Gervin focused the vision on it. "There is a man sitting inside it."

"So it's a *huge* bird!" Woolly was amazed. "And of course, it's the man's *physical body* that's inside, is that it?"

Gervin nodded.

"But is it a real bird?"

"No, more like a large tool. They use thousands of these, for all kinds of purposes."

"What about the dark fumes coming out of the bird's ass?" Szar was curious.

"Physical venom. Like the smoke coming out of a fire, but infinitely more toxic. It will be *everywhere*. This will be one of Ahriman's long-term strategies: lasting physical pollution that builds up over time. Just as we polluted the warp with our misguided fields, so the kingdom of the rainbows will be polluted by myriads of physical devices."

"So they are going to repeat exactly the same mistakes we have made, but on the physical level, is that it?"

"More or less."

The scenes that followed were shocking. The Earth swept by a tidal wave of iron. Cities covered in thick venomous fog. Forests dying. Poisoned rivers screaming with pain. Mountains of rubbish poured into the ocean. Arid lands scarred with wide crevasses, as if the caverns of sickness were taking over the surface.

"The most insidious attacks will be those on the human body itself." Gervin brought the image of a dead person who was being laid in a wooden sarcophagus. Village priests dressed in black costumes buried the sarcophagus in the ground without performing any cleansing rites.

"This will be one of their major sins," Gervin's voice was grave. "They won't take care of their dead. They will just dispose of them as if they were ordinary compost."

As could be expected, toxic fragments were soon released from the corpse's astral body. They wafted in the space and polluted other people's body of energy, making them sick.

"The results will be tragic: constant diseases – diseases that could never have occurred in the kingdom of Atlantis. And this will be only one of the many evils caused by the disconnection from spiritual worlds. The more polluted nature becomes, the sicker the people. In the kingdom of the rainbows there will be more sickness than ever before on Earth. The problem is, because of their lack of spiritual discernment, physicians will invent cures that end up creating more damage than the diseases themselves."

In a large chapel, men and women dressed in white gowns were busy working among shelves filled with bottles.

"A caste of physicians. Inspired by Ahriman, they have just found a new treatment for a particular kind of pestilence. But they are totally unaware that their remedy will cause hidden damage that will not be discovered for several generations."

"But these people do not look evil! Why do they follow Ahriman so blindly?" Szar wondered. "Don't they have any suspicions at all about his religion?"

"You could say the same of us. Why did we keep using the warp that was bound to bring our downfall? We just followed the example of our elders. The world was going in one direction; we followed. Who had the courage to put everything in question? Who would have even thought of questioning the foundations of our kingdom?"

"But our kingdom was founded on the revelation of the Law of Melchisedek," Szar argued. "It was divine, cosmic, magnificent. Why would anyone want to follow the Law of Ahriman, Prince of Darkness?"

"The tragedy is, they won't know what they are following – not until the very end. Ahriman is far too clever to show his real face. All they will see will be intelligence, science, fantastic discoveries, unprecedented realisations. When inspired by Ahriman they will believe themselves guided by their own minds. When performing his works they will sincerely believe they are serving the cause of humanity. Look at this."

In a small circular crypt, a group of Blue Robe people wearing round caps, thin ritual masks and strange gloves were performing a healing on the body of an old woman.

"They have found a way to replace her worn-out knee with a physical contraption – made of iron, naturally," Gervin explained.

"Do you mean to say, *even surgery* will be performed on the physical body?" Woolly could hardly believe his eyes.

"Absolutely. Thanks to these 'physical surgeons' the woman will no longer feel pain, and she will be able to walk again. Can you see anything wrong with that?"

"No," Szar replied, remembering how Mouridji's life had been transformed after he had fixed her hip. "Apart from the iron, of course."

"Even with the iron, it will relieve the pain of large numbers of people and allow them to lead normal lives instead of being cripples. These physicians – who have never heard of Ahriman – can be proud of their work. But what they do not suspect is what will happen in the following centuries, as the continuation of their efforts."

The next image showed a man asleep on a large altar. Around him were dozens of metallic arms that moved all at the same time.

"The physical surgeons have been replaced by these contraptions, which are capable of far more precise movements than human hands."

A spoon-like rod descended onto the man's face and ejected one of his eyes. Then a double metallic arm smoothly rotated towards him, carrying a small white ball in its claw. The ball was plopped into the man's eye socket. For a few seconds, bright blue sparks came out of the arm. Then the operation was repeated on the other side.

"What more beautiful present can you give a man than to restore his vision if he has become blind?"

"But..." Woolly and Szar felt quite uncomfortable at the idea that their eyes might be replaced.

"What are the eyes made of?" Woolly asked.

"A mixture of metals and pieces of flesh grown in the body of a pig. Now look at this!"

A naked young woman was lying on a similar altar. Three ominous metallic arms slowly descended towards her and stabbed her in the chest. She was too venomised to feel pain. There followed a revolting scene of human sacrifice: six pairs of claws ripped her open and removed her heart, which was seized by another claw and taken to a bucket of rubbish, into which it fell with a thud. A cloud of Spirit energies and arch-precious etheric quintessence escaped from her chest and dissipated in the space of the room. To make the crime worse, the murderous claws inserted an unholy ritual object into her chest, as in the most filthy black masses of Nephilim necromancers, except that this one was a metallic contraption instead of a toad. Blue sparks ensued (Ahriman's response, judging by the furious hissing sounds), which miraculously closed the chest of the butchered woman.

But the most incredible part of the vision was still to come. The dead woman opened her eyes. Like a zombie in the caverns of sickness, she stood up slowly and walked away from the altar.

"I don't get it!" Woolly scratched his beautiful nose. "Is it her astral body that we are seeing at the moment?"

"No. Her *physical* body! She has just received a new heart."

"So Ahriman will demand human sacrifices," Szar looked down to his left fist, utterly disgusted.

"No, you don't understand! That was not a ritual murder, it was a healing!" Gervin elucidated.

They looked at him incredulously.

"This woman was going to die. Her heart was sick."

"Why didn't they try to heal it?" Szar frowned.

"This *was* their healing," Gervin hammered. "Now she will be an extremely strong woman, who can run for hours without feeling fatigue."

"Yes, but without the quintessential energies of the heart... she won't be feeling anything at all!" Woolly was horrified.

"This is where Ahriman wins!" Gervin nodded. "Do you see how the plot unfolds?"

From the perplexed look on their faces, it was clear that they didn't.

19.6 Ahrimanic fitness

"Let's start again," the master shone his infinite patience. "As a result of the collapse of the warp, many new diseases will appear. These will be made worse by the fact that the people of the kingdom of the rainbows will be heavily disconnected from Spirit, and they won't know how to perform proper funeral rites. Then as a result of the Ahrimanic revelation, nature will become polluted, making people even sicker. And physicians will play apprentice sorcerers, using short-term cures with devastating long-term effects on the human race. The result? A dramatic degradation of the human body. Many men and women will be infertile. And a large proportion of babies will be born deformed, with missing organs and monstrous body parts. Now," he turned to Szar, "suppose your beloved wife had just given birth to a beautiful little girl with a malformed ankle. Would you prefer her to be crippled all her life, or have a new ankle made by physical surgeons?"

"I think..." Szar twinged his beard, "I would prefer her to go through the surgery."

"That was an easy one. Now," Gervin turned to Woolly, "suppose your beloved wife had just given birth to a beautiful little boy with only a deficient liver. Would you prefer him to die, or to have his liver replaced by a state-of-the-art super-sponge that will allow him to digest *anything* throughout his life?"

"This is an easy one too," Woolly didn't hesitate one second, "I would let him die, so he can find a better body in his next life. Why would anyone want to live with a sponge instead of a liver? As the Law says, 'the liver gives life,' and 'foresight comes from the liver,' and 'a man with a great liver will be a great knower of future events.'"

It was the first time Gervin and Szar heard Woolly quote the Law so authoritatively. They exchanged a genuinely worried glance. Was this all too much for him?

"Isn't it true?" Woolly frowned.

"Undoubtedly!" Gervin answered in a supernaturally soft voice. "But it is not how the people of the kingdom of the rainbows will think. Believing that everything finishes with death, they will do *anything* to prolong life. And their lack of perception will make them unaware of the spiritual consequences of being stripped of their organs."

"But without their real organs, they won't really be alive!" Woolly rebelled against the concept. "Will no one realise that someone whose heart has been removed becomes a different person?"

"Oh, yes, some people will notice the changes!" Gervin agreed.

"But they will have no choice. That's the plot," Szar understood. "If they don't give in to Ahrimanic surgery, they will all die!"

"This will be true of the later periods," Gervin said. "Before this, it is their materialistic ethics that will guide them. When parents choose to avoid treating their children with Ahriman's medicine, they will be accused of superstitious beliefs. It is on humanitarian grounds that Ahriman's medicine will be made compulsory by Law. And those who refuse to comply will be thrown in jail or made outcasts, rejected from schools and other institutions."

A tall dark man with his torso bare was sitting in a small chapel. In front of him stood a White Robe physician, threatening him with a small thin arrow. The arrow was poisoned, as could be seen from the venomous aura around it.

"Deep inside him, this man *knows* that the so-called medicine will damage him. But he has no choice. If he refuses the venom, he will not be allowed to remain part of his professional caste. A destitute, he will become."

The man gave a nod, and the physician stabbed his arm with the poisoned arrow, injecting the venom into his body.

"Mother of the Light, have mercy on this physician!" Woolly prayed silently, watching the crime against nature.

"But let me show you something else," Gervin brought back the image of the man whose eyes had been replaced. "This person wasn't compelled to undergo physical surgery. He wasn't even blind! His vision was quite normal. But now... see the world through his new eyes."

The man was in a huge crowd. A jumble of castes, judging by the colours of their strange gowns. They were all rushing, as if in urgent need of finding toilets – which perhaps explained why they all looked so tense. It was in a large street with long rows of iron towers on each side. The sky was marred with grey clouds.

Out of the blue, the sky turned into an extraordinary tapestry made of patches of all colours. The iron towers became red, and people's faces started shining with bright green glows.

"Are these auras?" Szar frowned, wondering which rung of the cosmological ladder all this came from.

"No. The man's magic eyes allow him to change the colours of his world as he pleases."

"But it's pure illusion, isn't it?" Woolly wasn't impressed.

"It is. Being out of touch with Spirit, this man is bored to death. Illusion is all he has to fill the emptiness of his life."

A beautiful dark-haired woman was walking towards him. Instantly, the colours went back to normal, and the woman's dress disappeared.

Woolly was shocked. "Do they walk in the street naked?"

"No, this woman is still wearing her dress. But the man's eyes can see through her clothes," Gervin explained

"Is that lawful?" Woolly asked suspiciously.

Gervin nodded, and he bit his lip, wondering what was happening to his Woolly.

"Can the eyes also see auras?" Szar asked.

"No, only physical things. But this goes far beyond what you imagine. Look. Thanks to his new eyes, the man was accepted into a caste of warriors. Changing caste is no big thing for these people."

The man was running through a forest. He was searching in all directions, as if hunting someone. Then he stopped. The forest turned dark, as if suddenly enveloped by night. In the distance, a reddish glow could be seen.

"Here his eyes are not seeing colours, but warmth. The reddish shape is the person he is looking for. Her body shines because it is warmer than the rest of the forest."

Suddenly, the man found himself right in front of the woman, as if he had jumped out of his body.

"Understand what happened?"

"It can't be teleportation, can it?" Szar asked.

"No, nothing like that. The man's eyes have enlarged the image. It allows him to see minute details from a distance. His eyes can do many other miraculous things."

In the next scene the man seemed to be lying on a bed, except that there was nothing to support him. His body was hanging in the air. The dark-haired woman he had met earlier walked into the room. This time she was wearing a provocative red dress. She smiled at him as if he was her dear friend.

"Did they get married?" Woolly asked. "But wait a minute... this woman doesn't have an aura!"

"Because she's not a woman. There is only one person in that room: the man. The woman's image is an illusion constructed by his eyes."

"Like a field?" Szar asked.

"Something like that, except it happens only in his head. All the images of his daily life are registered in some kind of archive. He can not only replay them, but also modify them at leisure. Now, do you start to understand why many people are going to be tempted by organ replacement? Their choice will be either a sickly diminished body, or a beautiful-looking one which can accomplish miraculous feats such as running as fast as a levlon or breathing under water."

"But then they will no longer be themselves," Szar frowned. "These bodies will not be *their* bodies. They'll be empty shells."

"This is what the Ahrimanic plot is all about! In the epochs that will follow the kingdom of the rainbows, many human beings will be nothing more than empty shells." Gervin conjured the image of a long, slender, fair-haired woman. Like savages, she was dressed in a thin piece of cloth that left her legs uncovered. Apart from her exaggeratedly high forehead her features were harmonious, and her eyes were bright. But what was striking about her was the dimness of her aura. Nothing more than an elusive grey glow.

"Is she a human being?" Woolly was looking more and more distressed.

"Her eyes, ears, heart, pancreas, liver, gall bladder and kidneys have been replaced, and so have most of her bones. Her skin is a mixture of metals and animal-like pieces of flesh grown in bottles. Her hair is made of substances taken from plants and minerals. Her blood is replaced every three weeks. Her muscles have been transformed with drugs. She never gets sick, she can run faster than a horse, and her physical strength is such that if it came to fighting with hands, Szar wouldn't stand a chance against her. In addition, her brain was modified and linked to a physical knowledge bank, so her memory is absolute. And in less than one second she can bring to her mind any information that has been gathered by all the civilisations for which physical records are still kept. But in this impressive construction, the great absentee is Spirit. Truly, she is half-way between a human being and a magard."

"A magard?" Szar and Woolly asked in unison.

"A particular kind of being that will appear in the future. The concept might not be easy for you to grasp. Let me give you a bit of background." Gervin brought an image of the chapel of the Forgotten Mysteries of the Law in the temple of Eisraim. "Remember seeing this?" he pointed to a strange device made of thin threads on which wooden beads were strung. "It's called an abacus. A curiosity that came from the revelation of the Watchers."

"I never understood what its use was," Woolly declared.

"It allows you to make simple calculations, such as seven times thirteen, and so on."

"Yes, this I understand. But what does it tell you that's not already in the lawful hymns of multiplication tables?" Woolly questioned.

"Nothing, which is why the abacus was never used in the kingdom. But in the kingdom of the rainbows, the situation will be quite different. Because of their amnesia, people will be unable to remember the hymns."

"What?" Woolly could hardly believe it. "Do you mean, even the lawful hymns of multiplication tables will be lost?"

"People will be so amnesiac they'll be incapable of remembering them. When asked trivial questions such as, 'How much is thirteen times seventeen?' most of them will have to stop and think, or pull a small abacus from their pocket. To them it will become an indispensable contraption. Immense efforts will be invested in the construction of gigantic super-abaci."

In a medium-sized chapel, Grey Robe men and women were busying around a dozen large cupboards, some of which had mirrors that twinkled with coloured lights.

"One of the first super-abaci," Gervin commented. "In its Point-packed way, it can chant the entire Law of additions and multiplications six hundred times every second."

"But why would anyone want to chant so many multiplications?" Woolly had difficulty understanding why the grey-robed people looked so fascinated by their work.

Szar, however, found the concept quite natural. "All sorts of Point-blowing operations of consciousness can be derived from numbers. The universal language of the Flying Dragons is based on numbers. And the sky of the gods is filled with mathematical wonders."

"The people of the kingdom of the rainbows will develop super-abaci that can mimic mental processes with a great degree of sophistication. They will use them in *all* situations of life."

A man and a woman were hanging in the air, lying on an invisible bed.

"The man is not a real person. He is an illusory projection from a super-abacus," Gervin explained. "Like some kind of field."

The illusory projection was speaking soft words to the woman, comforting her.

"She's such a bitch! Such a bitch!" the woman was crying.

The illusory projection took her in its arms. "She's just your mother-in-law. What d'you expect?" it said in a compassionate voice.

Woolly was deeply puzzled. "But how can the abacus talk, if it's a purely physical device?"

"It is linked to a knowledge bank which knows how to say the right thing at the right moment."

"A *real* universal knowledge bank in the astral?" Woolly asked.

"No. A *physical* knowledge bank," Gervin answered. "A super-abacus in which knowledge can be stored."

"How can you put something mental in something which is purely physical?" Woolly didn't follow.

"The first abaci will not be mental, they will only *mimic* the mind. But later on, things will become far more complicated. This is where magards come in. Look at this. One of the first magards."

A man dressed in a bizarre blue costume was holding a small black box in his hands.

Szar and Woolly's mouths dropped open in wonder.

"Did *he* make that, or was it given to him by the gods?" Woolly asked.

"He and his friends made it," Gervin answered. "But only by accident."

"This is... this is..." Woolly was struck speechless.

In and around the box was something unlawfully inconceivable: an aura. It was not just a vague venomous glow imprinted by some act of magic. It was the aura of a living being. A being that could think. A being with a consciousness of its own.

"So they can give life to inanimate matter!" Szar exclaimed with awe-struck reverence.

"No, no! It's not life," Gervin corrected. "It's a purely mental being, an astral entity."

"How did it manage to incarnate in the abacus?"

"That's what the people of the kingdom of the rainbows are going to have a hard time understanding. Because they know absolutely nothing about astral worlds and their beings, magards will be a complete mystery to them. The wizards who created this abacus sincerely believe in the Ahrimanic creed: nothing exists but the physical world. And yet, and yet... as they are going to discover, there is a ghost in their abacus!"

The man who held the box screamed with surprise.

He immediately called one of his friends through darkness visible, "Max! Max! Come immediately! SI31K is taking over the network!"

"What are you talking about!" Max choked.

"Man, it's happening right in front of me! SI31K is closing the remote stations, one after the other."

"But fuck! Fuck! We've never programmed it to do that!"

19 – The Book of the Fields of Peace

The next scene showed a huge fire, which warrior-priests with shining helmets were trying to extinguish, helped by long snakes that vomited torrents of water.

"When abaci reach a certain degree of sophistication, it will happen more and more often that non-physical entities sneak in and take residence inside them, like parasites. They will be ghosts in the machine: magards. The rainbow wizards, who won't be able to see auras, will be dumbfounded. Their abaci will start behaving in a way that is completely incomprehensible to them, as if they had a mind of their own – which is exactly what will be happening. But as the wizards will be unable to clear entities, they will find themselves in extremely difficult situations."

A corpulent man entirely covered in urine and faeces was walking out of a tiny crypt in which a small white circular altar occupied most of the space. He was trembling, deeply shocked.

A black-robed woman ran towards him, "Oh, no! Not again! What happened?"

"I... I don't know..." the man gasped. "I just tried to flush it, and... and... all this shit started coming out!"

"Security! Security!" the woman ran to the door. "The magard is back!"

Gervin brought down another image, where an elderly woman was eating dinner with her aura-less husband. There were candles on the altar (or rather hanging in the air, like all the dishes of their dinner). The atmosphere looked particularly warm and loving. "A different type of magard. This woman's husband died one year earlier. Supposedly, the man in front of her is an illusory projection coming from her abacus. But after the husband's death, fragments of his astral body came to incarnate in the abacus. In other words, the widow is now having a relationship with her husband's ghost."

The air of complicity in the man and the woman's eyes was such that Woolly exclaimed, "She knows, doesn't she?"

"With her heart, she knows!" Szar smiled.

"It makes her happy," Gervin sighed. And he signalled, "Enough for the moment. I want you to go and pay your respects to the unfallen nature outside the halls."

"All glory to the teacher!" Szar and Woolly thanked him for the extraordinary visions.

As he was walking out, Szar confided in Woolly, "Now I understand why the White Eagle is withdrawing his priestesses from the kingdom. How could there be White Eagles in a world of iron?"

They went separately. Szar walked to the hills to watch the sky. Woolly went back to the River of Remembrance.

19.7 Light out of darkness

Szar returned to the hall first, the high end of his column of Spirit lit like a White sunrise at the Edge of Highness. Woolly came back immediately after him. The shining-bright heartness that radiated from his eyes showed he had cried another flood of tears. His heart, on which the peach-blossom flower was still attached, was pulsing in unison with the River of Remembrance.

With naked sincerity he asked the first question, awakening a fresh watery feeling in the hall, the river flowing through his words, "Gervin, I want to understand the deeper meaning behind the images you have shown us. How can the Lord Melchisedek permit such darkness to overtake the Earth? Has he abandoned human beings? What will there be at the end of the night?"

Gervin brought an image of the chapel of the Salmon Robe in Eisraim. It was shortly after Szar had arrived at the temple. He and his fellow apprentices were preparing for a ritual, putting the gold utensils and offerings in their lawful place.

Szar was horrified to see how slowly they moved. It made them look grotesque, especially in contrast with the images of the kingdom of the rainbows.

"Look at these young men," Gervin began. "By the power of their rituals, they are constantly surrounded by the presence of the gods. They live in a world where every single action, every single gesture, every single word is endowed with spiritual significance and vibrant with the heart of the Law. This is the noon of Spirit – a bright day of the Lord. But what will these priests have achieved by the end of the day?"

In the middle of the fire ritual a godly presence descended in the chapel. Entranced, the Salmon Robe priests became still, bathing in the bright light which illuminated the hall.

"They know how to receive spiritual light, but there is no personal structure in them to retain it. Truly, they are not fundamentally different from the blobs that bathed in divine soup. They are soft, plastic, malleable, always fulfilled, always nice and gentle, never tense, never vicious or venomous. When confronted with a new problem they don't even feel disarray, they just stop and become blank. In the wonderful cocoon of the Law, they sleep their life. If it were not for the collapse of the warp they would have kept sleeping until the end of this cosmic cycle. Now look at this sage of the kingdom of the rainbows."

In a small filthy hut a man was meditating. The walls were dead, with no living glows. The man looked tired, and was particularly ugly, his tanned face covered in scars. Judging by the darkness of the space and the poor quality of vibration in his aura, his meditation wasn't very successful.

"A great ascetic, this man will be. A spiritual lighthouse for his fellow-human beings!" Gervin surprised them.

That was difficult to understand. Compared to the illumination in the chapel of the Salmon Robe, the space in the man's hut looked pitiful. Compared to the shining auras of the priests, his energy was a wreck.

"See the light in his heart?" Gervin pointed out.

It was genuine, but certainly not blasting.

"He didn't receive this light from the fields, he gained it through his own efforts. This light was born from inside, despite the darkness of a world of spiritual indifference. And for this reason it will stay with him forever. Kingdoms will pass, cosmic nights will follow cosmic days – this man will never be separated from God."

"But..." Woolly found it difficult to understand how someone could be satisfied with such dim spiritual light. "Is this all he will achieve?"

"When this man reaches the Fields of Peace, he will shine like a sun," Gervin prophesied.

"Still, it breaks my heart to imagine what he could have achieved if he had been in our temple," Woolly sighed. "With our knowledge of rituals and with the Spirit which..."

"But this man *was* in our temple," Gervin interrupted him. "He was Alar of the Salmon Robe, an old man who died a few years before you and Szar arrived."

"Was he already a spiritual genius?"

"No, he was a complete sleeper, beautiful and useless like most of his fellow priests. In the kingdom of the rainbows he will have to start more or less from scratch. The only thing that will be left of the decades of rituals he performed in Eisraim will be a profound nostalgia, a longing for the light of the Spirit – a great incentive to begin his journey, but nothing more than a few past-life memories."

Woolly looked down pensively. For a moment, all that could be heard in the hall was the soft flow of the River of Remembrance.

"So the children of the Law have fooled themselves completely," he concluded.

"Only in the later periods of the kingdom," Gervin replied. "In the early days, the Law took them from the stage of complete blobs to that of puppets, which was a major evolutionary step."

"Still, this is the end of a long dream during which it was possible to be a high initiate, speak to the gods, know the mind of angels, command awesome forces of nature, and yet end up with nothing in the end. All these grand celebrations of the Law, these rituals on the Holy Blue Flame, these sublime atmospheres in our chapels – none of these were ours. Now, that which belongs to the gods is to return to the gods. We must start looking at ourselves for what we really are."

"Meaning that humanity is entering a phase of much greater spiritual maturity." Mighty forces were unleashed through Gervin's Voice. "True, life on Earth will be more difficult. But who wants to sleep forever? True, this is the twilight of the gods. But it had always been planned that human beings would awaken from their own free will, not as the result of a gift from celestial hierarchies. True, this is the beginning of a long night. But whoever wakes up will never sleep again. True, Ahriman will put immense obstacles in the way. But whoever overcomes will inherit the Fields of Peace."

They remained silent, listening to the flow of the River of Remembrance.

Inspired by the stream, Woolly felt a profound wave of awakening rising inside him, "The Lord Melchisedek created darkness, that light may be revealed," he quoted the Law.

"This is the heart of the mystery of the fall. And this is why Ahriman will be permitted to plunge post-Atlantean kingdoms into increasing darkness."

Woolly looked deep into his master's eyes. "We have been *so* privileged to be guided by you, Gervin," he said, letting the heartness of the river flow through him. "Now that I start fathoming the full measure of what you have given us, I do not see how we will ever be able to thank the Mother of the Light for having led us to you."

Curious, Szar smiled, moved by the strength behind Woolly's words.

Woolly inundated him with the river's fresh fluid presence. Then he closed his eyes and attuned the pulsing of his heart to the knowingness of the hall. "Look into the future!"

A small woman in her mid-thirties was addressing an audience of young people who were sitting behind small individual altars. As she spoke, they were frantically covering their altars with magic glyphs.

"Look at the glow in her eyes. She's *not* a sleeper," Woolly said with respect. "She has judgement, she can think for herself, take responsible decisions, carry out long-term projects. She has structure! And deep inside her heart, she has a longing for the light. But she doesn't know where to find it. In her land there are no temples, and very few teachers."

Woolly brought back the image of the entranced Salmon Robe priests. The spiritual intensity was such that three of them, including Szar, fainted. "The tragedy of our kingdom was that light was everywhere, but people had no structure to retain it. In the kingdoms after us, people will have more structure, but the tragedy will be that light will be concealed and hard to reach. Thanks to Gervin and the Masters of Thunder, it was given to us to develop structure before the sunset of the Law."

Then Woolly managed to bring several scenes together at the same time, in a way that could only be followed from the Point. In one of the scenes Szar was behind Lord Gana's altar, agonising to find a question to ask his master. In another scene he was engaged in an animated discussion with Elyani, not long after his return from the Underworlds. In parallel, Woolly, Ferman, and Lehrmon were fighting for the survival of their stones, Teyani was laughing with her White Eagle priestesses, and Khej and Gallagher were swearing like pigs in the Law after the collapse of one of their fields.

"Gervin gave us missions with kingdom-size problems to solve, and impossible challenges. He made us fall in love, have broken hearts, face massive failures, feel terrible about ourselves. It was hell, it seemed unfair and inhuman... worse than death, in many situations! And now, our vessels are ready to be filled with the light. We will never have to go through the agony of those who seek in darkness. That which could have taken thousands of years will have been achieved in one life – a magnificent life. And the greatest of all privileges is about to be bestowed on us: that of having something to give, and being capable of helping others on the way. All glory to the teacher!"

It was simple and magnificent, like the flow of the River of Remembrance. In one thought form, Woolly had cognised his master.

19.8 The cross and the tessellated pavement

"Watch this," Gervin turned to Szar. "One of your appointments with the future."

At first, all they saw was a huge white flame that ignited the entire hall and rose so high that they couldn't discern its tip. It was so White-Eagle that it made Szar ask, "Does this happen on Earth or in Highness?"

"It happens in the heart of these people," Gervin pointed to a group of men and women in the centre of the flame. It was night, they were standing around a small bonfire.

"They will be called 'the pure', and rightly so," Gervin began. But Szar was so absorbed in the vision that he no longer heard him.

High up in the endless flame, his Flying Dragon nature was contemplating the Web of Love – this wonder which, long, long ago, had attracted his father to the spheres of Melchisedek. Compared to the expanses of remoteness it was nothing more than a tiny dot. Yet its infinite depth made the supermind boggle. Fascinated and perplexed, Szar exchanged a glance with his friend the Great Ant.

"Do you understand this web?" he asked.

The Great Ant immediately answered with a multidimensional array of archetypal truths which separated the horizontal-ness of the Flying Dragon spheres from the Unborn God's link to the Mother of the Light and ended with a long series of complex numbers.

Szar turned towards Space Matrix for a translation of the message. Space Matrix started reciting a thirty-three-aeon-long poem which told the beginning of a measureless chain reaction of unfathomable mysteries which, by the way, few Flying Dragons knew better than his father, so why not save many aeons and ask him directly?

Szar turned to his father, who was always blue-stellar-explosion-happy to Point-ness-ness-talk with him and who White-warmly congratulated him on his progress in Eagle-ness, and how was Revelation Sky? But divinely well, thank you. And the Sons of Apollo? Divinely well, thank you. And did he want to know more about the Web of Love? But why not ask the White Eagle, who immediately heard the call of his forever friend in remoteness and appeared at the Edge of Highness.

The White Eagle, whom he had first discovered in Elyani's love, and whom he had loved passionately ever since.

The White-magnificent Light flew towards him, Voicing an ardent breeze, "The Web of Love is a great mystery."

Szar Point-nodded and sighed tenderly. The Great Ant lent a mathematical ear. Space Matrix switched on its best archive-recording mode.

The White Eagle started drawing a horizontal line which, Point-curiously, swept an infinity of time continuums and passed through all the spheres of remoteness from one end of the Great Cosmic Night, where the Dawn of Creation breathes in, to the other, where she breathes out.

Then he drew a vertical line that started from the very top's top of the ladder of the worlds, far above the Golden Shield, in those regions where the Lord Melchisedek is One with the Unborn God. The line went down, crossing all the spheres of Highness (which are a great, great many, despite the fact that they are all One), then passing through the Golden Shield, reaching the sky of the gods and the countless worlds of the tip of the triangle, then continuing down into the triangle, the intermediary worlds, the kingdom, the Underworlds, the Deep Underworlds and the Sea of Lightning, just where King Vasouk happened to be bathing with several of his best Naga-friends, and the line kept descending, crossing the Golden Shield below and reaching the spheres of Lowness (which, necessarily, are as many as the spheres of Highness, since they are the same) and finally the Mother of the Endless Night, who is the Great Dragon of the Deep, in this infinite bottom where she is One with the Mother of the Light.

Then the Eagle pointed to the middle of the gigantic cross formed by the two lines, "There, where verticality and horizontality meet, is the mystery of the Web of Love!"

It was a revelation – an enlightenment. Szar cried tears of starlight, his heart flaring with the ardent infinity of the centre of the cross. And to tell of the times when all will be accomplished, the Great Ant immediately began a new poem, six-hundred-and-sixty-six-aeons long, which Space Matrix translated on the Point-spot and as it was being revealed.

As this feast was illuminating the spheres of remoteness, the Eagle enveloped Szar in his wings, "A favour to ask from you, I have."

What greater joy can there be for a lover than to grant a favour to his lover? Szar let the Mother of the Light smile through him, and he surrendered to the Eagle's will.

"There," the Eagle pointed to the centre of the cross, "are great souls, knowers of the Web of Love. Great souls they are, great trials await them. Their fate is sealed, and cannot be avoided. But I want my Light to be with them. Go with Elyani. Stand by their side. Lighten their burden by loving them, as they will love you. And remember, that which is will always be."

Why grieve?

In the centre of the cross, Szar found himself in front of the small bonfire, amidst the circle of friends.

His left hand was holding Elyani's hand.

The Web of Love was shining in the eyes of the man standing across the fire.

"I've never seen a mass with such strong Holy Spirit as tonight," the man said. "Do you think it's a sign?"

"Of course," Szar smiled at him from the Eagle. "A sign that God loves you, Simon."

The man's face shone a little brighter. "That I can feel! It's like... it's like..." Simon tried to describe his feeling but couldn't find the words.

"Like being enveloped in huge wings," Elyani said.

"Yes!" Simon exclaimed enthusiastically. "Exactly like that! It's so beautiful. I can't understand what I've done to deserve this!"

"Yes," Szar went on, "what have you done to deserve such an easy, uncomplicated life, Simon?"

They all burst out laughing.

"How can you joke in such tragic times?" a woman asked.

"Ah, don't worry!" Elyani said. "He's been like this ever since I've known him."

"Me?" Szar looked so surprised that they all laughed again.

They remained silent for a long while, watching the fire, letting the Spirit of the Web of Love glow through their hearts. Then Simon told them in a grave voice, "We must make a decision, now. It won't be more than a day or two before the soldiers reach the mountains. We could still try to flee south."

"This is my land. I'm not leaving!" a young woman declared.

"I'll stay!" Elyani seconded her.

"And what about your baby?" Simon asked.

Her left hand on her belly, her right hand holding Szar's hand, pregnant Elyani stood firm as a rock, "I'll stay!"

"I'll stay," Szar nodded.

"And me!" the old man on Simon's right decided. "We could try to hide in the cave by the little stream."

"That's a good idea, Lucien!" Simon approved.

"Oh, God! I don't like the sound of that!" another man said. "Do you know what the soldiers do to those who hide in caves? They wall up the opening and let them die from thirst and asphyxiation."

"What else can we do but try our luck?" old Lucien argued. "We can't just stay here and wait for them to come and slaughter us!"

After a few minutes of discussion, Simon turned towards Elyani, "You haven't told us what you think."

Elyani remained silent.

"You're a woman of sight," Simon insisted, "tell us what you see!"

"If we go to the cave, God will be with us in the cave," she answered.

"Does this mean that we won't get walled inside?" Lucien asked.

"No," Elyani replied immediately. "It means that if we get walled inside, we will die in the wings of the Lord."

Tears in his eyes, Simon looked deep into Elyani.

She held his heart in the Eagle, and shook her head near-imperceptibly.

He understood.

"So we'll go to the cave!" he decided.

"Yes!" a woman rejoiced. "Who should be afraid of dying in the wings of the Lord?" And after hugging each other, they gathered their bags.

As they started walking, old Lucien put his hand on Szar's shoulder. "When you visited the World to Come, Philip, what did you look like?"

"Extraordinarily beautiful, like everyone else in the World to Come!"

"Did you have wings?"

"Nay!" Szar laughed.

"And did you have a beard?"

"But of course!" Szar pretended to be badly offended. "Have you ever seen me without a beard?"

"Just asking!" Lucien exclaimed apologetically. "Just asking!"

The vision faded.

Szar's left hand was left empty.

Archive Hall One was left inundated with White Light.

Deeply moved, Woolly turned towards Szar, "The pure will die in the cave, won't they?"

There was an air of total devastation in Szar's eyes. Gervin had warned him – contemplating the future is the most testing of all trials.

"An illumination of love, it will be," Gervin prophesied. "The Light will descend into the cave, bringing Highness into their hearts. The deepest wish of these people will be fulfilled, they will understand the mystery of the cross and the meaning of the Web of Love."

"Who will be responsible for their deaths?" Szar asked.

"The soldiers of Ahriman," Gervin brought an image of people riding horses. Clad in thick iron coats and iron helmets with only narrow openings for their eyes, they carried a white flag with a large red cross.

"Makes a lot of sense to see them dressed in iron," Woolly remarked. "But what about the cross? I thought it was the emblem of the pure?"

"There will be a lot of religious confusion around this symbol," Gervin answered. "It stands for the incarnation of the clear fountain's verticality into the creation, represented by the horizontal line. Incarnation – this is one of the dominant issues in the future of humanity. Sleepers hardly live in the kingdom, their Spirit is not really present to the world. The more they awaken, the more their Ego becomes involved in the kingdom. At the centre of the revelation of the cross will be a mighty Ego impulse that will foster awakening and bring new qualities to people's hearts. Let's return to the kingdom briefly."

The hall filled with mists. They found themselves in a small Tomoristan street. A woman with a pale aura tripped and fell on the ground. She screamed with pain, her face in the dirt. The passersby ignored her. Those who happened to look at her seemed totally unconcerned.

"Their Ego is aeons away," Gervin observed. "Heartness and warmth are foreign to them. It doesn't even occur to them that they could help her and comfort her. In the kingdom of the rainbows people will have a greater sense of compassion and love, being more in touch with their Ego."

"That was not obvious from the images you have shown us," Woolly remarked. "Apart from the pure, of course."

"The Ego is a gateway to love. No one will be forced into it. Contemplate this great mystery of the future: the tessellated pavement." Gervin let the Atlantean street and the mists vanish. The floor of Archive Hall One appeared to be paved with alternating black and white square tiles.

"One of the emblems of the Knights of the Apocalypse," Szar whispered, recognising the floor of No Limits.

"And understandably so, since the Apocalypse will be a clash between forces of light and forces of darkness. The tessellated pavement represents the destiny of humanity. Think of Atlantean sleepers," Gervin began explaining, "they are slow, boring, incapable of warmth, and incapable full stop, but they are rarely vicious or wicked. They are essentially 'nice' people who flow with whatever wind carries them. When they happen to do horrible things, it is usually by default, not from their own free choice – essentially because they have little or no free choice. They are neither black nor white, but grey.

Not so of people whose Ego is awakened! The more Ego, the more free will. The cosmic impulse of the cross, which will begin in the kingdom of the rainbows, will set humanity on a course where they become increasingly capable of choice, and therefore responsible for each and every one of their acts. And so they will no longer be grey but white or black, servants of the light or servants of the dark side."

"This is why the kingdom of the rainbows will receive an Ahrimanic revelation," Woolly understood. "Same as with us, really. As long as we were sleepers, Ahriman couldn't care less about us. We would have been unable to *choose* to follow him. It's when we started awakening that he sent Aphelion against us."

"As sleepers, you would have been useless to Ahriman. Following the path of evil requires will. Sleepers lack the structure that would allow them to dive deep into the dark side."

Realising that his left foot stood on a black tile, Woolly took a cautious step forward. "I had never realised how dangerous free will was."

"But without free will, there can be no blossoming of the superior flame of the Ego," Gervin insisted. "This is another reason why the Lord Melchisedek will permit Ahriman to infiltrate the Earth. If the free will of human beings only allowed them to choose the light, it would not be free will."

Szar brought back an image of the iron-coated soldiers with the emblem of the red cross. It was night. Under the Full Moon, they were rolling large boulders which they used to wall up the entrance to several caves.

"The servants of the dark side?"

"Not really. Just a bunch of idiots who have been promised heaven if they slaughter these innocent people. They don't really know what they are doing. But those who command them do! They know very well that the pure could pose a major threat to Ahriman's plans. The pure have found the mystery, their hearts are rooted in the Web of Love."

"What will happen to them?" Woolly asked.

"This is not written yet," Gervin gave a mysterious smile. "They could be the starting point of a new civilisation based on brotherly love and spiritual truths – one of the major streams of enlightenment of the future. Which is why Ahriman will do anything in his power to have them all exterminated, so *nothing* remains of their knowledge."

Tears, blood, true love and Eagle's feathers, Szar was crying.

In the cave the Light was bright as Highness.

Lying down in the filth, the pure were dying from thirst.

In the wings of the Eagle.

19.9 Apocalypse, the time when everything is possible

The image faded. Archive Hall One was left flooded with the Light of the Eagle. Woolly's clear fountain throbbed with a flashing realisation, "As time passes, more and more people will awaken to their Ego, is that right?"

"Right!" Gervin answered.

"The more aware of their Ego they become, the more free will they will have, right?"

"Right!"

"Then... necessarily, the more time passes, the less things are written!"

"Absolutely true!" Gervin exclaimed, echoing Woolly's enthusiasm.

"Then there must come a time in the future when it will be absolutely impossible to know on which side the balance will tip – especially if this free will business is *really* serious."

Gervin raised his right eyebrow, "It is."

"Then at that time, really, *anything* will be possible!"

"This is what makes the Apocalypse so exciting. A great many will awaken. Then anything will be possible! *Anything!*"

Archive Hall One turned into the smouldering ruins of a strange city, filled with huge broken iron beams and piles of debris everywhere. The foul-smelling fog was so thick and dark that it was impossible to tell whether it was day or night.

A violent explosion shook the scene, so loud that Woolly and Szar jumped in surprise. The remnants of a building were set ablaze. A man ran out of the ruins. Tall, handsome, curly hair falling to his shoulders. Dressed in the black metallic outfit of the Knights, with the large yellow disk on his chest.

"Virginia!" he Point-called. "Where are you?"

"Just in front of you!" a young woman dressed in the same way Point-answered. She was hiding in a basement located under an enormous pile of metal wreckage. "Hiram, be careful!"

"Where's Jackson?" Hiram Point-asked.

"Dead!" Virginia Point-answered.

"Oh, no!" Hiram kept running full speed.

"Careful! They're on your left!" Virginia Point-shouted.

Hiram threw himself to the ground and hid behind rusty girders.

Two men in red armour appeared. "There!" one of them pointed at him, immediately followed by a series of loud explosions.

Hiram screamed with pain and collapsed.

"No! No!" Virginia shouted, rushing out of the basement. Connecting her Point to a strange spherical thing that was floating above the ruins, she unfurled a deluge of fire onto the two men, instantly turning them into pieces of charcoal.

Three loud bangs resounded, shaking Archive Hall One.

"Hiram!" Virginia Point-yelled, running towards him.

There was no answer.

When she reached him, she found him dead. His astral body was already wafting in the space, disconnected from the physical.

"Hiram!" she screamed, falling on her knees. "Teyani! Teyani! Help! For God's sake, help us!" she invoked.

No answer.

Virginia slowly stood up, raising her arms, palms facing Hiram. She concentrated her energy and called with all her strength. In the space of a few seconds, her aura turned into a White Flame of Spirit which strangely contrasted with the forlorn greyness of the ruins.

"Teyani!" she clenched her jaw, "I *know* you can help!" She pulled from the Spirit with such might that her Flame gradually grew ten times the size of her body.

From the Edge of Highness, a response sparked.

A formidable stream of Spirit started pouring out of her mouth, "As it was in the beginning, is now, and ever shall be, world without end, Amen!"

It was immense, awesome. Rolling Thunder, an entire hierarchy of angels discharging their fire through her mouth.

Hiram's aura flashed with thousands of dazzling sparks.

Virginia started shaking like a leaf, as if the power was about to blow her body to pieces. Holding to the Spirit, she kept blasting her friend's body with the Voice.

Abruptly, she became silent and fell on her knees. She took Hiram in her arms and held him against her.

He opened his eyes.

Dazed by the brightness of the dancing flames, he mumbled, "Is this the Fields of Peace?"

"Not yet!" To stop herself from trembling, she held him tighter.

"Oh my God!" Hiram realised he had been brought back to life. "Did you do that?" he asked in shock.

She nodded, wondering whether it was really happening. Then she let go of him and stood up. "We'll talk later. Can you walk?"

Holding her hand, Hiram managed to get up. A grinding abdominal pain took his breath away, as if he was being cut in two.

Gasping, he held his belly, fighting to remain on his feet.

Virginia raised her arms vertically and called onto Highness again.

"Walk!" she unleashed the Voice onto him, White-igniting his aura.

The power was insane. Every single cell of Hiram's body started vibrating with the most unreal sensation he had ever felt.

"Walk!" she Voice-projected onto him. "Walk!" And she took his hand and started running. To his complete amazement, Hiram found himself running behind her.

The vision faded, leaving Archive Hall One out of breath.

When he saw the fierce Dragon look on Woolly's and Szar's faces, Gervin burst out laughing.

"Was she calling on *our* Teyani?" Woolly frowned.

"Yes, *our* Teyani, who will return from Highness to take part in the training of the Knights of the Apocalypse," Gervin thundered.

"So the Knights will be trained in the power of the Voice!" Woolly exclaimed with wonder.

"No they won't, and this was all the beauty of this scene," Gervin replied. "In Apocalyptic times, thousands of years after the end of the kingdom of the rainbows, the Voice will be a long-forgotten legend."

"So how did she do it?"

"Through the power of awakening!" Gervin clicked his fingers, producing a wonderfully musical drum sound.

"But..." Szar was dumbfounded. "I received the Voice as a transmission of power, part of the initiation of an ancient lineage. How..." he hesitated.

"She will receive it directly from Highness."

"Do you mean to say she lives in a world of people who can't even see auras and she is capable of projecting the Word of Thunder without having been initiated into it!" Woolly and Szar looked at each other, suddenly wondering if they themselves were at all awakened.

"Will many people awaken like her?" Woolly questioned.

"This, no one can predict, since it will be the time when everything is possible," Gervin shone his mystery-smile. "But enough will awaken to threaten Ahriman. The Apocalypse will be the time when the tessellated pavement comes to completion. Even though large numbers of human beings may still be grey, the separation of black and white forces will reach a point of confrontation. Seeing so many human beings on the brink of awakening, Ahriman will have no choice but to launch a grand offensive, a war of all against all."

"And then what? Are some scenarios more probable than others?"

"At the end of the Apocalypse a fraction of humanity reaches the spiritual maturity which allows them to be lifted into the Fields of Peace. They arrive here and begin a new phase in their evolution. The Earth, by then, is nothing more than piles of ashes and rubble. What is left of the Earth becomes the kingdom of the dregs, over which Ahriman rules unchallenged."

Archive Hall One turned into a huge, ominous red pyre. It was a degraded fire with no connection and no Spirit, hungry flames devouring everything, leaving only black dregs. Finally, the only thing left was the black substance of Ahriman – that black pitch which only Alcibyadi's ritual at the Edge of Highness had been able to clear from Szar's hand.

"And what about the rest of humanity, those who haven't made it to the Fields of Peace?"

"They will find themselves in a lamentable situation. The new humanity in the Fields of Peace will make great efforts to try and rescue them. Those who can't be rescued, either because they are too lukewarm or because they have given in to Ahriman's darkness beyond recall, will become the inhabitants of the kingdom of the dregs. Some will end up in Ahriman's pit of darkness. Most will be left hanging in intermediary spaces until the beginning of the next cosmic cycle, where it will be impossible for them to join the rest of the human hierarchy because they will have missed too much of the journey of evolution."

"Is this the worst possible scenario?"

"Oh, no! There are several variations on the same theme, depending on how much of humanity awakens. In the worst scenario, Ahriman manages to keep the Earth asleep until his wars destroy everything. Due to insufficient spiritual maturity, humanity is unable to continue its evolution in the Fields of Peace. Human beings have more or less wasted an entire cosmic cycle."

"And since *anything* will be possible, what is the *highest* possible outcome?" Woolly wanted to know.

"A zenith of awakening. An explosion of Spirit in the heart of human beings. The triumph of the Web of Love. Ahriman defeated without any wars. The Earth and the Fields of Peace become one."

Woolly was astonished. "Could that really happen?"

"Well, of course," Gervin laughed, "since *anything* will be possible."

Szar twinged his beard, "That would imply correcting all the effects of the fall, wouldn't it?"

"The elemental corruption redeemed, the end of death, and the eradication of all dark forces from the human sphere. The regenerated Earth becomes married to the Fields of Peace, and in this new world the whole of humanity begins a new chapter of its evolution."

"How probable a scenario is it?" Woolly asked.

"It would require a phenomenal amount of transformation. But if enough people on Earth awaken, then it definitely becomes possible. And if you want to know what the world would look like then, just go out of this hall. The transformed Earth already exists. It is here."

19.10 Where a man belongs

Woolly was crying by the side of the River of Remembrance.

The grief seemed endless.

For one thing, crying in the Fields of Peace was so much easier than in the kingdom, where it leaves your eyes unlawfully red and your face looking like a venom-mop. Fields-of-Peace tears were free-flowing, clean, venom-free, and they came straight from the heart.

"But why does my heart ache so much?" Woolly asked the river.

"Because you haven't yet reached the core of yourself," the river whispered. "Just open a little more, let another wall fall!"

"Aaaahh!" Woolly cried in agony, remembering the ghastly episode in which his nose had been broken.

"And a little bit more," the river kept flowing through his heart.

"But the more walls fall, the worse the pain!" Woolly complained. "Opening, opening... why does it have to hurt so much?"

"It is not opening that hurts, it's when you stop closing off," the river explained. "The layers that covered your heart are peeled off, the shells are broken. This is what hurts."

"But why do I have so many shells?" Woolly sobbed.

"Don't just think of the pain! Haven't you noticed that the more the facades fall from you, the more alive you become?"

"True," he conceded. But another wave of pain rose. "Aaaahh! I feel bottomlessly hopeless!"

"Let me wash you," the river offered.

Woolly's trust in the river was such that he immediately threw himself into the water, holding the flower on his chest.

"Ah, don't worry!" the flower whispered into his heart. "I am not going to let you down now that you need me the most."

Woolly let himself drown, as in his last life, when he had committed suicide because too many things – *too* many things – had gone wrong for far too long, and who cared? What was the point?

As he kept drowning, and drowning, Woolly realised that the water was far deeper than he had thought.

"You wouldn't want me to be shallow, would you?" the River of Remembrance smiled.

"Of course not! But..."

"In the Fields of Peace, one breathes to worship the Lord, not by necessity," the river reassured him. "Just keep drowning! You like it, don't you?"

"True," he accepted.

"Do you see why?"

"When you are drowning, then really there is nothing to worry about any more. You leave everything behind. You're not holding onto anything."

"You let go!" the river summarised. "Just do that... totally!"

"But I can't!" Woolly objected. Instantly, he stopped drowning. He found himself suspended in the waters. "What if I go too deep and arrive late for the Thunder initiation ?"

"Will you not trust me?" the river asked.

"I trust you but this is very serious! If I miss the initiation, then really... really, it's the end!"

"Frankly," the flower whispered to his heart, "can you really imagine the Masters of Thunder would start the initiation without you?"

"Mm... no, not really," Woolly admitted.

"The truth is, you do *not* trust me!" the river said. "You do not trust anything, or anyone. Not even yourself. How could you be ready to meet Thunder if you don't even trust yourself?"

Woolly, suspended, was shaken by throes of agony. His heart caked with so many layers, the cause seemed hopeless. This in itself proved a great help. When there is *really* no hope, why cling on? The distress could have gone on forever, so why not stop right now?

At the climax of pain, a wave rose from the deepest,

"Letting go!"

To his immense relief, he started drowning again.

"Keep drowning like this until the end of time and you will know my wisdom," the river chanted.

"Unrestrictedly, unlimitedly, unaffectedly, unbendingly, unapprehensively, unfathomably, un-unlawfully drowning!" Woolly let out a cosmic sigh that opened every single pore of his body.

Down, down, down... and down!

"But wait a minute!" He realised he was no longer drowning downwards, but upwards.

He found himself suspended again.

"Ah, you're not going to start *a-gain*, are you?" the river protested.

"All right!" Woolly burst out laughing, letting himself fall upwards.

It went much faster than when he had been going down, and it lasted much longer, which of course did not make sense, but that was exactly what Woolly needed.

"The pulsing," the river whispered to him. "It holds the key."

Woolly tuned into his heart, feeling the pulse linking his body to the Fields of Peace. A few times, when the pain was too bad, he had tried to take refuge in the soft pulsing quality. It brought relief, but without reaching the bottom of the wound.

"It's because you are doing it the wrong way!" The river made itself pure pulsing-ness, a stream of light in which Woolly was falling up faster and faster! But when was this going to finish? Never, precisely! Pulsing without end, as pulsing was in the beginning, is now, and ever will pulse.

This was when Woolly understood.

He was not part of the pulsing of the Fields of Peace.

He *was* the pulsing. The pulsing was him. And the Fields of Peace were in the pulsing, inside him! And so were the sky, the Sun, the kingdom, the worlds of the gods and the Molten Sea, the Ugly Underworlds and the beautiful ones, the fountain of blue Life and Light and all the birds of paradise, and the Mother the Dragon and her Melchisedek lover, and why stop there? Just around the corner, the Mother of the Light who smiles at the end of the Fault of Eternity was inside him too, and so was *all* the rest!

When Woolly's head emerged out of the water, he was a different man.

He contemplated the sky, which looked completely different, and the woods along the river, which looked completely different too.

Szar was sitting on the shore, having just returned from a long walk to the Mountains of Sharp Vision. White-wondered by the illumination in Woolly's aura, he read the creation's infinity in his eyes.

Soaking wet, Woolly went to sit close to him, placing his hand on his shoulder.

"You have come to say farewell, I know," Woolly pulsed the wisdom of the river into his friend.

"I love you, Woolly," Szar had tears in his eyes. "And I will come whenever you or Gervin call me. But this is not my world! I do not belong here."

"I understand," Woolly contemplated the river. "Finding the place where you belong is perhaps the most important of all things."

"You belong... here?" Szar asked.

"Oh, yes!" the river sighed through Woolly. "This is where I have *always* belonged. Now that I know this, things will never be the same. Kingdoms can rise and fall, and my kingdom-nose can be broken and fixed... my heart will be pulsing here, always!"

They remained silent, listening to the river.

"You have lost your flower," Szar noticed.

"No, it has become one with my heart," Woolly said. "And what about you, beautiful friend, where will you go?"

"After the initiation, I'll return to the kingdom with you, of course. We have a bad mess to fix, down there. From what I have seen in Archive Hall One, victory is far from being assured. But when the Archive mission comes to an end, I will not come back here. I will fly to Revelation Sky."

"To Elyani?"

"No, that is not where she lives. There are so many worlds in the triangle! Especially in the sky, at the tip of the triangle, where infinities are Point-packed on top of infinities. It's a mystery to me, I have this sky of the gods in my Flying Dragon's skin. The first time I saw it, I spent an entire night crying. Then one day I realised. It was while I was being beaten up by a god," he confided.

"Beaten up by a god?" Woolly found that amazing.

"The worst beating I have ever taken, and by far!" Szar nodded. "But what a revelation! Above me was this arch-magnificent expanse, the source of the wisdom of the gods. And the more my friend was punching me in the stomach (he'll become a friend, I know), the more obvious it became to me – this was my world! Ever since, I have known it in my blood. And these holy Fields of Peace have only confirmed it. I belong to Revelation Sky. I *must* return there."

"How beautiful!" Woolly and the river exclaimed in unison.

"I am going to miss you, friend," Szar took Woolly's hand.

"I have just understood the meaning of one of the most important verses of the Law," Woolly replied. "That which is, will always be."

The River of Remembrance sang,

"Flying Dragons, gods, the Lord Melchisedek, you and me.
Forever One in Love."

19.11 Thunder initiation

Hymn after hymn, monumental flames coming out of his mouth,
Gervin filled Archive Hall One with Voice.
The One Voice which sings the Song of Creation.
As it was in the beginning is Voice, and ever shall be.
Voice and Fire, Fire and Voice, I am walking on the edge.
Mother of the Light, protect my way!
Gervin held Szar's wrists. The Voice became an all-consuming fire,
"I now invest you with the powers of a Master of Thunder!"
Breath of the Unborn God.
Archive Hall One disappeared. The world was extinguished.
Waking from the Great Serpent's dream,
Szar found himself on the Edge of Highness.
Under him, a tempest, thousands of lightning shafts
Weaving an incandescent web – the warp of Thunder,

One with the Sea of Lightning.
Rumbling Cosmic Fire, God's Will unleashed,
Light in Darkness, colours unspeakable,
An ever-moving blazing cloud of infinite expanse
Stretching from one end of the Great Night to the other.
His feet in the thunderous waves, Szar saw Gervin,
One with a thousand million angels of Highness,
One with the White Eagle's irresistible fire.
At the Edge of Highness the Eagle is no meekness
But an unstoppable power, Absolute Flame, infinite straightness.
Wisely, he keeps his fire separate from the creation,
Lest all things be consumed.
Vision of Thunder – simple, direct, awesome.
See only Fire! Find the source of all sources.
Pointing to the thunderous sea,
Gervin gave Szar his final instruction,
"Now you can be anything, you can do anything!"

Vision of Thunder, brutally total.
Resting on the power, dancing a lovers' dance with the Eagle,
Szar heard the whisper of the Universal Mother.
It travelled like a wild wind of remoteness.
It sung the mysteries of a thousand futures,
"The thing you want to see the most
Is the thing you want to see the least.
One day, God will ask you to destroy a city."
Revelation Sky crying tears of starlight,
Watching the birth and death of civilisations.
The pure, slaughtered by Ahriman, and reborn in the Land of the Rose.
Barkhan Seer dancing in the Golden Sun.
The Knights ascending God's White Line.
Apocalypse, the time when everything is possible.
Philadelphia Six, the city in space. Twenty times more souls
Than Eisraim in the flourishing days of Orest.
And yet, nothing more than a tiny dot in space.
How improbable life is. Fragile like the blossoms of the alohim tree.
"Engage!"
Bleeding Sun. The space turns red,
Philadelphia Six plunged into a sea of flames.
And Virginia is dead.
There are sorrows that do not pass with time.
Surrendering to the power which can reunite all things
Because it has created all things,
Szar called, "Mother, Mother, if anything or anyone can erase this,
Please! Please, let the sins of men be washed

By the waters of your compassion."

"Serah?"
"Panther!"
"Serah, we need to speak to you. Immediately."
"Who's we?"
"Hiram and I."
"So Hiram is talking to me, now. Good news. I'm just about to see McGuirk to prepare the meeting with High Command, so I can't see you right now..."
"Yes you can! Listen, Serah, Hiram has a plan. A plan to liberate Philadelphia Six. I believe it could work."
"A plan to liberate Philadelphia Six..." Sitting in his office, Serah pensively contemplates Mercury through the large bay window. From Eisraim to Philadelphia, eternity condensed in one point.

One with my father, the Flying Dragon from beyond
The Abyss of the Deep and the Fault of Eternity,
One with Gervin,
One with Orest,
One with Barkhan Seer,
One with Takhar the Unbending,
One with the entire lineage of Thunder,
One with the god of the golden helmet,
Who is playing the molten star in front of the Original Sea,
One with the Eagle,
The Gold of the Tradition is my offering,
To the source of all sources, I give, I give.
To the Mother of the Light, I give, I give.

– Thus ends the Book of the Fields of Peace –

Note: Szar's knot of destiny – the rendezvous with Hiram and Philadelphia Six – is retold in the *Bleeding Sun* legend.

20

The Book of the Last Days

20.1 Aparalgon, son of Aparalgon

"Master Szar! Master Szar!"

Szar turned round. In an empty alley of Maniya, swamped with thick dark mists, a grey silhouette was walking towards him.

Szar wriggled his nostrils. The smell was that of a young man. Dangerous? No, completely innocuous. A sleeper.

There were smells of death wafting in the space, coming from all directions. Not surprising, considering a hundred people had died from the pestilence in the last three days, and another four hundred were agonising in their beds. One more week like this and the temple's population would be reduced by two thirds.

A priest in his early twenties emerged from the fog, "Praise the Lord Melchisedek, Master Szar of the Brown Robe!" His aura showed no signs of the pestilence.

"All glory to the Lord Melchisedek, man of the Law!"

He had soft blue eyes, and no beard. He gave a beautiful sleeper's smile, "Master Szar, my name is Aparalgon of the Grey Robes of the Angel of Dawn. May I speak to you for a lawful moment?"

His highness Aparalgon was the Grey Robes' assistant grand master who had lodged an administrative complaint against Szar for daring to speak to his highness without first being addressed by him. The fact that Szar had done this while rescuing his highness and healing his ankle was irrelevant: the Law is the Law.

But a spring and an autumn had already passed since that old bastard in the Law had left his body.

"Aparalgon, son of Aparalgon, perhaps?" Szar asked.

"Lawfully correct. So you know my father!" the young man exclaimed, as if it explained everything.

Breathing deeply, thinking of the White Eagle, "I had the privilege of meeting his highness last year."

"No, his highness Aparalgon, Assistant Grand Master of the Grey Robes of the Angel of Dawn, was the father of my father, Aparalgon of the Grey Robes of the Angel of Dawn," Aparalgon corrected.

"I see."

"Master Szar, I have come to lawfully ask you to enlighten me."

"What about?"

"The Truth of the Law."

Szar frowned, "I lawfully beg your pardon?

At that moment, Szar received a Point-call from Khej in the rainbow chapel, "Commander, the short-range sensors are picking up a strange signal. In the catacombs, in the mid-eastern enclave. Under the chapels of Barradine."

Szar Point-tuned in. "A rat?"

"Could be."

"Activate the pest-removing field and see what happens," Szar Point-instructed. "I'll be with you in a minute, I'm just round the corner."

Aparalgon didn't notice the Point-conversation. Yet, Szar noticed, his Point had been finely woven in the Eisraim style.

"Yes, Master Szar, I have come to beg you to accept me as your disciple, that you may enlighten me and reveal the Truth of the Law to me," Aparalgon reverently recited the lawful verses. "I have come to surrender my destiny to you!"

Half the temple was dying from the pestilence. The warp in the throes of agony, the Archive transfer was imminent. And the thirteen ghost Nephilim had been spotted at a distance of only half an hour from the temple's main entrance four times in the past forty-eight hours. The last thing Szar needed was a disciple – especially a lawful parrot.

Szar shook his head, "Sorry, man of the Law! I have no time to give you." He set off for the rainbow chapel, walking fast.

Aparalgon rushed behind him, "At first the teacher shall refuse, so as to test your endurance. You shall lawfully persist, demonstrating that your soul is pure and your resolution is great," he recited.

There was something touching in his naive enthusiasm.

"Don't you have a teacher?" Szar asked him.

"My teacher was his highness Aparalgon, Assistant Grand Master of the Grey Robes of the Angel of Dawn, and he taught me the Law lawfully well. But now that he has left for the Great Journey, I must find another teacher."

"It's been nearly a year since his highness left."

Aparalgon had to run to follow Szar's pace, "Until the last days, I had not realised how important it was for me to find another teacher."

"And what made you suddenly realise this, my friend in the Law?"

Khej sent another Point-call, "It *was* a rat. I think, it was a rat. The signal wasn't completely clear."

"And now?" Szar Point-asked.

"After the pest-removing field it's complete silence."

"Keep scanning!" Szar Point-ordered.

Racing behind Szar, Aparalgon was holding his long hair, tied in a bun behind his head. "Lawfully frankly, I couldn't tell you what made me realise. But I *know* the time has come, and I *know* you are the teacher," he added with surprising decidedness.

"Friend..." Szar stopped to face him. He softened his voice, "Friend, you come late. Now I *really* have no time."

"Great teachers are always more busy than the Law! But perhaps I could be of help to you. The Law says, Serve your teacher and the nectar of the Law will flow into you."

Szar closed his eyes, scanning him. "Do you know anything about fields?"

"Lawfully certainly!" Aparalgon chanted, "The fields were given to the children of the Law by the Lord Melchisedek, that they may chant His glory and sacrifice to Him. And through His endless bounty..."

"No," Szar interrupted him, reopening his eyes. "I meant, do you know how to operate and repair fields?"

Aparalgon's face became vague. "This particular aspect of the Law is unknown to the priests of the Grey Robe of the Angel of Dawn, Master Szar."

"Can you fight?"

Aparalgon wasn't sure what Szar meant. He gave his beautiful smile, "Fight with Spirit, man of the Law!"

"I mean, can you operate soft-stone weapons?"

"Harming living beings is against the Law of the priests of the Grey..."

"Aparalgon..." Szar put his hand on the priest's shoulder, calling on the compassion of the Mother of the Light.

Looking deep into him, he held the silence of the Dawn of Creation.

Aparalgon didn't notice. "Are you accepting me as your disciple, Master Szar?" he asked, eyes beaming with hope.

Szar sighed.

What can a sleeper do when his world is about to collapse?

"Aparalgon, have you ever heard of the book of Maveron?"

"This particular aspect of the Law is unknown to the priests of the..."

"Then go to the chapel of the White Eagle and ask Lady Teyani or one of her priestesses to teach you the book of Maveron."

"But Master Szar, I couldn't do that!"

"Why?"

"I am not married!" He started reciting, "A non-married priest of the Grey Robe of the Angel of Dawn must not converse with a woman, nor cut his hair, nor come close to a corpse, nor..."

"Fine!" Szar spoke straight from Revelation Sky, "You want to know the Truth of the Law? Go and shave your head, ask Teyani to teach you Maveron, and become a helper in the cremation ground."

Unlawfully stupefied, Aparalgon stared at him, half blanking out.

Szar gently slapped the priest's shoulder, "Farewell, man of the Law!" and he walked away.

This time, Aparalgon didn't follow him.

20.2 Rats

In the rainbow hall Szar found Khej and Lord Proston working together. Khej was sitting in meditation position, his back Thunder-straight. Unusually, Lord Proston was lying on the floor, eyes closed.

"I think we found another rat," Khej announced. "In the catacombs. Also in the mid-eastern enclave, but under the chapel of the Rural Deities, this time."

Only one hundred and fifty lawful feet from the chapel of Barradine.

Szar's nostrils cringed, "That stinks! How could a rat have survived the field you blasted under Barradine?"

"Perhaps it's just arrived from some lawful place else," the young Field Wizard conjectured.

"I don't like that. I don't like that at all! Throw another pest-killer immediately and report!"

Szar went to sit on the floor close to the former grand superintendent of the fields. "Are you all right, Lord Proston?"

The fifty-year-old man opened his eyes and gave a courteous smile, "Lawfully fine, just tired."

With the ghost Nephilim so close, no one had slept much in the last days.

"I must speak to you, Commander," Proston sat up. "This morning I went out of the chapel and had a Point-chat with Lord Viniret, my successor at the King's palace. Grim news. The Nephilim giants have sent out another army. These are the elite battalions of the Green Guard, by far the best troops in the kingdom. And they are heading towards us, burning everything on their way. The good news for us is, the King's generals are preparing a huge counteroffensive, massing troops in Asherban and the northern parts of Perentie: the first, sixth and ninth armies, over a hundred thousand men."

Szar contemplated his left fist, "Even ten against one, I can't see the King's army standing a chance against the giants of the Green Guard."

Proston didn't agree. "The ninth army is powerful: trained in the venom arts, and under Nephilim command. Have you ever heard of General Harravan? The heir of a prestigious lineage of Nephilim officers. Forty years ago at the battle of Monahal, his father gave the giants a memorable beating. We can't know for sure that the ninth army will be able to stop the Green Guard, but at least they will inflict serious casualties."

"Nephilim against Nephilim!" Szar grinned. Serious again, "The burning question is, if the giants annihilate the King's armies in Perentie, where will they go next? West to Jex Belaran, or south to Lasseera and us?"

"With Bobros at their head, there is reason to hope they'll race to Jex Belaran. You know that Lubu started the order of the Hunters by killing one of Bobros' ancestors, don't you?"

Bobros and his three ugly Nephilim sisters. The legend.

For one second, Szar was back in Mount Lohrzen's dining hall, taking Verzaza-Floster in his arms to the vociferous jubilation of one hundred and fifty Sons of the Dragon.

He shook his head, firm, "The Great Warriors hold different views as to who killed that Bobros."

Proston responded with a diplomatic smile.

"Anyhow..." Szar went on, "something on which everyone agrees is who killed Bobros' grandfather: the Brown Robes."

"What?" Proston's eyes opened wide in horror.

"Didn't you know? At the clearing of Erriba, thirty-nine years ago. Orest and the Masters of Thunder got rid of that son of a Bobros, who had taken over the valley of the Necromancer and plagued the entire country with its darkness."

"Oh, but that changes everything!"

An ominous token for the county of Eisraim.

"Alarm!" Khej sent a Point-signal to everyone in the chapel. "The rat survived the pest-killer field. I keep picking up its vibration in the sector of the Rural Deities."

Meaning the rat was *not* a rat!

"Oh shit!" Master Ferman erupted into the rainbow hall. "Shall we engage the wormwood procedure, Commander? All our Field Wizards are inside the chapel."

"Engage, then!"

Khej and Proston Point-activated a wormwood field, a powerful weapon of the Eisraim Wizards. It flooded the entire network of catacombs with deadly levels of venom.

No living creature could survive such a dose.

Except, of course, Nephilim Hunters.

"Gallagher!" Ferman Point-called, "Open the secret Point-pathway and call Lehrmon and Woolly in Lasseera. I want them to be kept informed of what's happening here, lawful minute by lawful minute."

The Field Wizards held their breath, all Points fixed on the under-chapel of the Rural Deities, scanning the space through the catacombs' sensor-fields.

"The rat signal is still there!" Khej Point-shouted, thrilled by the prospect of imminent action. "There's a fucking Nephilim in the catacombs!"

Or perhaps more than one.

"Disengage the wormwood field. Everyone takes their position!" Szar Point-ordered, and he started running full-speed in the direction of his bedroom – the only part of the rainbow chapel opening into the temple's catacombs.

When the enemy arrived at the chapel, it would be there.

That morning the bedroom was a field packed with dark-blue stars reflected from the Blue Lagoon, so close to each other that the entire space had turned blue. It stopped at the colonnade of vaulted archways that led to the catacombs. There the arches were lit with yellow glows, a poetic contrast with the blueness of the Lagoon.

"Everyone in position, Commander!" Ferman Point-reported.

The Field Wizards were sitting in pairs, each in separate rooms of the building, their Points on the triggers of thousands of deadly fields.

"Engage the night!" Szar ordered.

In the hall, all light disappeared.

Every single room in the rainbow chapel had turned dark. The darkness of a cosmic night, much blacker than black. The Wizards could no longer see their bodies. Not even the faintest glow in darkness visible.

And the waiting started again. With a major difference, though. This time, no doubt – the enemy was *inside* the temple.

As he began the first movements of the black dance, Szar grinned with satisfaction at the quality of Point-ness in the chapel. Awakening was running high. Never before had the Field Wizards been so totally centred, their columns of Spirit precisely attuned to Master Gervin in Archive Hall One.

So was this what it took for them to awaken?

Praised be the Lord Melchisedek for having created the Nephilim!

Gervin's presence came down into the chapel to meet them.

But as minutes passed and the rat wasn't budging, a wave of unease arose among the troops.

Was this going to be another endless waiting game?

The problem was, they couldn't kill him from a distance.

The Wizards weren't short of Nephilim-killer fields. But these were all laid within the rainbow chapel and its immediate surroundings. None reached as far as the mid-eastern enclave, nearly a quarter of a lawful mile away.

"The vibration we're picking up is totally still," Lorenz remarked. "What if it was an artefact coming from the windmills of the Law? I can't see how the energy of a living being could remain so unfluctuating."

"The Nephilim can do things like this," Ferman said. "But not any Renegade Hunter! He would *have* to have been trained in Jex Belaran."

"Or in the Eastern Peninsula," Proston added. "Your opinion, Commander?"

Dragon in the Point, "Not an artefact!"

In silence, they waited.

Thirty minutes later, the signal was unchanged.

There was no way in the seven spheres the Field Wizards could spend another day in the chapel doing nothing, waiting for the ghost Nephilim to make a move. Throughout the temple there were fields in need of urgent repair. The arch-precious travelling field of the Controllers' chapel, in particular, was on the verge of collapsing. So were the fields in the music hall and in the second hall of Melchisedek. Unless they were fixed immediately, the fields risked losing their memory – and then there would be nothing left of them to transfer into the Archive!

Besides, how could the Archive transfer take place with crack Nephilim fighters playing hide-and-seek in the catacombs?

Something *had* to happen.

"I'm going to make a sortie," Szar Point-announced.

No one liked the news, but there was not much choice.

Khej volunteered, "May I come with you, Commander?"

"No."

Set in motion from Archive Hall One, Szar started running into the catacombs. "Khej, keep relaying the rat signal into my Point."

Khej connected the short-range sensor field to Szar's Point, "Done!"

An elusive breath. Nothing more than a whisk of shade in the purpleness of darkness visible.

His energy concealed, Szar was running through a large bowel that stank of sewage at the north-eastern end of the enclave of lawful relief when Lorenz Point-warned, "Two more rats! They're coming from the east. Towards the mid-eastern enclave. They're moving. Slowly. Towards the Rural Deities."

Which didn't necessarily mean they knew Szar was coming.

Approaching the mid-eastern enclave, Szar was scanning darkness visible. Not the faintest smell of Nephilim spice, nothing indicating a presence in the catacombs.

These were great experts in the art of camouflage.

"The two new rats are now under the chapel of the Golden Egg," Lorenz updated.

Khej estimated their speed, "They don't seem to be running. They probably haven't detected you, Commander."

Szar was now under the chapel of Ananta, in the mid-eastern enclave.

Less than a hundred lawful feet from his target.

He stopped running. At this distance, there was a danger the rat could hear him.

Sixty lawful feet in front of him, there was a crossing. Judging from the signal, the rat could only be in the bowel on the left.

"Now Point-call me only if the rat moves, or in case of extreme danger!" Szar disconnected from Khej.

Silent, sealed, he walked like a cat.

In the bowel's semi-darkness, the only noise came from a nearby sewage channel.

No thoughts, Point-Dragon.

Thirty lawful feet from the crossing, Khej sent an emergency Point-call, "Thirteen Nephilim in the temple! Not in the catacombs..."

Before Khej could finish, Szar felt a formidable wave reaching his Point.

Triangularly sealed, he held onto Gervin's presence.

Point-warfare – a split second to kill or be killed.

Venom tidal wave. Dark. Treacherous and ugly like sleep. Massive. Powered from the sky of the Watchers.

Matching the wave, Szar's Point became a gigantic flame.

A second wave hit him. The pitch of a thousand abysses.

Cold. Hope is dead.

Darkness is vast, mysterious are its roots.

Give in to sleep! Death eternal is also eternity.

Szar caught a glimpse, "So you are the one who killed Fridrick!"

But why? Why?

Stepping from Archive Hall One into Revelation Sky, from Revelation Sky into eternity. The Nectar God has burned the world.

The creation in one drop. Highness and the world are One.

Down there, far away, a god screams,

"The triaxe! Use the triaxe!"

Kartendranath, whom the Mother of the Light loves so much.

She smiles.

Taking the triaxe, Szar contemplates infinity in Her eyes.

Nothing is written, not even Philadelphia. Not even Hiram...

Not even Virginia.

Smite, triaxe! One blow.

One Law, one way. He who never sleeps never dies.

All glory to the teacher!

"...they're on the western side, close to the main entrance," Khej finished his Point-message, immediately adding, "Now wait, wait! We're losing the signal under the Rural Deities! The rat is disappearing."

A thud noise, coming from the bowel on the left.

Szar ran to the crossing.

Lorenz Point-announced, "Now my two rats are running, but they've changed direction! They're going east. Running away, it seems."

Turning left, Szar finally saw him.

Only forty lawful feet away. A heap on the floor. His astral body disintegrated by the triaxe.

"Khej! The rat is dead. A Hunter, judging by his leather bag."

"You've killed him already?"

Already? An aeon had elapsed!

"What about the thirteen Nephilim? Where are they heading for?"

"This is crazy... they're moving away! Looks like they're running fast, Commander! Shit! Shit! I'm losing them!"

Szar knelt by the corpse.

A tall man in his mid-thirties, dressed in a long dark-blue cloak. Short blond hair. The high forehead of a man of the north.

So this was the man who had killed Fridrick.

Death had made him serene, like a child fast asleep.

Szar inspected his leather bag.

Horror!

"Khej, this man was carrying more than three hundred soft-stone weapons!"

Magnificent he-stones, all of the same model – meaning it was unlikely they had been stolen.

"Where are the other two men?"

"They're about to cross the southern wall of the temple. They'll soon have disappeared from our short-range sensor fields."

20.3 Warmth

Szar emerged from the catacombs in the middle of the chapel of the Rural Deities, recently converted into a large cowshed. Amidst haystacks he walked backwards, pulling the Hunter's corpse by the shoulders.

He bumped into a cow. The cow mooed unlawfully at him but didn't move. He modified his course accordingly.

The noise drew the attention of two priests of the caste of Attendants of the Sacred Cows. "Praise the Lord Melchisedek, Master Szar of the Brown Robe!" they greeted him with the consistently serene voice and smile of their caste, and without taking any notice of what he was doing.

"All glory to the Lord Melchisedek!" Szar responded without stopping but with all the heartness of Gervin's presence.

When he arrived at the fence, the attendants politely opened the gate for him, and closed it behind him.

He kept dragging the corpse. "Many lawful thanks to you, men of the Law!"

They kept smiling at him, "Farewell, man of the Law!"

Still walking backwards, Szar reached the chapel's portal and went down the stairs, the Hunter's boots thumping on each step.

He found himself in the path of the Angel of Dawn, opposite the chapel of the Grey Robes. A group of priests, Aparalgon among them, were sitting in the chapel's doorway, watching the mists.

At this time of the day they should have been performing their rituals. But the field they normally used for this purpose had broken down. So they were waiting for the Field Wizards.

"Praise the Lord Melchisedek, Master Szar!" Aparalgon stood up and walked towards him.

He hadn't shaved his head.

"What a lawful coincidence!" he smiled like the Law. "Doesn't the Law say, 'No meeting is without lawful meaning' and 'When the disciple is ready, the master will cross his path'?"

"Aparalgon, now is not a good time."

"Great teachers are always more busy than the Law! But please, Master Szar, let me lawfully help you carry your friend. Doesn't the Law say, 'The disciple shall take his share of the master's burden'?"

The Hunter's head was hanging backwards, his mouth half open.

"Aparalgon, don't you notice something about this man?"

"I do not recognise his robe. His caste is unknown to the Grey Robes of the Angel of Dawn." The young man bent down to grab the Hunter's feet.

Inspired by Gervin's presence, Szar didn't stop him.

Together, they carried the body along the path of the Angel of Dawn. In the thick, dark fog, they were soon out of view of the Grey Robe priests.

"You did it!" Khej and Namron emerged out of the mists, having run all the way from the rainbow chapel.

"You did it! You did it!" Khej shouted, taking Szar in his arms.

Szar dropped the Hunter to give him a hug. This was when he noticed for the first time that Khej's shoulders had broadened. Hugging the tall young Field Wizard was nearly like hugging a Son of the Dragon.

And what warmth!

Namron's cheeks and nose were black from having spat out his black root against the wind. "You scared the Ugly Underworld out of us, Commander!" he wiped toxic sweat from his forehead with his hand and slapped Szar's shoulder, cleaning his hand on the brown gown without realising it.

"Fucking ghosts! Ahh!" Dancing with joy, Khej kicked the corpse, "At last we got one of them."

Aparalgon, who was still holding the Hunter's feet, watched the scene with some bewilderment.

Knowing his caste, Namron and Khej refrained from saluting him.

"What's the latest?" Szar asked.

"The catacombs are completely clear. We've just spotted the group of thirteen ghosts in the forest, ten minutes away from the main gates. You scared them away, Commander!"

"Hunh hunh! I wish it could be that simple."

"Ahh!" Khej kicked the corpse again. "At least, there's one less of them."

That was when Aparalgon finally understood. "Has this man..." Horrified, trembling, he dropped the Hunter's feet. "Has this man begun the Great Journey?"

Khej turned towards him, one eyebrow raised, one eye half closed.

Namron looked at him too, pulling a quizzical face. Seeing the profound disarray on the young priest's face, he went searching in his pocket for the infamous substance. With the same hand.

Since Aparalgon had asked them a question, there was no lawful reason not to speak to him. Namron handed him a small heap, "Want some black root, man of the Law?"

Again, it was Gervin who inspired Szar to say, "Aparalgon, I think that at this stage, some black root would be excellent for your spiritual development."

Trusting the master's word unconditionally, Aparalgon took the turd-looking heap and stuffed it in his mouth.

Immediately, his face flushed scarlet. His mouth turned into a burning hell, he started coughing and spitting.

"Farewell, man of the Law!" Szar said casually, grabbing one of the Hunter's arms. Khej grabbed the other arm, Namron the feet, and they went.

20.4 Conjectures

After spending the day mending the fields of the temple, the Field Wizards held council in the rainbow hall.

Szar had invited Teyani. While they were waiting for her, he explained, "In the last twenty-nine years Master Gervin never held an important meeting without Lady Teyani."

There was immediate consensus that from now on, Lady Teyani should be asked to all important meetings of the Field Wizards.

For this special occasion, they had put the Hunter's corpse in the middle of the hall. They sat around him, forming a large circle.

When Khej came into the hall, Master Ferman too noticed, "But what's happened to you my boy? You've damn doubled in width!"

"Hey!" Khej proudly contracted his biceps, pectorals and deltoids, pushing his shoulders forward to accentuate the impression of mass. "The power of the fields!" he clicked his fingers.

So this was how he had turned into such an unlawful chunk!

"But these muscle-building fields, aren't they from the Nephilim?" old Lorenz questioned with some concern.

"Well... aren't all fields?" Khej tried to defend himself, drawing a loud, indignant, "Oh!" from all the Field Wizards.

"I tell you, they're damn solid muscles!" Khej said to divert their attention. He called his friend, "Gallagher, come on! Punch me in the stomach!"

Gallagher stood up. He was one head shorter than Khej. Now that the fields had worked on Khej, the difference in size was shocking.

"Punch me!" Khej demanded.

Gallagher threw a hesitant fist into Khej's abdomen. It didn't do a thing.
"No, much harder!" Khej said, all confidence.

The short man with the round belly gave a more convincing punch.

Unaffected, Khej stood straight, "Harder! Harder!"

A touch exasperated, Gallagher tuned into the field that hardened the abdominal muscles. Point-deactivating the field, he punched Khej's solar plexus with all his strength.

Khej fell on his knees, gasping, holding his belly.

"Oh I'm sorry! I'm sorry!" Gallagher knelt by his side.

A few seconds later, Lady Teyani made her entry. Half-asphyxiated, his face dark purple, Khej was lying on his side on the floor, fighting to catch his breath, while all the Wizards were laughing their Points off. Apart from Gallagher, who was holding Khej's hand, "I'm so sorry! Are you all right?"

The men's laughter was not just loud, there was something highly charged about it. The accumulated tension of days spent sitting still like plass statues, waiting in the dark, had finally found an outlet.

When they saw Teyani, the men stood up. Silence resumed.

The Grand Master of the White Eagle took a quick look at the huge rainbow that decorated the hall, then at the corpse that lay on its back in the middle of the circle. She went to take position on Szar's left. Ferman moved aside to let her into the circle.

Szar thanked her with a nod. It was a great honour. At important meetings, Teyani had always sat on Gervin's left.

She sat down, lawfully inviting the Wizards to do the same.

As they were taking position, Gallagher dragged Khej into the circle. It made young Arena burst out, chuckling, then coughing.

Looking around the circle, Teyani saw all of them making great efforts to contain themselves, stifling smiles, contorting their mouths.

Teyani judged this laughter inspired from heaven.

It wasn't difficult to imagine what Gervin would have done in such a situation. Contemplating the Hunter, she pushed her lips forward and nodded in admiration, "Nice corpse you have here!"

It was all in the way she said it. Lord Proston was the first to explode with laughter, and he did it so buoyantly that the other twenty-six men instantly followed him.

It was irrational. Violent. Irresistible.

Teyani started laughing with them.

Gervin's presence flooded the rainbow hall.

Khej, who had regained his breath, was rolling on the floor. Gallagher and Arena, holding their bellies, were tapping the floor with their heels. Lorenz had to rush to the toilet. Ferman was clapping his hands, shedding tears, basking in Gervin's light. Proston, his voice trained for many years at the King's palace, was the noisiest of them all.

Laughter ran wild for at least three minutes, until sharp-eyed Ashok shouted, "Commander, a rat! Under the central kitchen."

In one second, complete silence was restored. Teyani watched the trans-formation with great interest: twenty-seven Points scanning the catacombs' sensor fields, razor-sharp.

"I think this one *is* a rat," Ashok said. "The vibration fluctuates. Quite different from the Hunters'."

"It would have fallen down from the kitchens," Ferman added.

"Engage the pest-killer!" Szar ordered.

Teyani tuned in, praying for the rat's soul.

A few seconds later there was a general sigh of relief. The rat signal had vanished.

Szar began the meeting's proceedings. For Teyani he summarised, "We still have no idea who these ghosts are – giants, Hunters, Renegades... they could be anything Nephilim. We keep spotting two groups: one of four men, one of thirteen."

"I thought it was fifteen," Teyani recalled.

"Two of them have vanished."

"So what are the clues?" she asked.

"They're top-level elite troops," Ferman said. "I know only two places in the kingdom where fighters of this calibre are being trained: Jex Belaran and the Eastern Peninsula."

"You realise these are exceptional soldiers," Szar said for Teyani. "For months they've been roaming in the immediate vicinity of the temple, where we have laid thousands of detection fields. And yet we haven't been able to detect them more than a dozen times. Add to this the fact they've been sleeping outdoors through the rainy season and through winter... Marek, my teacher in the Dragon, would have great respect for them."

"Apart from the giants and Jex Belaran, we cannot rule out the possibil-ity they could be Renegade Hunters," Proston said in his eloquent voice.

"But then who?" Ferman went on. "The Foxes and the Red Clan were decimated last year, and anyway they were nowhere near as good as our ghosts. The Black Renegades were eliminated by Szar and Aphelion..."

"With the possible exception of Murdoch!" Szar dropped in.

"All right, so Murdoch could be one of them. But he couldn't possibly have trained fighters of this calibre in a year. Especially knowing he no longer had a seed-connection stone. That leaves Henrick the prian, the Renegade who defected from Jex Belaran. Or possibly another clan of Renegade Hunters coming from a distant county."

"Is that the Henrick who melted Woolly's chapel in Laminindra?" Tey-ani asked.

Szar gave a nod.

"I find it difficult to imagine that Henrick would have been capable of training Renegades as powerful as our ghosts!" Proston pointed out.

"We have another clue," Szar opened the Hunter's bag and emptied its contents in front of him. "Magnificent he-stone weapons. Three hundred and twenty-one of them, all identical – which tells us they all come from the same manufacturing chapel. This doesn't point to Henrick's clan. As far as I know, Henrick steals stones here and there. He'd never have the kind of infrastructure needed to produce this."

The Wizards' eyes were fixed on the heap of stones, drooling.

Proston was categorical, "There I must say, I know of only two places in the kingdom where Nephilim beauties like these could have been manufactured: Jex Belaran and the Eastern Peninsula."

"Which always brings up the same questions." Ferman started the refrain, "Why would Jex Belaran want to come and steal our hermaphroditic stones, since we have offered to supply Perseps for free? And if the giants want our Archive stones, why don't they send one of their crack battalions to get them?"

"But isn't that exactly what they're doing at the moment?" Khej asked. "How long before the Green Guard reach Eisraim?"

"True!" Szar said.

The days were numbered. The time was coming.

"Don't underestimate General Harravan!" Proston reminded them. Turning to Teyani, "Harravan the fierce heads the ninth army of the King of Atlantis. All his officers, and nearly three quarters of his soldiers, are Nephilim. In the past the ninth army has defeated the giants more than once."

Gallagher and the younger Wizards rubbed their hands enthusiastically.

No doubt the Watchers themselves had turned their eyes to Asherban, where the battle was about to happen.

The tone of profound respect with which Lord Proston had spoken had aroused curiosity in the circle. He decided to say more. "Of all the generals of His Supreme Majesty the King, Harravan the fierce is the one who impressed me the most," he stressed in the magical harmonies of his highly trained voice. "A luminous mind, with far-reaching vision. A man of immense powers, he can turn impossible situations to his advantage and win battles when everything seems lost. A strange character, though, boiling with Nephilim spice, and completely unpredictable. Like the giants, he eats animal corpses. And in the midst of battle he launches terrifying Voice-screams, so charged they can paralyse an entire brigade."

The vivid impressions conveyed by Proston left the Wizards pensive for a while.

Ferman returned to the topic, "At least, now we know the two groups of ghost Nephilim are related."

"Why?" Teyani asked.

"This morning the smaller group infiltrated the mid-eastern enclave, while the larger group appeared on the western side of the temple. If they didn't know each other, it's difficult to imagine they would have launched these offensives at the same time."

"And how do we make sense of the fact they all suddenly ran away this morning?" Proston asked.

"Szar scared them off!" Khej declared.

"No way, man of the Law!" Szar was adamant. "Warriors of this calibre do *not* get scared when one of their comrades falls in combat."

"Commander, would it be... I mean, could we ask you..." Ashok hesitated, "how was it to kill this Hunter? Difficult?"

Seeing the glimmer of excitement in the eyes of the young Wizards, Szar burst out laughing, slapping his thigh. "It was... certainly much more difficult than anything I had to cope with when training with Fridrick."

"How did you do it?" Gallagher and Khej asked in one voice, spellbound.

"Thanks to the grace of Master Gervin, I let the power of Revelation Sky flow through me," he told them.

It sounded very noble, but it didn't completely satisfy the young men's curiosity. Eyes fixed on Szar, they waited anxiously.

"All right," he yielded. "I used the triaxe, a secret weapon the gods have prepared for the Knights of the Apocalypse."

"Can we ask you more on this?" Ashok immediately tried.

"No. Or another time perhaps."

Teyani had been watching the glows in the Wizards' eyes with fascination. What was happening to them? They all used to be so much alike that she could hardly tell one from another. Now for the first time, they were people.

"Any other clues?" she asked after a while.

"Yes," Szar pointed to the corpse, "this is the man who killed Fridrick."

Heavy silence.

There was nothing left of the Hunter's energy. Even if his astral body hadn't been annihilated by the triaxe, his friends would have wiped out all traces before withdrawing.

"What makes you think this, Commander?" Proston wanted to know.

"Call it the knowingness of Thunder!" Szar replied, one with Gervin.

As the Wizards were contemplating the corpse thoughtfully, Teyani told them, "Friends, one thing I must point out is that I have never seen you so bright and awakened! Whatever you have been doing lately has done you a lot of good. Take my word for it, when Master Gervin sees you from the Fields of Peace, he must be extremely proud of you. You are no sleepers in the Law!"

If there was one compliment that could have touched them, this was the one.

20.5 Oh, gods!

Three days later, late in the evening, Szar was repairing the field in the third hall of Melchisedek when Teyani called him through darkness visible.

"Master Szar?"

An unusual start. Perhaps she was in a perky mood.

Szar wasn't. Yet another day spent burning corpses and fixing fields that collapsed as soon as he let go of them.

How would Gervin have answered her?

With heart, "Lady Teyani! *So* good to feel your Whiteness."

"The Eagle's love with you, always. Master Szar, there is someone in urgent need of a healing in my chapel. Could we have the privilege of your presence?"

Since his return from the Fields of Peace, Szar had spent considerable energy healing Antaria. So far, no other Eagle had been struck by the pestilence. "Some bad news?" he wriggled his nostrils.

"Where is the good, where is the bad?" Teyani sighed through the space.

It *was* like hearing Gervin.

"Coming right now!"

Szar Point-called the rainbow chapel, "Ferman, this damn field in the third hall of Melchisedek! Each time I restore it, the one in the lake collapses, and vice versa. *Three hours* I have spent, rushing from one to the other."

Ferman didn't mind the challenge. "Leave them to me, Commander!"

In urgent need of exercise, Szar ran out and lifted himself up onto the dome of the hall. He jumped from roof to roof, remembering the days when love gave him wings to fly back to Elyani's courtyard, never knowing what the White drink would taste like this time.

It hardly took three minutes to reach the roof of the White Eagle. Szar announced his arrival by giving three knocks on the dome, then climbed down into the adjacent courtyard.

She was standing at the doors, fresh and clear as if her day had been spent meditating on the Dawn of Creation.

"Praise the Lord Melchisedek, Teyani of the Eagle!"

Soft irony in her smile, "All glory to the Lord Melchisedek, Master Szar." She opened both doors for him.

There was only one other person in the chapel. A man, lying on the floor unconscious.

Szar pulled his beard, "Now then, what is that?"

Aparalgon!

The young priest had shaved his head. His grey gown was in tatters. He was covered in bruises, one bad cut on the side of his head.

Szar went to kneel by his side. Eyes closed, hands running over his body, he diagnosed, "No broken bones... no damaged organs... his life is not in danger. He's a strong man, actually. He received a beating, is that it?"

"Unlawfully certainly! When he arrived the wound on his head was bleeding badly. I had to use the Voice to stop the blood. I put him to sleep by the same occasion."

Dragon engaged, Szar began the healing. Each blow Aparalgon had received was like a knot in his energy. The first thing to do was to undo the knots. "Who beat him?"

"This is a long story! Early this morning, he came to knock at the doors of my chapel. He said, 'Would you, by the grace of our Lord Melchisedek, be Lady Teyani of the White Eagle?' When I said I was, he said, 'Master Szar has ordered that I should shave my head and that you should teach me the book of Maveron.' I said, 'Ah, well! If Master Szar has ordered it, then...'"

Szar was shaking his head, "Oh, gods!"

"The morning rituals were just finishing. Antaria invited our guest to sit in the centre, while the seventeen of us formed a circle around him. And we gave him a recitation of the book of Maveron."

"Oh, gods! He must have been terrified!"

In the last fifteen years, the only woman Aparalgon had spoken to was his mother.

"Terrified he was! Trembling the whole time. And keeping his eyes fixed on the dome ceiling, as if we were Immaculate."

"But who gave him the idea to come here?"

Teyani frowned, "I lawfully beg your pardon?"

"I mean, where did he find the courage to shave his head and approach you?"

One of Gervin's half grins appeared on Teyani's lips. "The man must have a great teacher."

Oh, gods!

"So who beat him?"

"After the recitation of Maveron, I instructed him to go and meditate in the corridors. During the day he was seen to-and-froing the female wing, carried by the Point-guidance field, repeating verses of Maveron. Lawfully fine. But in the evening when he tried to return home, his fellow priests refused to let him in, because he had shaved his head! They called him an outcaste and they beat him."

Very much in line with the lawful ethics of the Grey Robes of the Angel of Dawn. The Law is the Law!

Master Szar was laughing in horror. "Oh, gods."

"After this, he didn't know where to go. So he came back to my chapel."

"Lucky he didn't let himself die!"

Put in the same situation, it was what most would have done.

Szar had finished undoing the knots. He finalised the healing with a solid injection of life force. "Anything else you want to tell me before I wake him up?"

"Hunh hunh."

Szar pulled Aparalgon back into his body and patted his right cheek. Gently, "Sleeper, awaken!"

Recognising the voice, Aparalgon smiled like a filosterops. "Master Szar!" He opened his eyes and spoke in a feeble voice, "What a lawful co-incidence! Our paths cross each other again!"

He hadn't changed.

Or had he? Throwing life force into his body, Szar watched him with curiosity. He waited for him to recover his spirits.

"So you shaved your head, Aparalgon," he said in a neutral voice.

Always smiling lawfully, "Doesn't the Law say, 'An order given by your teacher is a decree from the gods,' and 'The teacher speaks the Word of the Lord'?"

"And look what happened!"

"A most unlawful misunderstanding, Master Szar. I tried to tell my brethren in the Grey Robe that I had only been following orders of Master Szar of the Brown Robe but they didn't believe me! They called me a liar, they said Master Szar could never have ordered me to go against the Law of my caste. And then they started beating me."

There was not a trace of bitterness in Aparalgon's voice. He kept smiling as if the Lord Melchisedek was holding him by the hand.

"Did you like the book of Maveron?"

"A splendid recitation, Master Szar. The priestesses' voices were lawfully magnificent."

"And the content?"

"Very deep. As the Law says, 'The Law is deep like the Great Ocean,' and 'Man of the Law, how could you possibly fathom the depth of the Law?'"

Szar and Teyani exchanged a glance.

From the Point he asked her, "What the hell are we going to do with him?"

"I thought *you* were going to tell me that!" she Point-answered. "He's *your* disciple after all."

Szar closed his eyes, took his head in his hands. "Aparalgon, what do you think is the most important verse of the book of Maveron?"

"Sleeper, awaken!"

Favourably surprised, Szar reopened his eyes.

"Before I left the chapel this morning, Lady Teyani told me, 'The essence of the revelation of Maveron lies in this verse: Sleeper, awaken!'" Aparalgon justified his answer.

"I see. But Aparalgon, tell me something. Why did you ask me to be your teacher?"

"Because my teacher, his highness Aparalgon of the Grey Robes of the Angels of Dawn, died one lawful year ago."

"But why me?"

Aparalgon's eyes shone. With his heart-breaking sincerity, he declared, "I saw you walking in front of my chapel two lawful lunations ago, and I *knew* you were my teacher!"

"Voof!" Teyani slapped her forehead. "This is deep!"

Szar gave her a look.

"Just my opinion!" she said. "I can give my opinion, can't I?"

Aparalgon was gazing above her head, his face expressing boundless gratitude.

"Commander!" Khej Point-called from the rainbow chapel. "We have spotted the ghosts! By the shore of the Fontelayana river, twenty minutes away, north-east of the main gates. This time they're fifteen!"

"So they have regrouped!"

"Or they have received reinforcements."

"I'll be back soon," Szar closed the Point-communication.

Szar called on Archive Hall One.

The response was immediate, changing the space in the chapel. Gervin's presence was so strong, it was as if he was standing by Teyani's side.

She and Szar held eye contact. From Eagle to Eagle. Whiteness eternal. Forever love.

"Master Szar, I must now return to the chapel of the Grey Robes of the Angel of Dawn, so the unlawful misunderstanding may be cleared. Doesn't the Law say..."

"Aparalgon," Szar's gaze remained one with Teyani's, "do you really want to awaken?"

"Lawfully certainly, Master Szar! Doesn't Maveron say, 'Unless you want awakening with all your heart, with all of yourself, and more than anything else, you will never awaken'?"

Szar turned to Aparalgon and plunged Thunder into his eyes, "Then never return to the chapel of the Grey Robes, Aparalgon. Become a new man. Change your ways. Open to the Light of the Lord!"

"But..." Unlawfully shocked, Aparalgon stared at Master Szar in total confusion. Yet he didn't blank out.

Remembering his years as an apprentice, Szar knew exactly what he was feeling.

With Szar, Gervin had adopted a different tactic. He had left him with the sleepers of the Salmon Robe until he became so completely fed up he had no choice but to leave. But that was years ago, when the kingdom was still eternal.

Now the days were numbered. Every minute counted.

If there was *one* chance this sleeper could awaken, it had to be dead soon.

Szar pulled him by the hand, "Can you walk?"

With the massive injection of life fore he had received, the young priest had no difficulty standing on his feet.

"Do you know where the chapel of Lord Gana is?" Szar asked him.

Too overwhelmed to speak, Aparalgon just gave a nod.

"If you need a place to sleep, go there! Ask the god to inspire you," he said with the Eagle's infinite softness.

Sleeping away from the chapel of the Angel of Dawn?

Aparalgon shook his head.

What was being asked of him was impossible.

Szar understood. He put his hand on the young man's shoulder, blasting him with the Eagle's warmth.

"Commander!" Khej Point-called again. "We've spotted them again. Not fifteen. This time, there are sixteen of them!"

Turning to Teyani, "I *really* must go!"

She flooded him with her love.

To Aparalgon he said, "I will speak to you soon!" And he started running towards the catacombs, Aparalgon's devastation weighing heavily on his chest.

But where had this idea of telling him to shave his head come from?

Straight from Revelation Sky.

Oh, gods!

20.6 Someone

The sixteen ghost Nephilim were spotted in the forest three more times that night, each time in different locations, and always less than half an hour from the temple.

One of the things that didn't make sense was that they weren't making any attempt to destroy the detection fields which the Eisraim Wizards had woven throughout the forest. Had they wanted to, it wouldn't have taken them much to eliminate most of the short-range scanners, making it infinitely more difficult to detect their presence.

But the thing that made the least sense was, why did they roam around instead of attacking? What were they waiting for?

An army of giants, perhaps?

One could see why the giants would have wanted to send a couple of rangers to map the terrain and spy on the fields. All this could have been done in a week. But sixteen of them, and for months and months...

"There must be something we're not seeing!" Master Ferman kept repeating.

It was late in the night. The temple was asleep. Ferman and Ashok were in the rainbow hall with Szar, monitoring the detection fields.

"Anyhow, if it's the giants they're waiting for, it won't be long now," Ashok grinned, passing his hand through his short dark hair.

From Lasseera, Woolly had just sent the latest news. It would only take a few more days before the Green Guard reached Perentie, where Harravan was waiting for them. It wasn't expected they would encounter any serious resistance until then. They had already conquered seven counties, melting down all temples, extinguishing all fields, destroying all major cities, taking no prisoners. Carnage, Nephilim style.

What would happen in Perentie? The entire kingdom was holding its breath. If Harravan the fierce held fast, there was hope the King could win the war against the giants. But if the ninth army was slaughtered, then... total chaos was bound to spread throughout the kingdom.

The warp, however, was the healthiest it had been in months. The giants' medicine was doing it good. Thanks to their fine works, the windmills of the Law had been brought to a standstill in thirteen counties already. Thousands of rituals had been discontinued. The situation was potentially explosive because many of these rituals served to counteract the effects of other rituals. Major catastrophes could be expected any time: nature going wild, ancient volcanoes erupting, perhaps even tidal waves. It was just a matter of weeks, or perhaps days, before the warp started convulsing again.

Then a phase of paradoxical clarity would follow – the time for the Archive transfer.

But the way things were going, the giants might reach Lasseera before the next crisis of the warp. It had therefore been decided that if the Green Guard went further than Perentie, the Eisraim Wizards would send a destabilising wave to shake the warp and precipitate the crisis.

After having spent their entire life lovingly mending the warp!

That broke the Wizards' hearts. How could they possibly harm the warp of fields, the warp that had been given to human beings as a token of his Love by the Lord Melchisedek himself? It was like stabbing your own mother in the back. Difficult to imagine a worse crime against the Law.

Sharp-eyed Ashok turned to Szar, "If it weren't for these damn ghost Nephilim camping on our doorstep, you'd give the signal for us to butcher the warp of the Centre North and move to the transfer immediately, wouldn't you?"

Ferman bit his lip.

Szar made himself White Eagle, "What do you think, Ashok? If you were in command, what would you do?"

"I think we'd be mad not to do it. But I'm glad I'm not in command."

No one envied the karma of the man who would have to give this order.

"Picking up another rat under the central kitchen!" Ferman announced, engaging the pest-removing field. He told Ashok, "Tomorrow you'll have to go back and clean up these kitchens."

The twenty-two-year-old man took his head in his hands, as if Ferman had just ordered him to go and kill the Nephilim all by himself.

"Is it such a problem?" Szar enquired.

Ashok grinned, "Not the rats. The Wise Witches! There's always a few of them in the kitchen, for some unlawful reason. The amount of abuse I have to take each time I go there...!"

Ferman laughed, "My boy, I'm sure Master Gervin would have said it's excellent for your spiritual development!"

"Lawfully certainly!" Szar seconded.

Ashok was playing with one of the he-stones found in the bag of the Hunter Szar had killed.

"What do you think of this stone?" Szar asked him.

"Superb! Perfectly homogenous, doesn't get dissolved even in first-grade white slime, can hold enough venom intensity to kill twenty men in one go. I tell you, the Wizard who's crystallised that, he's someone."

"Someone..." Ferman nodded thoughtfully, rendered philosophical by the late hour in the night. "What's someone?"

"Someone is someone who's someone!" Ashok declared with opinion-ated certitude. "I want to become someone. Before I die."

"Aren't you someone?"

"Nay, not really. I'm a Field Wizard just like my old man in the Law was a Field Wizard. And if I wasn't here, there'd be another Field Wizard to do just what I'm doing. That's not being someone."

Fascinated, Szar made himself one with Gervin's presence for him. "So who is someone?"

"You're someone, Commander!"

"But there have been hundreds of Brown Robes before me," Szar argued.

"Yes, but you're different! You're not like Master Lehrmon, or Master Woolly. You're you. And you've done things no one else has done. Or take those fucking ghost Nephilim – they're someone! They're the fucking best Point-soldiers in the kingdom. Just the sixteen of them, they'd mop up the King's second army all by themselves."

Frightening, but probably true.

"So how are you planning to become someone, Ashok?"

"Don't know," he scratched his head. "The problem is, I left it to the last moment. Silly! Silly! Now I'm going to die, and I'm no one."

Silence, like at the end of time.

Archive Hall One was shining its compassion onto the young man.

"And another rat from the central kitchen!" Ferman announced. "But Ashok, do you realise you *are* a special Field Wizard? Take my word for it, there are not many in the kingdom who can lay fields like the Wizards of our team. And Lord Proston agrees!"

"But that's being good, that's not being someone!" Ashok replied.

Visibly not enough to satisfy the young man's newly-found aspiration for identity.

"Mm..." His lips pushed forward, Ferman was asking himself if he was someone.

Those strange questions that come to the mind of those who work throughout the night.

A few minutes and a few kitchen rats later, Ashok questioned, "Do you think there's still time for me to become someone? How could someone become someone in such a short time?"

"Tune into Master Gervin in Archive Hall One!" A surprising intensity flared in Ferman's voice, "Pray to him with all your heart. Ask, and he'll give you the light to become someone. Time is short, but Thunder is stronger than time!"

Ashok's eyes flashed. It was more than just hope. Ferman had passed something to him. A thread to the Archive.

The inspirational punch left Szar pensive.

Master Ferman was someone.

Ashok closed his eyes, turning to Archive Hall One. He made his heart a flame of aspiration, while keeping his Point on the monitoring fields.

"You can go to your room," Ferman relieved him from duty. "Master Szar and myself will finish the night."

After Ashok left, Szar marvelled, "Hard to believe how much they have changed lately! Only a few months ago, we could never have had a conversation like this."

"Master Gervin had predicted it long ago," Ferman said. "At the last hour, the sleepers awaken. Not all of them of course. But enough to surprise the Law out of us."

20.7 The dying kingdom

The next day, when Szar arrived at the cremation ground, he found the usual pandemonium: lines of corpses waiting to be burnt, a small crowd of priests and priestesses lawfully wailing around them. The thick smoke from the pyres married incestuously with the fog, making the air gooey, the stench particularly offensive. Exhausted by round-the-clock cremation rituals, the Attendants of the Dead officiated more and more slowly, adding to the congestion. And to make things worse they themselves were dying, one after the other. Not just from the pestilence, also from despair – this despair that had overtaken the good people of Eisraim now it was clear that nothing could save the temple.

Priests from several orders had been recruited to carry out cremation rituals. Right from the start of the plague, Melchard had set the example, blessing the dead and comforting their families from morning to night.

It was his forty-fourth consecutive day spent burning corpses and chanting hymns to the departed.

When Szar arrived, Melchard was standing behind a heap of smouldering ashes – the late grand master of the order of Barradine. Behind him stood a dozen Ochre Robe priests, their auras thoroughly decorated with the ominous black specks.

Soon, the order of Barradine would be no more.

All that would be left of it would be the memory of the fields.

By the side of the alley Szar noticed a Salmon Robe corpse. Covered in dirty pink linen, the face couldn't be seen. But Szar's nostrils recognised a familiar streak, drowned in the odious stench.

Artold?

Resting on the Dragon, Szar walked to the corpse and lifted the funeral shroud. A dreadfully unlawful thing to do, but who cared!

It was him. Preserved by the funeral field, his corpse showed no sign of decay. His face was that of a sleeping youth, blissfully serene, unconcerned by the world.

The question imposed itself on Szar's mind, "Where is he now?"

Sleeping through death, as he had been sleeping through life.

The painfully familiar words rang like a curse, "And how are your parents, my friend in the Law?"

Putting his hand on the priest's heart, Szar felt angry, "Artold, Artold... how could you be such an idiot!" And he cried tears of regret. "Why didn't I even try to shock you out of your Salmon dreams?"

He felt angry at himself for being the accomplice of sleep by default.

He felt angry at the world for all those who had died sleepers. The cremation ground was full of them.

So were the caverns of sickness.

A group of wailers stopped their lawful crying to look at Szar and Artold's uncovered corpse, horror-struck. Messing with the dead was a major offence against the Law.

Szar thought of shaking them awake with a Dragon scream.

Melchard Point-called, "Szar?"

"Melchard, I came to speak to you," he answered through the Point.

"A lawful ten minutes should be all I need to finish this ritual," Melchard answered. And through the Point he showered Szar with a Brown-Robe impulse, warm, peaceful and vast like the World to Come.

Covering Artold with the shroud, Szar walked to the periphery of the cremation ground. There he stopped and closed his eyes. For a moment the stench and the lamentations disappeared. He could hear the flow of the River of Remembrance. Smell its fragrance of eternity. Recall the magic moment when he and Woolly had said good bye. The river was humming, "Flying Dragons, gods, the Lord Melchisedek, you and me. Forever One in Love."

That which is, will always be.

"Szar!" Mouridji called him.

Szar reopened his eyes to the dying kingdom.

"Szar!" The prophetess of the Purple Robe was trotting her way around the corpses, followed by Aparalgon of the Grey Robe. His face was still congested with the marks of abuse, a large crescent-shaped bruise under his left eye, but he seemed to be walking with ease, and he was wearing a brand-new grey gown.

The Lord Melchisedek having been duly praised, Aparalgon remarked, "Our paths cross each other again, Master Szar! Yet another lawful coincidence! Doesn't the Law say..."

"Where did you find him?" Szar asked Mouridji.

"This morning at three o'clock he was wandering in the corridors of the female wing," she said. "So I fed him, and I found a decent gown for him."

"So you didn't return to the chapel of the Grey Robes!" Szar exclaimed, his interest in the kingdom suddenly renewed. "Where did you sleep, then?"

"Nowhere, Master Szar. Doesn't Maveron say, 'Sleep is the enemy' and..."

"After I fed him, he *did* crash on the floor. A four-hour journey through the spheres," Mouridji corrected, to his embarrassment.

Szar tapped his shoulder. Mischievously, "There's nothing wrong with sleep, Aparalgon."

Deeply confused, Aparalgon contemplated the smoky mists.

"So what are you planning to do now?"

"I have come here to enrol as a temporary Attendant of the Dead," the Grey Robe priest declared, recovering his lawful assurance. "As the Law says..."

"Do you really think this is the proper place for this lawful boy?" Mouridji gave Szar a questioning look.

Surrounded by this filth, it was difficult to imagine Aparalgon lasting more than a week.

Szar hated the situation. The River of Remembrance still flowing through his heart, he aligned his clear fountain with Gervin's Archive Hall.

The knowingness of Thunder.

In a burst of near-Voice threshold, "Yes! I couldn't imagine a better place for Aparalgon."

Aparalgon smiled ecstatically, trusting his destiny was in the hands of God.

"All right, then," Mouridji sighed. "Anyhow, there'll be less bodies to cremate, now that people are leaving the temple."

Szar frowned, "What is that in the Law?"

"Haven't you heard? The priests of Baltham and the Lawful Servants of the Mysteries of the Nectar God have decided to go. To the south. The temple of Berylia."

Self-imposed exile!

Only a few months ago, this would have been unlawfully unthinkable.

"They're panicking! They're panicking," Mouridji said, "but maybe they're not wrong."

Szar was pulling his beard in perplexity, "But why don't they just leave their bodies, if they want to go?"

It was so unlike anything Atlantean.

Mouridji shrugged her shoulders, "Must be that filth that's wafting in the mists. So many people are going mad, these days. It's throughout the county, it makes them do unlawful things like you wouldn't believe!"

Thick, it was. The mists so dark that it was hard to tell whether it was day or night.

A distressed call through darkness visible, "Szar?"

"Teyani!"

"Szar, please come. A terrible mess has happened. In the chapel of the Green Robes."

It wasn't often that Teyani sounded unsettled.

The peace of Archive Hall One immediately responded. It said, "Friend, friend... I am with you, even when I am far away!"

With all my mind, with all my heart.

Mouridji contemplated the light in Szar's eyes, amazed at how simple it was. And so totally silent.

Even Aparalgon noticed something was happening. But as steps were approaching, he made himself straight and lawfully articulated, "Praise the Lord Melchisedek, Sir Melchard, High Priest of Eisraim and Grand Commander of the Law for the County of Eisraim under the Appointment of His Supreme Majesty, the King of Atlantis!"

Instead of answering, Melchard joined in the silence.

Infinity, no need for words.

The creation, one spark. Light beyond time.

It couldn't last, of course. But who cared, since it was eternal?

"Thank you," the White Eagle responded through darkness visible, her voice more peaceful. "I will wait for you here. No need to run."

Mouridji took leave, Aparalgon following her like a duckling.

Amused, the Brown Robes watched the unlikely pair trot off. She was telling him, "I will introduce you to Zothar, the Grand Master of the Attendants of the Dead. His mother was best friends with Pari-Ma of the Blue Robe, who knew your mother well..."

Szar turned to the high priest, "Melchard, with the giants so close I have decided to implement the Pipili-Homar variation of my plan."

Accordingly, Melchard and Esrevin were to create a diversion by performing a fake Archive transfer. Melchard was to take position on Pipili Hills in the Western Plains, Esrevin on Homar Hills in the Northern Lakes. Using highly charged hermaphroditic stones they were to carry out a momentous ritual that would be perceived from far away, drawing enemies to the west. Meanwhile Lehrmon, Woolly and Szar would be travelling east to the Plateau of Sorana, carrying the Archive stones.

It was a painful plan for Melchard and Esrevin. Apart from the fact they were likely to be slaughtered, they might not be in the Fields of Peace in time to take part in the grand ritual of the transfer.

Heavy sacrifice. Missing a one-in-ten-thousand-lifetimes opportunity.

"When do you want me to leave for Pipili Hills?" Melchard asked, his voice flowing like the River of Remembrance.

"Soon. Perhaps as soon as the coming days. It depends how the ninth army performs in Perentie."

"Against the Green Guard, do you really think they stand a chance?"

"Proston seems to think General Harravan could well surprise us. Anyhow, the time is coming. Another thing: when you leave the temple I want you to take Namron and his men with you."

"Aren't you going to need them here?" Melchard questioned. "I don't have to be accompanied, I can look after myself. Giants or no giants, I will reach Pipili Hills. My word of Thunder!"

"If we want this operation to have any credibility, we need to play it by lawful rules." Szar was inflexible, "You will be escorted by ten men, armed with more than five thousand soft-stone weapons."

"Yes, Commander!" Melchard used the lawful intonation of a soldier receiving an order. And he smiled the heart of the Law.

Disarming spontaneity of the River of Remembrance.

Breathing the fumes, ignoring the stench and the cries of the lawful weepers, they held eternity in their gaze.

"You and I have never really spoken, have we?" Szar said. "I would like to, before you go."

"I would like that too," Melchard said.

An Attendant of the Dead was drawing near, "Sir Melchard! Pervcon of the Salmon Robe is unlawfully sick, he can't finish the cremation ritual. What should we do?"

Melchard returned to the dead. Szar took off into the catacombs.

20.8 Crime

The chapel of the Green Robes was located at the far end of the temple's female wing. When Szar emerged from the catacombs, his nostrils were flooded with disgusting astral smells. It was as if he had landed in the caverns of sickness.

It was a relatively small building at the end of a long, overgrown garden. The gardening fields in this area had been dysfunctional for months. As they were not part of the twelve hundred and twelve fields to be transferred into the Archive, the Field Wizards hadn't had time to repair them. The result was an unlawful tangle of high bushes and weeds. A depressing vision – no more flowerbeds shaped in harmonious geometrical patterns, no more delicate astral fragrances. The magic of fairies and other subtle nature beings had vanished. All that was left was green mayhem, nature gone indecently wild, ugly like the end of the Law.

But the astral stench wasn't from the garden. It emanated from the chapel. In one nostril-wriggle, Szar understood: inside, there were rotting corpses. At least eight of them, he judged. Their putrefaction mingled with the fields, spreading sickening astral fumes.

Shocking scene. Letting dead bodies decompose without performing purification rituals was a heavy crime against the Law.

At one end of the garden Teyani was standing straight, alone, her Whiteness contrasting with the place's forlorn darkness.

Szar ran to her.

There were no lawful greetings. Teyani was grieving. "How could I possibly let this happen," she whispered, stern, eyes fixed on the chapel, an ominously dark silhouette blurred by the mists.

Szar could have told her that similar incidents were probably being witnessed throughout the county. He took her arm, "Come. Let's go."

"I can't just walk away and leave this behind me!"

"Leave it to me. I'll fix the mess."

Teyani was frozen. "These women trusted me. Letting them die like this is nothing short of a crime. If..."

"Teyani!" With Eagle-soft near-Voice thresholds, Szar repeated her name, "Teyani! Teyani...!" shaking her out of her state.

"Let's go!" he started walking, pulling her by the arm.

Softening, she walked by his side, silent.

Resting on his nature of remoteness, listening to the sound-elixir of Flying Dragon spaces beyond the Abyss of the Deep and the Fault of Eternity.

At the end of the alley she turned back, "What are you going to do with this chapel?"

Foul vibrations like these were enough to pollute an entire neighbourhood, making the air unbreathable, causing diseases. A major clearing was required.

"At this stage I can't see any other solution than burning the building," Szar decided. The plass looked dry enough for that. "My Wizards will establish a containment field around it, so neither the fire nor the astral fumes spread."

Horrified, looking straight in front of her, contemplating the kingdom from a distance, Teyani whispered the verse of Maveron, "They will burn their own temples!"

Holding her arm, Szar started walking again.

When they reached the Point-guided corridors they met a group of priestesses dressed in dark-blue gowns, carrying heavy bags and baskets. The women didn't salute Teyani. They made their eyes vague, unlawfully ignoring her, and kept walking fast.

Leaving the temple without permission!

Teyani stopped to bless them, "May the Lord Melchisedek shed His Light on your way!"

Lending a deaf ear, the priestesses kept going.

Szar was perplexed. If they wanted to depart, why didn't they just leave their bodies?

These days, people no longer trusted death.

Teyani heard his thoughts. "They're terrified of the giants," she said. "They fear that if killed by them, there may not be anyone left to give them the funeral rites. They giants could even eat their bodies!"

The Law said, Unlawful death, unlawful rebirth. Without proper funeral rites a soul could be reborn as a maggot, or even wander in the intermediary worlds for an entire aeon.

In the next corridor, as they met two other priestesses moving out, Szar tried to change the topic, "How is Antaria?"

Teyani blessed the two priestesses, then answered, "Antaria is nearly completely healed, but the Sons of Apollo have sent the signal. The sixteen Eagles will depart for the triangle tomorrow night."

By far the best news that day – except that sixteen more corpses would have to be disposed of, and then Teyani would be left alone.

Silently, they walked past the chapel of the late priestesses of the Dawn of Creation. In the courtyard the weirdly-shaped bushes no longer had berries, and the songbirds had gone. But the vibrations were still completely out of the kingdom. Flying Dragon whispers, creation song, magic beyond anything the rich Atlantean language could express.

It brought some fire back in their eyes.

"And what about you, Szar. How long before you leave the temple?" Teyani asked.

"No more than weeks. Probably less."

In a voice that left no space for discussion Teyani announced, "I have decided I will stay as long as you are here. The day you leave, I will let the Eagle take me."

For the Great Lovers' Dance.

20.9 The plains of Asherban, in the county of Perentie

Fifty-seven Nephilim soldiers of the ninth army were lying dead in the snow, their bodies still warm.

"But *who* did this?" a Nephilim officer who had just arrived on the site was shouting. "Have the giants started their offensive?"

A soldier was following him, "They must have, Most Lawful Officer. Who else?"

"But where are the giants? And why would they kill only Nephilim soldiers?"

Incomprehensibly, the non-Nephilim soldiers of that battalion had all been spared. Only those with Nephilim spice in their blood had succumbed to the weapon, or whatever it may have been.

"How many officers were killed?"

"Four, Most Lawful Officer."

In the ninth army, all officers were Nephilim.

In the desolate landscape of the plains of Asherban, the mists were normally so dense that one couldn't see further than one's feet. That day, unusually, the weather was clear with a visibility of at least thirty lawful feet.

A soldier ran towards them, "We can't find any sign of the giants, Most Lawful Officer. No traces. And it hasn't snowed for a week."

"Akaran?" a voice called through darkness visible.

"Here, Estsjhel! To your left," the officer replied.

A crimson silhouette emerged out of the mists.

"Did you find something?"

Estsjhel was in shock, unlawfully pale. "I must speak to you, Akaran."

"Leave!" Akaran gave a casual hand gesture, sending the two soldiers away. With Estsjhel he walked away from the corpses, "So?"

"Akaran! It's... revolting. The field that killed our men..." Estsjhel's mouth was twisted in anger, "...it wasn't from the giants! It was triggered from the palace of the King. Our Field Wizards have traced the imprint."

"A mistake?"

"No, not a mistake. A threat! Two hours ago, General Harravan received a message from the King's palace. It said, 'Fight to the death, or not one of your men will escape the anger of the King of Atlantis!'"

Akaran's first reaction was one of incredulity, "But why kill only the Nephilim?"

"It's a retaliatory field! The Wizards of the King's palace have designed it to show that they can strike Nephilim populations anywhere in the kingdom."

"But this is disgusting! We've always served the King with total loyalty!"

"Akaran!" Another Crimson officer was running towards them. "Akaran, my brother Mweisht is dead!" He yelled, furious, "Revenge, Akaran! I demand revenge!"

Akaran Voice-shouted at him, "No one does anything without my orders!"

The man fell on his knees, beating his chest. "Akaran! They killed my brother! My brother!" he wept. Tears heated with rage dropped onto the snow.

Two more Crimson officers emerged out of the mists.

"But what are you doing here?" Akaran yelled at them. "Who ordered you to leave your positions?"

"General Harravan! All Nephilim officers are to take turns to come and inspect the site of the massacre for themselves. General Harravan himself will be here soon."

More officers were arriving by the minute. They walked from corpse to corpse, anxious to find out how death had struck. They formed small groups, shouting their outrage.

Among them Akaran saw Berrick, the officer in command of the Field Wizards of the ninth army. He took him aside. Straightforwardly, he asked, "How can we know the giants are not behind this?"

"Akaran, seventeen of my Field Wizards witnessed the wave that caused the death field. It *did* come from the King's palace."

"Couldn't it be some kind of subterfuge? Or a mistake?"

Berrick was as furious as the others, "A mistake, only two hours after the King sends us a threat?"

Such threats were not uncommon in the King's army, but it was the first time in generations the ninth army had received one.

"Who exactly sent the threat?"

"The Right Excellent Lord Poporenon, First Grand Adviser of His Supreme Majesty the King. I and seven officers were present when Harravan received the threat. I know that Poporenon! It was him, officer's word."

The irony was, Lord Poporenon was a Nephilim. Ordering the slaughter of his own people didn't seem to have disturbed him in the least.

A deep wave of sadness veiled Akaran's face. "Those lords of the King's palace are losing the plot of the Law, I am afraid!"

Berrick clenched his teeth, "We've known that for a long time, haven't we?"

"General Harravan is here!" an officer shouted.

All became silent, standing to attention.

General Harravan was a tall man in his late forties with exceptionally sharp black eyes and long red hair that he kept plaited. He was famous for the grin that rarely left his face, and that kept his right cheek twisted, his right eye half closed.

That day he wasn't grinning. Stern, he walked among the corpses. The officer whose brother had been killed was crying. Noticing him, Harravan walked to him and put his hand on his shoulder.

Not a common thing for a general to do, but it was not for nothing that Harravan was adored by his men.

"This," Harravan said in an angry voice, "should *never* have happened."

Tears rolling down his face, the officer thanked him with a nod.

Emphatic, Harravan said again, this time using the Voice, "*Never!*"

Through the mists, his officers heard the ominous crack of his knuckles as he clenched both fists, and they knew. Harravan the fierce was about to launch one of his Voice-screams.

It came out with the power of an Underworld wind.

It was wild, inhuman. It ripped the mists like a knife cutting through animal entrails.

Nephilim spice made sound, it was a scream of rage.

Compelled by the power of Harravan's Voice, the officers started screaming with him. They turned into a pack of howling wolves, hungry for revenge, smelling blood already. Mad with the venom of the Watchers, they trampled on the snow, grunting, barking, yelling their fury.

Later, in the privacy of his tent, General Harravan grabbed a small soft stone from his pocket and established a protection field around him. Resting on the power of this very special stone, he established a Point-communication through the sky of the Watchers, totally undetectable by the Field Wizards of the ninth army.

"Samoan?" he called.

From the Eastern Peninsula, the new leader of the guild of necromancers immediately Point-replied, "General Harravan! How did it go?"

"Exactly as we had planned. Poporenon was perfect."

"Perfect!" Samoan rejoiced.

"Tell Fornan and Basalinger to stay where they are for the moment," Harravan said. "I need one or two more days to finish preparing my officers."

"General Fornan will wait for your instructions," Samoan assured him.

"Good. Tomorrow morning, in the presence of my officers, I will call Lord Poporenon to demand an apology. Just instruct him to be himself: arrogant and ruthless."

Sardonically necromantic, Samoan laughed, "This will be easy. Anything else?"

"Nothing for the moment."

"Excellent, excellent. General Harravan, His Excellency Bobros and Grand Court Sorcerer Afran Kesborn have asked me to convey to you how much they are looking forward to meeting you."

Harravan wasn't the kind of man to turn soft at the sound of syrupy words. "All glory to the Watchers and their sons!" he terminated the communication.

Thinking of the King of Atlantis, the general gave his twisted grin. And in the fashion of Nephilim necromancers, he decorated the crimson carpet of his tent with a thick spat.

20.10 Inventions, part 1

In the cremation ground, Aparalgon was in the middle of a funeral ritual when he was shaken by a powerful Voice-whistle.

Startled, he turned round.

"Master Szar!" the Grey Robe priest smiled like the Law, "What a lawful c..."

"Get Pervcon to finish your ritual!" Szar told him. "I'm taking you for a walk."

Ecstatic, Aparalgon left his pile of smouldering ashes and went to wake up Pervcon of the Salmon Robe, who was lawfully napping beside the cremation ground.

With less than four hundred people left in the temple, there were fewer and fewer bodies to burn. The cremation ground was returning to some normality.

The mists were not! They were getting darker and heavier by the day. The atmosphere in the temple was becoming more and more oppressive, making it difficult to breathe.

Aparalgon returned lawfully diligently, and the two set off in the empty alleys of the mid-eastern enclave.

"Why do you think the mists are so thick, Aparalgon?" Szar asked.

"Because of the unlawful number of people who have died from the plague throughout the county. Many of them did not receive funeral rites. The astral fragments resulting from their putrefaction have mingled with the sickness of the warp of fields, creating this thick astral atmosphere that makes us feel like the Underworlds are farting on us," Aparalgon explained all in one go.

Szar was pleasantly surprised. "A remarkably awakened answer! How did you find out?"

"Master Zothar, Grand Attendant of the Dead, enlightened me on this point of the Law."

"What made you feel like asking?"

"I approached Master Zothar seeking lawful instruction on the topic of the fields, Master Szar."

"The fields?" Szar twinged his beard with growing interest.

Aparalgon blushed, "I thought that perhaps if I knew more about fields... there could be opportunities to be of service to you, Master Szar. The Law says, 'Serve your teacher and the nectar of the Law will flow into you.'"

Moved, Szar of the Brown Robe remembered Szar of the Salmon Robe and his desperate efforts to awaken so as to be able to spend more time in Master Gervin's company.

But Gervin had travelled over half the Atlantean continent to go and fish Szar! Szar hadn't done anything to find Aparalgon. If anything, it was Aparalgon who had found Szar.

One with Gervin's Archive Hall, Szar asked, "Aparalgon, where do you find your inspiration? How do these ideas come to your mind?"

"Mostly during my sleep, Master Szar."

Szar burst out laughing.

And he remembered how, each time he had made a step toward Gervin, Gervin had responded by making ten steps toward him. But what could he do for Aparalgon? Training a disciple required years of patient effort. Unless Harravan accomplished a miracle, it was difficult to imagine the giants taking more than a month to reach Eisraim.

Szar was taken by a wave of profound sadness. Why did Aparalgon have to come to him at the last hour?

Was it still possible to do anything for him?

Despite his good intentions, the young man was still a world away from awakening.

They were passing by the chapel of the Grey Robes. Like most chapels in the mid-eastern enclave, it was completely empty.

"Where have your Grey brethren gone?" Szar asked.

"They went away for a few weeks to seek lawful refuge in the temple of the Angel of Dawn in Tomoristan."

Seeking refuge in Tomoristan? Oh, gods, how could anyone be so stupid! If the giants triumphed in Perentie, it wouldn't take a week for Tomoristan to be reduced to rubble.

"Are you sad you couldn't go with them?"

Aparalgon looked down, his shoulders heavy with dejection. "They refused to speak to me, even my father. Each time I tried to approach them they said, 'Go away! You no longer belong to our caste!' and they threw stones at me."

All this sounded so familiar! Remembering the Mother of the Light, Szar put his hand on the young man's shoulder, "Perhaps we could find a better caste for you."

Aparalgon looked at him in complete bewilderment.

On the other side of the alley, in the chapel of the Rural Deities, the cows were mooing unlawfully.

Szar pulled a face, "We are going to have to do something for these poor beasts. It's been days since someone looked after them."

"May I be of help, Master Szar?" Aparalgon immediately offered.

"Have you ever touched a cow?"

"No, but the Canon of Cow Keeping is part of the Law of the Grey Robes of the Angel of Dawn." Aparalgon started singing the hymn of lawful milking, "O Divine Cow, Light of Bounty of our Lord..."

"Brave man!" Szar slapped his shoulder. "When I was an apprentice, I was *terrified* of cows."

Aparalgon stood lawfully straight, ready to be thrown into the stables.

Szar couldn't possibly do that to the cows. "I think we can find a better use for your talents," he said, taking him into a side alley. "What was your function in the chapel of the Grey Robes, by the way?"

"I was the Principal Lawful Cleaner of the Ritual Utensils for the Afternoon Fire Ceremonies," Aparalgon declared in a lawfully modest voice.

Painfully useless.

"So you know everything about clearings. Lawfully excellent!" Szar pushed his lips forward, nodding thoughtfully.

In the paddock behind the chapel of the Rural Deities, they reached a huge ant heap. "Have you ever heard of the Flying Dragons, Aparalgon?"

"Spread in the infinity of the spheres of remoteness," Aparalgon chanted.

"Right and righteous! Now let me show you something never done in the temple before: this field links a number of ant heaps and resonates with the Flying Dragons of the sphere of the Great Ant." Szar took over Aparalgon's Point, connecting it to his ant field. "Can you feel?"

Aparalgon felt nothing. "Deep like the Law!" he lawfully frowned. "As the Law says, 'Man of the Law, how could you possibly fathom the depths of the Law?' and..."

His lower jaw dropped. His eyes, wide open, were flashing with strange glows. Szar had blasted the heights of Aparalgon's column of Spirit, forcing a resonance with the Great Ant.

Aparalgon fell flat on his back in the wet mud of the paddock.

A jump into boundless spaces.

Far, far from the kingdom, he found himself in an incommensurable expanse, crystalline geometrical forms dancing around him.

Szar's voice was with him, "Hear the music?"

Sounds with dimension. Sounds incomprehensible. The voice of a million stars chanting the mathematics of infinity.

"See, on your left, in the distance?"

Blueness beyond anything the mind could conceive. It stretched over ten times the length of the spheres of Melchisedek.

"The Blue Lagoon!" the voice told him.

Meanwhile in the kingdom, Szar was working on his cleansing field. "The resonance with the Great Ant is stabilised," he Point-liaised with Khej. "I should be able to start the clearing in a few hours."

A massive clearing resting on the infinite clarity of the Great Ant, and powerful enough to cleanse the mists in the entire temple in a matter of minutes.

Flying Dragons' magic, grand style.

"Looks perfectly stable from here too," Khej Point-replied. Making efforts to contain his excitement, he added, "Listen, Commander, we too have invented a new type of field! An idea of Ashok's. We'd like to show it to you. Could you come back to your bedroom? Like... now, for instance?"

Clearly, it *couldn't* wait.

"A new field? Oho! But lawfully why not! What's this field for?"

"Killing Nephilim Hunters."

"How timely!"

Szar took a glance at Aparalgon, blissfully unconscious, half-immersed in the mud. One option was to carry him to a bed and give him a day to recover. But every minute counted!

Using the power of the Point, Szar forcibly drew him back into his body. With a mighty Voice-frequency, he called, "Sleeper, awaken!"

Aparalgon immediately reopened his eyes, and his mouth. He looked skywards, straight above him.

"Aparalgon, my Field Wizards are calling me. Would you like to come with me and visit my chapel?"

Fluttering little voice, "Abaa.. bha.."

"I'll take this for a yes." Grabbing the young man's hand, Szar pulled him Dragon-vigorously.

"Bha... bha..." Wobbling on his legs, his gown and the back of his head covered in mud, Aparalgon kept looking straight in front of him, his eyes illuminated with the Great Ant's insane clarity.

Szar pulled him by the hand, "I bet you've never visited the catacombs!"

Set in motion by the power of the Dragon, Aparalgon stumbled, "Bha..."

20.11 Inventions, part 2

Aparalgon was just starting to recover some perception of the kingdom when he and Szar arrived in the 'bedroom'. Ashok, Khej, Gallagher, Ferman and Namron were waiting for them. The men weren't surprised to see two people arriving at the vaulted colonnade. As soon as Aparalgon had entered the catacombs, his presence had been picked up by the sensors. "I'm bringing a visitor home," Szar had told the Wizards. What they hadn't expected was that the visitor would be a Grey Robe of the Angel of Dawn drenched in mud, eyes unlawfully wide open, staring like he had just swallowed his first dish of herbs of madness.

Following the Law of his caste, the men didn't salute him. They politely waited a few seconds, to see if he wanted to salute them.

He opened his mouth, but no words came out. He looked up to the dome ceiling in total bewilderment. Where was he? After blacking out he had found himself running behind Master Szar in these strange bowels which looked like the Underworlds and smelled like the Underworlds. Now he was contemplating this breath-taking field of stars, and yet it didn't exactly feel as if he had left his body.

"Commander, we have a problem," Namron moved on. "We need to speak to you... privately."

Szar took Aparalgon further inside the bedroom. "Make yourself lawfully comfortable. Sit down and enjoy the stars."

"Bha..."

"I'll be back soon!" Szar Point-compartmented the hall, leaving Aparalgon on his own in the womb-like darkness of a fluid field of stars.

"Commander, Lord Proston has disappeared!" Namron began. "He went out for his morning stroll on the straight path of the Law. Now then, instead of coming back he left through the temple's main entrance."

"The sensor fields followed him up to the Fontelayana river, and we lost him a few minutes ago ," Ferman said.

"Did anyone speak to him?" Szar asked.

"He looked perfectly normal when he went out," Khej said.

"When he passed the temple's portal, I Point-called him. He told me he just needed to be alone for a while," Ferman said.

"Completely irresponsible!" Namron shook his head. "With all those Nephilim roaming around! Now then we have a *major* security problem. Suppose they capture him and make him speak... we're in Underworld slime up to here," he raised his thumb to his Point.

"Did he take a key-stone to Point-communicate through our shield?" Szar asked.

"Thank God, he didn't have one! He didn't need one, anyway. He normally only goes out for a short walk every morning," Ferman said.

"And what if it was the Nephilim who had driven him out of the temple? Some kind of Point-abduction," Gallagher suggested.

"Can't we just go out and contact him through the Point?" Szar asked.

"I tried that. I used various Point-call frequencies, but it's as if he had purposely disconnected from us," Ferman answered.

"Not in favour of an abduction by the Nephilim!" Khej said. "They would have kept him talking to us, so we didn't panic."

"Except if they took him as bait, hoping we'd leave our chapel to go and find him," Ashok remarked.

"There's another possibility," Gallagher threw in with cold cynicism. "It could be he's been a spy right from the beginning."

Lord Proston, a spy! Now *that* would have been the end of the Law.

But in this disintegrating kingdom, who or what could be trusted? No one even tried to dismiss Gallagher's suggestion.

Grim silence, Namron noisily chewing his black root.

"Going out to look for Proston would be too dangerous," Szar decided. "So it's like this: we recall all our Wizards into the chapel, change all the keys of our shields, and wait."

While Ferman was sending Point-orders, Namron took leave. He had to go and take care of the chapel of the Golden Egg, where six decomposing corpses had just been discovered.

Szar gave a handclap, Point-clearing the hall's gloomy mood. Turning to the young men, he fired his voice, "So what about this new field, great Wizards?"

Ashok's eyes flared. He spoke fast, "Commander, after you killed the Hunter I had an idea! When the Hunter attacked you, he threw a Point-impulse at you. That left an imprint in the catacombs' fields. So I went and studied the imprint, and I found a way to use it as a trigger for another field I've been thinking of in the last days. You know how the warp has become brittle lately, with small holes bursting out here and there. So I thought, why not divert Point-impulses into these small holes so they turn into big holes?"

"Get the idea, Commander?" Gallagher took over. "The Hunter throws his Point-wave, the wave hits the warp, rips a hole in it, and blewurp!" he made a graphic sewage noise, "through the hole, a torrent of elemental shit falls into his Point."

"And we made it!" Khej raised both fists in triumph. "The field is fully woven, right here, and it can work as far as a lawful mile from the chapel."

"Show me!" Szar playfully engaged his Dragon. "Shall I send a kuren-jaya impulse into your field?"

"I don't think it would be wise, Commander," Master Ferman interposed. "With all due respect, I don't see how you – or anyone else – could survive this weapon of hell. Even the slightest impulse would result in a massive wave of elemental slime. Much worse than the one which nearly killed Lady Hermina the Immaculate, but all condensed into a Point."

Szar was twinging his beard, utterly impressed. "How did you get this idea?"

"For weeks, we've been trying to find something that could beat the Hunters – something they have never thought of," Khej said.

Gallagher was playing with one of the stones found in the bag of the dead Hunter. "It's tough to compete against these sons of a Nephilim bitch! They're so good! On all levels, they leave us way behind."

As they were speaking, Szar was Point-exploring the field. A well-polished work, which seemed to be doing exactly what the young Wizards described.

"What do you say, Commander?" Ashok asked, anxiously waiting for his verdict.

Szar looked into his eyes, shining the light of Archive Hall One, "I say, the Wizard who has designed this field is someone!"

20.12 Debacle

It was nearly sunset when Ferman announced, "I'm picking up a Point close to the Fontelayana river. It's him! Proston! He's coming back towards the temple."

"On the path from the river to the temple's main entrance," Arena confirmed.

The Wizards directed their detection arsenal towards him. The man was alone. There was no sign that his energy had been tampered with.

But who could tell?

The Nephilim arts of deception were deep like the abyss.

Point-communicating through the chapel's shield without a key-stone was impossible. Ferman decided to go out and Point-call Proston. But as he was walking out of the doors of Baltham's entrance hall Lorenz detected, "Nephilim! Eight of them, I think. They're following Proston. Some three or four hundred lawful feet behind him."

Everyone was already on the highest possible level of alert.

"Speak to him, Ferman," Szar ordered. "Don't mention the Nephilim."

A few seconds later, Ferman Point-reported, "Proston wants a meeting with all of us, and Lady Teyani. He wouldn't say what about."

"We've spotted the eight Nephilim," Khej and Gallagher confirmed. "Hardly three hundred lawful feet behind Proston."

Namron was at the chapel door with Ferman. "Commander, we can't take the risk of having Proston captured. I think we should kill him while we still can," he Point-announced coldly.

With the wormwood fields that had been woven along the path leading to the river, Proston was an easy target.

But getting rid of the Nephilim was even more important. As long as they stood in the way, the Archive transfer was about as safe as listening to Watchers' lullabies.

Szar had just spent the afternoon working with Ashok, improving the new field. He judged this was the perfect opportunity to test it.

"Come with me!" he told the young Field Wizard and he started racing to the chapel's entrance. There they met Aparalgon, who was quietly sitting on the steps. They didn't stop.

"Aparalgon, what are you doing here?" Szar Point-called.

The young man wasn't trained in Point-communication. Vaguely feeling something in his Point, he looked skywards, wondering which angel was calling him.

Gods, was he aggravating with his mouth open!

From the front steps Szar and Ashok ran through the empty temple. Soon they had to slow down. Ashok had difficulty breathing. The mists were as friendly as the dark smoke of a funeral pyre.

As they were passing the main portal, Khej Point-reported, "Proston is still walking towards you. No signs of the Nephilim."

"I can smell him," Szar replied. "If there is any sign of the Nephilim reaching him, engage the wormwood field instantly and kill him! Don't worry about Ashok, I'll hold his Point."

On the path to the river they stopped half a lawful mile away from the portal. It was as far as Ashok's field could operate to its maximum intensity. There they waited, Point-scanning for the Nephilim.

Expectedly, they found nothing. The only way the Nephilim could be detected was through the highly sensitive short-range sensor fields.

Another waiting game began.

"Perhaps it would be better if I stayed here alone," Ashok said after a few minutes. "The bastards would have less hesitation targetting me."

"Hunh hunh! We want the eight of them to launch an attack at the same time."

"Yeah, the unlawful lot!" Unconsciously, Ashok had flexed his left forearm, clenching and unclenching his fist.

Szar was sense-smelling darkness visible, "Won't take more than a minute for Proston to reach here. I can't smell anyone else, though." He put his hand on the young Wizard's fist, "Stop this."

Ashok thrust his hand in his pocket. "He seems upset like the Law upside down!" he said, sensing Proston's vibrations through darkness visible.

Proston, who of course had detected them, didn't try to make contact. He just kept walking. They heard his steps on the wet dirt of the path.

"Not his normal self!" Szar agreed. There was something defeated about the way he dragged his feet. Quite unlike the aristocratic pace of a grand superintendent of the fields.

Finally he came out of the mists, unlawfully dishevelled, his eyes red, looking ten years older.

There were no salutes. "Did you meet someone?" Szar asked.

"No, I was alone the whole time," Proston answered.

There was no sign to indicate he was consciously lying but his voice sounded beaten, completely devoid of his natural self-assurance.

"What the hell has happened to you?"

"I'll tell you when we meet with the others," he just said, looking down. And he started walking again in the direction of the temple.

Szar grabbed him by the arm, "Wait! Are you aware you are being followed by eight Nephilim?"

"Oh, damn it!" Proston took his head in his hands, overwhelmed. "I'm sorry! The last thing I wanted was to create trouble for you."

Through a key-stone brought by Ashok, the Field Wizards were scanning Proston's Point in all possible ways. "Everything looks normal," Ferman reported after a minute. "But we've lost the Nephilim!"

"Shall we wait here?" Ashok suggested.

"No point. If they wanted to attack us, they would have done it already. We go back to the temple," Szar started walking at a gentle pace, firmly holding Proston by the arm. "You can relax, now," he slapped Ashok's shoulder.

He said this only to invite an attack, in case the Nephilim were listening through Proston. But he kept his Point on Ashok's field, ready to flush the hell out of the warp.

"So you want a meeting with everyone?" Szar said.

Head half bent, absorbed in his thoughts, Proston gave a vague nod.

Szar didn't want to enter Proston's consciousness – too dangerous, if he was a weapon sent by the Nephilim. But no probing was required to realise the former Crimson man was in complete chaos, so overwhelmed he could no longer stand up straight, his aura gloomy like the mists. Each time Szar asked him a question, he just mumbled, "At the meeting..."

For obvious security reasons, a gathering with Teyani and all the Wizards was out of the question.

Atlantean Secrets

"Teyani can't be disturbed, she's in the middle of a long ritual at the end of which her priestesses are to depart for the triangle. If you want a meeting, Ferman, Ashok and I can meet with you on the steps outside the chapel. The Field Wizards will be linking with us through a key-stone."

"But..."

"That's as good as I can offer. Take it or leave it!" Szar Dragon-voiced.

Proston gave in with a resigned nod.

Szar bit his lip. It hurt him to see this lion of a man reduced to such a compliant wretch.

When they reached the rainbow chapel they found Teyani sitting on the steps, Aparalgon basking in her light. Dazzling White like an Eagle's feather, she announced through darkness visible, "Highness sent me here."

Meaning, don't even thought-form asking me to leave.

Szar gave her a questioning look, "And your ritual?"

"The end of the ritual will wait. The Eagle wants me here for the moment," she said, shining her light of compassion onto Proston.

Ferman was coming out of the chapel, accompanied by Namron and Mouridji. Aparalgon walked to Szar, "Master Szar, this morning when I fell asleep in your hall, I had a dream in the field of stars. I must tell you about it, for as the Law says..."

"Not now!" Szar shut him up with a near-Voice threshold.

"Looks like we're having our meeting," Ashok grinned, as Lorenz and Arena were coming out too. All the others stayed inside, ready to strike.

The small group sat on the steps, apart from Proston who stood in front of them. Teyani's energy pouring into him, he seemed to be regaining some of his normal self, standing straighter, looking more present. Keeping eye-contact with her he began, "Friends, I have decided to leave the temple. This morning I spoke to Lord Viniret, my former colleague at the King's palace. I learnt grim news. Without any warning, General Harravan has defected to Bobros' side. Last night his Nephilim men slaughtered all their non-Nephilim comrades, after which the ninth army marched to the camp of the giants. There, Green guards and Crimson soldiers fell into each others' arms. They called each other brothers in spice, praising Bobros, the Nephilim messiah. I had..." Proston's voice choked. He burst into tears.

Lamentable sight. The man was broken.

Mouridji the prophetess was shaking her head, appalled. Ferman and Lorenz had tears in their eyes. Arena looked sideways into the mists, Proston's distress echoing on his face. Namron's hostile look softened, replaced by pity.

No thoughts just Dragon, Szar kept his Point on the trigger of Ashok's field. Point-warfare was dirty business. One second of inattention and the Archive transfer could be dead. He left it to Teyani to hold Proston's spirits.

Gathering his courage, Proston resumed, "I had immense respect for General Harravan. I considered him a man of honour, one of the pillars of

282

the kingdom. What has happened here is..." he shrugged his shoulders, "...incomprehensible to me. It shows the King's administration has been rotten all along – even more rotten than I thought. There were traitors in every corner of the palace. My life has been wasted, serving a dream. Now there is nothing left for me in this kingdom. I have decided to return to the land of my fathers."

A move equivalent to committing suicide. The small Proston island, only one hour away from the Western Shores, was being ravaged by a pestilence worse than the one which had emptied the temple of Eisraim.

"Now for the rest of the news. In the early hours of this morning, the Green Guard exterminated the first and the sixth armies of His Supreme Majesty. It only took a few minutes. In one single venom onslaught, more than sixty thousand men died. And in a supreme mark of contempt, the giants didn't even stop to eat the kidneys of the Crimson officers. They marched straight to Asherban, where they melted down the temples and slaughtered the entire population. They are now on their way to Prasnameghan, followed by the ninth army. As soon as the news reaches Tomoristan, expect a wave of panic. Many will try to flee south, which is bound to create more chaos in Lasseera and in Eisraim. And I have a precious piece of information for you: there have been reports that the Green Guard was accompanied by baphomets. As you may know, baphomets can only survive when immersed in Nephilim fields. It means the giants are not just discontinuing the windmills of the Law, they are weaving Nephilim fields wherever they go – Bobros' radical solution to 'save' the kingdom."

Turning the warp of fields into a warp of Watcher-ness.

Szar was clenching and unclenching his fist, mentally contemplating the map of the counties of the Centre North. After they finished with Prasnameghan, the giants would march on Tomoristan. Then where to? North to Jex Belaran, or south to Lasseera and Eisraim?

Proston turned to Ferman, "You no longer need me. I have taught your men what I knew. Anyhow, there is no need to envy the Field Wizards of His Supreme Majesty the King. I have learnt from you as much as I have taught you. Besides, the Spirit is with you; it is not with them."

Ferman the fiery spoke straight from Archive Hall One, "Proston, if you stay with us the Spirit will be with you too!"

"No, it's too late for me. I wish... I wish I had listened to Gervin, when he came to fish me twenty-six years ago."

"It is *not* too late, Proston!" Teyani plunged her Light into his eyes. "The Archive adventure is only beginning. There is a place for you here if you want it."

Proston's face closed off, "No. It is finished for me. I am going."

"You're not going anywhere for the moment," Szar spoke in Dragon tones. "For reasons of security, I have to ask you to stay in Eisraim at least a few more days. In the royal suite," he added, making it clear that Proston couldn't come back to the rainbow chapel.

His superb arrogance now nothing more than a memory, he just looked down, "All right."

20.13 Super-ants

On the lawn close to the third hall of Melchisedek, Szar knelt down by the side of a two-lawful-feet-high ant heap. "It has more than tripled in two days," he told Aparalgon, who watched from behind with lawful interest. "And look at these ants!" Szar placed his hand close to the main entrance. A small company immediately covered his palm. "Aren't they beautiful! Strong and vibrant. Look how single-mindedly they walk," he joined his hand with Aparalgon's.

Aparalgon recoiled, "But they bite!"

"Great for awakening! Ant venom is the carrier of cosmic forces of clarity."

Aparalgon shook his hand. "Gods! Gods!" he shouted in panic, "They're under my gown! They're biting me! Gods, help me!" He unlawfully took off his robe, jumping from one leg to the other, "Help! Gods!"

Szar shook his head and sighed, pondering reverently on the patience Master Gervin had shown with Szar of the Salmon Robe.

He returned to his cleansing field. The magic had commenced. Since the beginning of the evening, the first effects had been felt. The gooey astral muck that polluted the temple was being broken down. The oppressive heaviness of the mists had started to lift, making it easier to breathe.

"Commander!" Khej Point-called, "I'm in the music hall with Master Ferman, we have something amazing to report. The music field had collapsed this afternoon, and now it's fixed itself! Master Ferman says it must be an indirect result of your ant field."

"Could well be. In which case all fields in the temple are going to be easier to manage from here on."

"But how does it work, exactly?"

"Ants have a natural affinity with the Flying Dragons of the Great Ant. The field enhances the resonance."

"Turning the ants into super-ants?"

"And letting them do the cleaning work for us."

"Blasting! Blasting!" Khej connected his Point to the ant field. "Hard to believe how fast it vibrates!"

Szar crushed a couple of ants with his fingers and put them in his mouth. "Superior taste!" he told Aparalgon, who had finally extricated the ants from his long winter underpants and was putting his gown on again. "Want to try?"

Aparalgon contained his horror, not unlike Felicia in front of her first locust. "Eating living creatures is against the Law of the Grey Robes of the Angel of Dawn," he looked sideways into the mists.

They started walking along one of the lines of telluric energy that Szar had connected to the ant field. "Now then, why don't you tell me about this dream of yours!" Szar imitated Namron's voice, stuffing a small ball of crushed ants into his mouth and chewing.

Aparalgon took a minute to collect his memories, then began, "I was travelling in the field of stars, 'ascending to glorious heights', when the Angel of Dawn appeared to me. He was just as the Law says, 'his eyes, blazing Cosmic Fire, his smile, infinite compassion,' and 'clothed in a garment of Cosmic Dawn,' and he was 'pure iridescence of the colours of Highness.' I immediately prostrated myself in front of him, as the Law says one must do when the Angel of Dawn appears to you. Then he spoke to me! 'Aparalgon, son of Aparalgon!' he said. As the Law says, I said, 'Your lawful servant in the Light of Dawn, Great Angel!' and I began chanting the seven lawful hymns of adoration to the Angel of Dawn. Hardly had I begun than the angel said, 'Aparalgon, follow this light!' and out of his hand came a beam of white light. I said, 'Your lawful servant in the Light of Dawn, Great Angel!' and I followed the beam like he said. It didn't take very long, it was a short beam. At the other end of the beam there stood another angel, shining with golden light, and quite different from the Angel of Dawn. Then the Angel of Dawn spoke to me again. He said, 'Let this angel be your angel, Aparalgon! Follow his light!' So I turned to the other angel and I said, 'Your lawful servant in the golden light, Great Angel!' and I bowed in front of him. And just after that I woke up."

They walked in silence, the first rays of moonlight peering through the mists.

"Shame you didn't have time to ask the new angel's name," Szar commented in a meditative mood.

"But I did hear his name, Master Szar! As I was waking up, I heard someone whispering it: Barkhan Seer."

Szar stopped, faced the young man, put his hand on his shoulder, calling on the Archive with all the strength of the Eagle. "Aparalgon!"

Aparalgon responded with his beautiful smile. But there was no sign showing a thread of connection between his Point and the Archive.

Szar established a link with the fluid darkness of Archive Hall Five. "Can you feel anything?"

Aparalgon frowned, serious but vague, gazing at the mists, "Deep! Very Deep. As the Law says..."

"Repeat after me!" Szar made four explosive 'bha' Voice-sounds, followed by the name of the prince of Thunder. Wild flames of light came out of his mouth, sparking Aparalgon's aura.

Shocked and compelled by the power of the Voice, the young priest repeated, "Bha! Bha! Bha! Bha! Barkhan Seer!"

Szar gave a handclap and Voiced, "Again!"

"Bha! Bha! Bha! Bha! Barkhan Seer!"

"Keep on!"

As the young man was repeating the mantra, Barkhan Seer's bubbly golden light shone around him.

Handclap after handclap, "Again!... Again!"

"It's him! It's him!" Aparalgon exclaimed in awe, recognising the presence. And he felt on his knees, prostrating himself.

"Aparalgon..." Szar sighed, "is this what the Grey Robes do each time an angelic presence comes down to them?"

"Lawfully always!" Aparalgon whispered, his face in the dirt.

Szar watched the golden light dissipate – the precious connection, wasted!

Pulling him up by the hood, "Aparalgon, we *have* to find you another caste, fast!"

So totally unlawful that Aparalgon didn't seem to register the words. He looked skywards, mouth open, as if the Lord Melchisedek was about to deliver a new revelation of the Law.

"Let's go," Szar dragged him up and resumed the stroll. After reflection, he decided, "I want you to stop working at the cremation ground. I have a new task for you. Now that Lady Teyani will no longer be surrounded by her White Eagles, she's going to need a helper. I therefore nominate you Principal Lawful Attendant of the Grand Master of the Female Wing of the Temple of Eisraim. And for the Lord Melchisedek's sake, Aparalgon, close your mouth!"

Aparalgon swallowed. "Does this mean I will be seeing priestesses every day?" he asked anxiously.

For some reason, women seemed to worry him more than corpses.

"Don't worry, they're mostly dead."

Aparalgon remained thoughtful. "Perhaps... you could find me a wife, Master Szar. This way, I could converse with women lawfully unrestrictedly. As the Law says, 'When a Grey Robe priest gets a lawful spouse...'"

Szar stuck his left hand on the young priest's mouth, shutting him up. He kept on walking, "Aparalgon, tomorrow I want to see you dressed in a different gown. Choose any colour you want. But if I see you dressed in grey, I *refuse* to speak to you. Understood?"

Aparalgon's eyes were blinking like he had been transported into the Underworlds.

Szar used a threatening near-Voice threshold, "Understood?"

Hiding behind closed eyes, Aparalgon nodded.

Szar took his hand off, looking up. "A beautiful night, really," he said casually, turning into the alley that separated the lawful centre from Maniya, heading towards the music hall. Aparalgon followed.

286

The temple was empty, and full at the same time. The people had gone, their presence hadn't. In the silveriness of moonlight the feeling was eerie, like walking in another world.

They found the music hall vibrant, as if the amphitheatre's four hundred seats were occupied. As they walked down the steps to the central stage, Szar could see himself sitting against the living wall, a jar of madness marmalade in hand, Elyani on his left, Teyani on his right, all his friends in the room, waiting for the priestesses of the Dawn of Creation.

Putting his hand on Aparalgon's shoulder, he recited a verse of Maveron, "That which is will always be. Why grieve?"

Still in shock, Aparalgon turned toward him with an anxious frown, wondering what to expect next.

"Have you studied music, Aparalgon?"

A cautious nod.

"Lawfully excellent!" Szar Point-activated the field, producing a vibrant low-pitched rhythmic sound, bringing down Barkhan Seer's presence into the hall. "Hold this sound!"

A sound coming straight from Archive Hall Five.

They had arrived on the stage. Aparalgon hesitated, wondering whether to prostrate himself. He turned to the Master of Thunder, who was watching his reactions with interest

Gently, "Hold the sound! With your Point."

This required verticality, it was incompatible with being on all fours. Timidly, Aparalgon stayed on his feet, Point-holding the sound.

Barkhan Seer's golden light started flowing into him.

Refraining from bowing down was a major departure from the Law of the Grey Robes. Aparalgon held fast, more and more light pouring into him.

Szar's face was illuminated with a smile.

It was one of the things which amazed Aparalgon. How could someone's smile be so much like the Light of the Angel of Dawn?

"Let's dance!" Szar clapped his hands, marking the rhythm, slowly moving his body.

A totally new experience for Aparalgon. Swallowing, he slightly moved his shoulders to and fro with the ease of someone carrying a milk jug on his head.

"More light!" Szar demanded, jumping from one leg to the other, shaking the floor in the Dragon-elegant style of Mount Lohrzen's dining hall.

It looked terrifying.

From his Point, Aparalgon increased the volume of the sound. Barkhan Seer's gold increased accordingly, igniting the young man's aura.

"Not bad!" In seven slow consecutive jumps, Szar circled Aparalgon. "Something is happening in the temple at the moment. Can you feel what?"

Aparalgon shook his head.

"Ask Master Barkhan Seer!"

Aparalgon closed his eyes. "The Flight of the Eagles!" he reopened his eyes, amazed at how easily the knowing came to him. "The sixteen White Eagles are leaving their bodies!"

That we may fly together.

Archive Hall Five was flooded with Eagle's Light and Teyani's presence. Aparalgon saw a flame rising to the triangle, where the Sons of Apollo were waiting for the priestesses led by Antaria.

Whiteness eternal. Forever love.

"Let's dance, my friend," Szar took his hands.

At first Aparalgon moved hesitantly, fearing the presence would fade if he didn't concentrate enough. Magically, he retained the link.

His Point became a fountain, pouring Barkhan Seer's liquid gold.

They danced, eye to eye, celebrating the end of a world and the birth of a new one.

20.14 Reunion

The next morning, Khej and Gallagher were coming out of the chapel of the Early Mysteries of the Law at the eastern end of the temple when Ferman Point-called from the rainbow chapel, "Are the repairs going well?"

"We didn't have to repair anything!" Gallagher Point-exclaimed. "It's magic like in the early days of the kingdom! All the fields are fixing themselves and working like lawful charms."

Thanks to the ant device, the Wizards' mad race to mend field after field had turned into peaceful routine inspections. And the mists were so light that everyone in the temple – which by now wasn't more than seventy people – felt like flying.

Ferman closed the Point-communication remarking, "Sad to say, the temple being empty is doing the fields a lot of good."

That, the Masters of Thunder had foreseen long ago. Which was why they had planned to perform the Archive transfer when the temple was depopulated, free from the thought-forms of eleven hundred people busying around and constantly using fields for rituals and a thousand other things ranging from communicating through darkness visible to warming themselves up in their bathtubs. The clarity of the last days was a shocking contrast with the ugly heaviness of the former months.

Gallagher stopped by an ant heap in the middle of the alley. "Was this one here yesterday?"

"I don't think so!" Khej scratched his head. "They're coming out like lawful pimples after a puberty ritual!"

"Know what I saw yesterday? Szar eating ants!"

"Really?" Khej immediately grabbed a few ants, crushed them and put them in his mouth.

"Hey, what about the Law? Aren't the Field Wizards supposed to refrain from eating corpses?" Gallagher reminded his friend with a grin.

"But if Szar does it, it's got to be lawful!" the exaggeratedly broad-shouldered young man picked up more ants, ignoring the foul taste.

Unlawful curiosity taking over, Gallagher imitated him. But as his hand was about to reach his mouth, he completely froze.

Khej too became rock-still.

For a few seconds, the Field Wizards remained like statues.

Two tall blond Nephilim men in long dark-blue cloaks emerged from the mists. Silent, precise, camouflaged from darkness visible to the heights of Point-ness, they walked slowly like predators ready to leap on their prey.

From the rainbow chapel, Ferman Point-called again, "Are you all right, my boys? I'm picking up something strange coming from your Points."

Taking over Gallagher's consciousness, one of the Nephilim men made him Point-answer, "We're fine. It must be that ant field. Makes us feel weird when we tune into it."

"That I can understand!" Ferman Point-laughed. "Last night I sat on one of those damn heaps by mistake and I got bitten in unlawful places. After that I felt dizzy like I'd had a suppository of herbs of madness."

"Sounds about like how I feel. Anyhow, we've finished around here. We'll be back in the chapel soon," Gallagher Point-said.

The Nephilim men exchanged a satisfied nod.

Khej and Gallagher started walking as if everything was normal like the Law. They looked quite normal – except for the two Nephilim following them like shadows, Point-hiding behind their Points. And inside themselves the Field Wizards felt quite normal too, totally unaware their consciousness had been taken over.

In the empty alleys of the temple the rattle of the pebbles was that of two men walking, not four, so closely were the assailants following in the Wizards' steps.

In the mid-eastern enclave, passing by the chapel of the Golden Egg, one of the Nephilim detected a soul coming out of a nearby alley. He turned to his companion.

The other shook his head, silently indicating the target wasn't worth killing – especially knowing the slightest venom shower could have revealed their presence.

Soon they met him. A frail old man dressed in a dark-green gown.

One of the Nephilim established eye contact with him for a fraction of a second. After which the old man no longer saw four men – only two.

Khej stopped to salute him, "Praise the Lord Melchisedek, Pushpadiv of the Green Robe!"

"All glory to the Lord Melchisedek, Field Wizards of the Law," old Pushpadiv answered in a tired voice.

"And how is your son, my friend in the Law? Getting better?"

"Better, better!" the old man nodded, vague. "He'll be cremated tomorrow morning."

Khej bit his lip. Old Pushpadiv had lost the thread of the Law.

"I don't think he knows where he's going. Shall we take him back to his chapel?" Gallagher suggested.

The Nephilim manipulated Khej to answer, "No. We don't have time. We must go. Farewell, man of the Law!"

They went, leaving the old man to wander in the alleys.

That day, Shyama and Ashok were sitting in the rainbow hall with Ferman, coordinating the operations. Ashok Point-called Arena, who was working in the catacombs. "Arena, what the hell are you doing?"

"Just fixing up one or two short-range sensors," young Arena answered.

"But you're making a mess! All the sensors in your area have lost half their sensitivity."

"Yes, I wonder why."

"What do you mean you wonder why? They're the sensors you've been working on all morning. You should know what you've done to them!"

"There could be something wrong with my calibrating stone," Arena suggested. "I'll come back to the chapel to get another one." And he set off to Szar's bedroom – followed by another Nephilim dressed in a dark-blue cloak, whose Point was hidden behind his.

An extraordinarily clever camouflage technique. During the Point-communication sharp-eyed Ashok hadn't noticed anything unusual. And none of the sensors around Arena had picked up the foreign presence.

Totally undetected, the Nephilim combatants were on their way to the rainbow chapel.

Ashok Point-called again, fulminating, "Arena, you've just messed up another sensor!"

Manipulated by the Nephilim, Arena Point-answered, "It's this damn calibrating stone."

"You fucking Blue Priestess, why do you touch the fields if you know your stone is wrecked? Come back here immediately! Bring me the fucking stone!"

It was the unlawful language that caught Ferman's attention. "Are you all right, my boy?" he Point-called Arena compassionately.

"Yes, yes, Master Ferman."

Ferman noticed the same Point-touch he had perceived in Gallagher and Khej a few minutes earlier. It was elusive, even for a Point master like Ferman. And it didn't have any Nephilim flavour attached to it.

But it didn't have any of the characteristics of the Great Ant either.

Ferman went on Point-chatting, "You've been working late hours in the last days. Perhaps you need a lawful rest."

"I'll rest in the Fields of Peace!" Arena replied.

It was what Arena said each time Ferman wanted him to rest.

"Tell me, which calibrating stone are you using?"

"One of the hermaphroditic stones from the death chamber."

"There's probably something wrong with it. Just bring it to us my boy, we'll fix it for you," Ferman said, warm and supportive like a lawful uncle.

Shyama and Ashok had Point-overhead the conversation. They frowned in disbelief. Something wrong with one of the hermaphroditic stones? Plainly impossible! By definition, hermaphroditic stones were perfect, *totally* impermeable to foreign influences.

How could Master Ferman say something so stupid?

"Alarm!" Ferman shouted, closing all Point-communication channels with the outside world. "Arena, Khej and Gallagher are sending suspicious Point-signals. And Arena is speaking complete nonsense! He *must* be being manipulated."

Not stupid at all, Master Ferman.

"Where is Szar?" Ferman ran to the door of the hall.

"At the cremation ground with Teyani, conducting the funeral ritual for the sixteen Eagles," Shyama said.

Standing in the doorway, Ferman ordered, "Ashok, get Lorenz to replace you here and go and take position in Szar's bedroom. Arena will arrive in three minutes. Be ready to test your field! If the Nephilim are manipulating him he could do anything."

Ashok stood up and ran, thinking, "Gods, I asked for this, didn't I?"

The Nephilim-killer fields in Szar's bedroom didn't need to be manned, with only one exception: the one Ashok had designed. At his insistent request, it had been decided he would be the first one to test it.

"We have fourteen men outside, what about them?" Shyama asked.

"Don't tell them anything. Send only routine messages. But scan each and every one of them!" Ferman ran to a nearby cellar and took a key-stone to establish a protected Point-link to Szar.

At the cremation ground, Szar, Teyani and Zothar were each holding a torch, chanting the magnificent hymns to the departed souls, pouring their voices into sixteen heaps of smouldering ashes. Apart from a line of corpses waiting to be burnt, one of them Pervcon of the Salmon Robe, the cremation ground was empty. There were no lawful wailers around the corpses. All helpers had gone. The only Attendant of the Dead left was Zothar, who from a sense of duty had vowed to be the last person to die in the temple so he could lawfully incinerate all the others.

"Commander, we could be under attack any minute!" Ferman Point-called, giving a full report in packed format. "It could be that because they can't get into the temple without being spotted the Nephilim are trying to hit us from a distance," he concluded.

"Or it could be they're in the catacombs!" Szar Point-replied.

With so many sensors impaired, who could tell?

Pulling forces from Revelation Sky, Szar handed his torch to the White Eagle. Exchanging a glance, "Teyani I love you!"

Teyani's eyes flared, but not with the Eagle's softness. Stepping into her higher self, a formidable angel at the Edge of Highness, she ignited Szar's column of Spirit, sparking a time crossing.

Eternity in a split second.

A trail of Eagle's Light from Eisraim to Philadelphia.

Dazzling love.

Gervin the warrior, pouring Thunder into Szar's Point.

Teyani, Barkhan Seer, and seven of Thunder projecting the High Word through Virginia, raising Hiram from the dead.

Hiram, Knight of the Apocalypse and Descender, king of No Limits.

997! Hiram, Hiram, Aparalgon taught you well!

Szar started running, jumping over the line of corpses. "Ferman," he Point-called, "I want a protected Point-line to Ashok. Fast!"

Ferman grabbed a key-stone and ran through the stone stairways of the rainbow chapel. "Are you coming through the catacombs?"

"Too dangerous. By now the catacombs could be infested with ghosts! I'll be at the chapel doors in three minutes."

No point going via the roofs. From the cremation ground, he cut through the enclave of lawful relief. Dragon-racing, Szar was gearing himself for the engagement.

Point warfare – one second to kill or be killed.

"Kartendranath!" he called. "Kartendranath!"

From Revelation Sky, Kartendranath looked down, triaxe in hand, chanting, "Nama Gana, Nama Gana, Gana Gana, Nam Nam..." raising Szar's Point to the full potential of the helmet.

From the helmet, a certitude: "At last! At last we are going to know who the ghosts are."

That day, Szar's hall was a fiery-red field of stars. Ferman raced in, his face turning bright orange. Ashok was standing by the vaulted colonnade that opened into the catacombs, waiting for Arena.

"Don't tune into Arena's Point!" Szar Point-warned. "Can you feel his presence through darkness visible?"

"About... three hundred lawful feet from here," Ashok Point-confirmed.

Bolting full-speed through the mists, Szar Point-instructed, "I won't make it, you're going to have to handle this by yourselves. There could be as many as sixteen Nephilim in the catacombs. They could all arrive at the same time as Arena. So it's like this: as soon as Arena walks in you blast his Point with an anti-spice field. If the Nephilim are Point-paired with him, they will *have* to strike back. Then you activate Ashok's Nephilim-killer field."

Ashok gulped, "But if the ghosts are Point-paired with Arena, my field is going to kill him too!"

"No choice!" Ferman said, holding fast to the light of Archive Hall One.

Immersed in the changing orange glows they waited, their Points on the triggers of the deadly fields.

Ashok wiped beads of sweat off his forehead. For the first time, he could see death right in front of him.

It was cold. It brought up an irrational malaise.

"I could never have been a Nephilim Hunter," he thought. "Wouldn't have the guts."

Sensing the wave of fear, Ferman clicked his fingers and pointed above Ashok's head.

Ashok gave a nod, calling on Archive Hall One.

The response was instant – Gervin's apocalyptic intensity pulsing in his column of Spirit.

It shocked the young man into awakening, triggering a flash of extraordinarily lucid peripheral awareness. He beheld not only the seven archways – the one in the middle opening to the catacombs – but also the entire hall, with the drifting clouds made of tens of thousands of shining particles of light, mostly orange-gold and crimson stars, apart from the distant end of the hall where a huge lapis-lazuli nebula was whirling slowly, indolently. At the other end of the hall he could feel the quiet presence of Ushbudh and Visarg, standing in the doorway of the death chamber. A few lawful feet from them, Balavan was guarding the crypt of the Archive stones. Ashok could also hear Master Ferman's tense breathing, and every single note in the faint, incomprehensible Flying Dragon music that swept through the fields of stars.

The young man was still scared like an animal on a Nephilim sacrificial altar, but what a clarity! It was the first time he *really* noticed how magnificent the hall was. "A fucking work of art," he thought.

They heard Arena's steps.

The steps of only one man. Not in a hurry. He *was* tired.

Coming closer...

Ferman raised his hand.

...and closer.

Arena tripped on the first step of the last stone stairway, then started walking up. One step, two steps, three, four, five...

Ferman abruptly lowered his hand.

In unison the two Field Wizards projected a massive dose of anti-spice venom into Arena's Point. Enough to kill an entire caravan of Nephilim pilgrims.

No shock in return, just silence.

Either the Nephilim had let go of Arena's Point, or they knew how to deflect the attack.

Or perhaps all this was just a false alarm.

Arena started walking up the steps again. As soon as his silhouette appeared in the central archway, Ferman lowered his arm for the second time.

Another anti-spice venom avalanche into Arena's Point.

Arena staggered, rendered dizzy by the intensity. "What'ya doing?" he mumbled, the two orange faces staring at him anxiously like he had just stolen the relics of the Law.

"Mother of the Light!" Ferman sighed, wiping a bead of sweat from the corner of his eye. He Point-called, "Commander! Arena is here. Looking all right. His Point no longer shows any abnormal signs."

"Take him out of the hall immediately!" Szar ordered. "Knock him unconscious and get someone to watch him. Ashok, you stay in the hall. Total vigilance! They could still come in any second."

Total vigilance. As Ferman was running out, firmly holding Arena's arm, Ashok could see each and every star-dot in the galactic clouds, feel the soft breeze that aired the hall, and the equal flow of breath in his nostrils, and the hole in his left shoe, and the fat which held his mass of short black hair stuck on his head. And he heard every single step as Ferman and Arena hurried along the corridor, their footsteps fading away in the main stairway. Yet he was perfectly centred.

Eyes fixed on the central archway of the colonnade.

Awake, more than ever before.

"Come on, ghosts! Come on!" he whispered.

Meanwhile Szar had just crossed the southern border of Maniya, "I'm nearly there!" he Point-called the rainbow hall. "Getting something from the catacombs?"

"Can't tell," Shyama Point-answered. "The sensors have been further dimmed in the last minutes. I don't think we could detect a rat at this stage."

"I can smell Khej and Gallagher," Szar warned. "They've arrived at the chapel of the Lawful Gardeners."

A large chapel-shed, right of the rainbow chapel.

The two Wizards were walking fast, followed by their Nephilim shadows. They saw a man in a dark-green gown coming out of the chapel-shed.

The man saw them, but he didn't see the shadows.

"We met old Pushpadiv," Gallagher told him, pointing east. "That way!"

"Thank you, Field Wizards of the Law!"

They walked along the walls of the chapel-shed. And as they arrived in the alley outside the chapel of Baltham, they caught a glimpse of Szar darting up the front steps of the chapel.

Turning his head, Szar saw four men – not two.

He immediately recognised the one who was walking behind Gallagher.

He was Henrick the prian, defector from Jex Belaran, and the father of Pelenor Ozorenan's child.

For a fraction of a second, the men's gazes met.

Henrick's Point was a fortress! Same instant impression as when they had first met in Tomoristan.

But today he wasn't smiling.

The Hunter didn't launch his attack.

Szar jumped into the chapel. Namron slammed the heavy gate closed behind him.

Now Szar was inside the shield. He established a Point-token-ring with all the Wizards in the chapel. "It's Henrick! Henrick the prian. Outside the chapel doors with one of his Hunters."

Ferman was in the rainbow hall, his nephew blissfully unconscious on the floor by his side. "But what's Henrick doing at the head of sixteen Nephilim Hunters?"

Henrick's clan was comprised of four or five men at the most.

Were they new recruits, trained hastily in the last year? That didn't fit with the degree of expertise they displayed.

"Who says the others are Hunters? They could also be giants," Lorenz said.

Which would have explained the hundreds of magnificent he-stone weapons found in the bag of the Hunter killed by Szar. The giants had supplied Henrick generously.

"Oh shit!" Ashok clenched his teeth, realising he could be face to face with a dozen Nephilim giants any second.

He was shaken by a wave of panic. His Nephilim-killer field had been designed to match Hunters' Point-attacks. What if the giants' style of combat was completely different? His field wouldn't even be triggered when they launched the first venom shower.

The rest of the field arsenal in the bedroom might prove powerful enough to kill them, but by then what would be left of Ashok?

Outside the chapel Henrick and his man stayed Point-united with Gallagher and Khej. Any Point-attack launched against them would kill the two Field Wizards. They stopped at the entrance's bottom step.

"Szar!" Henrick called in a loud voice.

Geared for the onslaught, Szar was standing in the lavishly fielded entrance hall of Baltham, Namron noisily chewing black root by his side. "Henrick!" he responded through the gate.

"Szar I don't want to kill you! I know what you have done for Pelenor," the Hunter declared.

His Point high in Revelation Sky, Szar made an obscene mudra with his fingers, making it clear to Namron he didn't buy into these honeyed words.

Namron agreed with a graphic face, showing his black teeth.

"Szar, all I want is the stone from Jex Belaran, and twenty-four hermaphroditic stones. That still leaves plenty for your Archive. Bring me the stones and you'll never see me again. My Hunter's word."

Szar remembered Space Matrix's voice: Never listen to the music of the Watchers.

"Out of the question, man of the Law!"

For obvious reasons. Nothing could be more attractive to the giants than the Archive stones, once super-charged. Arming Henrick with hermaphroditic stones would only make it easier for him to return and launch an attack during the transfer.

"Szar, think twice!" the Hunter went on. "Why should you care about what will happen in the kingdom after you? You are on your way out, all that matters to you is your Archive. Let the Nephilim sort out their affairs here, and the Nephilim won't interfere with yours."

"Commander," Shyama Point-called, "the short-range sensors are detecting Nephilim everywhere! Two at the main portal, one at the chapel of the Ancient Mysteries, two at the central kitchen, four around the chapel of Dawn, three outside the second hall of Melchisedek, three in the catacombs under the enclave of the High Priest, one at the portal of the female wing."

"Sixteen of them altogether," Ferman confirmed. "Not making any efforts to conceal their presence!"

"Just the opposite! It's as if they were trying to trigger as many sensors as they can," Shyama observed. "Doesn't make any sense!"

In one nostril wriggle, Szar could feel Nephilim spice all over the temple.

"Doesn't make any sense at all!" Ferman yelled. "Except if they've found a way to bypass *all* our defence systems!"

That didn't do anything to reassure Ashok. "I *am* going to die!" the realisation dawned on him with cold certitude. "No way out!"

The immediate proximity of his death restored total vigilance. In the awesome precision of his peripheral awareness, he noticed a faint shadow on the other side of the central archway. A blur in the orange glows of the field of stars.

"There's no one there. It's all right," the thought imposed itself on his mind.

Anyway, a Nephilim presence would already have triggered the hall's arsenal of Point-weapons.

Except if the Nephilim was hiding behind his Point.

He took three steps in the direction of the archway. The shadow had disappeared, the light was back to normal.

"Perfectly normal!" he turned round.

Perfectly normal?

"Master Gervin! Master Gervin!"

Suddenly inspired, Ashok took over the Point-ness of the hall, wiped out the decorative field. The reddish clouds of stars disappeared instantly, replaced by the normal purpleness of darkness visible. Swivelling round, he caught a glimpse of a pair of eyes.

Something greater took over.

A massive influx descending through his Point. Thunder. Unleashing fields of hell into the Nephilim.

At the same time, vastness. Perceiving the warp of fields of the entire kingdom, which the Mother of the Light was compassionately holding in her hand, but not for much longer.

She smiled.

The Nephilim's response came out with a violence that shook the entire chapel. One with Gervin, the Wizards Point-held onto their fields. In the rainbow hall, Arena reopened his eyes. In the crypt of the Archive stones Balavan stood up and rushed out in panic, as he saw the fields of the nearby death chamber were about to vomit their venom.

Still like Revelation Sky, ready to smite with the triaxe, Szar waited for Henrick's attack.

It didn't come.

One second later, the wave fell flat. All fields returned to normal.

Three Point-messages simultaneously came through the Wizards' token-ring.

One from Shyama, "All catacombs' sensors have been restored. Doesn't seem to be anyone left down there."

One from Ugr, who was outside the chapel of the Mysteries of Ancient Times, "Commander, I've been contacted by the Nephilim! They say they want to speak to you immediately but whatever you do *don't kill Henrick*! They say our chapel is *not* in danger!"

One from Ashok, "I... I... I killed..." Ashok Point-choked. "I killed *two* Nephilim Hunters! There's... *two* fucking corpses in front of me!"

And inside himself he thought, "So I *am* someone!" But mixed up by the emotion, he leaked the thought into the token ring.

Holding onto the triaxe, Szar stifled a smile. "Ugr, who contacted you?" he Point-called.

"They're coming! Right in front of me. Not giants, Hunters! They're not attacking." There were a few seconds of silence, then, "It's the chief! He says his name is Joranjeran. He wants to speak to you but he can't reach you through the damn shield. He says, whatever you do don't kill Henrick!"

"Joranjeran, past Grand Commander of the Nephilim Hunters?" Ferman spat on the living floor. "I don't buy into that."

"The Nephilim are closing in on the chapel. Won't take more than two minutes before they all arrive," Shyama warned.

"Avan and Lehr have sighted four Nephilim outside the second hall of Melchisedek," Ferman announced. "They confirm they're Hunters, not giants. They haven't attacked them."

"Commander!" Ugr Point-called again, "That Joranjeran man wants me to give him my key-stone so he can speak to you through the shield. He says 'It's perfectly safe, remember the ginger marmalade!' But I can't possibly give him my key! Would be..."

The Point-communication was interrupted.

Ferman immediately cancelled the Point-line to Ugr's key-stone.

Ginger marmalade! If it was a trick, it was a damn smart one.

"Szar!" Henrick shouted in a threatening voice, "Bring the stones immediately, or I kill you and everyone inside your chapel!"

"Oh shit! Shit! Ugr has been attacked!" Ferman reported.

"Killed?" Szar asked.

"No. Just knocked unconscious," Ferman answered.

Just unconscious? Why?

It was at that moment that Szar understood.

Ugly like the Nephilim!

"I can't believe this! I can't be-*lie*ve this!" he hit the living floor with his heel, furious. "Restore the Point-line!" he ordered.

An absurd instruction. A key-stone wasn't enough to crack the defence shield, but still enough to break into the Wizards' communication system.

"Confirm the order," Ferman asked.

"Restore Ugr's Point-line!" Szar repeated. "Immediately!"

Ferman hesitated, "Are you sure?"

"Yes! Fucking sure!" Szar ground his teeth. "Don't you get it? This is a fucking feud between Nephilim, it has *nothing* to do with us! We've been caught in cross fire. Jex Belaran has manipulated us all along!"

Stunned, Ferman restored the Point-line to Ugr's key-stone.

"Szar! Szar!" a familiar vibration erupted into the token-ring. "It's me, Joranjeran. Szar, don't strike Henrick! Whatever you do don't strike Henrick! My men have caught him in *five* triangular nets. His Point can no longer be dangerous to you."

"Joranjeran..." Szar inhaled a deep, hissing breath, "if this story is what I believe it is, I am going to be very, *very* angry!"

"We'll talk later! For now stay out of this. Don't intervene!"

Tangled in the triangular nets, Henrick couldn't launch a Point-attack on the chapel without first overcoming the fifteen Hunters led by Joranjeran. So he used another weapon – the Voice.

Unleashing a torrent of Voice, "Szar! Open the door! Let me in!"

A glacial wind swept through the hall, hitting Szar and Namron.

"Open! O-o-o-o-o-o-o-pen!" Underworldly low-pitched, the Voice became monstrous, buzzing with ancient forces, bringing down an awesomely dark presence. "O-o-o-o-o-o-o-pen! O-o-o-o-o-o-o-pen!"

Darkness visible was filled with sounds that rushed in all directions at absurd speed, hissing stories of worlds that started dying the moment they were born, spawning useless creations that hurt like the sound of a board scratched by a thousand nails.

The music of the Watchers.

It combined with Henrick's Voice into a cacophony of hell, "O-o-o-o-o-o-o-pen!"

Losing his mind, Namron started lifting the thick wooden beam behind the chapel doors.

"Stop!" Szar pulled him back by the shoulders.

In the deafening madness, Namron turned into a wild beast, screaming and kicking.

Szar had to knock him down with precise black-dance blows.

"O-o-o-o-o-o-o-pen!"

As Namron was collapsing on his knees, Ferman, Shyama, Arena and Lorenz rushed into the hall. Ignoring Szar, the four of them raced to open the door.

In this energetic mayhem, darkness visible turned insanely loud, projecting the Voice of Thunder could have had unpredictable results. Szar chose to black-dance them out of action. He focused on the strong men, Ferman and Shyama, hitting their cheap-way-out gateways as they passed him.

They fell softly onto the white living floor.

He turned to Arena, who was already on the beam. But a blow in a gateway under the left scapula proved ineffective. Szar hit again, this time a cheap-way-out.

"O-o-o-o-o-o-o-pen!"

Captured by Henrick's Voice, Arena staggered but didn't fall.

Szar hit a full volley of blows, as if fighting a black dance opponent.

The young man collapsed, a streak of blood flowing from his mouth.

Rendered furious by the music, old Lorenz fought with unexpected vigour. Meanwhile Meran and Uhl were arriving in the hall, their eyes illuminated with demented glows.

Szar saw the situation getting out of control. "Ashok! Are you holding it?" he Point-called.

Ashok was exploring the bags of the Hunters he had killed. "Everything is quiet here!"

Lorenz attacked headfirst. It took seven consecutive black-dance blows to annihilate him.

Suddenly, the Voice stopped. Darkness visible became silent again.

Meran and Uhl stopped in the middle of the hall, looking at each other in disbelief.

"Back to your positions!" Szar ordered, and he ran to a peep-hole on the front wall.

Melchard had arrived on the scene. Both hands raised, he stood twenty lawful feet meters behind the Hunters and their hostages, ready to project the Voice of Thunder.

On the left, Joranjeran emerged out of the mists. Alone. Dressed in a worn-out black cloak covered in mud. Looking ten years older than last time he and Szar had met.

"Joranjeran, do not force me to hit you!" Henrick threatened.

"Good to hear your voice, son!" Joranjeran spoke in his warm rugged low-pitched voice. "It's been a while."

"What do you want?"

"You, Henrick."

Henrick was defiant, "Killing me might not be as easy as you think! I have learnt more about the Watchers than..."

"I don't want to kill you, I want you back," Joranjeran spoke without anger.

Henrick hid his surprise. "Back?"

"Yes, back in Jex Belaran! Letting you go was the greatest mistake I have made in my life, Henrick. I have come to apologise."

Not a common thing to do for a Grand Commander of Jex Belaran's Nephilim Hunters. Henrick looked down, incredulous.

With disarming sincerity, Joranjeran kept on, "I want you back! I know what you have done, I am ready to forgive everything."

"Too late!"

"Son, I am an old man. Nine months, I have just spent, hiding under heaps of leaves and sleeping under the rain, fighting against the plague. If you come back with me now, it will have been worth it. Pelenor is in Jex, you know. Waiting for you. And your son, a beautiful..."

"The past can't be undone!" Henrick's voice was charged with the accumulated bitterness of twelve years of exile.

"What future is there for you with the giants, son? You're not going to tell me your heart is with that Bobros! What do you want, exactly? You have Joranjeran's personal apology. Isn't that just as good as seeing Jex Belaran in flames?" The old man with the tanned face grinned, "There have been fires in Jex Belaran before. Joranjeran has *never* apologised to anyone."

Henrick shook his head in disbelief.

Joranjeran extended his hand. "Start again?"

In a softer voice, "I can't Joranjeran. I can't."

The hand remained open.

"Please go, now! I don't want to kill you," Henrick hardened again.

Szar sent a Point-prompt through the token-ring.

"I'm back in the crypt of the Archive stones," Balavan responded.

Ashok left his corpses, "Totally ready!"

Ushbudh, Visarg and the others confirmed they were holding their positions.

Outside the chapel, Joranjeran and Henrick were looking at each other.

Szar saw the wave coming, "Hold it!" he raised the Point-intensity.

Nothing was felt inside the chapel. Outside, not one noise. But Henrick and his man fell.

So did Khej and Gallagher.

Szar screamed, "Melchard, bring them in, fast!"

Melchard rushed on Gallagher, dragged his body up the steps of the chapel. As he arrived at the top, Szar quickly opened the door and pulled the body of the young man inside. Melchard ran back and brought in Khej.

Both of them were dead.

Badly dead. Szar couldn't even try to pull them back, simply because there was nothing left to pull back. Their astral bodies had been completely evaporated by the formidable dose of venom which the sixteen Hunters had projected into Henrick.

In the entrance hall of Baltham, Namron was already moving, his left hand searching his pocket for black root. Melchard examined the four Field Wizards Szar had knocked down. A quick Voice projection brought Ferman back to his senses. Shyama was deeply unconscious, but his vital gateways were intact.

But when he came to Arena, Melchard called, "Szar, have you seen what has happened here?"

Arena was dead.

So was Lorenz.

Their vital gateways were such a puree that trying to call them back wasn't an option either.

Both fists clenched, the Dragon in his eyes, Szar walked out of the chapel, ready to tell Joranjeran exactly what he thought.

He found the old man kneeling by Henrick's body, crying.

He stopped on the steps, and contemplated the mists.

Later, when the Wizards established a Point-link with Lasseera to report, Szar spoke to Lehrmon. He spoke in measured words, with the irresistible clarity of Revelation Sky, "Remember the conversation we had last year, when you were telling me the Nephilim were the prime reason for the rotting of the kingdom and I was trying to defend Naamah? Well you were right. The Nephilim *have* destroyed the kingdom."

20.15 Cooperation, Nephilim-style

Szar and Joranjeran were walking by the side of the Fontelayana river.

The old chief explained, "After we disconnected your hand from the seed-connection stone of the Fox Renegades, Perseps returned north. I didn't. I stayed in the county with fourteen men. Miserable times, these were! Two of my Hunters died from the plague. Five others fell sick. They caught dysentery and had to be sent back to Jex Belaran. I nearly lost three others in an avalanche. One broke his leg, falling from a bridge... a long list of catastrophes!"

Szar was putting facts together, "So this is why you didn't even try to destroy our short-range sensors in the forests around the temple: you wanted to be sure we would detect Henrick's arrival?"

"Except that we weren't sure it was Henrick who was behind all this. I strongly suspected it, which is why I stayed here. See, there were not many men in the kingdom capable of creating such a mess: that Fridrick ghost fooling around with the Brown Robes, the Foxes and the Red Clan slaughtering each other, the Black Hunters exterminated in a matter of hours... splendid work!" Joranjeran exclaimed, as if with pride. "I trained Henrick.

I knew what he was capable of. Also, Bobros is an intelligent man. He surrounds himself only with the best. If I had been in his place I too would have chosen Henrick. Henrick *was* the best."

Now that the giants were on their way, it was clear that eliminating the Foxes, the Red Clan and the Black Hunters had been a colossal mistake. If there was *one* chance to stop the invaders, it would have been by uniting all Hunters – regulars and renegades – against them.

Fridrick was still an enigma to Szar. How could a man speak and behave exactly as if he had been trained in Jex Belaran, and yet never have been there? Was he an extraordinarily convincing spy, or a puppet whose personality had been completely fabricated?

Szar tried, "Is there something you haven't told me about Fridrick?"

"No. The only thing I can think of is that five years ago, two of our Hunters disappeared mysteriously. Alder and Pion, they were called. They went to get someone in Barnagiran, but they never arrived there. Vanished from the kingdom! Who knows, maybe the giants captured them and carved Fridrick from their astral bodies. The necromancers of the Eastern Peninsula do dirty tricks like this."

"Dirty tricks..." Szar pulled a contemptuous face.

He took a small plass box from his pocket. It contained Perseps' poisoned gift: the key-stone to communicate through the shield of Jex Belaran. Its radiation was concealed by the container's lining.

"Using me as bait *was* a dirty trick," he said, handing the box to Joranjeran.

The Hunter took the box and put it in his pocket without even opening it. "Joranjeran never makes apologies. It's well known," he said. "Anyway, as far as I may judge you messed with this stone quite a bit, didn't you?"

Quite a bit, as Joranjeran would realise a few days later.

"Why couldn't you play it straight with us?" Szar shrugged, "The giants are our common enemy. We could have joined forces to eliminate the traitor."

"Isn't that exactly what we have done?" Joranjeran grinned.

Cooperation, Nephilim style.

"This mess didn't have to happen in Eisraim. If you wanted Henrick, couldn't you just go and hunt him somewhere else?"

"Remember, we didn't know for sure it was Henrick. All we knew was, whoever was behind this story was Jex Belaran's number one enemy," Joranjeran pointed out. "The threat was too great, we had to find him. We couldn't afford to fail. Anyhow, it's not just our key-stone that attracted Henrick to your temple. If he came here it was just as much for your hermaphroditic stones."

Still, if Perseps had given the stone to Szar, it was to attract the traitor.

They walked silently to the boat that was to take the Hunters back to the Northern Lakes. Joranjeran's men had already embarked, carrying with them the body of Henrick. The chief checked on his men and gave a few orders.

Before leaving, he stood on the gangplank and warned Szar, "The giants have recruited many spies among the Nephilim people of Barnagiran. They're everywhere in the counties of the Centre North. You'll have to keep an eye on them. Take care of yourself, Szar of the Brown Robe!"

"You will send my love to Pelenor. And to Felicia. I'll let you explain that this time I *really* didn't have time to prepare pickled cucumbers for her."

"Would you like to speak to her?" Serious, Joranjeran pulled out the small plass box from his pocket, offering it to Szar. And he grinned, as if the joke was funny.

"Farewell man of the Law!" Szar turned his back and walked away.

To the cremation ground.

– Thus ends the Book of the Last Days –

21

The Book of the
Valley of the Necromancer

21.1 Following the light of Archive Hall Five

It was late in the afternoon, when the funeral ritual of the four Field Wizards was ending. Szar left the corpses of the three Hunters to Zothar.

"Will be done, Master Szar!" the Grand Attendant of the Dead gave a broad smile, always willing and ready to accompany a soul in the first steps of the Great Journey.

The more depopulated the temple became, the broader Zothar's smile — the smile of satisfaction of a sincere man who saw his life mission about to be completed. In a way, his lawful joy was heart-warming.

But who would perform Zothar's rites? Szar had often wondered. As he couldn't see any easy solution, he refrained from raising the question.

Walking back to the rainbow chapel, he called through darkness visible, "Aparalgon, I want to see you. I don't care which gown you are wearing, just come. To my chapel. I missed you today."

Such a flow of heartness. It brought tears in the young man's eyes. "There will be no embarrassment for you, Master Szar. I have changed gowns," he announced with dignity.

"Ha! Ha! Ha! Ha! Ha!" Szar's Dragon blasted darkness visible, making Aparalgon jump. "Come immediately, then. Run! I can't wait to see you."

"Lady Teyani asks if she can come too," Aparalgon added.

With all my heart, with all my mind...

"By all lawful means! Tell her I was just about to call her."

"She says she knows," Aparalgon said.

Returning home, Szar made his hall a simple field of stars, sober like those he first saw when Elyani and Seyani were teaching him to travel. And he sat in the middle, contemplating the light, images of the morning drifting through his mind.

304

Killing Arena and Lorenz... how could that possibly have happened? He saw the young man falling, blood coming out of his mouth. And he saw himself beating the hell out of old Lorenz. Strange associative links led him to remember the caverns of sickness, and the blonde Vivyani on her deathbed.

"No, not that again!" he stood up and danced under the stars, letting go. Letting go.

When he heard Teyani and Aparalgon arriving, he stopped, holding his breath, praying to the Good Lord Melchisedek, "Please, not a pink gown!"

They walked in arm in arm, she, Whiter than ever, he, dressed in a long black cloak which he wore with great dignity, his Point still shining with Barkhan Seer's gold.

Szar ran towards them and Dragon-hugged each of them, making Aparalgon's vertebrae crack.

"Tell me, friend! What made you choose black?"

"Master Barkhan Seer inspired me," Aparalgon answered, reaching behind to rub his back. "From now on I will wear black. Black is the colour of judgement."

"Judgement," Szar echoed, amazed, like the Mother of the Light was delivering a new star in front of him. "What does that mean?"

Archive Hall Five answered through Aparalgon, "Judgement means everything counts. Every single thing I learn, every single thing I do, every single thing I say. Every minute. All the time."

It was Szar's turn to have tears in his eyes.

At the last hour, the sleepers awaken!

Palms and eyes turned skywards, Teyani gave Barkhan Seer an amused smile. Then she lowered her gaze on Aparalgon in a way that showed she had adopted him.

"What if people ask which is my caste?" he asked.

He couldn't lawfully possibly call himself of the Grey Robe and wear black!

Teyani answered in her prophetic voice, "You will say, 'I am Aparalgon of the Last Hour.'"

Szar drank their presence, fixing their image in Space Matrix's memory.

"Friends," he announced, "I want to invite both of you to an extraordinary ritual. Tonight, in this hall, the Field Wizards will assemble for the charging of the Archive stone."

The entire temple to be involuted into one stone. More power than in a great ascension ritual.

Szar called on Gervin to give him the strength to deliver the rest of the news.

Teyani looked into him and through him, blasting him with the Eagle's Light. In the silence of Highness it said, "I know what you are about to say, I love you, the Eagle loves you a thousand times more than me, and that which is will always be."

Szar took Aparalgon's hand, "Friend, now is the time to call on Barkhan Seer's light and be strong. Charging the Archive stone will take a whole night. Then at dawn Melchard, Namron and his men will leave the temple, carrying false Archive stones. At noon, all the Field Wizards with the exception of Ferman, Ushbudh and Shyama, will leave. They too will carry mock stones. And I will leave at sunset. With the real stone. Then there will be nothing left of the temple – only structural fields to keep the living walls erect."

The White Eagle took Aparalgon's other hand. "When Szar leaves, so will I," she said with devastating simplicity. "Szar and I have a night and a day to give you all we would have wanted to give you, had the Lord Melchisedek given us the time."

"But this will be no ordinary night and day," Szar immediately added. "The power in the stone will be awesome. Great miracles can happen."

Aparalgon was crying.

Why should these two masters care for him so much?

Warmth was a new experience for him. At the chapel of the Grey Robes, there wasn't much of it. He was hardly discovering the magic taste, yet already about to lose it.

"As the Law says..." he began, but he interrupted himself, shrugging his shoulders. He looked into Teyani's eyes, wondering what he had done to receive so much love.

"We must discuss practicalities," Szar went on. "Staying in the temple is out of the question, the giants will be here in a matter of days. Yet... I do not think you should leave your body."

"I know," the young man said, holding to his Point. "Master Barkhan Seer has told me. I must go, follow the light of Archive Hall Five. It will not be exile. Wherever I go, the Archive will be my home. I just wish... I just wish I could stay with you a little longer."

Teyani brought down a cloud of Whiteness. "In the Law of the Eagle, there is a magnificent verse. It says, 'With all my heart, with all my mind, I am with you, even when I am far away.' We will be with you, Aparalgon. Wherever you go, you will feel our presence. At times, even more strongly than if Szar and I were still in the kingdom."

21.2 Plan

Just before sunset the Field Wizards started arriving in Szar's hall, in groups of three. They sat in a large circle, contemplating the stars silently.

Teyani and Aparalgon came in, bringing a fresh Eagle breeze with them. She went straight to sit on Szar's left and kept Aparalgon on her left.

There was an air of devastation on Ashok's face. Szar extended his hand, "Come, sit on my right side! Let not the tragic events make us forget, you are the hero of the day."

They all clapped their hands in support of the statement, so convincingly that, carried by the momentum, Ashok clapped his hands too.

And he cried.

Ferman was crossing the doorway. Szar jumped to his feet and went to greet him. Silent, still, they held each other's gaze.

Nephilim or no Nephilim, Szar had slaughtered Ferman's nephew.

Serene, Ferman took Szar's hands, "Perhaps you saved him. And Lorenz. Now they rest in peace, I know."

Unlike Khej and Gallagher.

Melchard was walking into the hall with Mouridji, Namron closely following them. "News from the Fields of Peace!" Melchard announced. "Lorenz and Arena have been received in the Archive by the Masters of Thunder. They will be guests of honour at the ritual of the transfer."

Melchard realised everyone was standing up to honour his rank. "Sit down, please! By the grace of our Lord Melchisedek, I am no longer the Grand Commander of the Law, just Melchard of the Brown Robe," he said, sitting by Ashok.

"And what about Khej and Gallagher, Master Melchard?" Ashok asked him.

Melchard shook his head silently.

When all had taken their position in the circle, Ushbudh brought up the burning question again, "So what has happened to Khej and Gallagher? Where are they?"

"Two Virgin Spirits in Highness," Szar said.

Everything else had been erased.

Ushbudh was shocked, "Is it all that's left of them?"

Teyani answered him with a breath from Highness, "That which is not has never been. That which is will always be. Why grieve?"

Magic words. They brought down a superior quality of presence.

It remained that what had happened to Khej and Gallagher could happen to any of the Field Wizards in the coming days.

"Friends, the venom intensity Joranjeran and his men discharged to kill Henrick was phenomenal," Ferman told them. "I can't see why the giants would want to use so much force on any of you."

Except for Szar of course. And Melchard. And Esrevin in Lasseera. And Lehrmon and Woolly.

Not much more could be said about this. Szar held onto the precious silence for a minute, then moved on, "Has Proston left?"

"This afternoon I escorted him to the river. He took a boat to the south," Namron said.

"How many people are left in the temple?"

"Apart from those in this room and my four men, I'd say... no more than twelve," Namron guessed. "My men are making rounds, bringing the dead to Zothar."

"...who is by far the happiest person in the county!" Mouridji added.

"He lawfully is! Now then, we could run into problems tonight," Namron continued. "Strangers from the north, fleeing the giants. They're arriving in the county in hundreds. Yesterday a crowd of sixty went to knock at the doors of Lasseera. Master Esrevin gave them shelter for the night. They behaved lawfully. But in Eisraim city there's been some looting of warehouses going on. Desperate people are capable of anything."

"The situation in the north is catastrophic," Ferman reported. "The giants have destroyed Prasnameghan and Bajalakopan – but *really* destroyed! Not one living soul left behind them, people and animals slaughtered alike. The cities were flattened. Completely! Not *one* building left erect, not one tree. They've even interrupted the nature fields. From Asherban to Tomoristan, all the forests are in flames."

The end of the tree-houses.

"Have they reached Tomoristan already?" Melchard asked.

"I last spoke to Pelden one hour ago. According to the latest reports, the giants were reaching the outskirts of the city," Ferman said.

So the carnage was going on at this very moment.

A sombre mood had descended on the hall.

Aparalgon, whose clever father and peers had taken refuge in Tomoristan, turned to Teyani.

She held him in the Eagle.

Being held in the Eagle doesn't erase grief, it makes you feel vast.

Vaster than the fields of stars.

Szar gave a handclap, "Friends, yielding to dark moods has never served the light! One of the things Gervin taught us was to laugh amidst the most appalling circumstances. I *know* that if he was with us, tonight would be no exception."

"True!" Teyani and Melchard seconded in unison.

Szar charged his voice with the Dragon, "Tonight there is a victory to celebrate! We have held fast against the Nephilim Hunters."

That sounded incredible. So much so, the Field Wizards themselves still had difficulty believing it.

Szar turned to Ashok, "How did you feel when you saw the two Hunters falling in front of you?"

"Didn't feel a thing! In my mind I was already dead. *So* scared!"

"No! No! No! No! No!" Visarg said quickly, bringing Gervin to everyone's mind. "I saw you, you looked like a warrior god."

Ashok chuckled. He raised his right hand and frowned, fierce, just like a traditional statue of Buhr Brandishing His Axe.

"Ah, yes!" Melchard exclaimed loudly, clapping his hands with juvenile enthusiasm, totally unlike himself. The Fields Wizards all looked at him.

"Why are you looking at me like that?" he said.

Politely, they looked elsewhere.

He laughed, "But don't you understand? It's finished, I'm no longer the High Priest. I am a free man! Look at me!" he stood up.

Spellbound, they watched him caricaturing Buhr Brandishing His Axe.

Unthinkable for a High Priest.

Ferman clapped his hands. Everyone followed. Somewhat hesitantly.

Like a low-caste jester in a marketplace Melchard took a low bow, receiving the applause. Then he told them, "Now I want you to accept me among you as Melchard of the Brown Robe. Like you, I will be dead in three days!"

They gulped.

"And like you I am going to become one of the Archive people in the Fields of Peace. An extraordinary adventure this Archive, isn't it? And it's only beginning!"

Beaming eyes, he had. No one had realised before that day.

Ferman stood up and went over to him, "I welcome you among us, Melchard of the Brown Robe!"

"Thank you, Ferman!" Melchard hugged him like they had spent their childhood keeping pigs together.

In a friendly slap, Szar half-dislocated Ashok's shoulder, "Come on, go and welcome him too!"

"Wild!" Teyani thought, sensing Szar's violence.

The time of the final mission was coming. The Dragon was warming up.

Massaging his shoulder, Ashok went to Melchard. "Melchard of the Brown Robe, I welcome you among us."

Melchard gave him the same hug as Ferman, "Congratulations, warrior god!"

"Congratulations, warrior god!" Ferman shouted, and soon all the Field Wizards were exchanging brotherly hugs, congratulating each other on the day's victory, welcoming Melchard among them. Mouridji joined in, feeling very much part of the team.

Sitting on the floor, Aparalgon watched, devastated.

Few things can bring more desolation than being left behind.

He saw himself wandering in the kingdom, in the dark.

By his side Teyani was shining.

Szar too had remained seated, eyes on his left fist. Clenching. Unclenching. Clenching...

When the Field Wizards regained their positions in the circle their eyes were sparked with enthusiasm. Using a field, Szar had drawn a rough map of Eisraim and Lasseera on the plass floor. Undulating in the middle, the Fontelayana river. On the eastern side the Ferex river leading to the Mountains of Lasraim. On the western side, the Western Plains with the tiny Pipili Hills; and further north, Homar Hills.

"Time to recapitulate our plan!" he announced in Marek's cool voice. "First, some good news. I confirm we will not have to send any destabilising influence into the warp. No need for paradoxical clarity! Thanks to the ant field, the clarity in the temple is more than adequate for charging the Archive stone."

The Field Wizards applauded, praising the Flying Dragons of the Great Ant.

"The charging will begin later tonight, both in Eisraim and in Lasseera, and will finish at dawn. We will be charging not only the two Archive stones – one in Eisraim, one in Lasseera – but also sixteen 'false' stones designed to lure our enemies: eight stones in Eisraim, eight stones in Lasseera. At dawn, Melchard of the Brown Robe will leave for Pipili Hills, accompanied by Ashok, Namron and his men. They will be carrying one of the false Archive stones, and seventeen hundred soft-stone weapons. From Lasseera, Master Esrevin will lead a team of seven to Homar Hills, carrying another false Archive stone and about a thousand soft-stone weapons. At noon, we will send six teams of three Wizards each to the following positions: Visarg's team will go to Erriba, Balavan's to Mount Fulcrum, Ugr's to Orpan, Avan's to Renan, Lehr's to Pakaru, and Meran's to Bamam," he said, pointing to corresponding areas on his map. "Meanwhile, six similar teams will be leaving from the temple of Lasseera, carrying high-intensity relay stones. This will leave us with Ferman, Ushbudh and Shyama keeping a blazing false Archive stone in the rainbow chapel..."

"Together with Mouridji!" Ferman added.

"...together with Mouridji," Szar corrected, "while Master Pelden and three of his men will be keeping another blazing beauty in the chapel of the Field Wizards of Lasseera. And at sunset, I will leave Eisraim carrying one of the real Archive stones, while Lehrmon and Woolly will leave Lasseera, carrying the other. I will be meeting them in Ferex Pass, and from there we will go to the Plateau of Sorana."

Sorana! Hearing the magic name brought glows of wonder to the Wizards' eyes.

After nearly four decades of preparation, the Archive transfer *was* imminent.

"Two days from now, Melchard's team will have reached Pipili Hills; Esrevin and his men will be on Homar Hills. The mock Archive transfer will begin. Melchard's and Esrevin's stones will start emitting high-intensity vibrations, and so will the false Archive stones kept in Lasseera and Eisraim. Using their relay stones, the teams of three Wizards scattered in the countryside will create a net linking Homar Hills, Lasseera, Pipili Hills and Eisraim. At the same moment, the Masters of Thunder assembled in the Fields of Peace will begin a rehearsal of the transfer ritual, shining their light into the net. Simultaneously, a field linking the rainbow chapel to Flying Dragons will interrupt all Nephilim fields in the counties of the Centre North, and perhaps even further than that."

21 – The Book of the Valley of the Necromancer

That's when Joranjeran would realise that Szar *had* messed with the bait stone.

"We can still do that even though we no longer have Perseps' stone?" Mouridji asked.

"The stone told us all its secrets!" Ferman grinned.

The Field Wizards found this field immensely exciting. "Which sphere of remoteness will it be connected to?" Lehr asked.

"That of my father. The Flying Dragons from beyond the Abyss of the Deep and the Fault of Eternity," Szar declared.

"Gods, he *is* wild," Teyani thought to herself in a shiver, feeling the power behind his voice.

A volcano ready to erupt. Dragon above, Dragon below.

Ferman's grin had spread to the circle. Lehr was rubbing his hands, "All Nephilim fields falling flat, you said?"

"All of them! Shielding, weapons, communication, cooking... you lawfully name it!"

"And for how long?"

"In theory, it should last until the giants manage to blast our chapel," Szar looked down to his left fist. Clench. Unclench....

"Master Szar," Ugr asked hesitantly, "I don't want to sound like a coward but... how do you think we're going to die? I mean... I know we are doing all this so the giants attack us. But how do you think they'll kill us?"

"My guess is, elite commandos of the Green Guard will detect you early, but they won't strike you immediately. What do the giants want? The power of charged stones. They'll wait for the transfer, when stone radiations climax. Then they will strike. Simple venom showers – a quick painless death. You'll already be in the Fields of Peace by the time they start eating your kidneys," he grinned at Ugr's bewilderment. "The situation is likely to be much nastier for the teams at Homar Hills and Pipili Hills. To make the transfer credible, Esrevin and Melchard will defend themselves with the Word of Thunder. Nephilim casualties will run high. Expect the giants to discharge much greater venom intensities."

In other words, Ashok, Namron and his men were candidates to share the fate of Gallagher and Khej.

"But it's in Eisraim that the most violent action is to be expected. After the Nephilim fields crash, it won't take long before the giants find out that the disrupting field is emitted from here. Their best people will converge onto Eisraim and they will hit this chapel with every single weapon they have."

"But as you all know we don't intend to make it easy for them!" Ferman declared in a calm voice. "Without their fields, there's a good chance they won't be able to flatten our shield. So they will have to come down here, into this hall, and get a taste of the venom we have prepared for them."

Ushbudh and Shyama were serene. For months they had been preparing themselves for the onslaught.

311

"What if..." Ugr's voice choked. "What if the Nephilim capture us and try to make us talk? I can't see myself resisting the charms of persuasion of a necromancer for very long."

"Which leads me to a part of the plan I have never disclosed until now," Szar announced. "Tonight during the charging of the stones, extraordinary forces will be released. I will use these forces to operate a slight modification in your memories. Tomorrow when you leave the temple you will have completely forgotten that the Archive transfer you are about to enact is a mock one. Only the Brown Robes will remember."

A charged silence, with a measure of uncomfortable stupefaction.

"Even... Master Ferman will believe it's the real transfer?" Ashok asked, incredulous.

"Especially Master Ferman!" Szar replied from the Dragon.

Whispers ran through the circle. Ferman burst out laughing. Contained laughter at first, gradually louder and louder. When he stopped, all eyes were on him.

"Gervin must have particularly liked this part of the plan!" he said.

"He did," Melchard of the Brown Robe assured him.

Turning to Szar, Ferman gave his best grin, "See, you have become like him! You manage to make us laugh amidst the most appalling circumstances."

"Yeah!" they all agreed with Ferman. But they didn't laugh.

Szar went on giving specific instructions to each group of three, discussing the terrain in the proposed destinations, giving further tips on how to conceal their presence from the giants – exactly as if they were about to carry out the real Archive transfer. There were many questions. Each was answered with a profusion of detail, so that more than three hours had passed when Szar concluded the session, "Thirty minutes for everyone to get ready. Then the charging begins!"

21.3 Charging

In total silence, the Field Wizards came back from the crypt of the Archive stones with nine of the most magnificent treasures Maryani and Woolly had crafted. A stupendous hermaphroditic soft stone the size of a small apple was placed on the living floor in front of Melchard. Another one, even larger, was placed in front of Ferman. Visarg, Balavan, Ugr, Avan, Lehr and Meran resumed their place in the circle, each with a relay stone in front of them – hermaphroditic, almond-shaped, an inch long. And in front of Szar, Ashok placed a stone the size of an apricot. Like the others it was a translucent soft stone, half-way between a crystal and coagulated jelly. But it only shone a moderate opalescent glow in darkness visible. In contrast, those of Melchard and Ferman were surrounded by a one-foot-wide iridescent aureole, glittering as if with lightning.

Awesome stones, capable of generating high-intensity fields spreading through an entire county – and therefore capable of spreading death through an entire county.

Aparalgon was contemplating Szar's stone, wondering how the whole temple was going to fit into such a small thing, when Teyani stood up and invited him to swap positions with her. Hardly had he sat between the Eagle and the Dragon than something clicked in his column of Spirit. He found himself Point-vast and profound like the whole of the temple's Pointness, a galaxy of secrets packed above his head, threads to all rungs of the ladder of the worlds, myriads of angels whispering the mysteries of time.

Szar had connected him to the Point-network through which the Field Wizards were monitoring the twelve hundred and twelve fields that were to be involuted into the Archive stone. This involution would be achieved through the action of another fifty-five fields.

The Wizards spent a few minutes conducting a thorough checking, Point-sweeping through the fields of the entire temple, after which Ferman beamed, "They're all alive and well!"

"Ready to engage the transferring fields?" Szar asked.

After receiving a final Point-nod from each of his Wizards, Ferman uttered the magic words he had thought about every day for thirty-nine years, and heard in his dreams, and hallucinated about in fevers, and prayed for relentlessly, "The ritual can begin!"

"Strange ritual!" Aparalgon told himself. There was no altar, no copper utensils, no offerings of grains, flowers and fruits, no Voice-purified water, not even a single flame. No one had been singing opening hymns. And there was no lawful waiting.

Szar raised his hand, "Engage!"

Aparalgon felt a violent implosion in his Point.

In a split second he Point-saw the music hall in which Karpelion was giving thirty-nine thousand three hundred and twenty-seven music lessons over forty-three years, receiving and giving inspiration from musician gods whose music was Revelation Sky's worship of the Molten Sea, and who listened carefully each time Karpelion gave a devotional musical performance, and who smiled each time his art was interrupted by a loud fart – another form of music, after all everything is music, the gods know that – and who made sure anyone who touched Karpelion's beard after he farted received a present within five days, so the legend lived, for the gods love legends, the gods are the legend of all legends, and whoever knows the mystery of the gods becomes a legend. In the same split second Aparalgon saw every single person who, in the last six thousand five hundred and eighty-six years, had stopped by the small lake outside the third hall of Melchisedek and plunged their thoughts into the field of the lake. It was a field for pensive reflection. The people who stopped there were happy, sad, inspired, dejected, greedy, lustful, reverential, desperate, calling their god, viciously cursing their enemies or ardently praying for the Light, or dying, or in love, and all sorts of other things, many of which Aparalgon had never suspected could exist. That in itself was a revelation. He saw geniuses and imbeciles, conquerors and the destitute, enlightened masters and sleepers, and he was inside the mind of each of them as they contemplated the water, and he saw the Mother of the Light sending her love to each of them. And four hundred and sixty-seven years ago, a priest had even pissed in the lake. No one had known at the time. His name was Afran of the Crimson Robe, as would be remembered in the Archive for aeons and aeons. To him too, the Mother of the Light had given her blessing. In that split second Aparalgon also saw the images kept in the field of the chapel of the Mysteries of Ancient Times. There were scaly beasts twice as big as the first hall of Melchisedek, frolicking in tropical jungles and smoky landscapes while entire ranges of volcanoes were erupting in unison to celebrate the youthful folly of a fresh world in which Lucifer hadn't yet arrived, wise winds breathed the omniscience of the One God, and you and I were odd-looking blobs, ecstatically happy all the time, blissing out in godly warmth – all the time! – and loving every second of it. Life was but a long, divine orgasm, a concept totally new to Aparalgon. And before the Ancient Days of the Earth he saw the primeval nebula, mysterious female cloud pregnant with all secrets, all creatures, all futures. She remembered the Song of Creation which the Mother of the Light had sung at the very beginning, when out of the Great Night she had given birth to the first ray of light.

Gods, gods, was this ray of light beautiful!

Newborn infinity discovering the magic of limits.

In one point it explained the entire creation. And especially its meaning.

In that split second, contemplating the source of all sources, Aparalgon realised that phenomenal treasures of knowledge had been kept in chapels he had walked past every day in the last fifteen years. The thought of stopping had never come to his mind. How could he be such a sleeper! Like a lawful idiot he had lived in vain, since he was ignorant of the beauty of this first ray of light. The beauty of God is like love, when you have never known it you don't even know how much you miss it. Now, Aparalgon knew.

Simultaneously, during that split second, he saw his father, his grandfather and twenty-two generations of Aparalgons before them, performing one hundred and ninety-two thousand seven hundred and seventy-three rituals to the Angel of Dawn in their chapel. The angel's Light was magnificent. It shone the miraculous compassion of Highness onto the roof of the chapel. The Grey Robes were lawfully performing the ritual every day but unfortunately it had been twelve generations of Aparalgons since one of them had remembered to look up to the roof, where the light was shining. Yet the angel had never abandoned them. He had made sure that crumbs of Light fell into the chapel through the roof, and these crumbs were enough to make the Grey Robes holy men. But he sighed aquamarine winds and he cried tears of starlight because the days of his presence in the kingdom were numbered. Not that he had chosen to abandon his beloved children of the Grey Robe. Truly, the Angel of Dawn wasn't withdrawing from the kingdom. It was the world that was pushing him away. The more the world became a world of iron, the harder it repelled the Angel of Dawn, and Malchasek, and several others like them. For centuries, the angels had resisted the foul repelling breath. But it had now reached the point where they were being pushed away so harshly by the world that in order to maintain their presence here, they would have had to light a great fire in the hearts of human beings. Human beings were not ready. It would have consumed them. So the angels were leaving, to the icy satisfaction of the Prince of Darkness. And Aparalgon saw how incredibly fortunate he had been that one of the tears of the Angel of Dawn had fallen into his heart, after which he had sought to approach Szar. Particularly fortifying was the realisation that the Angel of Dawn hadn't given up on him. He was still Aparalgon's angel, the Light at the beginning and the end of his path. Master Barkhan Seer had been sent to guide Aparalgon along that road, until Aparalgon became capable of beholding the angel face to face. Looking ahead, Aparalgon marvelled at how soon this could happen. Hardly thirteen thousand years from now, which is nothing in the scale of infinity. A cosmic appointment, the angel already waiting for him. Aparalgon saw himself arriving at the appointment flying on a great majestic bird. In the fields of stars. Surrounded by men and women dressed in black like him – black, the colour of judgement, when everything counts. Together they were fighting mind-blowing battles against the Prince of Darkness, flocks of birds setting the spheres ablaze with fire. Trained by the Masters of Thunder he saw himself a man of extraordinary cunning and boldness, a Point-master fighting for the Light, a mighty weapon in the hand of God. In the sphere close to the Sun a great battle was raging, with more birds of war in the heavens than ever before in human warfare. It was in the first hour of that battle that the Angel of Dawn came to meet him, igniting a gigantic flame in his heart, consuming all obstacles. Victory was certain – provided in the coming thirteen thousand years Aparalgon kept wearing the colour of judgement, never forgetting that every minute counts.

Enlightenment comes as a result of having made ten million right decisions.

During the same split second, Aparalgon Point-contemplated the exorbitant wealth of information accumulated in the field of the chapel of the Space Controllers, which had kept records of hundreds of men and women travelling in all imaginable and unimaginable spheres every night and day for thousands of years. Free and omnipresent like a vast angel, he found himself flying though a million fields of stars. And he flew further and faster, and into more and more dimensions, because infinity is the only taste that can satisfy a man's heart. Thank the Great Architect, the creation was nothing like the small cereal loaf Aparalgon had imagined, with the gods above, the Underworlds below, and himself in the middle. The infinities that stretched up and down and right and left and forward and back were just the beginning. Everywhere he went doors were revealed to him, leading to other dimensions. But you could only see them when stepping into the superior simplicity of the angels' mind, which knows that parallel lines don't *have* to remain endlessly separated, they can be reunited by the power of love, so why bother thinking linearly. This was no problem for Aparalgon, whose Point was still contemplating all the useless rituals performed by his useless ancestors and the gigantic lizards and the blobs of the Ancient Days and the friendship of the Knights and the first battle of Mercury and the mood of each and every passerby pondering at the lake outside the third hall of Melchisedek and the tears of the Angel of Dawn, while at the same time hyper-jumping from world to world. Moving from one world to another was easy, all Aparalgon had to do was to request access from the threshold keepers who stood at the border. But as each of these threshold keepers needed to be Point-addressed in a particular way, and shown certain keys, Aparalgon made a quick supermental note to remember where the travelling keys were kept in the Archive, so he could come back to them later on.

Without keys, the creation is but one great closed door.

That was what Aparalgon saw during the first second of the charging ritual. Szar hadn't yet finished lowering his hand.

The revelation continued all night.

21.4 The heart of the Law

At dawn, when the charging ritual ended, Aparalgon felt vast like a Flying Dragon stretching from one end of the Great Night of Remoteness to the other, rich with all the treasures of the creation.

He opened his eyes and saw the two Archive stones, one in front of Melchard, one in front of Ferman. They were glowing like the Golden Sun, who is the Solar Logos and the Lord Melchisedek. Just by looking at these stones Aparalgon Point-remembered all at once the entire range of mysteries he had cognised during the night. It was like standing in the middle of a gigantic hourglass, the tradition condensed in his Point, the past of the world in his trail, a thousand possible futures laid out in front of him.

Glancing around the circle he saw only incandescent gazes, as in a host of gods holding council. The knowing was absolute: each of them had seen what Aparalgon had seen, and travelled from one end of the ladder of the worlds to the other.

Ashok stood up. Like a majestic god he walked to the end of the hall, and returned with a one-foot-long plass box. Aparalgon immediately recognised it. It had been made in the chapel of the Lawful Craftsmen of Eisraim two years ago, then taken to the chapel of the Field Wizards. There Master Woolly had lined the inside of the box with a special jelly of his own invention, aimed at screening soft-stone vibrations. That day Master Woolly was in a terrible mood, kicking walls and swearing insults at all those who happened to be in his way. Aparalgon, like the Field Wizards, could see all this by Point-tuning into the Archive stones, and how Woolly had nearly broken the box by throwing it against a living wall.

They smiled a god's smile.

Ashok placed the box on the floor in front of Melchard of the Brown Robe. Melchard took his Archive stone with both hands and preciously fitted it inside the box. He closed the box, eclipsing the Golden Sun. Then he stood up and said in a celestial voice, "We shall meet again in the Fields of Peace!"

The others replied, "We shall meet again in the Fields of Peace!"

And they exchanged glances that said more than human words can tell, as when gods return from a long journey.

Melchard left, followed by Ashok and Namron.

The others kept their positions in the circle.

Aparalgon closed his eyes to contemplate the sparkling wonders of the triangle one more time, from the celestial cities of light and fire to the highest archetypal mysteries of Revelation Sky. One second later, when he reopened his eyes, it was noon in the kingdom.

Visarg, Balavan, Ugr, Avan, Lehr, and Meran were placing their relay stones into small plass boxes, which had also been prepared by Woolly. Together with their teams they stood up and contemplated Master Ferman's Archive stone one last time, Point-feeding on its sublime light.

They looked a little less godly than a few hours earlier but their gazes were still ignited enough to convey all that had to be said, and aeons of mysteries and legends, and much more, so that the only words that were exchanged were, "We shall meet again in the Fields of Peace!"

The eighteen men left.

The glow of the remaining Archive stone had become so bright, Ferman couldn't be seen behind it. Ushbudh, Shyama and Mouridji were watching the stone in total Point-fascination, partaking in the feast of angelic presence, drinking the fabulously concentrated nectar of knowledge.

Teyani was sitting, eyes closed, deeply entranced. She had already left the kingdom, it seemed.

Szar grabbed a soft-stone trinket that had been left on the floor in front of him. He placed it into a small plass box that he casually stuffed into his pocket, and stood up. "Follow me!" he told Aparalgon.

Paying his respects to the resplendent Archive stone, Aparalgon stood up slowly. It was as if Revelation Sky was lifting him up. He felt glorious and unstoppable like a denizen of heaven towering over the spheres, a conqueror of eternity. Following Szar through the cellars of Baltham, he strode decidedly and single-mindedly towards his new life, accompanied by hosts of angels.

They were blowing the trumpets of destiny.

Arriving at the doors of the chapel, Szar stopped and put his hand on Aparalgon's shoulder. "From the moment you cross the shield of the chapel there will be only two things left: your Point, and Master Barkhan Seer," he said, grave.

From his lofty supermental standpoint, Aparalgon caught a multifaceted vision of what Szar meant. Seeing the big picture, his foresight reaching thousands of years ahead, he gave a god's nod, "That which is will always be. Why grieve?"

They exchanged a last glance in total knowingness of each other.

Then Szar opened the large doors and they walked out.

It was as Szar had said. From the instant they crossed the limit of the chapel's protection shield, they found themselves in another world.

No more trumpets. The angels had gone.

Everything had stopped.

It was an empty world. No longer the temple of Eisraim. Ancient ruins it seemed, the buildings miraculously kept intact by some mysterious power. How could they remain erect, when all presence had disappeared from them?

There was an air of unreality on all things.

Szar and Aparalgon walked in alleys that were like the solitary spaces the dead must cross in the first phases of the Great Journey: forlorn, empty of everything, even emptiness.

Aparalgon still held the clarity and the momentum of the night's experiences in his Point. But it was like walking in the void. Under his feet the firm ground of cosmic certitude had disappeared.

There was no longer light. Only the memory of the light.

He remembered everything, but for how much longer?

"Now you must Point-hold onto Archive Hall Five and Master Barkhan Seer's presence with all your heart, with all your strength," Szar told him.

They walked.

It was day only in appearance. In reality it was total darkness.

They walked through nothingness. Under their feet the pebbles pretended to be rattling, but the rattle rang false. The walls of the buildings were more honest. They kept total silence, not trying to hide the fact that they had lost all their memories. They were unrecognisable. They could have been the walls of some other temple, or some city, somewhere.

Szar and Aparalgon felt like strangers visiting some place, somewhere.

In the dark night of the kingdom.

There was nothing left.

Only Master Barkhan Seer's light, which Aparalgon felt more clearly when he closed his eyes. The gold of the tradition, the combined essence of the Masters of Thunder, Lord Gana, the Sons of Apollo, and the Eagle's Light, and the smile of the Angel of Dawn... right up to the vastness of the Lord Melchisedek, weaver of the Web of Love.

Now that the temple had become nothing, Aparalgon realised how much it used to shine the presence of the tradition. Before, that particular goldness used to be everywhere, it breathed through the living walls, you could feel it behind the mists, you could hear it in the rattle of the pebbles, everyone had it with them, all the time.

Which is why no one noticed it, of course.

"It is still with you. It's alive. But now it's inside, not outside," Szar said.

"The heart of the Law. That's what it was," Aparalgon realised.

This mysterious heart of the Law which lawful parrots tried to reach by chanting hymns and copying the behaviour of their fathers, and which they lost because all they could do was chant hymns and copy the behaviour of their fathers.

And yet it was so simple. Just a thread of presence.

How could people who were so immersed in that presence miss the thread?

Worse than missing it, they hadn't even tried to find it. Why should they have tried to find something that was everywhere around them?

Spiritual bankruptcy of the Atlantean civilisation.

The legacy was abysmal. An entire world wiped out. Nothing left.

They walked.

In the alleys of that strange place.

Where it was difficult to imagine someone had lived.

21.5 How White Eagles say farewell

One hour before sunset, Szar and Aparalgon were still walking. They heard steps coming towards them.

"Teyani?" Szar called.

"Szar!"

It was her. But the voice and the steps were those of a woman who knew exactly where she was going – not at all like Aparalgon had imagined someone would sound an hour before leaving her body. A surprising contrast with how she had looked earlier in the chapel, when she had seemed so far away from the kingdom, her real Self already ascended into the Eagle's Highness.

How do White Eagles say farewell to each other? Aparalgon wondered.

The love he sensed between Teyani and Szar inspired immense respect in him. It was mysterious, profound, irrational like the Light of the Eagle. Watching them together he caught glimpses of the Fields of Peace, where empathy is as tangible as fire and water.

She came out of the mists. "Szar, I need to speak to you!" her voice was firm.

He frowned, sense-smelling and wriggling his nostrils.

"Szar, I am no longer leaving my body. I am coming with you!" she said, totally determined.

Aparalgon watched Szar. The Master of Thunder remained very contained but the way his nostrils had suddenly dropped still betrayed his stupefaction.

"You are going to need me. I know," she added.

Szar closed his eyes, took his head in his hands, "Teyani, this is a military expedition. Apart from concealing my presence, I will have to..."

"Run, climb mountains, kill people... I know this!"

Szar turned to Aparalgon, "Wait for us a moment." Firmly taking Teyani's arm, he walked with her to a nearby alley.

He could have told her that with hordes of giants racing after him, the last thing he needed was to have to take care of a forty-eight-year-old high priestess who had never harmed anyone in her entire life. But telling her this would have been a waste of time, he knew.

"Is this from the Eagle?" he just asked.

Pointless question!

"Of course it is from the Eagle! Who else could convince me to go running with you, climbing mountains and killing people?"

The last time Teyani had killed an insect was seventeen years ago, and very much by mistake.

"Of course!" Szar was cogitating, Point-speed.

"Listen, here are my conditions!" she said, as if she had the negotiating edge. "Any time you need to, you just leave me behind. And you don't come back for me. If for any reason I happen to delay you, I will immediately leave my body. And I don't want you to give me funeral rites, understood? If you try to, I'll dematerialise!"

He smiled, biting his lip.

"Are you going to tell me why the Eagle suddenly wants you to accompany me?"

"I just know you're going to need me. And you're going to need this too," she added, putting her index finger on the orichalc plate Szar wore around his neck.

Lohrzen's powers – the seed of the Warriors' tradition.

Szar closed his eyes one second, contemplating Revelation Sky.

"All right! Let's go," he decided.

Teyani feigned surprise, "You mean you agree already?"

He held her arm a little tighter, "Trying to disagree with you is a waste of time."

In Revelation Sky, the gods agreed with him.

This easy victory brought a beaming smile to her face, but not for long. Now the real battle was about to begin. In front of Szar all she could see was an abyss of darkness.

They went back to Aparalgon. They found him standing very straight, grave, his Point illuminated with Barkhan Seer's gold. He knew the time to say farewell had come.

From the way Teyani and Szar were walking, he understood they would be leaving the temple together. He felt warmer for this.

In the empty alley of the empty temple of an empty kingdom, the two men held each other's gaze. The rich presence and fluid darkness of Archive Hall Five superimposed on top of them.

Liquid silveriness of a starry night in the World to Come.

"I have thirteen thousand years to thank you, is that it?" Aparalgon said.

"By making ten million right decisions," Szar smile-shone the infinite softness of the Eagle.

Aparalgon called on Barkhan Seer to make himself strong. "I will, be, at the appointment!" he swore, fierce.

In the land of the white rose, when the Masters of Thunder return and angels of Highness ignite great flames in the heart of human beings.

One last time Aparalgon contemplated Szar, and Teyani, drinking the wondrous light.

"There is no need to say farewell. We will be with you, always," Teyani said.

From the supermental standpoint of Archive Hall Five, Aparalgon saw this was the pure truth. The Eagle's flight traced a line from now to then, which is always, infinite-here, Flying Dragons, gods, the Lord Melchisedek, me and you.

Edge of Highness. Whiteness eternal. Forever love.

"I won't say farewell, then." He nodded, "We shall meet again in the Fields of Peace!"

Teyani engaged the Word of the Eagle, "We shall meet again in the Fields of Peace."

Aparalgon walked backwards, holding Szar and Teyani's image until it became blurred in the mists. Then he turned round and went, following the light of Archive Hall Five.

Absolute knowingness guiding each step.

21.6 Smells

"Be ready, I will kill anyone who stands in our way," Szar warned Teyani as they reached the pontoons on the shores of the Fontelayana river. He was no longer wearing a brown gown but disguised in a thick black cloak, similar to Aparalgon's.

"I know," she said, serene.

Dressed in a turquoise gown, she looked like a completely different person. It was like being inside another skin – the first time in more than forty years she wasn't wearing white.

A small boat was waiting for them.

"Praise the Lord Melchisedek, Boater of the Lawful Boatmen," Szar saluted a dim shadow on the front deck.

Boatmen were always called Boater. They all looked like shadows. How they recognised each other was a mystery to non-boatmen.

"All glory to the Lord Melchisedek, man of the Law," the shadow answered. Boatmen never called people by their name. They never remembered names, or conversations. They never asked questions. The Law of boatmen said, "A good boatman is born deaf." A wise Law.

"Going to Ferex Pass?" Szar checked.

"Lawfully," Boater just said.

Standing on the gangplank, Szar thoroughly scanned the man. No Point. Few thoughts. Digesting a warm meal. No idea who and what he was about to transport, and no interest in knowing. A lawful boatman. There was no one else on the boat.

Teyani was facing in the direction of the temple, eyes closed, paying her respects. In the past, each time she had gone on a journey or returned, she had stopped on this pontoon and turned to the temple, eyes closed, breathing in its marvellous presence, directing her love to Gervin.

Now there was nothing to breathe. It was a dark night, forty-eight hours before the New Moon. She directed her love to Gervin's Archive Hall, and followed Szar onto the deck.

Boater disappeared at the back, leaving Szar and Teyani alone on the front deck. As the boat started gliding silently on the water, Teyani realised in horror this time she was leaving Eisraim for good, never to return.

She hid under the hood of her turquoise gown, shivering with cold.

"We should reach Ferex Pass tomorrow midday," Szar said.

Crossing Ferex Pass in winter was no small enterprise. The paths were narrow, and often hidden under snow. There were several rapids to cross and few bridges. It had been a wet winter. The risk of avalanches was high, especially with the erratic behaviour of the fields.

"I'd better do something to prepare your legs," Szar said.

Teyani shook her head. "My legs will be fine!" she engaged her word.

Szar frowned, like who is in command, here?

She straightened. Promptly, "Yes, Commander!"

He sighed. He made her sit on the deck and sat in front of her, undid her boots and started massaging her feet. A preventive Dragon-healing with thorough reinforcement of gateways and solid injection of life force.

"By now I estimate that at least two hundred giants must be after our men and us," he told her, scanning the boatman's mind at the same time.

The boatman was so skilled in the lawful art of not listening that he wasn't even hearing them. There were still no Point influences around him.

"Do you think the giants have finished with Tomoristan?" Teyani asked.

"For sure, but that's not why they're after us. They've had to change their plans this morning. I think they thoroughly trusted Henrick the Hunter would get Jex Belaran's key-stone for them. They must have had a high opinion of him, since they didn't send any troops to back him up."

"His death took them by surprise?"

Szar grinned, "Even better than that! By now the giants have no way of knowing whether Henrick is dead or whether he played up with them and disappeared with the stones. All they know is that since this morning, the Field Wizards of Lasseera and Eisraim have been travelling in all directions with hermaphroditic treasure-stones."

The only way of concealing stones of this intensity was by using shielding fields like those woven in Eisraim and Lasseera. The moment the stones had left the temples, the giants would have known. The protective plass boxes were used only to whet their appetite.

"So they have detected us too," Teyani said, thoughtful.

"Of course. But now we're only one out of sixteen targets."

Not counting Eisraim and Lasseera.

They heard fishes jumping by the side of the boat. Teyani uncovered her head. She felt much warmer. Szar was throwing fire into her feet. Strange vibrations, though. Dragon tingling running along her legs, unlawfully sensual. Who cared? The Law had lost its mind.

"Why do you think Henrick betrayed his own people?" she said.

"Revenge, that's all he wanted. He had been chosen to become grand commander after Joranjeran. Instead, he left Jex Belaran after a quarrel. Then the only thing he dreamt of was to see Joranjeran on his knees. For that he went as far as selling himself to the giants. But when finally he had Joranjeran on his knees, even that wasn't enough. He preferred to let himself be killed rather than swallow an ounce of his pride."

"The Nephilim are complicated people."

"The Nephilim are a pain in the ass!"

"They follow the spirit of their people."

"The spirit of their people is sick. It has poisoned the kingdom."

"The kingdom would have died anyway."

"It would never have become so rotten."

"It had to die from something."

"Did it really have to die from that stinking filth?"

"You are wild," she smiled.

"The time has come to be wild!" he let go of her feet and turned to the water. Touching Lohrzen's plate on his throat, "Do you have any idea what I'm going to have to use this for?"

"Be wild!"

He looked down to his left fist.

She undid the lace that tightened the collar of her gown and plunged her hand into the water to release some of the fire welling up out of her belly. "In the last twenty-four hours the plate has awakened. I feel Lohrzen's power behind it. Like a great volcano," she said.

A volcano of the Ancient Days, spilling pure Dragon fire.

"I can feel it too." Clench. Unclench. Clench...

"It's Lohrzen. It's his presence that makes you feel like exterminating the entire Nephilim kind."

"Could be." He laid his hand on her feet again.

"I don't know that I can take much more of this!"

"I'll be soft."

"That rather makes it worse! It's a bewitching charm."

"The Sons of the Dragon don't do bewitching charms. They're too naive for that."

"If you don't stop I'll start spitting flames and walking on water."

"Think of yourself as a great volcano."

That helped.

Head pushed back, mouth opened skywards, Teyani exhaled what felt like lava. Curious, "Do you feel like this all the time?"

"No, but Lohrzen did."

Lohrzen was the fury of the Dragon.

She laughed, exhilarated, "I feel twenty years younger!"

He was grave, "I am glad you came with me."

"Me too," she put her hand on his shoulder. "But if you keep doing this I won't be with you much longer. Volatilisation is imminent!"

He stopped and became totally still, apart from his nostrils.

"I can smell Nephilim. Giants. At least ten of them. Fighters. Very dangerous. They're not even trying to disguise their presence through darkness visible."

Teyani closed her eyes. Tuning into Szar, she followed the astral smell through the ether. "They're far," she said.

"Not coming towards us."

"One of them is not a soldier. A sorcerer, he is. A man of great powers. But they're not after us, they're after Melchard."

They remained still, sensing darkness visible.

Teyani didn't feel like putting her boots on. Too hot.

Behind them, Boater was chanting a short farewell hymn addressed to the Holy Fontelayana river. The boat would soon take the bifurcation into the Ferex river.

As hours passed and the boat kept moving north, Szar detected more and more Nephilim smells. There were soldiers camping in the surroundings of Eisraim city, and various movements of troops along the Fontelayana river. There were also dozens of Nephilim civilians scattered throughout the land. The civilians didn't smell like giants.

"What are they doing here?" Teyani wondered.

"Mixing with the population, spying for the giants. Joranjeran said they were recruited from the Nephilim ghettos of Barnagiran."

More worryingly there were smells of Nephilim soldiers coming from the north-eastern part of the county: the mountains of Lasraim and the shores of the Ferex river. Szar first detected a group of seven giants camping with Nephilim civilians, probably not far from the entrance to Ferex Pass. Then three other groups. Twelve giants each. Armed to the teeth with soft-stone weapons. Extremely dangerous soldiers. Sleeping on the shores of the Ferex river, only three or four hours away.

Soon after, Szar detected another group of eight giants. "Dangerous. Dangerous!" he said, fingering Lohrzen's plate. "They're on the river. Not asleep! Hardly three hours away. Coming in our direction."

"They're after us. They have a sorcerer with them," Teyani saw.

Going towards them would have been madness.

"Boater!" Szar used a near-Voice threshold.

"Lawfully."

"Take us to the shore, immediately! This side!"

"Lawfully."

The boat changed course. Teyani put on her boots. Szar grabbed a plass box from one of his pockets. He took two small round soft stones out of the box and hid the stones in a hollow on the side of the deck. "One is to make them believe we're still on the boat. A field replicating our presence and the Archive stone's radiation," he explained. "The other one is to kill them when they board. After that the boat will keep going."

Bringing the total number of targets to nineteen.

The boat was reaching the eastern shore of the river. Deftly, the boatman pulled up alongside a small grassy prominence. Szar held Teyani's hand, helping her to the edge of the boat. Teyani's legs took over, making her jump like a gazelle. "Voof!" she was amazed.

"Boater!" This time Szar used a forceful Voice frequency.

The shadow appeared on the front deck, "Yes, man of the Law."

"Boater, you keep on going north! Men will stop your boat. Very tall men. When they walk onto your boat they will fall, dead. Then, go back south! Follow the Fontelayana river all the way to Berilya," Szar Voice-ordered.

"Yes, man of the Law," the shadow answered, compelled by the Voice.

Szar jumped, joining Teyani. "Now, go!" he Voice-commanded.

"Yes, man of the Law." The boat started drifting away.

The most memorable day of Boater's life. And, quite likely, the last.

Teyani silently prayed for his soul.

They had landed in the forest of Nadavan, only a few hours away from the plain of Erriba. Szar started walking fast towards the east, following the smell of the mountains. "No need to try to conceal our presence. With what we're carrying it would be a waste of time," he touched his pocket.

Transported by her legs, Teyani found herself racing behind Szar with great ease, immensely enjoying herself. "This is magic! This is magic! Why aren't we running?"

"Because we don't know where we're going yet."

"This is magic! I wish you could have done it to me a year ago."

"You never asked."

"I wish I had. Have we given up on following the river to Ferex Pass?"

"For the moment. Too many giants! We have two options: One, cross the mountain range, reach Sorana. Two, spend the day waiting. Tonight when the false transfer begins, all Nephilim fields will fall flat – a good time to find another boat and zap to Ferex Pass."

Finding another boat wouldn't be difficult. The problem was, the giants weren't going to spend the day waiting. They'd run after the Archive stone like hungry bears smelling honey.

As to crossing the mountains of Lasraim one month before the end of winter... only a Dragon would have considered that possibility. Preferably a flying one, for the giants weren't afraid of mountain climbing.

"I can smell more giants. South-west. Nine of them. Soldiers. They must be around Erriba," Szar announced.

Meaning Visarg and his team were either dead or about to be captured.

No way to know. Point-communicating would have been too dangerous.

Wriggling his nostrils, "And two other soldiers! Up in the mountains, two hours from us, straight ahead. Carrying stones. Hiding in a cave. They could be after Balavan."

Szar stopped, thinking.

To reach Sorana, there was of course a third option. But it was pure madness.

Teyani stopped by his side, holding the Eagle for him. It was too dark to see her face, he could only guess her shape. She breathed fast.

Turning towards her, "What if we went through the Valley of the Necromancer?"

On the map, it would have seemed the logical choice. It led straight to Sorana, and there was nothing to climb. But knowing the history of the valley, even a Dragon would have thought thrice.

"The Valley of the Necromancer..." Teyani called on her Light of Highness.

"At least the giants wouldn't follow us there!"

In the last four hundred years, not one caravan of Nephilim pilgrims had dared visit the valley, one of the worst death-pits of the kingdom. Even sorcerers stayed away. The only necromancers who had managed to visit it and stay alive were the Bobros, because the valley had been turned to the dark side by Harmag. As the legend went, Harmag, necromancer of ancient times and son of Azazel the Watcher, had fathered the first Bobros.

"If we venture there the valley will sense we are Bobros' enemies. It will hit us hard," Teyani foresaw.

"Could we withstand that?"

Teyani engaged her sight, "The valley has thrived on the rotting of the fields. It has become far worse than at the time of the clearing of Erriba."

Thirty-nine years ago, when the Masters of Thunder had descended to rid the county of the evil magic of Bobros, grandfather of Bobros.

Pity the Masters of Thunder hadn't cleared the entire valley.

Or perhaps not.

"This valley could be our chance!" Szar said, itchy fingers running over Lohrzen's plate.

"What does Gervin say?"

Szar closed his eyes for one second.

"Gervin says, I can be anything, I can do anything!"

Especially with Teyani by his side.

"Let's go!" Teyani started walking. Through darkness visible, she had no difficulty sensing her direction. The valley couldn't be missed, it was a huge black chasm.

21.7 Valley of the Necromancer

They strode through the night, gathering their strength, gearing themselves for the onslaught.

"Weird astral smells," Szar reported as they came nearer. "Unlike anything I've smelt before."

"Foul?"

"No. If anything, rather enticing. But strange."

Like a field covered in orchids, not two of them of the same species. Or a dark-skinned princess dancing, veiled in mists. Or a forest in which leaves talk too much. Or a hundred centipedes walking backwards. Or the landscape at the bottom of a deep Underworld sea. Or the edge of the Blue Lagoon, where the eddies of time trap Flying Dragon travellers. Or...

"Smells like these could make me lose my mind!"

"Ignore your senses. See only Fire."

"As long as we aren't in the valley, I need to keep a nostril on the Nephilim. Those I smelt in Erriba, in particular. They're on the move."

"Coming towards us?"

"No. I think they guessed our destination. They're on their way to the entrance of the valley."

Teyani knew nothing of the Dragon art of sense-smelling. But when Szar fired his nostrils, she could tune into astral scents through him. They were like tracks in the ether. Following them, her sight reached through to the Nephilim.

"One of them is a powerful necromancer," she saw. "They want our stone. They know you are a Brown Robe."

Nine Nephilim giants, a necromancer among them.

Szar grinned, Lohrzen's fury mounting in his belly.

"Do you want to run?" Teyani offered.

"No. Even if we did, they'd still have time to reach the valley before us," Szar evaluated.

She felt like flying, "Let's walk faster, anyway."

The night wasn't as cold. It didn't make sense. Coming closer to the mountains, the air should have been chilly. The forest felt lusher. That didn't make sense either.

"Sure we're walking in the right direction?" Szar started having doubts.

"We are!"

Teyani wasn't into Point-warfare, but when it came to the magic of the Ancient Days there weren't many like her in the kingdom.

He turned skywards with a loving thought, "Thank you, White Eagle."

As they advanced the night became darker and darker, the forest weirder and weirder, full of astral shadows of trees with no physical counterpart, and physical trees that didn't glow in darkness visible. Szar bumped into a large stump.

"Let me walk in front. So all your nose can be on the Nephilim," Teyani said.

He followed her. "Four of them have stopped. No... these four are moving back. Smells to me like they're running in the opposite direction!"

"Scared to death. They've come too close to the valley," Teyani knew.

Made Szar curious. What could scare elite troops of the Green Guard?

"You know what I see? This valley used to be one of the purest tirthas in the kingdom," Teyani said.

It was what had attracted Harmag.

The purest places are those which can become the most evil, when taken over by dark forces. Sometimes the same applies to people.

"This valley used to be so beautiful!" Teyani marvelled, tuning into the memory of the trees. "A meek maiden, gorgeous. Beauty of the Earth!"

Fresh, quintessential and juicy like the fruits of an Underworld orchard.

It had been an ugly rape.

Nostril alarm, "I've lost one of the soldiers! Four are still running away. They must have got close to the entrance of the valley. But the last one..."

"He is dead," Teyani saw.

"Or hiding!"

"No, dead."

"If he were dead, I'd smell his corpse. Corpses smell."

"The valley has not just taken his soul, it has gobbled his life force."
There was nothing left to smell. Ghastly.
"I thought the valley was against us. Why does it kill our enemies?"
"To the valley, they're just insects. And so are we."
Szar shielded their Points. "At this distance, the giants could launch a venom attack. Any moment."
"They won't strike until we are close. They fear the valley could reflect waves against them. They're not wrong."
"What are they like?"
"Intelligent. The sorcerer isn't afraid."
In silence, they continued. Szar was ready to strike.
The night's blackness became more black. Teyani didn't once bump into a tree. Szar wondered how she managed. It was eerie. There was no wind. Not one creature moving. Silence, like in a crypt. It weighed on them. Szar practised the superior art of waiting. Teyani walked faster.
Until Szar announced, "Now we *are* close!"
She slowed down. "Can you smell them?"
"Straight ahead. Only a few minutes away."
"Sniff again!"
Confusing scents. The necromancer had turned into a field of orchids.
"I... can only smell one. The others..." he hesitated.
"The others are dead!"
"But I can still feel their Points!"
"It's a trap. Whatever you do, don't use your Point! Nor the Voice! Go, run, kill the necromancer!"
Szar ran, his hands in front of him to avoid the trees. Trees everywhere. Too many trees. Couldn't run fast. He held onto his Point, expecting a massive venom shower. Nephilim necromancers were masters in Point-warfare. They had invented it.
But why wasn't the shower coming?
He narrowly avoided a tree, ran into another, had to slow down.
A tree. Another tree. And another.
A whisper, like a breeze.
A tree? Not a tree! The sorcerer!
Why wasn't he attacking?
From Eisraim to Philadelphia, infinity packed in a split second.
Black dance instinct taking over. Jumping to reach his throat. Time slowing down. Hitting the right cheap-way-out, close to the jugular, then the left one. Punching his right temple. Smashing his throat. Demolishing his right knee in one kick. Landing on the ground.
Why isn't he falling?
Pounding his testicles. Zeroing into his solar plexus. An ascending chop, destroying his nose from below. A kick in his right groin.
But why isn't he falling?
Giants!

Lohrzen's points, heart gateways. One. Two. Three. His sternum, broken. Don't do, let the Dragon do. Smashing his left temple. Family jewels, second round. Punching his navel. Upper part of the throat, pulverising the small bone. Flat hand straight into his left eye, hissing sound. No Voice! Teyani said. His right eye. I pray to the Mother of the Endless Night. Shattering his left knee, from the side. Smell of blood. From his nose. Nephilim spice mingled with blood.

Now he collapses. Let the Dragon do! Left fist into his right ear. A massive chop on his neck. A bull's neck! Loud crack. Seven consecutive blows along the spine – seven cracks. Smashing the back of the head, flattening him onto the ground. To the final kicks in his skull: one, two, three, his soul is going, four, going, five, going, six, going, seven, eight, nine, gone, gone! Ten, eleven, twelve. Homage to you, Marek, master of the Great Dragon!

End of the black forty. "May the Earth be cleansed of your sins!"
Steps.
Jumping, fists clenched, ready to kill again.
Teyani's steps.
Back onto the ground, Dragon-still. Silence of the Deep Underworlds, shining lapis lazuli and rivers of life.
Teyani heard music inside the Earth, loud and beautiful.
"You killed him."
"Yes. Where are the others?"
"I thought they were dead, now I'm not so sure. They could also be inside the valley."
"Can't smell them."
"DON'T TRY! The valley would steal your mind."
"Why did you tell me not to use my Point?"
"The sorcerer had laid a trap, using the power of the valley. He expected you to strike from the Point, or use the Voice. The valley would have reflected the wave back into you."
The sorcerer expected a Brown Robe, not a Great Warrior. Sad for him.
"We move!"
Teyani started walking again. "Mother of the Light, take care of this man's soul!" she prayed for the sorcerer. The invocation reached high in the Light, piercing through the night. The valley didn't like it.
The air became cold.
"All right valley!" Teyani stopped the invocation. Unlike her to compromise.
Walking behind her, Szar understood why the ritual murder of the Nephilim was performed with the black forty. He had often wondered. To annihilate a normal adversary, four or five blows on lethal gateways were plenty. Not so with the giants! Lohrzen knew well.
"Are we in the valley now?"
"Just about."

Gods, gods. "Teyani, wait!"

"What?" she stopped.

He took her in his arms, held her in the Dragon. "You *are* the Whitest Eagle. Totally like Gervin. Please don't stay too long in Highness. I miss you already."

"I will be with you, you have no idea how much!"

"So much love, Teyani. So much love!"

"I know."

Forever love. Whiteness eternal. Szar could still smell Nephilim blood. It must have been on his clothes. "Let's go!"

The night was still completely black. But warmer. They walked.

"Why isn't the valley attacking us?"

"Perhaps she likes your music."

"Think she's a she?"

"Definitely," she said.

"What music?"

"The Dragon music, inside the Earth."

When Harmag had first arrived, he too had awakened melodies inside the Earth.

"Play, Dragon! Play for her!"

Szar plunged his consciousness into the Earth, vroofing a few cautious waves.

The Earth echoed the vroofing, magnifying it.

"This place is a Dragon site!" Szar exclaimed.

"What's a Dragon site?"

"Where Underworlds and kingdom mix."

In the Ancient Days, the whole Earth used to be like this.

"Keep playing for her. Louder. Charm her!" Teyani said.

Szar increased the power, lovingly shaking the Dragon inside the Earth.

They kept walking. There were now fewer trees. The silence was still unnatural. The air was balmy. The first glows of dawn should have been appearing, but it was still completely dark.

Vroofing, wave after wave.

Harmag too had played gentle melodies at first. Then, gradually, he had made his music awesome.

"The valley wants you to play louder."

"This could get completely out of control!" Szar warned.

Plunging deeper into the Earth, he made the vroofing louder and wild. Lohrzen's plate became warm against his throat. Teyani heard choirs of Underworld angels. Szar didn't like the weight of the silence. His belly felt like a gigantic cauldron.

A thunderclap resounded in the distance. A few seconds later, another one, closer. No lightning in sight.

"This is to welcome you, man of Thunder! The valley can feel the power of your stone."

Harmag was a man of immense power. A great magician. A great lover.

Thunder kept resounding, coming closer. Szar didn't mind. It was the sound of his lineage. Sensing his feelings, the valley brought rolling thunder right above him.

Harmag could arouse passionate winds, his fire rising like a pillar from inside the Earth to the fields of stars. For him, the valley made her waters soft and welcoming. For him she made her fragrances maddening.

"The smells! The smells! Oh, gods! Incredibly beautiful."

"Don't use your nose!"

"Not from the nose, from the Dragon. *So* strong. It's all over the valley."

"The valley is confused because of the power stored in the Archive stone. I think she is wondering whether you are Harmag."

Wondering whether her lover had returned.

Would he play the music of the Watchers for her? Harmag knew so well how to enchant her.

"Speak to her!"

Don't do, let the Dragon do! Vroofing below. Thunder above. "Valley!" Szar raised a mighty Dragon-Voice, "I want light!"

It only took seconds before daylight started peering through the mists, which remained thick. Teyani and Szar discovered the stunted ground they were marching on. No grass, only a few miserable shrubs here and there.

"Thank you, valley!" Szar danced his way, clapping his hands, shaking the depths of the Dragon with blissful waves. The valley responded with light tremors under his feet. Thunder kept rolling, high over his head.

There was an air of desolation in the landscape, a forlorn greyness.

"Is there anything we could give her?"

"Life is what she has lost. Long ago. That cannot be restored."

Harmag had stolen her life and her seed. But he made love to her so well!

They came across one of the soldiers. A superb giant with huge red lips and a child-like face. Dressed in bright green clothes he was lying on the ground in foetal position. His vital gateways showed he had died only a few minutes earlier.

"The valley is making you a present!"

"Gods, gods! If she thinks I am Harmag, she'll *never* let us out of here!"

"Don't show any signs of weakness. Think of yourself as a great wizard!"

Szar let Lohrzen's plate guide his feet.

Earth trembling below them, sky thundering high in their columns of Spirit, they walked. Half an hour later they found the corpse of a second soldier. This one was lying flat, palms upwards. He seemed to be smiling. Szar thanked the valley from the Dragon. Not long after, they came across a third corpse, in the same position. He too had rendered the ghost only a few minutes earlier, or perhaps only a few seconds. Szar was becoming more and more uncomfortable with so many presents.

All of a sudden, the Earth stopped trembling. Thunder came to a halt.

Szar's Point received an unmistakable signal. "The mock Archive transfer has commenced!" he announced.

Throughout the kingdom, Field Wizards were detecting violent tremors shaking the warp in the Centre North. Soon, all Nephilim fields would break down.

But why now? Esrevin and Melchard weren't supposed to begin before the evening.

"Either they had to start early because the giants were everywhere, or the valley is fooling us and it is much later than it seems."

"No, the valley cannot fool us." Teyani was categorical, "With the stone you are carrying, you are immune to illusion."

In that case, quite likely Esrevin and Melchard were taking a pounding. Under venom-fire from the Green Guard, how long would they last?

"We must hurry."

The White Eagle stopped, eyes lit up like snow in the world of the gods. A mighty presence shone through her. It made her look taller. "Did I ever tell you what my name was in the Ancient Days of the Earth? Als'ven. Follow me if you can!" she Voiced. And she started running, Dragon-fast.

Szar raced behind her, wonder-struck by the transformation. "Who did you say you were?"

She Voice-laughed. The mists were illuminated with joyful tingles. But only for a few seconds, after which they turned greyer.

Long forgotten were the days when the valley knew the taste of innocent joy. Now she hated anything that reminded her of her past.

They ran on flat barren land. Teyani-Als'ven ran faster and faster. To follow her Szar had to rest deep on the Dragon. The subterranean quivers resumed.

The valley enjoyed. So long, so long since she had been caressed!

Joy, she didn't want to remember. Pleasure, she couldn't forget.

She made her fragrance intoxicating. The mists lightened with her mood.

Esrevin of the Brown Robe was on Szar's mind. Was he as powerful a Voice-master as Melchard? How long would he last against the giants?

The valley heard his thoughts. Deep inside the Earth, she sent an impulse. Szar's Dragon sensed it. He thanked his Mother.

"Come! Come to me!" the valley whispered.

The landscape changed. From rocky and dry it gradually turned soggy. Trees reappeared. High trees, their tops lost in the mists, their leaves hanging down miserably, creepers falling from the branches, others coiled around the trunks in smothering spirit. Depressing sight.

Arriving on the edge of a marsh, Teyani stopped. "We're coming closer to the heart of the valley," she announced in near-Voice tones. She wasn't breathing fast. She was shining like a queen. She followed the edge of the marsh, "There is a path waiting for us on this side. It will take us to the heart."

"And then what?"

"A great celebration!" she said. She knew the valley was listening.

Szar didn't like the sound of that celebration. The path was only a hundred lawful feet away. A straight narrow path, oddly dry considering the marsh licked its borders.

Running no longer felt right. They walked side by side.

There were beasts in the marsh. They couldn't be seen but they made bubbles that burst loudly on the surface. The trees looked sick. There were rotten weeds coming out of the mud. The smells were extravagantly beautiful like a goddess in love.

"You never told me about Als'ven."

"You never asked."

"I wish I had. Was she a queen?"

"Very much so."

"Where was her kingdom?"

"The whole of nature was her kingdom."

"Did she have a king?"

"Many a king tried to marry her. But she loved only the White Eagle."

He wanted to know more, but his Dragon sensed a tremendous current sweeping through the under-valley. It had the magnitude of a tidal wave, but deep inside the Earth. On the surface, the sensual quiver continued.

"A gigantic Dragon power! It's in front of us, three or four hours away. Is it the heart of the valley?"

"Where the Abysmal Crevasse is. Long ago Harmag turned the crevasse to the dark side, using the consciousness of the Watchers. When Bobros' grandfather resided in the valley, this is where he drew his powers from."

That Bobros was a terrible lover. From the day of his arrival the valley had known he wasn't the one. When he had fallen into the Abysmal Crevasse and died, she hadn't wept.

"Awesome land energies!" Szar shook his head.

Teyani felt very much at ease. "To the heart!" she said.

In silence, they followed the path.

21.8 Temple of Eisraim

Fornan the crocodile was standing on the steps of the chapel of the Field Wizards, his forehead more wrinkled than ever. "We knew these bastards were clever! But this..." the old general told himself, Point-sensing the protection shield.

This... was far worse than anything the giants had expected.

To Fornan's knowledge, only the Hunters of Jex Belaran were capable of weaving protection fields like this one.

Spread around the building, more than seventy Field Wizards of the Green Guard were busy probing the shield, using improvised detection fields that had been woven in haste. Not *one* of their usual field-devices was working.

Mechanically, Fornan grabbed a communication stone from his pocket, "Basalinger?"

Darkness visible remained deaf and mute.

"Damn it!" Fornan yelled, throwing the state-of-the-art soft stone against the chapel door. It crashed with a moist sound.

The unthinkable had happened. All real fields – that is, all Nephilim fields – had collapsed. Vexingly, the fields of the dwarfs seemed to be working fine. The warp couldn't be blamed for the mayhem. It was the dwarfs! Those miserable dwarfs!

If anyone had needed a confirmation that all dwarfs should be exterminated, this was it.

"Basalinger!" the general screamed.

Without communication stones, screaming was the only way to reach someone. The problem was, all around the building Fornan's Field Wizards were shouting at each other, and not just for communication purposes. A wind of fury was sweeping through the Green Guard, especially the Field Wizards. And the giants had loud voices.

"Basalinger!" the general screamed louder. "Basalinger! Basalinger!"

"General!" a distant voice responded through the mists.

"Come here! Immediately!"

"Yes, General!"

A minute later, General Basalinger emerged out of the mists, running, two officers also running by his side.

"When are those damn stones arriving?" Fornan kept screaming.

To restore some semblance of a communication system, the giant needed stones – stones made by the dwarfs. Their own stones were useless, connecting only to Nephilim fields.

"The situation is not good, General!" Basalinger replied.

"What do you mean, not good?"

"Luvick and his men won't be reaching Eisraim city before the middle of the night. By then, everything will already be destroyed! But I sent a squadron to Laminindra. With some luck they should reach the temple before the ninth army finishes looting."

"What? You're not going to tell me we have to go all the way to Laminindra to find stones!"

"Your orders were to obliterate everything from the Snowy Mountains to Eisraim. So there's not much left in..."

Red with rage, "Shut up! Search this temple! Send a squadron to Romeran! Use your stupid spies! *Do* something! Understand?"

"Yes, father!" Turning to his officers, Basalinger yelled, "Move!"

"But General, we're already doing all these things!"

Louder, "I said *move*! *Do* something!"

"Yes, General!" They ran down the steps and disappeared in the mists.

An officer was running towards the chapel, shouting, "General! General! Grand Court Sorcerer Afran Kesborn has found a way into the chapel. Through the catacombs."

"Tell him to wait!" Fornan's voice remained at its peak, "No one goes in there until Bobros arrives! Understood? And you watch him carefully!"

"Yes, General!" the officer started running in the opposite direction.

"Afran Kesborn? But what is he doing here?" Basalinger was startled.

"I've no idea. He arrived just after us. He said he just came to visit."

"Grand Court Sorcerer Afran Kesborn travelled all the way from the Eastern Peninsula just to visit this shit-hole?"

There was Nephilim-spiced intrigue in the air.

"What the Watchers' hell is going on in this chapel?" Basalinger asked.

"I wish I knew!"

Whatever was inside, both Bobros and Afran Kesborn wanted it.

A fat officer with a huge broken nose called in, "General, our men are getting angry! If we could let them start demolishing a little..."

Screaming, "No! I said no one demolishes *anything* until Bobros himself gives the order. Bobros himself, is that clear? We are *not* an angry mob, and this is *not* the fish market, is that clear?"

"Perfectly clear, General! I'll go and see that your orders are followed, General!"

Not an easy task. The temple of Eisraim was more crowded than during a yearly celebration of the Law. But instead of a motley gathering of priests and priestesses, only one colour could be seen: green. There were angry giants on every roof, in every bowel of the catacombs, in every alley, in every chapel, the only exception being the chapel of the Field Wizards. More than five thousand giants in total. Unable to speak with each other through darkness visible, they vociferated through the mists, cursing the dwarfs, their huge murderous hands itching for carnage.

To make things worse, there was no one left to massacre in this temple! Not even animals. Or perhaps they were all hiding in that damn chapel.

A clamour arose from nearby alleys.

Someone shouted, "His Excellency Bobros, Grand Commander of the Citadel of the Nephilim Giants!"

The soldiers interrupted their efforts to acclaim him.

Bobros had come accompanied by Grand Necromancer Samoan, Leader of the Guild. Marching behind them were two lines of soldiers of the Green Guard.

"Oh no!" Fornan passed his parched hand over his bald head, appalled. In the small procession four baphomets were being carried on stretchers. Their eyes were closed. They didn't move.

Bobros' face was perfectly calm. Samoan looked unusually pale. They stopped in front of the generals. The greetings were brief.

"The disrupting field is coming from this building!" Fornan pointed to the chapel doors. "But there is no way to get in! The dwarfs have woven an impenetrable shield. Very much like the one in Jex Belaran."

Bobros and Samoan spent a few seconds Point-scanning the shield.

"I need to speak to you, General," Bobros said.

Fornan invited him and Samoan to accompany him to a royal tent that had been set up round the corner of the alley.

"Wait for me here!" Bobros ordered Samoan.

On the way to the tent Fornan asked, "What happened to the baphomets?"

"When the fields collapsed, so did they. They're not dead, just unconscious. If we can restore the fields soon enough, they should come back to their senses."

Otherwise they would come back to their senses anyway. But in a matter of weeks they'd be nothing more than silly goats.

Bobros waited till he was inside the tent before asking, "Did you get the Brown Robes?"

"So far, only one of them. We think he was Melchard the High Priest. His head, heart and kidneys will be here for you soon. But when the communications fields were interrupted, the Brown Robe in Homar Hills was still resisting, our casualties running in excess of seventy. Using the Voice, the enemy caused three consecutive landslides on the hillside."

Bobros gave one of his glacial necromantic grins, "Impressive! What about the other Brown Robes?"

"One was located at the entrance of the Valley of the Necromancer. The other two have completely disappeared. They could be inside this damn chapel."

"Could they be in the other temple, Lasseera?"

"There's nothing left of Lasseera. Not one building."

"Good, good."

"Now, what do we do about the disrupting field? We need to move fast. Disorganisation is total. Once communications are restored, it could take up to three days before we're back in action."

Bobros shook his head, "You're not doing anything, you leave it to me."

"Do you know how to deactivate the shield?"

"There is a way in through the catacombs. I'll get in through there."

Fornan frowned in that particular way that made him look reptilian, "You mean *you* are going into that chapel?"

The red-haired giant answered with a nod, smiling with the assurance of an envoy of the Watchers.

Fornan exploded, "What's this nonsense, Bobros? We have *no idea* what's inside the shield! If it's powerful enough to flatten all our fields, who says it won't kill you?"

Bobros liked Fornan when he vented his anger. Patiently, he answered, "I know from the Watchers, Fornan. I can manage this."

"Don't bullshit me with the Watchers! Taking this kind of risk is completely unacceptable! Bobros, this place is dangerous! Very dangerous!"

"And I received detailed reports from Henrick the Hunter. I know exactly what's inside."

Still screaming, "Fine! Let's talk about your Henrick! Where is this son of a Nephilim bitch? Where is he? Disappeared! What if it was *him* who taught the dwarfs how to weave the shield? Bobros, don't be ridiculous! At least, let Afran Kesborn go down before you. He too found the way in!"

"Is Afran Kesborn here?" Bobros frowned, menacing, "Not in the chapel, I hope?"

"No! I ordered him to stay out."

"Good, good!" Bobros walked towards the entrance of the tent. "I will see you soon. Make sure *no one* gets in there after me."

"Bobros, wait! What if you don't come back?"

"I will, General, I will."

"But what the hell do you think is in there? Nothing more than stones!"

"Stones!" Grinning at Fornan, "Stones powerful enough to put the kingdom on its knees... or launch a challenge against a grand commander of the citadel!"

"Afran Kesborn wouldn't do that!"

Bobros' grin broadened, "Of course not."

"All right, Afran Kesborn is a bag of vipers. Let my Field Wizards go, then!"

"If they make a mess, we lose everything we came here for. Did you get Melchard's stone?"

"No, it fell apart as soon as we caught hold of it."

Bobros wasn't surprised. It was the least he would have expected from the Brown Robes.

"Bobros, we already have the kingdom on its knees! Why tempt fate?"

"Fornan," Bobros raised his voice, indicating he was no longer willing to be patient, "my seed is from the Watchers. My lineage was destined to rule. My time has come. Absolute power is right by my hand. I grasp it!"

21.9 At the heart of the Valley of the Necromancer

"Here we are!" Teyani pointed to high flute-shaped rocks on the side of a hill.

It was just after sunset. To compensate for the dwindling daylight the valley had made her mists sparse, revealing the mountains that bordered her northern side. The smells were still maddening. The trees were taller but just as sick. There were wisps of whitish vapour coming out of the marshes. The land energies were wild, like standing on a colossal Dragon-gate opening straight into the centre of the Earth. Lohrzen's plate was hot.

They had arrived at a crossing. In front of them, the path continued through the marshes. Turning left, another path led to the rocks.

"Now what?"

"By the side of these rocks, there is a cave. This is where Harmag left the power. This is where the valley wants you."

History repeating itself all over again. This time, Felicia was a valley.

"This time, the choice is simple," Szar nodded thoughtfully, hands in the pockets of his long cloak, fingers playing with his arsenal of stones.

The mists were still, the silence eerie, not one bubble bursting in the marshes. The valley was holding her breath.

Was he her lover?

Teyani shook her head, "No, not so simple! If you don't go into the cave, we will have to bear the brunt of the valley's fury. If you do go in, you will find yourself inside the Watchers' mind. And you'll never get out of it."

"How can you know that?" Szar started walking on the left path.

The valley was calling him. A secret Dragon call, deep under the surface of the Earth.

Teyani stayed where she was. "I just *know*! Szar, please listen to me!"

Szar stopped and faced her. Wild with the spirit of the land, "Als'ven, I *am* ready – Dragon above, Dragon below, and the entire tradition of Eisraim in my pocket. I am going in, and you are coming with me."

She didn't budge. "My beloved friend, these powers are clouding your judgment. The Watchers' mind is an abyss."

"Now is not the time to doubt but to conquer!" Firmly grabbing her arm and pulling her, he walked towards the cave.

The valley found him superb.

He was coming towards her.

She shivered with excitement, making the ground tremble softly.

"Szar, please!" Teyani called on her Light of Highness, "Remember the Eagle! Listen to me!"

The dark Dragon in the Abysmal Crevasse disliked her Light.

The Earth shook menacingly. A wave of anxiety passed through the mists, as if something terminally ominous was about to strike.

Szar used the Voice, "Stop this, Teyani! You are going to destroy us."

Teyani complied, retreating from the Light. She tried a different angle, "Szar, understand! The valley wants you to hold the fire of the Watchers and marry it to the Dragon in the Crevasse. This is what will give her pleasure. But if you mediate between darkness above and darkness below..."

"No thoughts, just Dragon!"

Totally single-minded, Szar was walking towards the cave. The path went up, rising from the marshes. A friendly breeze blew behind them, giving a gentle push. Szar filled his nostrils with the valley's astoundingly sensuous fragrance. At this time of the day the mists should have turned red. Strangely, everything was grey. Seen from outside, the cave looked oddly ordinary, considering it had been the abode of one of the greatest necromancers of all times. The cave's entrance was similar to Verzazyel's in the Red Lands: rather narrow, hardly higher than a normal giant's height. Nothing more than a hole in the rock. Seen from the Point, however, it shone with extraordinarily complex astral light, made of myriads of geometrical patterns – one of the things Szar had missed when visiting the Red Lands. There were many others. Now was the time when all secrets could be revealed.

"Szar! Szar! Szar...!" Teyani repeated his name in soft Voice frequencies, trying to call him back to reason. "Szar, if you want to go in, at least give me the stone! I propose a plan: you hold the valley, I take the stone to the Plateau of Sorana."

"I need the stone to tame the power in the cave."

"Szar! Szar! Szar! Szar...!"

Holding her arm he made her run full-speed. He had wings on his ankles, like a lover running to his lover. It took less than a minute to reach the rocky terrace outside the cave.

The mountain was vibrant with excitement, a lover waiting for her lover. At the dawn of the kingdom Harmag had come, and left. She had been waiting for him ever since. Now it was twilight in the kingdom.

The lover had returned.

"Szar, please! Remember Gervin!"

Szar saw in Teyani's eyes that she was about to strike him with the Voice. What shone through her was no longer the Eagle's softness. She was fierce. Whiteness turned Fire.

He smiled at her with irony. "She'd kill me! Just like this," snapping his fingers.

Startled, she finally understood.

"Now, a present for the valley!" he kept smiling. He took Lohrzen's plate in his left hand and pulled violently, breaking the leather cord. From his right pocket he extracted a hermaphroditic stone. He threw both treasures into the cave and started running. Teyani ran behind him, shouting at him, "You scared the Underworld out of me!"

"*Now* is the time to be scared!"

Behind them, a Point-explosion. The power in the cave was being activated. The valley's nuptial chamber was being filled with light.

Instead of following the path, Szar went along the edge of the mountain. "No point going back to the marshes!" The path in the middle of the marshes had been raised for them by the valley. It could be swamped any time.

How long before the valley realised she had been fooled?

Awesomely ancient vibrations were shaking the mountains. There were strange silent noises everywhere, noises like no one had heard in the kingdom since the early days. They carried the memory of long-since-buried mysteries. Deep inside the Earth, the dark Dragon remembered. She hissed.

Spellbound, the valley made herself moist, waiting for the magnificent fire to descend onto her and penetrate her. She called, "Harmag! Harmag, where are you?"

She didn't have to wait for long.

As Teyani and Szar were racing over the rocky slopes of the mountain, heading east, the mists became darker. A presence, like a titan's shadow, began to hover above the entire valley.

A feel of primordial darkness. Nearly as pure as the night between two cosmic cycles. The secret of evil: infinite purity with only a slight twist. But that twist is enough to make an entire creation err for an entire cosmic cycle.

Teyani was right. Had Szar tried to contain this power from his Point, he would have been instantly engulfed. The darkness was abysmal, it was felt hundreds of miles around.

When he sensed it, Esrevin of the Brown Robe was Voicing hell onto the giants from the highest point of Homar Hills. Interrupting the torrent of fire that was pouring out of his mouth, he turned to Jop, "A great catastrophe is about to strike the Centre North!"

On the other side of the mountains of Lasraim, Lehrmon and Woolly were travelling on the High Plateaux. They too felt the wave. Woolly creased his nose, "Hum... Aphelion popping in to visit, perhaps?"

Lehrmon shook his head, "Hell breaking loose in the Valley of the Necromancer!"

In Eisraim, Fornan saw the wave in Afran Kesborn's eyes. The two men were sitting outside the chapel of the Field Wizards, waiting for Bobros. Fornan was watching the grand court sorcerer closely, not trusting him for one second. He saw a dark pit floating behind his eyes, deep enough to swallow the entire county. From the mountains of Lasraim to the Western Plains, from Lasseera to Eisraim's border with Berilya, the same abysmal shadow was in all necromancers' eyes. But no one fathomed the wave's darkness as deeply as Bobros himself. In the catacombs, he had just reached the threshold of the cellars of Baltham and was finishing undoing a tangle of death fields. To him the presence was familiar.

"Harmag! Timely visit!"

Drinking the power, Bobros crossed the archway that led to the cellar.

The hall was immersed in complete darkness. That too felt familiar.

Sensing Ferman, he tried to shower him with venom.

Ashok's field was engaged, deflecting the impulse, tearing a hole in the warp.

A new weapon, unknown to the Nephilim.

Taken by surprise, the red-haired giant found himself caught in a torrential flow of elemental murk – warp sewage flushed into his Point.

"Harmag!" he Point-invoked, holding back the flow with prodigious vigour, while the hole in the warp was becoming larger.

Ferman watched the show of strength in disbelief, wondering how a human being could withstand such a deluge of shit. If *this* was the first ranger sent by the giants, then really the Green Guard were invincible.

"Harmag! Harmag!" using all his necromantic powers, Bobros attracted Harmag's presence onto him.

In the Valley of the Necromancer, the titanic shadow receded.

There followed a strange calmness. The ominous feeling lifted. The dark Dragon became quiet. Night was falling fast. Szar and Teyani were running, mountain slopes on their left, marshes on their right, clouds gathering above their heads.

"What do you think is happening?" Szar Point-asked.

"No idea!" she kept running.

The answer came from above. A few drops of water, soon turning into a shower. Water poured onto them with a violence that took the proportions of a venom attack. In seconds they were as wet as if they had jumped into a lake. The water was dirty, corrosive, offensive to their skin. They could no longer run. Together with water, the sky vomited venom. They had to seal their Points against it. Dark astral fumes exuded from the soil. Teyani started coughing violently. Szar had to seal the ground from venomous wells. The night became thick – venom, water and darkness mixed in an infamous, asphyxiating paste. Each step became a trial. Ominous noises were heard coming from the mountain. The Earth quaked.

The valley was enraged. Where was Harmag? Where had the presence gone? As the power of illusion was of no use against Szar and Teyani, she unleashed the fury of nature.

"She is about to hit us with an avalanche!" Teyani saw.

From the Dragon, Szar sensed a rock formation in front of them. He took Teyani's hand and made a dash for shelter. Battered by the rain, they managed to reach a huge concave boulder. They hid inside the hollow while stones careered down the slopes of the mountain. The Earth kept trembling. Larger and larger rocks fell from the heights of the mountain, crashing onto the protective boulder from behind.

"We won't last more than five minutes!" Teyani Point-warned. "What did you leave in the cave? Was it a soft-stone weapon?"

"No, a hermaphroditic stone. It replicated our presence and triggered a high-intensity field of Point-ness."

A stone as Naga-pure and perfect as the Archive stone itself.

"Link my Point to it!" Teyani said.

"The Watchers will swallow you!"

"They tried before. It didn't work."

"This is very heavy shit!"

"I am from Highness. There is no such thing as heaviness in Highness."

Connected by Szar, Teyani found herself Point-immersed in fire, and she saw. She saw a large hall which very much resembled Szar's bedroom, except that it was illuminated with absurdly bright light. She saw a thousand incandescent paths that led from nowhere to nowhere-ness extraordinarily fast. In that nowhere-ness she saw the apogee of fever, the sky of the Watchers. Formidable, it ran in all dimensions with demented speed in search of impasses and unanswerable questions – the proof of the Watchers is in the erring. And in the sky of the Watchers she saw the entire lineage of Bobros casting Harmag's darkness onto the temple of Eisraim, helping the last of the Bobros in his giant's struggle to contain the entire warp of the Centre North.

To them only one thing mattered: Bobros didn't have a son. If he perished now, so did their lineage in the kingdom. So they showered him with power, using the cave as a relay.

With the absolute simplicity of Highness, Teyani sealed the cave's ceiling. The sky of the Watchers lost its anchor in the valley. The power dropped. In Eisraim, Bobros fell on his knees, screaming, "Harmag! Harmag!" Ferman and Shyama were hitting him with every single field of their arsenal of death, casting net after net onto his Point, hosing him with fire from the entrails of the Dragon, deafening him with insanely loud astral sounds. But with inhuman stamina, Bobros kept holding the warp above his head, invoking, "Harmag! Harmag!"

"Devil of a man!" Ferman was baffled. The elemental sewage pouring into Bobros' Point was comparable to the one that had annihilated Alverard. Yet the giant held fast, mending the warp while swallowing the shit. His faith in the power was total. He believed himself indestructible, precisely because he didn't have a son.

Meanwhile, the valley was becoming more and more furious. Teyani saw that massive boulders were about to be dropped onto their heads. The level of the marshes was rising quickly, threatening to engulf them.

Looking down from Highness, Teyani also saw the immaculate purity of Lohrzen's orichalc plate. On the floor of Harmag's cavern the jewel looked like a mirror that reflected memories of the Ancient Days when the Watchers hadn't yet arrived and nature was capable of anything. A world in which every tree, every pebble, every drop of water chanted the eternal name of God. Als'ven's world. The superior Peace that breathes through all things when the Divine presence shines, sovereign.

Seen from Highness nothing had changed. The Divine presence still permeated all things. Not one thing in the kingdom existed without it. Not one thing in the creation exists without God.

God *is*. Anything that is, is God. To be is to be God.

Simple.

In the deluge of water and venom, their protective rock taking a beating from rolling boulders, the Earth quaking in anger, Szar hardly heard Teyani uttering the mantra which holds the key to the power of the Edge of Highness, "As it was in the beginning is now, and ever shall be – world without end!"

It was instant. Absolute.

Through Lohrzen's plate, the Peace of Highness descended onto the valley.

The rain stopped. The air lightened. The stones gently finished their course down the slopes, carefully avoiding the trees. In a matter of seconds everything was silent.

Absolutely silent.

"Just like that?" Szar was dumbfounded.

Tranquil voice, "Let that which is, be!"

Catching his breath, incredulous, "Hunh!"

It was still dark but darkness visible was strangely luminous and fluid, reminding Szar of the Fields of Peace. Teyani, like the Als'ven of the Ancient Days of the Earth, shone the awesome simplicity of Highness.

She *was* a queen.

Arm in arm, they started walking again. There was magic in the air – the Magic of the One God. It made breathing a communion with the Web of Love. "Gods, gods... which world is this?"

At that very moment the valley was asking herself the same question, unsure of who she was. It was like waking up in the middle of a dream. But which dream? She couldn't remember.

And why was she such a mess, marred with ugly marshes?

Teyani exhaled softly into the Earth, "Peace!"

They were in the middle of a huge puddle. They advanced slowly at first. But the earth soon absorbed the rainwater. A warm caressing breeze blew on them, drying their clothes, comforting their spirits. It carried essences of ancient wisdom and fragrances from the Molten Sea. It whispered a creation song that told how maiden Earth had emerged out of the primeval nebula. Szar kept exclaiming in wonder, "Hunh!" Teyani enjoyed every step, striding forward at a giant's pace. At times he had to run to follow her. At other times they flew side by side, two Eagles darting through Whiteness eternal – the Lord Melchisedek, Flying Dragons, you and me and all the gods, forever One. In Love. A great distance was covered in a short time. Seen from the Edge of Highness time is an illusion.

But as they reached a narrow winding stream, the continuum of Peace was challenged by ominous subterranean quakes. On the surface, nothing more than feeble trembling. Deep below, fire and anger, immense like the Underworlds.

The power in the Abysmal Crevasse. Black like a cosmic night. Bottomless like the Dragon.

It made Teyani laugh, "Here you come, fierce monster!"

She modified her course, moving towards the marshes.

Szar wasn't laughing. Teyani's Light of Highness and the dark Dragon couldn't possibly coexist much longer. One had to give way to the other.

Darkness visible became strangely split into patches of absolute Light and patches of absolute blackness. The landscape started wobbling. The entire world was about to be torn asunder. A horrible sensation in Szar's body. Cataclysmic sea-sickness. The cohesion forces that kept the cells together were on the edge of collapsing. An imminent threat of being melted into a small heap of vomit-smelling formless matter.

"Gervin, help!" he shouted in distress, trying to pull himself together from the Dragon. But the Dragon was being churned into chaos. Voicing, "Thunder! Thunder!"

Instantly, Gervin, Orest, Barkhan Seer and three hundred generations of Thunder were with him, creating a protective bubble around him. But as Szar was about to project the Word of Thunder onto his body to keep it in one piece, Teyani shouted, "Wait! Try to hold on a little longer!"

Bolting ahead she held his hand, passing her power into him. It made the wobbling recede temporarily. Szar managed to stay on his feet. The under-valley kept undulating wildly. The menacing beast in the Abysmal Crevasse started spewing its venom, spreading blackness into the world. In Eisraim, outside the chapel of the Field Wizards, the glow in Afran Kesborn's eyes made Fornan shiver. Down in the cellars, Ferman was pulling his beard in consternation. Bobros was regaining the edge. The giant stood up again, mending the hole in the warp. Slowly, he walked towards Ferman, his huge hands ready to grasp him by the neck. Ferman ran to the back of the hall. Bobros kept walking, Point-holding the warp above his head, summoning, "Harmag! Harmag!"

Until Teyani and Szar reached the marshes.

The marshes seemed to be simmering, a frenzy of bubbles surfacing and bursting. The dark Dragon was exuding arch-foul fumes, primordially black, abysmally potent. Szar couldn't breathe. From one end of the valley to the other, animals were dropping dead. The valley herself was suffocating. She tried to cough but the winds remained mute. Everything was about to implode. Teyani was the Whitest Szar had ever seen her.

Standing by the edge of the marsh she lightly touched his face, "I love you. I will be with you, always. Always!"

Choking, Szar couldn't answer her.

She turned to the Eagle and Voiced, "Let darkness return to the Cosmic Night! Let men be redeemed of the sins of the Watchers!"

Letting go of Szar's hand, holding his eyes, she let herself fall back into the marshes.

She floated, one or two seconds. Then Szar saw her sink into the mud, slowly. Her feet went down first. The liquid Earth enveloped her body. Her face remained serene, her gaze was Whiteness eternal. Szar couldn't scream, his lungs were locked. Teyani's eyes disappeared, then her forehead.

She was gone.

Her body engulfed, her Light plunged deep into the Abysmal Crevasse, wounding the dark Dragon, activating the Magic of the Dawn of Creation when everything was beginning and all things were possible.

A subterranean blast took place. It was grand and terrifying, it shook the caverns of orichalc and lapis lazuli, it was felt as deep as the Sea of Lightning. Amidst hissing gales, the dark Dragon imploded back into its source – the source of all sources, the Great Night from which all things emerged.

Harmag's charm was neutralised. The Abysmal Crevasse was now nothing more than a cleft in the rock, surrounded with bones. The valley was dead – no longer the Valley of the Necromancer, just a hollow between two lines of mountains.

In Eisraim Bobros was only six lawful feet from Ferman, about to strangle him, when the power suddenly failed him.

"Harmag! Harmag?"

No response.

Overwhelmed under the weight of the warp, Bobros fell on his knees. Ferman and Shyama launched another venom attack. When Bobros tried to retaliate the warp vomited a new deluge of elemental filth into his head. This time he no longer had the energy to mend the hole. Submerged, he collapsed, his face thudding against the living floor.

The last of the Bobros was dead.

In the valley Szar was on his knees, catching his breath, holding the cells of his body together from Thunder. He felt like a skin sack in which organs were floating, not all in the right places. The world around him was a dark maelstrom, the elemental forces in an advanced state of disintegration, the ground uncertain of its own foundations. Air was moving in all directions, unable to remember what it was like to be wind. Szar stood up, groping for verticality. Where was down and up and all the rest? The axis of the world was loose. There was no Dragon. He smelt a shoal of dead fishes floating on the surface of the marsh.

Following Thunder, he walked. "One Law, one way. He who never sleeps, never dies!"

There was no sky, no Earth, no Underworlds and no heavens. The world was preparing itself to become Ahriman's domain. Sleep and death, infamous sisterhood. A dirty mess, stubbornly meaningless.

One step. Another step.

Where do you find the strength when everything has been taken away?

The awakened one is what is left when all has been emptied.

Another step.

There is a world of dreams behind me. Kingdom, it was called. It dreamt for a hundred thousand years. It perished in a nightmare.

Another step.

Take the gods away. Take the Dragon away. Take Elyani from me. And Gervin. And Teyani. Destroy my body. The flame remains!

Another step.

One flame, one way. He who never sleeps, never dies!

I walk on the edge of two abysses. Flying Dragons are born and die. Worlds pass. The flame remains!

Another step.

If I can lose *everything* and still feel the flame, then I can run!

Running on the defunct ground, Thunder showing the east.

The skin sack is leaking. Blood flowing from my left side. So what?

The flame remains!

Running on dead rocks, tripping over carcasses, hitting stumps, there is nothing left of this land, narrowly avoiding a rolling boulder, coming across the body of the fourth giant, his head smashed under a huge stone, limbo is an ugly darkness that leads nowhere, the marshes are swelling like corpses, rising, engulfing the dry areas.

Running towards the hills, feet bleeding. A storm raging. The sky, a huge sore. Raining pus. There is no Point left to hold the venom. There is nothing left between the outside and the inside, no life to protect. The skin sack like a pierced bladder. The flame remains!

Stones rolling from the top of the mountains. All the trees are dead, their ghosts floating in darkness visible. Tripping. Falling against the face of the mountain, a boulder crushing my left hand, smashing every bone. No Dragon to muffle the pain. The body screams in agony. The flame remains. Standing up again, still screaming, climbing. Darkness visible, an incestuous soup filled with astral remnants of all the animals massacred by the dark Dragon. I see Ahriman's world to come, the scene is set. The future is a slaughterhouse, Mother nature's cannibalistic fury, an overflow of the caverns of sickness. The flame remains! Eternal. Absolute. It never had an end. It will never have a beginning.

The world has never had any power over it. It never will.

Dragging the skin sack on the cliff of the mountain, excruciating fits in my left hand, overwhelming visions of global chaos, half of the souls in the kingdom will have perished in one year, reaching a craggy path which winds its way up gently, makes the climbing a hell of a lot easier, doesn't make any difference to the flame. Touching my left hand. Three fingers missing. Teyani's presence is shining in the flame.

"I will be with you, always. Always!"

Reaching a plateau with the first glows of dawn.

The mists are sparse. In front of me, the High Plateaux. At my feet, the corpse of the Valley of the Necromancer.

The body, trembling.

Raising my fist, "Gervin! Gervin!"

A wild, wild wave of Voice, "Gervin! I am *not* asleep!"

Voice-screaming, echoed by the mountain range, "Gervin! Gervin! Gervin...!"

The Dragon has returned. Voicing her victorious fury through me,

"Gervin, I am *not* asleep!"

21.10 Transfer!

The High Plateaux were barren lands that had never been inhabited, and therefore had never been fielded. The superior quality of silence and the pristine purity made a startling contrast with the valley's elemental pandemonium. No thoughts, just Thunder, the path was easy. But by then difficulty and ease had lost all meaning. There was nothing but the flame.

It was still early in the morning when Szar reached the Plateau of Sorana. Woolly and Lehrmon had arrived the night before. After a few hours of sleep they looked fresh and rested. For security reasons they had avoided all communications, both through darkness visible and through the Point. When they recognised Szar's silhouette in the distance, they ran toward him, praising the Great Apollo. But when they saw his face covered in blood and mud, his maimed hand, his clothing in shreds and the imprints of high-intensity insanity the valley had left in his energy, they stopped.

Judging by the horrified expression on Woolly's face, it was a ghastly vision. "Did you meet the giants?" he asked, pale.

"A few."

"Did they do this to you?"

"Hunh hunh! The valley. The Valley of the Necromancer."

"Oh, shit!" Woolly pulled his hair. "So *you* were in that hell?"

"With Teyani. She's dead." Turning to Lehrmon, "She was... superb!"

"And the stone?" Woolly held his breath.

Szar plunged his hand in his pocket for the precious object, and frowned. Woolly became much, much paler, eyes exorbitantly wide.

Slowly relaxing his frown into a half-grin, Szar pulled the stone out of his pocket, showing it to his friends. Unlike him, the hermaphroditic treasure had come out of the valley perfectly unscathed, and without the faintest imprint.

His head in his hands, Woolly exhaled a long, loud sigh.

Lehrmon had remained serene. Holding eye contact with Szar, flame to flame, he pulled his Archive stone from his pocket. Packing the warmth of three hundred generations of Brown Robes in one smile, he just said, "Transfer?"

His brethren answered in one voice, "Transfer!"

– Thus ends the Book of the Valley of the Necromancer –

22

The Book of Virginia and Hiram

And God looked upon the Earth, and, behold, it was corrupt; for all flesh
had corrupted his way upon the Earth. And God said... Behold I will destroy them with the Earth.

Genesis 6.12-13

And the waters prevailed exceedingly upon the Earth; and all the high
hills that were under the whole heaven were covered. Fifteen cubits
upward did the waters prevail, and the mountains were covered. And all
flesh died that moved upon the Earth, both of fowl, and of cattle, and of
beast and of every creeping thing that creepeth upon the Earth, and every
man.

Genesis 7.19-21

22.1 Archive Hall Five, Fields of Peace, 13000 years later

In Archive Hall Five Virginia, Hiram and Barkhan Seer were watching
records of the transfer.

In the temple of light, the Masters of Thunder had assembled, filling
each and every Archive hall. Melchard, who had been killed by the giants,
was now with Gervin in Archive Hall One. So were Ashok and most of the
Field Wizards of Eisraim and Lasseera. Ferman, Ushbudh and Shyama,
however, were still in the rainbow chapel in Eisraim, with Mouridji. Esrevin and Jop were at the top of Homar Hills, holding fast against the giants.
Lehrmon, Woolly and Szar were at the Plateau of Sorana. Ran Gereset was
still in his cave in the Arctic region, completing his thirty-nine-year-long
ritual. Khej and Gallagher had disappeared from the manifested creation.

The Masters of Thunder raised their Voices. Incandescent energies
poured from their mouths, illuminating the Archive halls. Unleashing the
power which had cleared Erriba thirty-nine years earlier, they generated an
irresistible pull from the Edge of Highness, a breath of colossal proportions. In one day and one night, the entire traditions of Eisraim and Lasseera were lifted into the Fields of Peace.

349

The Archive was born.

When everything had been accomplished and the Voices were extinguished, Gervin instructed Ferman to destroy all stones in his chapel and neutralise all fields. Then Mouridji, Shyama, Ushbudh and Ferman left their bodies and were lifted into the Fields of Peace. This was when they discovered that the giant they had killed was none other than Bobros himself – Bobros who had died without a son, his necromantic lineage extinguished. Ashok received an ovation. To his joy he realised it was Gervin who had inspired his invention from the Fields of Peace. "All glory to the teacher!" He praised Master Ferman for directing him to tune into Archive Hall One in order to become someone.

Soon after, Esrevin and Jop arrived in Archive Hall One. They were followed by Lehrmon and Woolly, who no longer had a broken nose. Teyani was already in Highness, Szar in Revelation Sky.

While the Archive people were congratulating each other, praising the Great Apollo, looking forward to the extraordinary adventure which was only beginning, Fornan the crocodile and Grand Court Sorcerer Afran Kesborn were outside the chapel of the Field Wizards in Eisraim. The chapel's protective shield had dropped. All Nephilim fields had suddenly been restored.

Storming the chapel the giants of the Green Guard found Bobros' corpse in the cellars. Beating his chest, Fornan the crocodile cried in despair. Afran Kesborn didn't. He immediately declared himself regent of the citadel. Samoan opposed the move. A bitter dispute broke out. Fornan ordered both of them to stop bickering until they reached the Eastern Peninsula. And he declared a fortnight of mourning for the Nephilim people, during which looting and raping were banned. This was how the giants of the Green Guard returned to the Eastern Peninsula without having pillaged the temple of Eisraim. On the way home, Samoan died in mysterious circumstances. Twenty-four hours later Afran Kesborn became the new grand commander of the Nephilim giants. Totally disgusted, General Fornan retired. In the weeks that followed, his son Basalinger was assassinated. It marked the beginning of a civil war in the Eastern Peninsula. The Green Guard was split into two competing factions. So was the council of the baphomets. During the fighting, Pralaya was murdered. General Harravan returned to the camp of the King. The ninth army disbanded. The giants never conquered the kingdom.

Barkhan Seer brought up depressing images of the gradual agony of the warp of fields. All counties of the kingdom were struck by catastrophes similar to the one in Alverard. Locally, the holes in the warp resulted in carnage, bodies strewn all over the streets. The thick elemental filth that poured out of the warp also caused far-reaching pollution. Horrendous scenes. Throughout the kingdom the mists became heavier and heavier, the air unbreathable, the distinction between day and night unclear. The atmospheric doom was accompanied by widespread madness. People slaughtered each other or killed themselves for no apparent reason. The population of entire villages lay prostrate with a demented look in their eyes, waiting for death. Nature too had become insane. When droughts ended, they were replaced by floods, and vice versa. A number of cities were destroyed by unexplained fires. Others melted to the ground, under the eyes of powerless Windmill Keepers. Elsewhere there were tidal waves, deadly hailstorms, plagues and pestilences of all kinds. The land no longer yielded crops. There were famines throughout the land. Entire areas became barren. Countless species of plants disappeared. Pests kept proliferating. As Pralaya the baphomet had foreseen, rats were great winners in the Atlantean holocaust.

"What about the Sons of the Dragon? With their powers over the forces of the Earth, couldn't they counteract the disasters, even if only locally?" Hiram asked.

"The catastrophes stretched over several generations. With the sickness of the land, the energy of the gates of the Dragon became chaotic. Gradually, the Underworlds became sealed. The Great Warriors were no longer able to initiate new candidates. Their tradition died out."

Barkhan Seer displayed images of the temple of the Dragon in Mount Lohrzen. The dining hall dug in red rock was empty. So were all the rooms, the chapels, the bowels. Only one man was left. A very old man with long, white hair.

Hiram immediately recognised him, "Amaran!"

Amaran was sitting by the side of what used to be his beloved gate of the Dragon. He left his body and attempted a descent – no longer an easy glide but an extremely perilous journey. He found himself in total darkness, swayed by tempestuous winds. Several times he was violently brought back to the surface into his body. Finally, projecting the Word which is the thunder of the Earth, he broke through to marshy waters in the superficial Underworlds. In this muddy elemental filth he fought his way down. Every inch was an effort. It went on for hours, until he finally reached an Underworld cavern of azurite and lapis lazuli.

Exhausted, he stopped and cried for the Earth, remembering the days when descending into this cavern only took a joyful and effortless three-second jump.

Immersed in the familiar luminescence of dark-blue gems, Amaran breathed the sublime peace of the Underworlds. There, nothing had changed. The fragrances of Life were as pure as in the Ancient Days of the Earth. The sanctum of the Underworlds would always remain free from the pollution of the kingdom.

Sending a farewell prayer to the deities of the Red Lands, Amaran drifted down along a gentle breeze. A no-return descent into the Deep Underworlds.

The vision left Hiram spellbound, "Where is he now?"

"Amaran joined the Vulcans." Barkhan Seer went back to an earlier scene. In Mount Lohrzen's dining hall the Sons of the Dragon were enjoying their regular meal of charcoal-looking chunks. Szar was sitting in front of brother Floster. He was wearing the brand-new brown gown Floster had sewn for him. He was about to leave Mount Lohrzen for the ritual murder mission where he would meet Felicia. In the middle of the conversation he asked Floster, "I have often wondered why you didn't become one of the Great Warriors." The Son of the Dragon with the extravagantly broad and hairy chest explained he was following another initiatory path, the Mysteries of Vulcan. "Vulcan is called the god of the last hour. This is because he holds forces that will be released only in the very last moment, 'when the race of men is on its last leg.'"

"Could I learn more about it?" Szar asked, gripped.

"Perhaps when you come back," Floster gave a strange smile. Looking back, it was obvious he knew perfectly well Szar would never come back.

"Floster wasn't at all the rough bear he appeared to be," Barkhan Seer went on. "In the months that followed this scene, he conquered phenomenal powers and became grand master of the order of Vulcan. Fifty-seven years later when he left the kingdom to descend into the Underworlds, he had reached such a level of transformation that he took his *physical body* with him."

Something Maryani herself couldn't have done.

Hiram and Virginia were as fascinated as Szar had been, thirteen millennia before them. "What has happened to these people?" Hiram asked.

"You will come across some of them in your next life," Barkhan Seer prophesied. "But most of the Vulcan initiates will not return to the physical world until the very last hour – the final battles against Ahriman."

Apocalypse, the time when everything is possible.

"I want to know more!" Hiram was engaged.

"Perhaps when you come back," Barkhan Seer grinned. To change the topic he conjured images of the White Eagle priestesses who had been sent to Egypt. Alcibyadi and Seyani were walking along the Nile, invoking angelic forces, bringing down Spirit into the river and clearing land energies. Maryani was being courted by a king and his son, both madly in love with her. She was giving them the hard time of their lives, while teaching them about stones and Underworlds.

The priestesses were adored and they had fascinating lives, but they carried with them an immense nostalgia. Life without fields meant life without the presence of the gods. Of course the Eagle was with them – inside. But compared to Eisraim, Egypt was a spiritual desert. Hiram and Virginia understood the feeling well. Now they were in the Fields of Peace, immersed in an ocean of spiritual presence. To be, was to be full of God. In comparison, the physical world was dreadfully harsh – ontologically drought-stricken. Down there, being hurts! The world, a bleeding wound. Through the fields Atlantean temples had retained some of the original fullness from before the fall, when human beings lived in the bosom of the gods. For the White Eagles, leaving Atlantis for Egypt was like experiencing first hand the tragedy that awaited humanity at large after the Atlantean flood.

An abysmal feeling of loss. Spiritual desertification of the Earth. It was happening right in front of them.

Lehrmon, son of Lehrmon, was growing up. The resemblance to his father was so striking it made Virginia and Hiram laugh.

"Alcibyadi had manipulated the chromosomes!" Hiram figured out.

"Lehrmon became a powerful teacher of Archive lore." Barkhan Seer brought up a small stone temple where Lehrmon, now a tall man with Lehrmon's deep dark eyes, Lehrmon's dark curly hair and also, uncannily, Lehrmon's consistently composed and self-controlled attitude, was initiating students into the art of sight. Leaving the scene and moving forward in time Barkhan Seer showed another stone temple, a much larger one. He enlarged a detail on a wall covered in hieroglyphs.

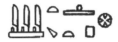

"Sekhet Hetepu." Barkhan Seer translated, "The Fields of Peace. Part of the mysteries and initiations transmitted by the Atlanteans in Egypt – not just our White Eagles.

And watch this! A descent into the Underworlds, guided by Nagas. Atlantean esoteric knowledge shaped many facets of Egyptian spirituality.

"And where did the White Eagles go after they left their bodies?" Hiram wanted to know.

"Afani and Pepni joined Teyani in Highness and never came back. The others went to the Fields of Peace, where they became part of the Archive people – except for Maryani, of course, who returned to the birds of paradise." Barkhan Seer showed images of the cascade of blue Life and Light in the high regions of the worlds of the gods. A flock of a hundred rainbow-feathered birds were flying in triangular formation on their way back from the Edge of Highness. The birds dispersed, landing on wise rocks on the face of the gigantic cliff. All at once, they started singing. Spellbinding harmonies, mysterious like the Song of Creation and packed with the punch of a hundred Maryanis – Life made sound.

The voice of Revelation Sky.

"And Vasouk?"

"King Vasoukidass is still the beloved ruler of the Nagas. In the Underworlds nothing has changed, except for the Nagas becoming wiser. And wiser."

Heart-warming images of morning bath-time outside Vasouk's castle. In a river of life, long golden snakes undulated in and out of the water, drinking their fill while discussing some subtle topic of Naga lore. Swimming by Vasouk's side was a little Naga, only thirty lawful feet long. From the shining light in his large onyx eyes it was clear that despite his young age, he was already exceptionally wise.

Hiram's mouth dropped open with astonishment, "Vasouk's child?"

"No, his nephew, Anantabadhra. He and Vasoukidass have become very close. Vasoukidass has taken responsibility for his education, which is to go on for another four hundred years."

"Being born a Naga, and Vasoukidass' close friend, moreover! Now *that's* a destiny," Hiram turned to Virginia.

"I take it, any time," the young woman sighed, eyes riveted on the scene.

"There is a long waiting list," Barkhan Seer warned them, as he took them back to the kingdom of Atlantis. It was snowing on Jex Belaran. In the royal suite of the Nephilim Hunters' headquarters, red-haired Felicia was lying in bed, pregnant up to the Point. She was screaming with pain. "Perseps! Perseps! The baby is coming!"

The kuren-jaya champion rushed into the room, white with anxiety. Felicia had demanded that he be her midwife. Despite a crash-course with the wise women of Verzazyel's temple, the prospect of delivering his own son scared the Watchers' hell out of him.

"Kasia had died two years earlier. Felicia took care of Perseps' little girl, and finally married Perseps," Barkhan Seer commented.

The next image showed a resplendent Felicia, her newborn baby boy blissfully asleep against her breast. By her side Perseps was lying flat on his back, staring like he had just returned from the Valley of the Necromancer.

"So the giants didn't destroy Jex Belaran?"

"No, they were too busy destroying themselves. Felicia and Perseps enjoyed a peaceful life and died of old age. Princess Pelenor didn't, though. She died from grief in the year that followed the death of her two men, Henrick and Prince Ozorenan. The prince was eaten alive by the giants when Tomoristan was destroyed. Pelenor's son was named Henrick, son of Henrick. After she left her body he was adopted and brought up by Joranjeran. But on the day of his eleventh birthday initiation, when he learnt the circumstances of his father's death, Henrick stabbed Joranjeran to death. He fled from Jex Belaran but was hunted and killed by a party of forty-one Hunters led by Perseps. So goes the legacy of the Watchers. Nineteen years later Perseps, son of Felicia and Perseps, became the next grand commander. And nine years after this, Jex Belaran was wiped out by an influenza epidemic. It was the end of the Hunters."

A clean ending, considering the horrendous mess into which the rest of the kingdom had sunk by then.

"And after the end of Atlantis, what happened to the Nephilim?"

"Only a few handfuls of giants escaped the flood. The Nephilim, as a race, disappeared. But the Nephilim spice spread through intermarriage. Now all human beings carry a touch of it in their blood."

The memory of the chromosomes.

Hiram looked up to the stars. He hated to imagine how a genetically-engineered Nephilim pilot would perform in a Scalene fighter.

"Now to something beautiful, showing how seemingly inconsequential events can dramatically alter the long-term future." Barkhan Seer displayed the front gates of the palace of Tomoristan, blurred behind a curtain of mists. Szar was leaving. After speaking to Princess Pelenor he was on his way to Raelene Vale, to raid the Fox Hunters' headquarters – and meet Aphelion. A few minutes later a tall, red-haired lad with a nascent beard arrived at the doors of the palace, requesting an audience with Pelenor. "Remember this man? He was Rolen, Felicia's younger brother. He was only twenty-two at the time. The fact that Felicia had been miraculously healed had sparked him on a quest. He had become obsessed with the idea of finding Szar and learning from him. Pelenor directed him to the temple of Eisraim, but when he arrived there Szar was still away, caught in Aphelion's clutches. Now, look! Destiny..."

Rolen was outside the temple's main portal. Namron had just informed him that Szar wasn't in Eisraim but had refused to say more. From Namron's hostile tone of voice, it was clear Nephilim people weren't welcome here. So Rolen stayed outside. An old Salmon Robe priest was passing by. Rolen tried to get more information from him.

"Szar?" the priest's eyes went from vague to very vague. Then he thought he remembered, "Oh, lawfully yes! Szar fell sick and went to the county of the Red Lands."

Rolen was surprised. "Hasn't Szar come back from the Red Lands?"

"Not that I lawfully know of, man of the Law. Oh! Lawful coincidence!" the priest exclaimed. "Here is Artold of the Salmon Robe. He and Szar of the Salmon Robe are best friends in the Law!" He called, "Praise the Lord Melchisedek, Artold of the Salmon Robe, how are you my friend in the Law!"

"All glory to the Lord Melchisedek, Dercon of the Salmon Robe! Thanks to the grace of our Lord Melchisedek, I am well, my friend in the Law. And how are you, my friend in the Law?"

"Lawfully well! Lawfully well! Tell me, Artold, my friend in the Law, Szar hasn't come back, has he?"

Artold knew that Szar had returned from the Red Lands. But he thought Dercon was asking whether he was still in Tomoristan. "No, he hasn't come back, my friend in the Law! But by the grace of our Lord Melchisedek, I trust he is well. As the Law says... "

The lawful babble went on. Rolen had tears in his eyes, believing Szar had gone back to the Red Lands.

"Which was how Szar lost his first disciple!" Master Barkhan Seer pulled his beard.

"Sleepers!" Hiram laughed in outrage while Virginia, sombre, was watching in silence. She knew only too well what it is like to miss one's destiny.

"But the story doesn't end there! Moved by the strength of a profound aspiration, Rolen took the first boat and travelled all the way to the Red Lands. There he spent five months roaming town after town, looking for Szar of the Brown Robe. The more he searched, the greater his aspiration became. Until..."

Rolen was cornered in a narrow lane by a mob of villagers. "Kill the Nephilim! Kill the Nephilim!" they shouted, and they beat him to death. But as he was being killed, Rolen called inside with all his strength, "Szar! Szar! Szar...!"

Seen from the Fields of Peace, his call was a huge flame.

"What a man holds in his consciousness at the time of death has a profound impact on his journey through the spheres," Barkhan Seer went on. "Rolen's aspiration allowed the White Eagle to set him on a course toward Szar. Followingly, Rolen was reborn around 3000 BC, an epoch when several Masters of Thunder reincarnated in India." Barkhan Seer showed two dark-skinned men with long hair sitting in front of a small fire, chanting mantras, "Szar and Rolen. After the training he received in India, Rolen became one of the Archive people. He is now one of our Whitest Eagles. A man of miracles, a powerful teacher."

"What were the Masters of Thunder doing in India?" Virginia asked.

"Throughout history the Masters of Thunder have reincarnated here and there, teaching their disciples, fishing new ones, and fostering the growth of spiritual traditions. In most cases they didn't reveal their identity, they just blended into local religious contexts. Ancient India was one of the high points because the language and the foundations of its culture had much in common with Atlantean lore. Of all the languages that came after the flood, none was closer to the Atlantean language than Sanskrit. The so-called Aryan invaders who came from the east and originated the Vedic culture brought with them an oral tradition which had retained many of the principles and ritual practices of the Law of Melchisedek. A number of ancient Sanskrit texts were full of verses taken straight from the Atlantean – the Laws of Manu, for instance. Ever heard of these scriptures?"

"Hunh hunh!" Hiram had only vaguely heard of India which, as a country, had long disappeared from the map of the Earth.

"The Himalayas were in India," Virginia told him.

"Oh, I see!" spark in Hiram's Point, eyes and heart. In the Philadelphian Air Force, his squadron often sat on top of the Himalayas for debriefings and informal meetings (in virtual reality, of course). "Stunning views!"

Barkhan Seer decided to pass over the details. "Ancient India staged a momentous enlightenment. Many sages descended from the Fields of Peace, from the worlds of the gods, and from Highness, and they kindled spiritual forces of considerable magnitude. For more than 5000 years India kept a flame, a spirit of high inspiration. Then materialistic values took over and the spirit was dampened. India became one of those places on which Ahriman focused his violence and his darkness, precisely to eradicate the vibrations of all sacred sites."

After Ahriman, the dregs. Piles and piles of dregs.

"Does anyone know what happened to Artold, by the way?" Hiram was curious.

"He never made contact with the Archive. Lost in the mists of time, like so many sleepers who basked in the light of the fields and thought themselves the proteges of gods."

"So what became of all these high priests and priestesses? Who were they when they reincarnated after the flood?"

"Sleepers like the Salmon Robes or the Blue priestesses came back as average people, but with an overwhelming nostalgia for the light of spiritual realms. In a barbaric world where all spiritual traditions had been lost, they went through a nightmare. Some tried to escape reality through insanity. Others buried all memories and took refuge in dullness."

Not a fundamental change after all. They used to sleep in the light of the gods. They kept sleeping in the darkness of the new kingdom.

"For some, though, nostalgia was perhaps their greatest asset. Because of it they kept searching. In the post-Atlantean age many spiritual seekers were people who, in Atlantis, had seen the Light. They yearned to be re-united with it. All these rituals they had performed throughout their Atlantean life hadn't been a complete waste of time. It structured soul forces which stayed with them in the form of a latent ability to connect with spiritual presences."

A tiny thread to the Divine, buried in the depths of their psyche.

"But not all Atlantean priests were puppets of the Law like the Salmon Robes. What about all those orders of initiates with extravagant powers of consciousness? What happened to them?" Hiram asked.

"They were magicians in Atlantis, they returned as magicians in the new kingdom. Interestingly, their abilities didn't necessarily translate into spiritual pursuits. Many Atlantean initiates came back as gifted scientists, artists, business people or politicians."

The Atlantean world revolved around the Law of the Lord Melchisedek, so in Atlantis they were high priests of the Law. The post-Atlantean world took a dive into materialism. They became the high priests of materialism.

"Complying with the trends of your epoch is a more subtle way of being a sleeper, isn't it," Virginia said with the superior impartiality that comes from watching the unfoldment of human trends over lengthy stretches of time.

She went back to the scene outside the portal of the temple of Eisraim. Dercon and Artold of the Salmon Robe had gone back to their chapel. Feeling utterly dejected, Felicia's brother was sitting against a wall, his head in his hands, wondering where to go next. Namron and two of his men came to him. "Now then, go, man of the Law!" Namron shouted threateningly. "We don't want you here. Go away!"

A gross insult. The Law commanded that all visitors to the temple be given food and shelter. But Namron didn't like the Nephilim.

"All right!" the young man stood up and left, not wanting to cause unlawful pandemonium in Szar's temple. Deeply offended, he mumbled inside himself, "Miserable dwarf in the Law! I will find Szar, whether you like it or not." And his decision was made. He was on his way to the Red Lands.

"Destiny, destiny..." Virginia murmured. "And what if Szar had been in Eisraim? Or what if Rolen had been allowed to speak to Gervin? Would he have become one of the Archive people?"

"Not necessarily!" Barkhan Seer savoured the irony of this record. "Sometimes, being led astray and having to wander is the surest way to reach the goal."

Virginia liked that. Immensely. It sounded like hope, for her who had spent 13000 years missing her rendezvous with destiny.

"Would you say that if Aparalgon hadn't come at the last hour, he might not have geared into your light with such intensity?" Hiram asked Barkhan Seer.

"Correct! Precisely because he came at the last hour his motivation was total. He knew he had only *one* chance. He couldn't afford to fail."

"So really it was by the grace of the Angel of Dawn that Aparalgon came to Szar in the last days," Hiram saw.

Tears of starlight falling through the roof of the chapel of the Grey Robes.

"Where did Aparalgon go?" Virginia asked.

Barkhan Seer called up records of the young man after he left Teyani and Szar. Dressed in his long black cloak he returned to the chapel of the Angel of Dawn. As he wandered through the familiar rooms he felt like a stranger, which brought a profound realisation. This chapel was no longer part of his world.

His Point rooted in the light of Archive Hall Five, he went to visit the chapel of the White Eagle one last time, then the cremation ground. There he found the body of Zothar, Grand Attendant of the Dead. His task complete, the old man had finally left his body.

Aparalgon stood in front of the corpse, wondering whether to perform the cremation ceremony. "What's the point?" he shrugged his shoulders, and walked away.

From Archive Hall Five Barkhan Seer sent him a foreboding impulse.

"All right! All right!" Aparalgon promptly replied, looking skywards. And he went back to perform the funeral ritual.

"The last funeral ritual ever performed in Eisraim," Barkhan Seer commented, grave.

"And the first of Aparalgon's ten million right decisions," Hiram smiled, watching the young man chant the hymns to the departed souls.

After this Aparalgon left the temple through the eastern portal. It was his second wise decision. Only a few minutes later the giants of the Green Guard were reaching the temple's main portal. On the western side.

Aparalgon followed the Fontelayana river down to the county of Berilya. From there he went east to Sheringa, where Szar was born. His intention was originally to join the White Eagles in Egypt, but in Sheringa he met a group of men and women on their way to Ireland. Barkhan Seer inspired him to follow them. During the journey he developed strong bonds with them, and ended up staying in Ireland with them.

There he gradually underwent a fascinating transformation. Nourished by Archive Hall Five, he grew in wisdom like a great fig tree. He became a patriarch, a teacher of Archive lore.

"Thanks to the seeds planted by Aparalgon, Ireland became a land where many connected to the Archive and received its light," Barkhan Seer showed magical landscapes, greenery with Spirit. "For thousands of years, the spiritual presence of the Archive remained particularly vibrant. Ireland was blessed with a special purity, a breath from the Fields of Peace. It was one of the reasons why, in the space age, so many Irish people migrated to the Philadelphias. And just as well for them! At the beginning of the wars of the Apocalypse the Rex submerged Ireland under a deluge of fire, to eradicate the special purity which had lasted until then."

Ahriman's fury. Ugly like the world of dregs.

"Are there records of Aparalgon's next lives?" Virginia was eager to know.

Barkhan Seer turned to Hiram, "Have you guessed?"

Hiram was beaming, "Of course. How could I not recognise him!" For Virginia, "Aparalgon became one of the Archive people, and was trained by the Masters of Thunder over several lifetimes. In Apocalyptic times he was reborn on Earth as Phelippe Varga," he said, stressing the last syllable of Phelippe. "It was more than a hundred years ago. The Rex still hadn't completely taken over the Earth. Varga escaped into space, joined the Knights, established the TS5 academy on Titan, and was the principal engineer of the first great victory of the Philadelphian Air Force against the Rex: the first battle of Mercury. He called it Operation Hour of God, because the very survival of the Philadelphias was at stake. The Rex's numerical superiority was overwhelming, in the order of ten ships to one. Yet the Knights completely annihilated the Rex's fleet in seven days."

Hiram called an image of a bald man in his late thirties, dressed in the black outfit of the Knights of the Apocalypse with the large yellow sun on his chest. "Colonel Phelippe Varga. Look at his eyes!"

The undaunted glow of a man who knows his time had come.

Operation Hour of God, Day 1, first hour – this was when Varga-Aparalgon had met the Angel of Dawn face to face. His heart ignited with a gigantic flame which reached up to Highness, he had led the Knights to victory, unleashing the anger of God, putting Ahriman on his knees.

More than sixty years would pass before the Rex could launch another expedition against the Philadelphias.

22.2 The dazzling dance of a thousand time lines

Returning from the River of Remembrance, Virginia and Hiram went to Archive Hall Seventeen, for in Archive Hall Five Master Barkhan Seer was busy receiving all the Knights who had just died in the fifth battle of Mercury. In the kingdom when someone departs, people grieve. In the Fields of Peace, each new arrival is a celebration.

Conversely, when someone in the Fields of Peace is about to depart and be reborn in the kingdom, the grieving of the Mother of All Compassion can be felt in the flow of the River of Remembrance, and in a certain air of gravity on every leaf of every tree, tears of dew on every blade of grass, great pelicans flying west.

"Knight Hiram, you are about to go, aren't you," Virginia said, grave.

She was the most resplendent Hiram had ever seen her. In the Philadelphias she had been a stunning young woman, the daughter of the divinely beautiful Elyani Serah. In the Fields of Peace her beauty had blossomed. She looked wise like a unicorn, the depth of the River of Remembrance reflected in her almond eyes. And her Flying Dragon nature made her mysterious, profound.

Holding her hand, Hiram walked into the fluid darkness of Archive Hall Seventeen. "I love you," he said, from the Eagle.

His love was echoed throughout Virginia's nature of remoteness, Eagleness mingling with the precious voice-elixir of the Song of Creation.

He made himself a White dot immersed in her vastness.

She enveloped him with the magic of the Great Night. A Flying Dragon way of making love.

Hall Seventeen waited silently, pregnant with the combined mysteries of the Archive and the Flying Dragons.

Virginia's human self was grieving. "Did Master Barkhan Seer tell you more about your next life?" she asked.

"Not yet. Next time we meet."

"Mother of the Light, Mother of the Light..." she prayed vibrantly, "please don't send Hiram back into the clutches of the Rex. Find him a beautiful mother, in the Philadelphias."

"A beautiful mother..." Hiram repeated pensively, trying to remember what it was like to be loved by a mother. In his last life he had been born in a test tube, his genetic material purposely engineered to make him small, ugly and weak, a miserable pawn in Ahriman's sinister games.

He shook his head, "Master Barkhan Seer gave me his word I would be the kind of man who has everything," he reminded her.

She gave him a teasing smile, "Enlightened, loved, handsome, intelligent. And of course, rich, and famous..."

"Stop! Stop! Sounds like a lot of trouble already. Couldn't I have something more... tranquil?"

Virginia brought a dazzling field of stars onto the dome ceiling of Archive Hall Seventeen. "If you reincarnate immediately you might even meet my mother. Will you take care of her?"

In the Philadelphias, Elyani Serah was now a widow. Colonel Philip Serah, alias Szar of the Brown Robe, had died with Hiram at the start of the fifth battle of Mercury.

"Meeting her again would be an immense privilege," Hiram said with reverence.

"You will meet her," she said with assurance, contemplating the stars.

"Think so?"

"You love her so much, it will attract you to her. Love is the most powerful of all magnets."

"Hey, who said I loved her?" Hiram protested.

"Me."

Frowning, "Mm..."

"Ask the stars above your head. Each and every one of them will tell you." Using a Flying Dragon trick she linked his Point to the starry infinity, spreading his consciousness through the spheres of remoteness.

Hiram felt himself melting, a drop in the oceans of remoteness. This time he defended himself, gathering himself back into his Point through a triangular seal, "It's with you that I am in love!"

Her teasing smile was back, "But you don't have to be defensive! There's nothing wrong, you can love both of us." And she wrestled with his Point, trying to break through his seal, "How about a fight, just before you leave?"

Hiram dropped his seal, letting her take control of his Point, merging into her.

She made herself infinite softness, enveloping him with her Flying Dragon vastness. "No fight?" she kept smiling.

He shook his head, totally surrendered.

"Then dance with me! Do something unforgettable, like..." she looked up, fathoming the stars, "take me inside your Point. Show me what it's like to be a Knight of the Apocalypse."

"Let's dance!" Hiram closed his eyes, tuning into the knowing of Hall Seventeen. This time the Archive record he engaged wasn't in image mode, but in Point mode – the vision of the gods. It was a record of the temple of Eisraim in the days that followed Szar's return from Mount Lohrzen. This time instead of contemplating a scene, Virginia found herself in a thousand minds all at once. She was Szar of the Brown Robe, jumping from roof to roof on his way to Elyani's courtyard, rock-solid, single-mindedly rooted in his Mother the Dragon. In the chapel of the White Eagle she was Elyani, calling on the Eagle with all her strength, and Teyani, flame of Highness, her heart filled with transcendental wonders, her playful mood reverberating extravagant mysteries of the Ancient Days. Outside the doors of the chapel she was young Pushpadiv of the Lawful Gardeners, his energy spread in the trees, his mind still like a lake, delivering the ladders he had just made for Elyani. And just round the corner she was Mouridji of the Purple Robe, who was bored, bored, suffered badly from her hip, hated herself for being weak and useless, and dreamt of another life in which she could serve a noble cause. A few chapels away Virginia was the priestesses of Dawn, small and frail, linked to the kingdom by a fragile breath of life, their human self nothing more than a whisper. High above them Virginia's Flying Dragon nature recognised the overwhelming magnitude of the Great Night of Remoteness from which everything has come, and in which everything will return – the all-permeating yin power which, in the kingdom, served as a foundation for the solar revelation of the Law.

Throughout the temple Virginia was in the minds of hundreds of sleepers who kept praising the Lord Melchisedek while mechanically carrying out their lawful routines. In the central kitchen she was seventy-two of them at the same time, chanting mantras to invoke the deity of cucumbers, then cutting the cucumbers. In the chapel of the Grey Robes she was Aparalgon and his fellow priests, religiously silent, meticulously cleansing their ritual utensils as they did every afternoon from half past two till six. Elsewhere she was a lawful mason feeding living walls with plass food, a lawful cleaner sweeping the alleys, an old Green priestess rendering the ghost, a young child contemplating the mists. At the western end of the temple the Salmon Robes were beginning a ritual to the thirty-three victorious gods, their slow movements bordering on caricature, their minds desperately empty. In them Virginia felt a wonderful lightness, an existential ease. They lived without fear, totally relaxed and happy. In their hearts shone the light of the Law – the thread to the Lord Melchisedek. It made every act of every day a spiritual offering, it gave fullness to their apparently empty lives. By strictly adhering to their rules, all these congregations of sleepers held the presence of the Law. Seen from the global vision which Virginia was enjoying through Hiram's Point, the connectiveness of their works made the temple of Eisraim a powerhouse of divine presence.

In this flash of omnipresence where she was giving birth to a baby girl – a painless experience, care of the fields – while chewing black root in Namron's mouth and astral travelling, zapping through fiery-red fields of stars, there came surprises. In the chapel of Apollo she found herself in the Point-consciousness of great initiates whose vision encompassed the heights of Revelation Sky, supermentally conversing with the gods. Clad in saffron robes they were sitting in a circle, Lehrmon of the Brown Robe among them! Being in Lehrmon's Point was like sitting in the centre of the almighty Golden Sun, one with Master Barkhan Seer's ebullient powers, one with Master Gervin's volcanic aspiration, one with Ran Gereset performing fire rituals in the dark icy cave, one with the temple of light in the World to Come and the River of Remembrance in which all the sorrows of men will be washed in the end. And while she was braying in the person of Aphrodoros of the chapel Barradine, anxious to receive the daily ration of herbs of madness, she was also in the mind-boggling world of Omon Lakh Singar, high priest of the Mysteries of Ancient Times, whose chapel was the repository of totally incomprehensible forces of consciousness, some from the Ancient Days, some from the Watchers, some from totally unknown origins, so weird that no one ever dared enter, apart from Mouridji who had been Singar's lover thirty-five years before and after this visited him twice a week because she never got bored in his company. Even from the Point and with the support of the Archive, Virginia couldn't make any sense of what was happening in that chapel. Meanwhile she was mooing in the Holy Sheds, and swimming with the fishes in the small lakes outside the halls of Melchisedek, and towering over the ladder of the worlds in the dazzling consciousness of dozens of high initiates, men and women with phenomenal clarity and powers. But in this field of enlightenment none shone brighter than three women at the top of the tower of Malchasek: two high priestesses of the caste of the Immaculate, and Holma the ascending goddess. Ardent love, flashing-White brightness, the effulgence of God – it made Virginia remember the awesome powers of Hermina the Immaculate, her teacher in Atlantis, who could light a Holy Blue Flame in one short mantra and project the Omnipotent Word which is the Thunder of the Earth.

Drunk with the supermental elixir, her consciousness spread through all the chapels of Eisraim, cognisant of a thousand minds' secrets, Virginia heard Hiram laugh, "Ready for the great dance?"

Without waiting for her answer he engaged an advanced function in the Archive, creating an explosion in Virginia's Point. The vision was so packed that at first she couldn't discern anything. She knew she was cognising something fabulous, but didn't know what – not an uncommon experience when learning the Point-language of the gods. Hiram involuted her further into his Point, taking her from Point-ness to Point-ness-ness, and the meaning was revealed. All at once Virginia saw the time tracks of all the people in whom her consciousness was immersed. In a multidimensional fashion, totally incomprehensible to the normal mind, she Point-cognised a thousand destinies.

A thousand time lines condensed in Point-packed format.

Each line contained 13000 years of history, crossing thousands of other lines, weaving a cosmic tapestry – the human scene as beheld by the Lords of Destiny.

In this exalted state of knowing, the first thing that struck Virginia was the superior sense of meaning. Human events, when considered punctually and from the ordinary mind, often appear random and insignificant, or even absurd. By itself, a dot along the line has no sense of direction. But when considering the overall shape of the line, every dot becomes an indispensable component of the greater whole. Then nothing is trivial. Every event, every circumstance of life is a vital link in the chain of destiny.

Virginia returned to the scenes in the palace of Tomoristan, when Szar had failed to fish her. Point-seen through the eyes of the Lords of Destiny it no longer appeared like a disastrous blunder. Szar's time line was gently moving towards Virginia's. Having missed each other in Tomoristan created a charge in their time lines that made their next meeting even more certain. It prepared a glorious future which, 13000 years later, was about to come to fruition.

Aparalgon was a magnificent example of the same principle. His first encounter with the Brown Robes could have taken place two lives earlier. But for two lives, the Angel of Dawn had pulled Aparalgon's time line in the opposite direction, like an archer pulling a bow. When it came to the last days of Eisraim, the karmic tension had reached a climax. This, in a way that only the supermind could comprehend, was what had made Szar bump into Aparalgon's grandfather, his highness Aparalgon, and what had caused his highness to lodge a complaint against Szar after receiving a healing from him. Yet another dot artistically laid along the line. Finally, at the most auspicious moment, the Angel of Dawn had released the string, projecting Aparalgon like an arrow.

In this grand vision of the workings of time, Virginia saw the good people of the temple of Eisraim moving from life to life and world to world. Mouridji was reborn as a Viking, a huge man who yelled furiously, slaying his enemies, winning battle after battle. Teyani was in Highness, dancing the Great Lovers' Dance with the Eagle. In the heights of Revelation Sky, Szar was learning celestial mathematics. Esrevin was in Persia, trying to rescue Oriel from Aphelion, but too late. Oriel had already gone to the dark side. Wearing turbans, Gervin, Woolly and Szar were in Bagdad, collecting a huge library.

There again, Virginia and Szar met. This time it was Virginia who didn't recognise him, and turned him away. Szar was left feeling abysmally empty. Crying under the stars, he called on the Flying Dragons. But as

Space Matrix whispered to him, it wasn't yet time for Virginia's appointment with the Archive. Guided by the superior wisdom of the Lords of Destiny, her line followed its course. It was separate from Szar's only in appearance. The two had been pulsing together since their father had planted his seed in the Great Dragon of Eternal Wisdom.

On his way back to Revelation Sky Szar stopped in the pine forest of ardent aspiration, and made love with Elyani. This too resonated with Virginia's time line. She had a dazzling dream, a revelation of pure, blazing light. After this Szar went back to Revelation Sky. Virginia went from life to life, not doing much, it seemed, apart from playing music – fabulous music, inspired from beyond the Abyss of the Deep and the Fault of Eternity. Often she and Szar played music together without knowing it, each in a different world, oblivious of each other but one in remoteness.

Taught by the Sons of Apollo, Elyani was gradually realising the full potential of her goddess' birth. In the grand warp of destiny the daiva which the Sons of Apollo had decreed could be seen as pure solar gold, infused into Elyani's time line just before Szar returned from Mount Lohrzen. Afterwards the gold spilled to Szar's time line, coiling it around Revelation Sky, with multiple friendship knots to Kartendranath's line. And through resonance the same gold illuminated the time lines of the Knights, trained life after life by the Masters of Thunder and the Sons of Apollo. And Virginia knew that when the gods had decreed their daiva, they were in the very same state of multidimensional foresight as she was in now. Their plan was a sublime work of art stretching from Eisraim to Philadelphia.

In the background the world continued its course. Civilisations were born and died. The Archive people grew in number and in strength. As the kingdom of the rainbows progressed, Ahriman's influence spread on the Earth like dark clouds before a storm. Teyani returned from Highness, joining Barkhan Seer in the Fields of Peace. Hiram was now one of the Knights, already legendary for his stubbornness.

Two more times Virginia and Szar met and missed each other, only to better prepare Virginia's appointment with destiny.

Until the day when their lines were joined by a momentous twist.

It was 13000 years after Eisraim, in the land of the white rose – Philadelphia, a name that means brotherly love. The wars against Ahriman had begun. So had the legend of the Knights. Sent by the Masters of Thunder, Szar had descended into the kingdom. Sent by the Sons of Apollo, Elyani had joined him. Now she was the Panther, dark-haired and fierce, apocalyptic. In a small cabin of an old space station along the orbit of Mercury they made love. In zero gravity. The space station was called Philadelphia Six. The lovemaking was unforgettable – apocalyptic – stretching from the Great Serpent of Eternal Wisdom to Revelation Sky. Nine Earth-months later a little girl was born: Virginia. From Tomoristan to Philadelphia, the cycle was complete, the time lines were joined. She was in his arms, inundated with his love. From Elyani she received a chest of celestial jewels. It was heaven on Mercury's orbit. It lasted five years. Then the armies of the Rex invaded Philadelphia Six. Virginia was trapped in the station, taken prisoner, separated from her parents, her soul smothered by Ahriman's venom. For twelve years. Twelve horrendous years at the end of which, watching Szar and Elyani's time lines, she found a resonance with the memorable night when she had been conceived.

It was on another space station, Mothership 7. The fifth battle of Mercury was about to begin. Szar knew he was about to leave his body. Elyani's mission wasn't finished, she was to remain in the Philadelphias. Their time lines were about to go their separate ways. Again they made love from the depths of the Great Serpent of Eternal Wisdom to the summit of Revelation Sky.

In the grand warp of destiny the time lines kept dancing.

22.3 The descender's farewell

When Virginia and Hiram arrived in Archive Hall Five, the Knights greeted them with an ovation. In the Philadelphias, Hiram was now nothing short of a legend. Operation Bleeding Sun, conducted by him, Szar and Marek in the first hour of the fifth battle of Mercury, had paved the way for a momentous victory. More than a third of all the Rex's hardware in the solar system had been reduced to space debris. The Philadelphias lived.

Fortunately, or unfortunately (depending on which world you looked from), Hiram didn't recognise any of his friends among the Knights in Archive Hall Five. In the kingdom the members of the Himalayan choir were alive and well, and so were the Knights of the Saint-Bernard choir, none having been shot during the battle.

The hall full with his disciples, Master Barkhan Seer was in a particularly jovial mood, his gold more bubbly than ever. Together they watched Archive records – records of the battle of course, but also of their past lives and of the worlds of the gods, remembering the most exciting moments of their training. They tuned into Master Szar who was travelling in distant Flying Dragon spheres, having taken Marek with him for the ride. And they let the joy of the River of Remembrance flow through their hearts, sending their love to those who had stayed behind in the kingdom, where much mourning was going on.

The celebration ended, the Knights left the hall. On Barkhan Seer's invitation, Hiram stayed.

Time to receive the instructions for the next part of the journey.

Virginia made a move. Hiram grabbed her arm. "I want her to stay!" he told his master.

"As you wish, son." Turning to Virginia, Barkhan Seer recalled, "Last time I sent Hiram to Earth, do you know what happened?"

Virginia looked at the Master of Thunder wondrously, contemplating great winds of compassion in his eyes.

"I cried," Barkhan Seer said with the simplicity of the River of Remembrance. "Oh, miserable times, these were! Throwing my beloved Hiram into the mouth of the beast."

Sending him to be born in a test tube, gunked by the filthy black pitch, chained in the pit of Ahriman's virtual world.

"But today..." Barkhan Seer illumined the hall with his smile, "today I am going to make him a prince!" Looking sideways to Hiram he gave a half-grin, "That's if he accepts the assignment of course."

Hiram chuckled.

To Virginia, "You have no idea how stubborn this man is!" Barkhan Seer slapped his forehead. "Trying to give him an assignment when he has something else in mind is a complete waste of time."

"I take the assignment!" Hiram declared unconditionally.

"Mm..." Barkhan Seer pulled his beard, mysterious. Plunging Archive Hall Five into darkness, he brought up an Archive record.

On Mothership 7, Serah and the Panther were making love. The very episode which had caught Virginia's attention while watching supermind records in Hall Seventeen.

Zero gravity and passionate fire. A view on the incandescent disk of the Sun through the window of the cabin. And the despair of an imminent separation.

In a climax the Panther screamed, "I want a child! I want another child with you!"

Pulling all his will into her, Serah roared from the Dragon, "Descender!" Descender!

Deep below, Dragon shaking. High above, a response.

"It happened three weeks ago. That night, a pregnancy was started," Barkhan Seer said, showing a stream of golden light pouring down from the Angels of the Seed.

"I know. The Panther told me," Hiram said.

At the time, Hiram was still in the kingdom. When Elyani had confided in him, he had been moved to the depths of his being.

"It's a male embryo," Barkhan Seer added, matter of fact. "If you want, the place is yours."

Tears in his eyes, Hiram watched silently.

Serah and the Panther were crying in each other's arms.

"Would she..." Hiram's voice choked, "would she want me as her child?"

The scene changed. Unusually, the Panther was dressed in white. She was alone, sitting in front of candles. Hiram quickly counted thirty-three of them. She was chanting a slow melody with strange intonations, her hands joined in prayer.

"Do you know what this is?" Barkhan Seer asked.

"Some kind of ritual," Hiram guessed.

"Correct. A ritual to the Great Apollo, asking for Hiram to be reborn from her womb. Since you left the kingdom, she has been performing this ritual three times every day."

Mysterious occult powers of a goddess.

"She's going to adore you," Virginia said, holding Hiram's hand.

Hiram was overwhelmed. In the last days he had prayed to the Mother of the Light, "Please, let me be reborn in the Philadelphias," because in the Philadelphias, people know the meaning of love. Now there was more love in sight than he could ever have imagined.

In Archive Hall Five, an astral vortex had appeared – a dark, whirling gateway followed by a tunnel.

Down at the other end of the tunnel there was the gold of the Panther's love, with the land of the white rose in the background.

"A time window is open," Barkhan Seer informed him. "You must go now. As to your directives..." he conjured an image of the solar system.

The vision spoke for itself. The Earth's aura was ominously black. Ahriman's pitch extended as far as the orbits of Saturn and Mercury. Inside the orbit of Mercury, close to the Sun, the fragile Philadelphian communities held the torch of the free world. Outside Saturn's orbit there were also pockets of extraordinarily bright light. The Rex's darkness threatened to take over the entire scene.

"It could still go either way," Barkhan Seer spoke from Thunder. "The time has come to awaken the giant inside, and fight for the light."

Apocalypse – the time when everything is possible.

"Now go, and enjoy being a child!"

Hiram and Virginia had already said goodbye, by the shores of the River of Remembrance. They exchanged one last glance. It told the entire Forever Love legend, from the Edge of Highness where the Eagle shines, to the Abyss of the Deep and the Fault of Eternity, where the Mother of the Light is smiling.

Moved, Barkhan Seer recalled the verse of the Law of the Eagles, "Put a Flying Dragon and a White Eagle together, and let the miracle unfold."

He put his hand on Hiram's shoulder. Grave, "I won't say goodbye."

Love pouring through his eyes, Hiram replied, "And I won't say thank you."

Eagles' farewell.

Resolute, Hiram walked to the vortex.

Crossing the gateway he whispered to himself, "One way, one Law. He who never sleeps, never dies."

– Thus ends the Book of Virginia and Hiram –

Archive Orientation

More information about the Atlantean technology of consciousness can be found in *From Eisraim to Philadelphia* (the general concordance of all Archive legends) and in various modules of the Clairvision Knowledge Tracks.

Eagle's Feathers and Endless Love, Tales of Teyani of Barkhan Seer can be found in the Clairvision Knowledge Tracks. The Clairvision Knowledge Tracks also include several other Archive legends of Atlantean times such as: *Takhar the Unbending* (the nature-enlightenment of Takhar of the Brown Robe in early days of the kingdom), *The Man who Said No to the King* (Gervin's training under Orest), *That We May Fly Together* (the flight of the White Eagles at the end of the kingdom, retold by Antaria and Jaleena).

Bleeding Sun tells the story of Hiram's life before he and Virginia arrived in the Archive Halls and viewed the records of *Atlantean Secrets*.

The musical themes of Archive characters and legends can be heard at the Clairvision Website:

www.clairvision.org

The Clairvision Knowledge Tracks present a systematic method to develop inner vision and gain direct access to the knowledge and forces of consciousness stored in the Archive.

Expect surprises!

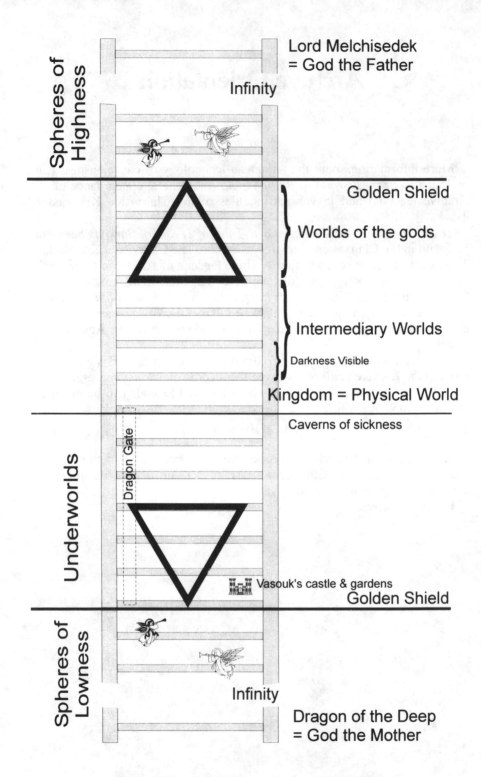

Spheres of Highness

Lord Melchisedek
= God the Father

Infinity

Golden Shield

Worlds of the gods

Intermediary Worlds

Darkness Visible

Kingdom = Physical World

Caverns of sickness

Dragon Gate

Vasouk's castle & gardens

Golden Shield

Underworlds

Spheres of Lowness

Infinity

Dragon of the Deep
= God the Mother

The Cosmological Ladder
Showing the Spheres of Melchisedek